The Split Sea: Book One

A HANDFUL OF SOULS

Stephen Rice

A HANDFUL OF SOULS

Copyright © 2020 Stephen Rice

All rights reserved

This edition was published in 2020 by Tiny Dice Publishing.

Cover Design: ebooklaunch.com

ISBN: 978 1 8381031 0 1 (paperback)

ISBN: 978 1 8381031 1 8 (ebook)

www.tinydice.co.uk

www.stephenrice.co.uk

This one's for Will,
the brother who started writing first

I

CHASING LARK

Dry Throat

Heat crept through the walls to coat Lark's skin with a slick of sweat. His eyes closed, chasing the peace he'd just lost.

'Are we alive?' The voice was soft, almost a whisper. 'Show me.'

Lark opened his eyes again.

'Good.'

The voice's owner was hunched over a nearby desk. He was fat and sweating profusely, scratching away in a book and mopping himself whenever his brow or squidgy nose threatened to blot the paper. He turned to Lark with a smile. 'It's a new beginning for you, my boy. Enjoy the blank slate while you can.' The man held the smile for a moment, then turned back to his book.

Lark didn't reply. He could wait. The world could wait. But it didn't and wouldn't and crept up on him with unwanted demands. He groaned as his skin stuck to the floor, each breath tightening a web of pain that gripped his chest.

The man coughed politely. 'What is your name, may I ask?'

'Lark,' he managed.

'Wonderful.' He scribbled away for a few moments, then dropped his quill with a satisfied flourish. 'Road greetings, Lark. My name is Terrano. My home city is quite far from here – in the Southlands, in fact.'

A land of spirits.

Despite the dozen or so oil lamps hanging around the room, Terrano raised one more to examine Lark's face. Fresh tears blurred the man's face to a painful halo. 'Can you speak, my boy?' he asked, lowering the lamp with an encouraging smile.

'Water.'

'Aha! Yes. Yes, yes, yes.' Terrano chuckled to himself, but made no move to fetch any. He set down his lamp and checked the book with a finger. 'An uncommon thirst on awakening, spasms of the back and neck, a fever unlike any other, visions and madness.' He held the lantern up again. 'Any spasms, Lark? Do you feel any spasms?'

'...water, please.'

Lark's hip ached, pressed down hard against the stone floor. Needles danced over his skin. Terrano was saying something else, but his voice sounded distant and tinny.

~

With a sinking sensation, Lark woke to find himself slumped in Terrano's chair, a coarse blanket draped over his shoulders. The wind had forced its fingers inside and pushed past the door to ruffle the strange man's book, which had been left open on the desk. Lark's hand crept out to still the fluttering paper. Sketches of his naked body littered the page, cut apart by arrows and smeared with letters. As he watched, the words tumbled and ran over one another, until only his name stood out clearly. It was written in Seatongue, and painted on using thick luxurious swirls of ink.

'One moment, my boy. I'll be with you in one moment.' Terrano's soft voice came from somewhere behind him. 'Sip some water.'

A bowl had been placed on the desk. Lark scrambled for it, spluttering and sobbing with relief.

'One moment. One moment.'

The empty bowl fell from Lark's hands with a clatter. He looked around the gloom, wiping a dribble of tepid water from his chin. Cobwebs draped angles between a snapped mill shaft and rotten crossbeams. Someone had dragged a crate through the dust to a far wall, but despite the lanterns hung all around it, it was still cloaked in shadow, and as Lark watched, the wood rippled and twisted, crawling, skittering closer on hidden legs, a yawning, cavernous moan rattling through its warped planks as it leapt at him.

The moment passed. Terrano knocked a fist against the crate and waited for a response. None came.

'Sere,' Lark croaked, closing his eyes against the visions. 'Where am I?' He heard footsteps and opened one eye a crack. Terrano had spread his arms triumphantly, as if to deliver a hug, and an old panic gripped Lark, sparking life into his aching limbs. 'Please! Please don't—'

'Such questions! I see you are recovering.' Terrano placed his hands, mercifully, on the edge of the table. 'I admit, I was worried when you collapsed. I thought I had picked a weakling at last, pushed myself too hard. But here you are. And truly, Lark...' Terrano dropped his voice to a whisper. 'Welcome back to the world of the living.'

He reached over and closed his book with a weighty thump. An ornate carving was fixed to the cover, and the title – An Encounter with Death – was etched above a magnificent and thoroughly fictitious rendering of Terrano, his chin raised and nobility radiating from a generous smile. Lark looked up at him. A plump, piggy-faced scholar beamed back, reading glasses dangling from his neck. He'd taken off his jacket and great puffs of lace bloomed over his clasped hands.

'To answer your earlier question, Lark, you are a day's ride north of the Split Sea. This was not my first choice of refuge, but the weather conspires against me.' He paused, allowing the howling wind to intrude on their conversation. 'The other subjects of my humble study are taking shelter nearby. Now, I understand from your papers you were volunteered for the tax patrol?'

He started rifling through Lark's pack, his new one with the crest of the Cerc Reno emblazoned on its side. Papers were held up to the light, then left to flutter to the floor.

'A real shame, a bright boy like you. But do not dwell on those who have wasted your talents. Those who shunned you.' Terrano peered through his glasses, frowning at the papers. 'You have a family with us now.'

'I already have a family, sere,' mumbled Lark. 'I saw them last week.' When had he lost his pack? The Taxer would be angry if anything was missing.

'If you can indulge me, my boy, what is the last thing you remember?'

Lark wriggled uncomfortably. After asking a question, Terrano's ever-curious hands would stop rubbing the desk edges, or fidgeting with his shirt collar. All of his attention would fix on Lark like he was a last, strange puzzle to solve, and nothing else came close to mattering. Lark clutched the blanket. 'I remember a noise. A moaning in my head.'

'Yes. You told me, you told me. I have that down here.' Terrano nodded, tapping his book. 'But think before that, can you recall any details? You are carrying papers from Cerc Reno. Was that where you were raised?'

'Branera, actually, sere. I'm due back in a year. If I'm welcome.'

'And why would you not be welcome?'

'I don't know.' Lark had no idea how to tame the quirks which caused his stepfather so much distress. The crush of Branera's upper circles was terrifying, and Little Indiscretions followed wherever he showed his face. Josef didn't do it on purpose, but Lark felt the old man's concerns like a weight on his back. 'I am to become a man first, sere. To grow out of my brain fevers.'

Terrano tutted. 'Brain fevers? Such ignorance dwells across the Long Path. You Northers are falling behind the rest of the world, I must say.'

'Is my patrol nearby, sere? I'm supposed to stay with them.'

'They are nearby, my boy, but you will not be rejoining them. How were things going?'

'We'd just started the triple draft. Food, gold and flesh—' His voice died in a feeble croak. Terrano urged him to drink, filling another bowl from a clay jug. 'Everyone hated us,' whispered Lark, wiping water from his mouth. 'The food they gave us at Dunford was horrid. Stew with bones in it, and wrinkled apples. Even the water tasted bad. It was sharp, sere, like sour wine, and it had a coppery taste, which the keeper said was from the river.' Lark rubbed his lips, tasting these memories. 'The Taxer didn't believe him. He refused to drink it and started shouting, but I'd already... I mean, I think there was a fight...' He trailed off, searching for more details but finding only confusion. The Taxer's furious face roared accusations at the grim, hooded men who'd filled the room. Pushing and shouting. A gut-wrenching pain so agonising that it seemed to slip from past to present. 'I think I was sick,' Lark said weakly, clutching his stomach. 'I don't remember.' Looking up from his knotted hands, he was relieved to see Terrano's attention had drifted again.

'Poor boy,' the scholar mumbled. He rubbed his finger over a chip in the wooden table. 'A taste like sour wine? Sharp on the tongue?' Terrano's face scrunched up, twisted to acrobatic feats by his distaste. 'You know, I suspected as much. I found the signs on you – this just confirms it. My boy. My poor boy. You were poisoned, you know that?' With a sympathetic tut he retreated to rummage through his lanterns and sacks. He eventually returned with some herbs, labelled and neatly bound with string. 'This should help,' he murmured. 'Pull off a leaf and chew. No, no, a bigger one, please.'

Lark picked the second-smallest one. The leaf was shiny and brown, and it didn't look at all good to eat; his sisters always said you could tell a good cure by its bad taste. After a bit of effort, he chewed it up into an awful, sticky pulp. A sweet pulp. With a tang of sour wine that prickled his throat and... copper? Terrano was wiping his hands down his shirt in long, deliberate movements, watching Lark over his reading glasses.

'Can... can I spit?' Lark asked, reaching for the bowl.

Terrano threw his bulk over the desk and clamped Lark's wrist, the table screeching in protest. His other hand seized Lark's jaw, fingernails digging into the flesh of his cheeks. He remained there, sprawled over the table, his eyes and hands pinning Lark in place.

'Swallow,' he whispered.

Lark's head clouded up. His leg jumped and rattled. He'd swallow, he'd beg, he'd bite just to be let go. He tried to scream, tried to slap. Wet air snorted and whistled from his nose as juice dribbled out over Terrano's fingers, but the grip tightened, and terrible seconds passed.

'Swallow,' Terrano repeated, a soft order Lark was too dazed to resist.

He swallowed.

Terrano let go and Lark's senses returned in a flood of tears. He choked and spat, frantically wiping away the sticky pulp that dangled from his lips and nostrils. When he raised his head, he saw Terrano tutting at the mess on the floor. 'No need to be so dramatic, my boy.'

'Sorry, sere,' said Lark, confused. 'I—'

'No, no, I am the one who is sorry. I apologise for touching you. I had a friend who was once beset by similar fears.' He mimed a hand over his leg, mimicking the jumping spasms that overtook Lark when people got too close.

'Someone like me?' Lark didn't dare believe it. 'With brain fevers?'

'I will tell you of him later,' said Terrano, waving a hand. 'Such things are past him now. But let us review the experiment. Did you recognise the taste? You did! I saw you did. That, Lark, was mortalus leaf, the very same toxic stems those fiends stirred in your water.' Terrano mopped at the mess on the floor with a handkerchief, squatting down easily despite his belly. He tossed the sodden rag aside and pulled a second one from his pocket to wipe his fingers. 'There is bad feeling in the Splitside villages. The triple draft is too much. The poisoning of a taxer is a message – a test of their boldness? Perhaps so.' Terrano stood and produced a third handkerchief. He offered it so Lark could wipe his mouth. 'You are mixed up in this, and through no fault of your own, I might add. My sympathies. It must have been a bad death.'

The blanket fell away as Lark reached out for the offered handkerchief. He froze, staring at his skin.

'Do not worry about those, dear boy.'

Lark pulled the blanket further back. Black veins throbbed on his arm. His chest. His shoulder. Horrified, he touched a hand to his jaw, feeling them bulge and wriggle.

'A fearsome look, but harmless.' Terrano patted Lark's hand. 'A lasting gift from your brush with death. Mortalus leaf running in your veins! And something more, perhaps?' He smiled.

'You just poisoned me?'

Terrano's laugh was almost too soft to hear. His shoulders shook but no sound emerged. 'I just proved it was impossible.' Terrano looked down at the scattered stems. 'That leaf would have killed five men, maybe six, all twice your size. It did, in fact! Your tax patrol is dead. I picked over their bodies to find you, sensing your suitability to be saved.' Clearing his throat, the scholar opened his book and placed an ink-stained finger on the first page. His arm slipped around Lark's shoulders, holding him tight while he shivered and bounced. 'See here, my boy? I record the experiences of every child who joins my family. I record them in meticulous detail.' He recited from his book in a hushed, proud tone. '"The most immediate observation is that the body of the dead will learn. Life cannot be taken the same way twice."'

Finger still in place, he turned to whisper in Lark's ear. 'You died, Lark. I brought you back and the deadliest of poisons cannot take you away again.' He gripped Lark by the back of his head, forcing him to look at the book. 'Last time I was in the Northlands, I was witnessed a young maid drown while washing her master's clothes. I found her and wrote her name in my book. Now she lives and no longer needs air to breathe. You? You were poisoned!' He shook Lark's head for emphasis. 'I wager you could choke down a whole bush of mortalus without breaking a sweat. Nibble on foxfell, dine on rotting flesh. Your body has learnt.'

Lark was only half listening, caught on a worrying thought.

'Do you understand, my boy?'

'What did you say happened to my patrol?'

'Dead. Do you understand all that I am saying?'

'I... don't, sere.'

'You will in time.' Pages fluttered past. Terrano recited the names that appeared at the top of each one. 'Amelle, Darren, Fay, Jodie...' He tapped the page with Jodie's name on it. 'Take care with this one, my boy. She gives me a new name each time we talk. However, I am not made of paper. She must make do with her first pseudonym.'

More pages turned, more names flicked by.

'It is clumsy work, with no science or theory to guide us. But who could claim to understand something as strange as this? My endeavours will change this world forever. And perhaps win my freedom.' He arrived at the page with Lark's name, and neatened off an embellishment with a scrape of ink. His quill rattled in the ink pot. 'You, young Lark, are the twentieth child to join our group.' The quill was dancing in Terrano's hand, noting down Lark's thirst, his aches, every objection he'd voiced and a dozen more he hadn't. The finished letters seemed to melt into nonsense.

'Sere, I don't—'

'Patience, Lark. I found you face down in a ditch – dead and abandoned. I implore you, answer my questions before voicing your own. Now, count backwards from ten, and tell me if you get a sensation of dizziness.'

Lips That Bleed

Young spat expertly on his rag and polished a smudge from the chipped glass. He inverted it and muttered a prayer, waiting a few seconds for the breath of Godearth to rise and fill it. Then a few more, because he was never quite certain how long such things took.

'What's all that muttering for?' Lester snapped.

'Blessings come from the Earth.' Young beamed at him. 'Look!' He showed him the empty glass. Not that this cretin was polite enough to pretend to see anything.

Young sighed and returned the tumbler to its shelf. His glassware shone with borrowed pinks and greens, cast down by the temple's stained windows. He thought it was very pretty and he moved the shelf to catch different colours each time a window shattered. The harvest tree creaked in apology; its barren branches flowed along the roof, seeking more windows through which it could escape. Young patted its trunk and leant back, putting his feet up on the altar.

'No god gives two craps about you, priest,' Lester said. His hand entwined with the hilt on his sabre, perhaps not on purpose. 'Or me. I don't give two craps either.'

Young tutted and gestured downwards. 'Careful now. He's always under you, always watching.' The tree groaned in agreement.

'Not you he's not, you old sot. Not me he isn't.' Lester spat on the temple floor and scuffed it in with a boot. 'See? See. So, knock it off.' A vicious kick snapped the lock off Young's cabinet. Lester tugged the door free from its stubborn frame and his hand drifted over the juni bottles. 'Have at this stuff, Leo. Should fetch a decent price.' He stood back and clipped his tag-along around the ear.

Leo dragged over a straw crate and started, reluctantly, to empty the cabinet. The boy hadn't grown much since Young had watched him storm tearfully out of choir practice five years ago. He crossed his knees over the altar. 'That belongs to Godearth, lad.'

Leo paused, his hands hovering over the next bottle.

'Your god.' Young stared up at the harvest tree. It creaked approvingly. 'The worst kind of god to annoy.'

The lad's brow furrowed. He stared at his fingers as if willing himself to disown them.

'Leo!' Lester snarled at him. 'The cause needs coin.'

'Careful now.' Young widened his eyes as Leo reached out again. He let his voice quiver, extending a finger. 'I feel him watching you!'

'It's just orders, Priest Young, just orders.' Leo looked between his priest and commander. He winced. 'It's for the good of the Northlands. It all is.'

Young could tell when a phrase had been beaten into a young man. The words tumbled out in someone else's manner, in this case obstructed by the bruises swelling on Leo's cheek. 'And Godearth smiles on your cause,' he said, letting the boy off. 'But stealing in a temple? Come, you know better. Give us your hand. Come on now.' He turned Leo's palm downwards and muttered words of forgiveness. Now, he normally made up these phrases, enjoying the sounds he could make in the pebble and soil of his god's tongue, but this time he stuck to the scripture, as the boy was clearly going to die in the coming months.

'There you go, young shaver.' He patted Leo's head. 'Blessings come from the Earth, remember that.'

It was the second rebellion of the year, and this one had teeth to it. The butchered remains of the last pitiful uprising – still nailed across a dozen signposts – had acted as anything but a deterrent. Weathered herdsmen slaughtered their last sheep and trudged down from the Mountain Feet. Starving woodsmen locked up their shacks and arrived with huge axes gripped in their sinewy arms. They'd heard rumours that Hillsford had food, and city-forged armour, and a turncoat general with a scar on his eye and a thirst for revenge.

Young hadn't seen anything like that. The same men said Branera was weak and drained of fighters, boasting of empty walls and rusted equipment. What truth came from the city of deceit and commerce? Mud, gold and lies. That's all you get in Branera.

'Take your time. There's a good lad.' Young watched as Leo fumbled another bottle, spilling most of it. He considered the stash he'd hidden in the brickwork of his well and allowed himself a smile. Charity begins with surplus. 'There's more on that shelf there, don't miss any.'

At the far end of his temple, the grand doors shook, halting the clink of glassware. Lester was hunched over a pew, caught with a bottle poised by his lips. He tossed it aside and sniffed. 'You bar that door, Leo?'

'I said I did, didn't I?'

Lester watched the dust settle around the doors. 'Then get back to packing that juni. Do as I say now.'

'I suppose it was the little door?'

'Beg your pardon, Priest?' said Leo, hands in the cabinet again.

'The door you barred. It was the little one? The pastor door?' Young inverted and blessed another glass. He set it on the shelf with the others. 'Because it's not the pastor door that's rattling.'

The doors shook again, dust and debris falling from the mantel. Young frowned at another chipped glass. How did he keep breaking them? He hid it at the back of the shelf where no one could see.

'Who—'

'I'm not expecting anyone,' said Young, smiling helpfully. The doors groaned. These were massive oaken slabs, with hinges so seized with rust that no priest had tried them for centuries. Cobwebs stretched to their breaking point as they thudded and squealed open, and Lester quickly moved to block the aisle. He stripped off his jacket, wincing as a formless voice bellowed past the doors. Despite the vaulted ceiling and stone walls, echoes were eaten and distorted in Young's temple; meaning was absorbed by the earth-covered floor and lost in mouldy hangings. To his guests, this greeting was an unintelligible roar.

'What the hell was that?' Lester snapped, turning on Young for answers.

With a thump and scrape, the doors opened another inch. The voice bellowed again. 'Priest Young? You in here?'

Young bent to whisper into the hollow behind his altar. 'Come in,' he said, and his words echoed and bounced around the room. The man who shouldered his way through the gap was a monster from cottage-wife tales – a giant, pale thing that would stand eye to eye with any shaved bear up on its paws. His naked body rippled with enormous quantities of fat, which shook as he raised his arms in prayer. Young whispered into the hollow again. 'Blessings come from the Earth.' The giant knelt and pressed his palms to the floor, then started trudging down the aisle.

'What did he say? Who the hell's that?' Lester was still blocking the aisle, his chin jutting out from under bulging eyes.

'That, I think, is Husker Tollworth,' said Young, grinning at the approaching figure. 'Have another drink and settle down? Or he might kill someone.' Husker returned the smile, if Young could call it that. Young's was the warm sort a priest liked to cultivate, with plenty of crooked teeth on show and a welcoming tip of the head. Husker's was a stretch of cracked lips that broke like a wound across his face.

'Hold up now,' snapped Lester, impressively sure of himself given the man looming over him. 'You don't know me, so I'll spare—'

'I've been released, Young.' Husker moved the swordsman aside with a sweep of his arm. He padded closer, his feet soft as snowfall on the groomed earth. The oversized fingers that took hold of Young's hand were even gentler. 'Feels good. You know the fields now lie right at the Mountain Head? Each season the cold crops climb higher.'

'You look well, my friend,' said Young. He patted him on the knuckles. 'And you have grown since I last braved the iron snows!'

'He's a prisoner?' squeaked Leo, a bottle in each hand. 'From the farms?'

'A released prisoner, boy. And I'm from here, same as you.' Husker dropped down heavily on a pew, legs spread in no attempt to hide his nakedness. He laid his hands on his knees. 'What's your name, anyway? Speak up now.' The giant's body was almost entirely hairless, bar a stubble of midnight-black hair and a scattering of grey whiskers on his chin. His face was squat and flat, as if ground against a stone, and he had honest eyes that Young had seen convert the most hardened prisoners to his side. And through some deft work a few years back, Husker's side was now the same as Godearth's.

'Leo, sere. Born to the smithy, by the village square.'

'Well, Leo, that makes us neighbours.' Husker's grin cracked and bled across his face. The boy shuddered.

'And friends,' added Young hastily. 'We're all friends.'

'No need for that.' Husker's lips puckered as he massaged them. His face seemed to be thawing out. 'He means well, Leo. You attend his sermons? You should. Your priest here climbs all the way to the Mountain Head to find a crowd to preach to. You might save him some bleeding if you came by once in a while.' He showed off the scars that covered his skin. 'The snow up there cuts you deep, but Young trudges through it wrapped in no more than bed linen and that flimsy robe.'

'What... what's that?' Leo's eyes were fixed on Husker's rock pendant. Husker bowed his head to take it off. The porous stone swung like a pendulum in front of Leo, and it might have been a precious jewel for all that it shone in the lad's eye.

'A rock.' Husker chuckled, tapping it so it kept swinging. 'Just a rock. But it stands for something more, and that's the trick of religion, isn't it?'

'What's it for?' asked Leo, confused.

Husker's hideous grin relaxed. Young could almost hear his skin creaking. 'Nothing. Our priest says I should mimic it.'

'One day, his hands will wear that smooth, and he will take my place at this temple. If he chooses.' Young frowned at Leo. 'You remember I offered you one, when you came of age.' There was a breath of steel as Lester drew his blade, so Young coughed and hastily stepped out of the way. Some men can only be ignored for so long.

'Now I know you.' The tendons on Lester's forearms bulged as he levelled the point of his rapier. He brandished the freshly stitched patches of rank on his jacket. 'I'm an officer in the uprising, and I know the name Tollworth, you monstrous fuck. You butchered a wife ten years back and we still whisper about it.'

'I didn't do it,' said Husker mildly. 'Anyway, I've been released.'

'Released?' Lester's eyes narrowed. The point of the rapier advanced an inch. 'Nah. That's not the point of the farms, is it? No one survives winter up there, so back up till you don't.'

Husker laughed, slapping his knees as he stood. 'I survived ten of them. But I've got better things to do than tend those slopes.' He moved without noticeable hurry, taking Lester's head and cracking it against the altar before anyone really noticed, grunting slightly as the rapier bit into his arm. Young watched a stupid grin spread over Leo's face. The boy was looking up at his new hero with unabashed admiration.

'Husker!' Young scolded. 'Blood on the earth! And on my altar too. It will take days to scrub that off.' He pulled his frock clear of the wet patch and scowled. 'Do not bring Goddeath to my temple. She and I had a falling out.'

'Ah, priest.' Husker waved a dismissive hand. He rehung his pendant, belatedly gripping it and muttering a prayer against impulse. 'He was a prick.'

Young slipped off the altar to set Lester upright, and checked the cut on his head. He was still breathing. Tedious. But then, the currents under his well were good at dragging tedious problems away. 'Goddeath is no stranger to taking others' turf,' he said firmly, wiping down the altar. 'I must ask you to control yourself in here.'

'Don't fret on it. I'll leave soon and take her with me.' Husker held up his arm, which had been badly cut by Lester's blade. 'You see this, Young? I'm still blessed by the Earth.' The cut was a deep slice along his forearm. It was weeping blood over his pale skin, and that skin was... wriggling. Creeping. Closing the cut up into a knobbly scar. Husker was trying to say something else, but he was dribbling like his mouth had been filled with plum stones. 'Bless...ings. Come from the Earth.'

Young took the liquor bottles from Leo's hands before he dropped them. The boy swore only faintly, but Young heard it and beat him round the ears. 'Bring the rake.'

'But—'

'Quickly now!' Young let his voice hit the warning tone that set his former choirboys moving – the one that said he was reaching for his birch rod. Leo winced and scurried off to get the rake. 'That's right, now hand it to Sere Tollworth.'

'He's not taking it, sere.'

'Give him a moment.'

Husker's eyes rolled back into view. He swallowed, wiping spit from his mouth. 'Thank you,' he said gravely, accepting the rake from the wide-eyed boy.

'So, the Earth still blesses you,' said Young. 'I am pleased. Though what is this talk of Goddeath? Have you not practised my teachings?'

'Never said I didn't. But all of the old three stalk those farms. You can't shake off Death on the Mountain Head, so I prayed to her most nights. Bargained a bit.' Husker used the rake to neaten the scuffed soil, and Young felt a flush of pride temper his mounting unease. 'They sent the smallest or oldest to me. I'd climb with them, haul their picks and shovels when their hands failed. Carry them home when their legs failed. Those wretches thought I was giving them life, but they didn't see Goddeath at my heels.' He finished raking and sat down heavily on the pews. 'If you were sent to me, you were weak. Weakness does not flourish up there, Young. Nothing does. Nothing except the cold crops.'

Young tutted and took down two of his most chipped tumblers. He filled them with juni and handed them to Husker. 'You're rambling.' He patted the man's leg. 'Have you eaten?'

'No.' Husker scrubbed his face. 'It's the heat. This place is a furnace after the snows. Come, preach to me. Am I unworthy of this blessing? I took your rock, yet I prayed to others.'

'Oh please,' Young said. 'Don't be so vain. The gods do not care if you kneel to others.' He tilted Husker's chin upwards. It was slippery with sweat. 'I have been a priest to all of the old three at one time or another. Trust me, Godearth is the one you need.' He took his empty tumblers and passed them to Leo, who was staring at the slumped form of Lester. 'Go throw these glasses on the midden – Sere Tollworth has hastened on the cracks with those big hands of his. Yes, now, please. Off you go. And light up the kitchens on the way back.'

The boy tried to linger, but the thwack of Young's birch rod against an altar put an end to that. He chewed his lip thoughtfully. With a bit of care, Leo could be kept too busy to be recruited again. A dirty temple was the most formidable weapon in a priest's arsenal, after all.

'I'm glad you found the time to visit,' said Young, pushing up his glasses to better examine the delirious freak sitting in his temple. 'Good gods. Look at the size of you. The blessing has indeed suffused you further.'

'Nothing can hurt me.'

'Blessings come from the Earth,' Young intoned. 'And the voice?'

'My angel sings to me. It moans in my head.'

'You are truly blessed. Though...' Young coughed politely. 'May I ask where your clothes are?'

'I left them on the slopes. The heat down here makes me agitated.' He shook his head. 'Young, I cannot stay. I need to see my children.'

'Of course.' His relief was uncharitable, but he could atone for that later. Away from the horrors of the Mountain Head, he'd forgotten how unsettling this man was. Let the world mellow him before he came back to serve. 'They are still in Branera, then?'

'Lily and Rose are. The letters from their stepfather tell me Lark was sent out last week to follow a Taxer.' Husker's smile cracked open an inch wider than before. His lips ran with blood. 'I'll be damned if my boy has anything to do with the Roaming Watch.'

'You will find him, I am sure. So, perhaps we can find you something to wear?' Young nudged Husker and winked. 'Hmm? Something that will make the city ladies comfortable?' His glasses were steaming up. The heat rising from this giant was palpable.

'Later. Tell me news, it took me weeks to descend.'

'Nothing changes in the villages.' Young paused. 'An uprising, perhaps.'

Husker looked up at the harvest tree. 'These towns are as rotten as the cities.' The tree creaked in agreement.

'Is it not as you remember?' Young tried to guide Husker to his feet.

'You know it isn't.'

Mud

L ily Kale-Tollworth pitched herself into an empty seat at the top table, breathless and a little flushed. Her hair was drenched, though she kept it too short for that to matter. Everything else was drenched too, which did matter in the Low Ends of Branera.

'Gentlemen.'

She ignored the whoops and catcalls, separating out her clothes and bending over to clean her feet. Foul-smelling mud coated her exposed toes and the hem of her dress had been dragged through enough filth that the stains reached her knees. Might turn a few heads on the boards later. Not that these idiots cared.

'What... the fuck... has happened to you?' said Ruckman, wiping tears of laughter from his eyes.

'Oh, just a little mishap,' Lily replied throatily, shaking some swill at the bottom of the table whisky. 'I see you all started early.'

The short, hairy mudder who ran this brothel kept her a permanent seat at his top table. Any lesser occupant was turfed down to the lower tiers, where the spirits thickened to slurry and men elbowed for space on crowded benches. Like most buildings sunk this far in the Low Ends, Ruckman's was a tall, cramped affair. It was more vertical than anything else, and too narrow to stand on its own, careering drunkenly against its neighbours. Knock the right building down and half the city would collapse.

'She's a dirty girl,' someone called out gleefully, inciting more laughter and whistling. Ruckman blew bubbles in his beer as he sniggered along.

It was busy tonight. Ruckman kept a rowdy crow – ageing letches who enjoyed a bawdy song, an ale or two, and a few seconds of exposed skin in the room upstairs. Nothing fancy, but the older crowd was reliable, easy money. Ruckman was their provider and role model, a proprietor with the breeding of a horny goat and about the same grasp of subtlety or tact. Even now he was playing up to the cramped table, licking his lips and waggling bushy eyebrows as he reached over to caress her foot with the same enthusiasm as if she'd flopped out a tit.

'Well, we can sort out those dainty little tootsies, Lils, no fear. Uncle Ruck will give them a wash...'

To the delight of their crowing neighbours, Lily planted her heel in his forehead and pushed him firmly away, faking a yawn. Down by her foot Ruckman continued to chuckle, leaning against her and waggling his fingers in a demented assault on her ankles. Not that he really touched her. He never did. He'd a soft streak hidden somewhere beneath those crusty clothes, even if the fool was so damn proud of his clowning it was impossible to see it. Or rise above it. Any attempts at composure were lost as he plumbed further and further into the depths of humour.

Ruckman muttered something to a neighbour, who sniggered and rubbed at his crotch.

'Are mishaps like this common, miss?' said a man with tanned, southern skin. His voice rolled with distant accents and rustled like leaves underfoot. 'I packed only one set of boots. I would hate to lose them.'

'Those old things?' Lily said, with a pout. 'Oh, sere, I'll have to help you find some local styles.' She turned her most wonderful smile on him, but found herself outmatched. The stranger's features were delicate and smooth, with high cheekbones and handsome, warm eyes. The moment was broken with a gasp as Ruckman poured ale over her foot, wetting it so he could massage her clean. She prodded him in the eye with her big toe. 'Gentle, you bastard.' Lily turned back to the stranger. 'A word of caution, sere. You should know that you're in the slums of our great city – I'd climb a few stairs before spending any real coin on footwear. This very brothel has been called the arsehole of the Low Ends on numerous occasions. You waded your way here, you know what I mean.'

Spluttering noises from Ruckman were accompanied by a bit of futile wiping of the table. 'I'll have you know—'

'Lils,' interrupted Withers, another lost soul hiding in this filthy place. 'Dren knows what he's doing. He's a great traveller!' The so-called traveller was preening under all this attention. Suddenly the warm image of climbing up the boardwalks with him to share a roof-top bottle was spoiled. It wasn't as if she lacked for arrogant men, and Withers continued to feed his clearly bloated ego. 'He tells wonderful stories, you know. They made me homesick, they really did.' He nudged Dren. 'The shimmering sands, the shifting waters? Eh? Eh, old man?'

This was a fairly common theme. Withers was a blinking, excitable sort from the continental spurs off the Wayward Coast. Any land there was thrown into place by the raging waters of the Split and torn up just as quickly. The proud, salt-skinned locals called it a nation, but the silt shifted so often that their lives were consumed by bitter border disputes. Withers had a grand name to match his diplomatic exploits there, even if no one could remember it beyond Withers-something-something.

'Imagine that, Lils.' Withers took a small sip from his line of drinks, embarking on a night that wouldn't end till dawn touched the roof far above them, and Ruckman's exhausted whores collapsed around him in the loft. 'Well, you don't have to imagine much, the way he paints it.'

'You flatter me,' said Dren, beaming. 'The world is a wonderful place, even I struggle to do it justice.' He gripped Withers by the shoulder. 'We both know that words are insufficient to describe someone's home. You cannot feel them, or taste them.' Dren closed his eyes, and Lily watched his smile spread with the urge to share this well-seasoned bullshit. 'We have both stood on those brazen beaches, Sere Withers. Erudite conversation. Bracing air. Exotic foods. The Nation has all the temptations of finery and flesh, and yet...' Dren's eyes met Lily's with a horrible sincerity. 'I still find myself missing the devious and beautiful people of Branera.'

Mixed flattery worked better than the obvious kind down in the mud, so his back was slapped, his knee was squeezed and an impromptu toast took place. 'Fine words,' Lily said, gesturing for her glass to be refilled. 'Though I wonder what a grand traveller like you sees in our humble city?'

He smiled at her joke.

Branera was the proudest, richest city in the Northlands, even if half of it was buried in rivers of mud and shit. The buildings that rose high enough were blessed by the greatest of the northern aristocracy, with boarded paths threading between these affluent peaks and reserved for the exclusive use of the fantastically well-off. Cerc Reno – their sister city on the shore – was a mean, harsh place in comparison, still clinging to a militant past and broken under poverty and stern rule. There were other cities, of course. It was hardly worth mentioning them.

'I know your home well,' Dren said, addressing the table as much as Lily. 'And I praise beauty as much as affluence. Women from Daren Dunn lack one and those from Cerc Reno lack both. It is Branera for me.' A glass of whisky was pressed into his hands. 'Too kind! Thank you.'

Lily snorted, annoyed at his effortless ability to snatch people's attention. His face was delicately featured, yet framed by wildly braided hair. He was young, but still strangely old, incredibly know-it-all seen-it-all, and his very accent drew out and enunciated syllables Lily never knew existed, twisting familiar words towards the exotic. Clearly, the man was insufferable twat.

'Perhaps you would like to hear a tale or two for yourself, miss?' said Dren, helping himself to someone's drink. 'It is how I earn my keep.'

'You tell stories?'

'I make stories, then tell them.'

Lily spluttered with laughter, and she was rewarded by a slight darkening of his eyes. 'Listen, Drake—'

'Dren, miss.'

She wiped her eyes. 'Really? Oh gods, it's too much.' Lily raised her hands in protest. 'Enough. I know your type. Wandering beggars with a scheme for every city. I expect you will tell me Dren is a fine name with a rich heritage. Perhaps you have an urgent legacy at stake?'

'Oh no, miss. Nothing like that. My name is ridiculous, old fashioned.' He twirled a finger in his ale. 'But your name sounds like a mystery, too – you dress in finery, yet go by a shabby handle from the villages. Have I missed a boardwalk trend, or is there a tale to your birth? Orphan, maybe?' His teeth glinted as he smiled. 'Yes. I think so.'

Lily's accent dropped, picking up the twang of the mudders around her. 'What a lovely, sharp wit. Go fuck yourself with it.'

'Lily, please!' Withers broke in with waving hands. 'Dren, she doesn't mean any offence.'

Neither she nor Dren had moved an inch, their eyes sparring over the table. Lily gave a tight smile. 'Who says I didn't?'

'Leave them be,' said Ruckman with a knowing nod. 'Look at them lock eyes, it will be lips later. I'm a soppy romantic, I know these things.' He lifted his mug and nudged Dren. 'The upstairs room's free. Two sarls if she messes the sheets – bet she's on the bleed with that mood.'

'Shitting gods, Ruckman!' Lily aimed a kick at his shin, but hit the table leg instead. He jerked his feet clear, cackling at her. 'You'll be blee—'

He slammed down his drink, joining her in mock outrage and disowning his muttered words. 'I heard it too! A slur on your honour. Who said that? Come on now!'

A few cheap laughs rattled around the table. Those drunk enough joined in with this pantomime, questioning their neighbours with waggled fingers and peering under the table to find the intruder. Lily crossed her legs. 'Really, now.' She recovered her accent. 'I'm a lady from the boardwalks. I wouldn't be seen dead lifting skirts in your filthy attic.'

'Not fancy enough for her mightiness.' Ruckman turned forlorn eyes on Dren. 'Afraid I ain't got any silk sheets for her to screw on. That's her problem. Got a rich stepdaddy.'

'Screw?' Dren seemed puzzled.

'Yeah. You know.' Ruckman humped the air a bit.

'What a strange phrase,' Dren said distantly. He rose with a bow and excused himself. 'And here I thought myself current with Norther dialect.' Dropping down to the next tier, he jostled for some space and announced his profession. Coins hit the table to the rhythmic thump of his fist, until he launched into a song loud and rude enough that the top table lost Ruckman as he tried to keep up with both conversations.

'So, really, what happened?' said Withers, growing serious.

'Nothing.'

'It's not nothing. You're out of sorts.'

'And you're prying, dear. I'd even say you sound sober. Is Ruckman watering down your ale again?' She dropped the boardwalk accent; it came and went when it pleased, just as she did. 'Don't fuss. I ran into trouble on the way here, that's all.'

'What'd she say?' Ruckman turned back round.

'Someone grabbed her,' muttered Withers, still watching her.

'What? They wouldn't fucking dare.'

Lily scraped some mud from her foot, slopping it into a bucket. 'Forget it. Was starting to think I wasn't worth grabbing, most others seem to be.' Her laughter sounded forced, even to her.

'You stop that.' Ruckman jabbed a finger towards her, nostrils flaring. 'Did they hurt you?'

'No.'

An unexpected grip clamping across her chest, another across her mouth. Massive groping hands squeezing tighter and tighter, parting cloth and finding skin. Arm hairs tickling her nose, her scrambling boots dragging twin trails in the mud. Stab. A warm spray splattered across her cheek. Stab again, wildly over her shoulder, her blade still trailing the straps that bound it to her thigh. Her assailant roared with pain, blood slicking both their grips.

'It's nothing,' Lily said distractedly. Her muddy lace was drying out, cracking off to reveal the stains she'd hidden beneath it. Better mud than blood, that's a mudder's saying. 'Going to skip the chimneys on Bakers Row from now on, that's all. Lots of people drinking, too few people working.'

Withers blew out air and leant back in his seat. Ruckman was standing, red in the cheeks and pointing a quivering finger at her. As if it were somehow her fault. 'You sit here. I'm going to find them.'

'Who you going to find, idiot?' Lily stroked her hair back and forced a smile to her face. He was going to do something stupid, of course. That's what stupid, kind people do. 'I didn't even say what they looked like. And you're swaying. Sit down and don't act like a prick.'

Dren's voice came from somewhere by their feet. 'Always good advice. And sadly, a Norther phrase with which I am more familiar.' He climbed back up to their table. 'Do you require a healer, miss? I have picked up a passing competency in women's therapeutics on my travels.'

She glared at him. 'Women's therapeutics? Seriously, where the fuck are you from?' Dren placed down two mugs, neither of which were his, and slid her the biggest one. Misplaced accusations and harsh words were exchanged on the lower tier as their owners noticed the theft.

'Somewhere else.'

'Well, I don't need your help.' Lily took the mug and drained it, letting the watery slop run over her chin and neck. She finished it with a gasp.

'What are you staring at? Don't you listen to this red-faced idiot. I spend enough time down here that I can look after myself. Plenty count me as more mudder than anything else.' Yet she gave him a haughty glare more suited to the boardwalks. 'Most nights someone would've been around to lend a hand.'

There were a lot of grey-haired, sallow faces nodding assent around the table. A few mutters about changing times. Ruckman didn't look all that convinced, so Lily played up to him. She didn't have much, but it was enough. Down here, almost anything was.

'Oh come on, Ruckers.' Lily leant forwards. 'Poor little man. You know the type, I drew a little prick of blood' – she waggled her small finger at him – 'and sent the oaf running home to his fat wife. I'm more concerned about losing my boot than some idiot pawing at my tits.'

Lily had abandoned it at the crossroads, unable to stop the sobs as she pulled and pulled at her ankle, which was stuck impossibly deep in the muddy soup. The city bells rang out around her, a cacophony of noise that drowned out the gutter splashes of rainwater and the bellows of her wounded attacker, but not her scream when a pale giant landed heavily between them. He roared a challenge and tackled the other man down, the two of them slapping and sliding in the muck. Between her tears and gasps, Lily managed to fumble her boot buckles free and splash off into an alley, but those few, trembling moments pressed against Ruckman's back door had done little to calm her nerves. Even now, as her foot tingled in the warmth of the brothel, she could feel it plunging again and again into the icy, rock-strewn mud.

Ruckman barked with laughter.

'Bloody bet you did. Bit off more than they could chew, eh, Lils?' He slapped Withers on the shoulder. 'Tougher than any of my daughters, this rich bitch is, and they were born right upstairs in the attic.'

Withers smiled half-heartedly, still watching Lily. He touched her hand when no one was watching. 'We can talk later if you want.'

She hated that. Perceptive old twat.

'Ruckman,' she wheedled, brushing Withers off. 'Fetch something from the top shelf, would you? I've got an hour before I'm up on the boards again. I fancy getting a tad pissed first.' They cheered as she pressed a hand to the cheek of her neighbour, taking his drink. 'Too kind. Someone's getting married tonight, you know. Not me, Ruckers, you idiot.'

~

Much, much later, Lily clattered down Ruckman's steps. The sounds of revelry at her back tempted her to linger, but unsteady feet warned her she'd stayed long enough. She swung past a platform, one hand on the post as snatches of song came from the window.

'My love from Darude, caught blue in the nude, feeling for her skirt on the bank of... shit.' Her feet were as clumsy as her voice. But what of it? There were no great singers in the mud.

Or tailors. The clothes Ruckman had found behind his bar pinched and rubbed at her armpits as she skipped down to street level. It was fair to say that a mudder's get-up could cause as much scandal as bloodstained finery; she had experience in such matters. But the dress was warm, and her head swam with whisky and kind words, so she really didn't care. Her fingers traced over the marks she'd cut on Ruckman's sign last winter. The dim lamplight revealed some unfamiliar scratches and she squinted at the newest name – it seemed Dren was a friend of Ruckman's now, too.

With a snort, Lily stepped down into the mud, feeling the chill rise against her borrowed boots. It paid to wear tall leather in the Low Ends. The aristocracy padded around upstairs in delicate slippers, never dreaming of trotting down to the sewer streets. She was the only lady in the mud, and she liked it that way. Even if tonight the Low Ends felt less welcoming than usual. Even if every shadow hid a pale shape, each alley a groping arm. She waded quickly to the nearest stairs, scraping her boots on the brush before climbing.

It was a long slog, exhausting even for the city guards. Not that they went down as much as Lily did, and certainly no one had run the ascent as quickly as she did this evening. At the top, the stair minder nodded sleepily to her. He gave her space on his bench while she caught her breath and fanned flushed cheeks. 'Evening, miss.' He tipped his hat and tried to look more alert, peering out over the rooftops.

'Hello, Daryl.' She accepted his water flask as gracefully as possible, resisting the urge to pour it all over her face and neck. This district of Branera was Lily's favourite. A girl could climb from nothing to everything on just one stair. By day, the layers of mudder shops were a riotous barrage of colour, thronging with shoulders and noise – she couldn't wade more than a few steps without getting sized up for her looks or purse. Then from dusk it was serene, balcony paint dimmed to soft pastels in the light of swinging lamps, wooden signs creaking in the wind. Climb any higher and you miss half the view, with glossed boards and thatched roofs sealing off the chaotic world below.

Someone called out from further along the platform, so she rose and smoothed down her skirts.

'Miss, hey there! I say, wait!'

Lily stood patiently while a slippered young man in an oversized waistcoat trotted towards her, flustered and gasping for air. She composed herself, placing one hand on her chest and dipping her head demurely. She caught the stink of whisky on her breath, so tried to keep her breathing light. 'Hello, sere,' she said. 'Did Papa send you for me?' She left her eyes averted, then raised them with a twinkle. 'I'm very grateful. Isn't it dark out tonight?'

'Indeed,' said the breathless gentleman. The stair minder retreated a few discreet steps. 'Indeed. Miss Kale, ah... I presume? Your stepfather is... is waiting at the hall. He said to come urgently. I was sent out, excuse me, to find you.'

And too timid to leave the boardwalks for this great mission, it seemed. His small chest puffed in and out, making his waistcoat flap around like a tent in a stiff breeze. He soon recovered enough to make a formal greeting, but after a few seconds of him whisking the air and bowing, Lily neatly intercepted one of his arms and pulled him upright. He seemed surprised at this, but rallied well, even when she started dragging him in the direction of the wedding hall.

'So, miss—' He was interrupted by a broken board and gave a squawk.

'Thank you for escorting me,' said Lily. Her boots clopped briskly on the creaking wood. 'Most kind. May I ask your name?'

'Tito Dale, Miss Kale. Oh, is that whisky? Has someone spilled their drink on you?'

'Sere Dale. It is the height of bad manners to smell a young lady while escorting her.' She let him excuse himself into knots, sensing the conversation would be dull anyway.

Josef Kale was waiting for them outside the wedding hall. Lily's stepfather was a man of advanced years, but also of great energy and image, unable to go two moments without striking a deal or filling someone's glass. She watched his hands go from pocket to pocket as he tidied himself, neatening his already smart attire. Lily called out as they neared, trying to interrupt the flow of nervous babble from her escort. 'Papa! Sorry I'm late.'

He gave a tight smile, but no reply. This curt response cut through the remaining warmth Lily had carried up from the brothel, leaving her exposed to the damp wind and his wary, bloodshot eyes. The rain had started up again, water rushing through the gutters around them and hammering down over the boards.

She tried again as they neared, ducking under the hall awning and out of the storm. 'I feel awful. Sere Dale told me you were beside yourself with worry.' Lily kept her questions in check as she gave Josef a peck on the cheek.

'Think nothing of it, my dear.' His hand touched her wrist, and held it, as if he were afraid she'd float off. It was then she smelt whisky on him too, his anxious fingers gripping her too hard.

'And Tito!' Josef found an offhand tone for Lily's diminutive escort. That marked him as someone approaching his equal, which was rare. Josef had taken a place in the city ministers several years back and his advancement had never stopped since. 'My thanks. Head inside and set us up a couple of sloshes, eh?'

'Of course, Minister. Need a word with the young lady, I expect. I did try to tell her—'

'Yes, well, Tito, you know how it is.'

'Goodbye, Miss Kale. An enjoyable, if brief, encounter.'

'Oh yes. Enjoyably brief, some might say.' Lily was too distracted to filter the little sarcastic poet who filled her head with such things. Tito's mouth worked circles of confusion as he processed her words, thankfully too slow or dull to press her on them.

'Good evening, Tito,' said Josef firmly.

'Of course. So... Miss Kale?'

Maybe in private Josef would return to his normal self? Of course, he was simply putting on a show for this idiot. Once they were alone, a smile would break out over his sly face, and they would laugh at his latest scheme to trap the daft midget in some political twist, joking over a glass of wine as his fingerprints faded from her wrist. She tugged on her arm, but Josef didn't let go.

'Miss Kale?' Tito took a step forwards, as if he'd earned some privilege by walking her two minutes down a sodding boardwalk. 'I'll be at the high table, Miss Kale. Maybe we can talk later?'

'Oh gods! Maybe you can fuck off, that's what you can do.' Lily turned to Josef. 'Papa, let me go.' She tugged on her arm again, but her step-father held her tight, so Lily whirled back to a spluttering Tito to vent her mounting frustration. 'Go on! Shoo! You really are an insufferably expectant idiot. Find some other skirt to hover around.'

Tito's nostrils flared. He'd caught up with her insults at last. 'How even dare you?'

'Tito, please,' said Josef, in a small, firm voice. 'Leave us.' That was a surprise even for Lily. She never got away with such tartness. Tito snarled and tapped his eye at recognition of the insult, then made a big scene of marching inside, ridiculous coat flapping around him as he went. Josef sent a platitude to his retreating back. 'My apologies. We have something urgent to discuss.'

'Papa, get off! You're hurting my wrist.'

'Oh.' He let his hand fall, distracted. 'Sorry. Sorry. I just wanted to… listen, we're leaving the city. Bit of an emergency.' His gaze was distant, like he'd already left. 'Your sister is waiting for us down in the coach.'

'What's wrong? I—'

'Don't worry. We'll sort it all out. Together. But we have to leave.' He noticed what Lily was wearing and tugged at a sleeve. 'What on earth happened to your clothes? What's all this?'

'Some beastly maid spilt a drink on me, Papa. I had to change into some mudder spares. But where are we going? Will we be long?'

Josef gave a small, urgent shake of his head. 'Later, I promise. I have your things in the coach. Come on, this way.'

Forgiveness

S wollen lids snapped open, revealing eyes made brilliant and wet by pain. The man screamed long and loud, but only an idiot would approach the hulking shape crouched at the end of this alley. A few windows rattled as more shutters closed.

'Come on, it's not so bad.' Husker pulled the knot tight with a savage yank. A bandage of bloody cloth trailed from the man's shoulder, with a matching rip torn from one of Young's old shirts. Well, several old shirts he'd stitched together then given to Husker as a parting gift. Two street urchins were watching him play the healer, half-frozen and huddled under an iron sheet; their crude shelter rattled violently under the driving rain, making almost as much of a racket as the man's chattering teeth. Lucky bastards. Husker's body played by different rules these days. He was calf-deep in muddy water and drenched in the same storm, but his skin seemed to prickle and burn. 'You still with me?' He mopped his eyes clear and poked the bleeding man in the face.

'I'm dying,' the man croaked.

Husker broke into laughter, and winced as his skin cracked.

'I'm dying,' the man insisted, eyes wide. He felt his wound. 'That bitch got my neck.'

'More your shoulder.'

'She cut me up! I'm gonna bleed to death—'

Husker slapped a handful of mud on the spluttering man's face. But, shit, he'd already heard too much. Steam rose from his back as he tried to scrape out Earth lines with his thumb, muttering whatever holy words he remembered. Heard them often enough, hadn't he? Crouched in mountain ruins as Young waved his arms and yelled over a snowstorm, but it wasn't long before that scripture sounded distant and tinny. With a grunt, he backhanded his patient across the cheek, leaving knuckle marks smacked out in stung flesh. He pulled him up, pulled him close, until that broken, bleeding nose bumped up against Husker's crushed slab of nostrils.

'Ugly bastards, aren't we?' he whispered. Their eyeballs danced inches from each other. 'Bet it's tough for you to turn a girl's head with that mug. Is that why you tried to grab my Lily?'

Weak hands flapped over Husker's face. A finger scraped his lip, another poked up his nostril, then he remembered Lily's frightened face and down the bastard went, down into Godearth's embrace. The man croaked as the slop of the alley closed over him, deep in panic, deeper in mud and shit. Husker's arms trembled. His heart found that unstoppable rhythm where everything looked breakable and he remembered Lily's frightened face. Her sobs. His heart pounded, pounded. Pounded.

The mud bubbled under his hands.

'Nourish the earth,' he gasped, arms shivering. 'Nourish it in death as you never did in life.' One of the urchins screamed. The other fled, wading for the street stairs. When the man floated up, his lifeless eyes were cleared of filth by the driving rain, and he stared up blankly at a thunderous sky. There were never any sodding answers up there, so Husker flipped him over. 'Blessings come from the earth,' he muttered, then clutched his head and squelched away. The man followed him, spinning slowly on the current of the sewer street.

Lily. Where had she gone? Her boot was still stuck in the mud, but she'd long since fled.

Deceit

'Rose?' Lily swung herself into the coach, wincing as she knocked a shin on the step. Her sister caught her, picking her up into a warm hug. That was new. Growing apart was just a part of growing up, even if Josef always prattled on about how they appeared on his doorstep. He'd grip his hands and grin, proud of how their tiny hands had been clamped fiercely together, with Lark bundled up in Rose's arm and screaming his lungs out. A kind-eyed, moustached captain of the Roaming Watch had managed to coax them over the threshold, but nothing could prise the sisters apart that evening. They'd woken up still holding hands.

'You took your time.' Rose recoiled, brushing a damp patch on her obnoxiously yellow dress. 'Gods, you're soaked. Papa, can we get some blankets from the box?'

Josef was outside, rain thundering over the hood of his cloak. He shook his head and slammed the door, dulling the storm with panels of wood and cushion, though it continued to drill an ominous tattoo on the roof. Lily shivered and cast around their luggage for something to change into. The mess was piled high, sliding around like they were off to tour the autumn markets with their unwanted junk. 'Urgh,' she said, edging past pots and utensils. 'Any idea what's going on?'

'Didn't Josef say?' Rose looked ridiculous, crammed into a corner like a pile of sacks Josef had found at the last minute. But, to be fair, there was little space for her anywhere else. She was taller than most men in Branera, and even Lily kept hitting her head on the ceiling.

'He said we were in trouble. Didn't elaborate much.'

'Same here. Careful!' Rose stretched out a steadying hand as Lily knocked over picture frame, dislodging a small avalanche of plates that sounded like they might have been expensive. 'Just sit down. Please? All your things are here, don't worry.'

'Seems like there's little which isn't.' Arm deep in a pile, Lily felt fabric and tugged out a dress. 'Look at all this stuff. Does he think they don't have cutlery outside the city?'

'Lils, can you change later? You should hear this.'

'I'm listening.' She struggled against soaked fabric as Rose covered the window and gave her an exasperated look. Lily grinned, pulling on dry clothes. 'Don't be like that. Honestly! I'm listening.'

She loved this dress. Snug and simple, with no room for petticoats, and it hadn't been washed since the warm months, so it still smelt deliciously of grass and trees. Rose's words grew muffled as she pulled it on. 'Well, he's been writing to us again.'

Lily straightened her outfit, briskly pulling wet hair free. 'I wish he wouldn't.' A trickle of rainwater ran down her back.

'I've only read these ones, but they seem years old.' Rose flicked through the sheets of paper on her lap, damp with drips from her hair. More letters were in a box next to her, a small, unassuming thing with a lock Lily had tried and failed to open a thousand times before. 'The key was left in,' said Rose, quickly.

'Put them back, you nosey bitch.' Lily leant over and slapped it shut. If she'd known what was in that stupid box she wouldn't have bothered fussing over it all those nights. 'Why'd you care what that madman has to say?'

'Lils! That filthy tongue. Have you been down in the mud again?' Lily shrugged and settled into silence. The box sprang open with a metallic twang, needing the lock to keep it closed. Rose rubbed some mist from the fogged-up windows. 'How's Josef?' she said, peering out.

'Like he's aged overnight.' Lily hugged her knees to trap a little warmth. A box like that should hold money or jewellery. Heirlooms. Fine tobacco. Instead, it was crammed with the bleatings of a psychopath. His top letter was curling up, peeking at her over the rim.

'I didn't get a chance to talk to him.' Rose was still watching the window, doing a fairly decent impression of Josef's dogs when he left for the city chambers. 'He found me at the back of the hall and dragged me straight to the coach. Do you think something bad has happened?'

They sat in silence for a few moments. The coach had that stuffy, steamed-up feel to it. Lily dried her hair as best she could on kitchen rags, and she was searching for a tie-up when Rose handed her an ivory clip. 'I'd thought he'd forgotten about us,' Lily said, tapping it irritably against her rings.

Rose shook her head and pressed the box into her hands. 'Read just one. The top one. One minute he's calm, the next... all I can say is he barely makes it to the end.'

Lily wiped the window and held his letter up to the light, squinting at the clumsy handwriting. He rambled on about his imprisonment on the farms. Snow and frostbite. Blood and ice. By the bottom, the words were big and shaky, making little sense as he ranted about death and the old gods, and then his name, Husker Tollworth, written carefully in cursive script. Her lip curled. 'He's nuts. What's that one you're dripping on say?'

There was a click and swing of the door. Josef climbed in, rain lashing the step behind him and blowing spray over Lily's toes. He shut the door quickly and banged three times on the front wall, his wet shirt sleeves slopping against the woodwork. The coach lurched into motion, hoof beats clopping over the rumble of raindrops on the roof.

'Sorry.' Josef sheepishly handed Lily a soaked blanket.

She put aside the letter, choking up at his troubled apology. He was a silly man at times. 'Papa, it's okay. I found clothes.'

He nodded wearily then paused, searching for something. Words or courage, or both. 'I think—' Josef spotted the sheets of paper on Rose's lap. 'Oh, you've read them.'

Rose relinquished them to his clicking fingers. 'When did he start writing again?'

'I suppose you could say he's never stopped.'

'Wait a minute,' said Lily, scrambling for the box as Josef lifted it and found the key underneath. 'Why didn't you tell us?'

He harrumphed rather than replied, gathering up the last scattered letters and stuffing them away. He took another one from his jacket and lay it on top, pressing the stack down so it would close. 'I'll tell you later.' The key clicked in the lock. 'Shall we get settled? We've quite some distance to travel.'

'I'm settled,' said Lily impatiently. 'Go on. What's all this about?' The coach shook as they hit the cobbles on the main parade, raised up from the muck and splatter of Branera's lower streets. Rose took Josef's arm and guided him to a seat before he fell.

'Oh, thank you, dear,' he said. 'Now, you are not to worry about your father. This isn't about him.' Lily ground her teeth. He lived and breathed for this sort of thing, tempting her to pry out his secrets like his stupid letter box. 'Gods, I'm weary to the bone. We can talk later, won't you let me get comfortable?' He fidgeted, settling his coattails around him.

They were in a queue for the Merchant Gate. Its legendary walls were deep enough to shelter several coaches, and three were already lined up for inspection. Lily caught the faint whiff of dung and rotting carcasses through the window – night carts and worse. No one respectable was riding at this time of night.

Josef folded his coat over his knees. 'Now, girls, I know this is all a bit much to take in but— Lily, what are you rummaging for?'

'A drink,' she said firmly. 'You're right, Papa, it's really all too much. Do you have anything to settle my nerves?' Her search was interrupted as their coach lurched forwards in the queue, dumping her back into the seat.

A wry smile, which had been conspicuous in its absence, played over Josef's lips. 'Are you drunk, little lush?'

'Not in the slightest.' Lily arranged herself out of her undignified sprawl with casual indifference, calmly adjusting her skirts. 'The floor seems slippery, Josef. You've carted half the weather in with you.'

'Young lady, you've been drinking.' He frowned. 'Please tell me you haven't been off the boards.'

'Of course not.' Lily dismissed his accusations with a sniff. 'You're one to talk, though. You practically twisted my arm off with your whisky fingers.'

'It's been a long day,' he protested. 'I'm old. I've earned the right to relax.' The coach jolted to a stop again, and a knock from the driver beat twice on the front wall. Josef checked his pocket watch with a grimaced. 'Now listen, I'd hoped for more time to explain, but we have two gentlemen joining us. They are paying good money, which I can't refuse. And they are both dear friends, whom I also can't refuse. Most of my fortune is tied up in wood stockpiles this time of year, so some loose coin wouldn't hurt.'

'Papa, where are—'

Josef's finger waggled in her face. 'Shhh, little lush, just listen. Our first guest is a...' He cleared his throat. 'Travelling man. A bit rough round the edges, but a fine fellow. I've known him for most of my life, and he brings me the best news from over the Split.' Josef rubbed his hands, as if to ignite the spark of business. 'In his care is a colleague of mine from the chambers, Minister Pearce. Pearce has been in an accident and he is in quite a state, so you are both to be kind.' He clambered over to the door. 'And tidy yourselves up, for goodness' sake.' With a click and rush of spray, he ducked out into the deluge.

Lily sighed and sat up straight, dragging crinkled gloves from her pocket. They'd also not been washed since a trip to Josef's summer house, and were happily decorated with river splotches and grass stains. A search through the trunks eventually produced a battered comb, but she soon tossed it back in defeat.

Rose reached out for it. 'Are you done with this?'

'Stupid thing,' said Lily, pulling pieces of ivory out of her hair. 'Why does Josef insist on collecting these antiques?'

'Don't look so sour, Lils.' Rose twirled up her raven-black locks, threading the rest of the comb through to serve as a pin. 'You look lovely, I'm sure.'

Before Lily could frame a retort, the door unclasped and Josef bundled through the gap. 'Sorry, sorry. Gentlemen,' he called over his shoulder, 'please come in.' He shooed Lily further along the seats.

Two soaked figures hauled themselves in after him, splashing water everywhere. The rain was whipping past in ferocious gusts, so Lily gestured at a pair of cloaked guardsmen outside to hurry things up. A conferred glance produced some hasty salutes, and they quickly slammed the door. No inspection was worth delaying a minister's coach. Or getting his daughter's feet wet.

Josef frowned as something heavy was thrown onto the roof, but he recovered with a flurry of bluster and handshakes. 'Horrid out there, isn't it?' he said, almost cheery as he pumped the hands of his guests and shooed them to their seats. 'May I introduce my step-daughters? This young lady is Rose Kale-Tollworth.'

The big idiot practically glowed, looking fresh from the bathtub rather than a thunderstorm. She even wore the soft, shy smile that came as naturally to her as breathing.

'And my second, Lily Kale-Tollworth.'

There was something about Josef's formal tone. It was the way he fired off her double-barrelled name, and it always prodded Lily into action. The Kale-Tollworth orphans had been raised to impress, with Rose gliding her way through years of boardwalk politics while Lily lied and cheated to keep up. Lark was as bad as her – a bit touched in the head, to be honest – but he'd been sent away with a tax patrol last week, which left Lily to struggle on by herself. So, as on a hundred occasions before, after climbing in through the wrong window or staggering back from Ruckman's to find shocked visitors in the hall, the mud fell away and the lady took over.

At least, as best she could. 'Hello.' Lily averted her eyes, reaching for sympathy over admiration. 'Lovely to meet you both.' She mumbled something else, then pretended to withdraw her gaze.

Minister Pearce didn't seem to notice or care. His troubled eyes missed her tugged down neckline, instead losing themselves about two miles behind her head. His drenched, blond hair was plastered down over a bleeding jaw, and it was too ragged to cover a neck swept with hideous burns. He wore no rings, no coat or ministerial pin, yet the blackened remains of a hat clutched in his white-knuckle grip marked him as one of Josef's peers. Minister of the poor, if Lily recognised it correctly.

The minister's companion flicked down a coat collar and bent over to shake out long, braided hair, which was thick with charms and feathers. 'You do go through a lot of outfits, miss.' Dren raised his head and winked at her. 'I am too loyal to this coat, but then I never was a man of fashion.'

And like that, Lily's evening came flooding back. The unexpected, groping hands. The driving rain. A spray of blood hitting her cheek.

'Ah splendid,' said Josef. 'You two have already met?'

'Oh yes, Papa,' said Lily brightly. Her stomach churned with a sour mix of whisky and unease. 'I must compliment Dren on his performance at the speaking stage today.'

'Strange,' said Dren, feigning surprise. 'As I recall we met over a bottle of whisky. You had lost a boot.' He was rifling through a leather satchel, fishing out endless packets to be moved into new compartments. He kept this up until it seemed the whole thing must have been out of order, or he was just doing it for effect.

'Lily?' Rose prompted, curious.

'Of course,' said Lily. 'In the Saints Rest, up by the bankers' district.'

'Even stranger!' The satchel continued to fold out in complicated patterns, each pouch exuding puffs of odd aroma – metals, spice and rotten plants. 'I would stake my reputation on us meeting in the mud. A brothel, if I recall. By the Low Ends? You must remember.' Dren's eyes were wide with innocence as he appealed to the coach. 'We linked arms to sing once or twice. She has a marvellous, if wandering, voice after a few whiskies.'

Lily burnt him with a glance. 'Yes. It's coming back to me now. You're the man with the stupid name. Drake, wasn't it?'

Josef spread his arms, trying to regain a little control. 'Oh ho! I sense a story here.'

'My friend,' said Dren, shaking his head. 'We must show a little sensitivity. Miss Lily had a misadventure this evening and may still be distressed—'

'Sere,' Lily snapped. 'If you want us to be friends, leave it there.' She took Josef's hands. 'Papa, I'm sorry. I'll explain later. I didn't mean to end up at Ruckman's.'

'Well, if you were there with Dren, I'm sure you were fine. He's a man of the world.' Josef patted her knuckles, missing her bristle at the implication of needing an escort in her own city. 'He's trained in magic, you know. Born in the Southlands.'

'Bloody gods, what a load of nonsense.' Lily snorted, snatching back her hands. As charades went, respectability was the most tiring. 'Are you really taken in so easily, Josef?'

'Lily Kale-Tollworth!' A warning shot. Both barrels of her name were loaded with shut-the-hell-up. 'I've known this man for years and you will not insult him.'

'Please don't argue.' Rose was impatient to hear more, flustered at the first hint of any romantic nonsense. 'You must tell us all about your magic! Please?'

'Yes. Yes, come on old chap.' Josef thumped Dren on the shoulder companionably. Their guest was busy trying to catch Lily's angry, averted eyes. 'Show us a spell. Should break up the journey a little.'

'I am sorry if I caused offence, miss.' He probably meant to sound humble. Except he damn well didn't. He probably couldn't be humble if he tried. 'I spend a great deal of time in my own company, and often forget myself.'

Ridiculous. Lily had never met anyone more self-aware. Every word he uttered was over-enunciated, his very accent celebrating each syllable in that stupid foreign purr. She watched out of the corner of her eye as Josef took a hip flask from his pocket and waggled it to tempt Dren away from his fruitless task. The two men shared a sip and a joke Lily didn't understand, then to her further annoyance Josef put the flask away without offering it around.

'Here!' Josef tapped the minister sitting next to Dren. 'Do you girls recognise my colleague?'

'I don't think we've been introduced,' said Rose, still trying to get into the conversation.

'But you have! Minister Pearce is my staunchest ally in the chambers. He sat with you at Year End dinner. This man' – Josef reached around to grip him awkwardly on the shoulder – 'is a voice of reason. A shining light that stands before the murky influence of the Roaming Watch.'

Pearce shifted on his seat cushion, still watching the panels behind Lily's head. 'I think he needs relighting,' she muttered, edging over so he wasn't looking through her so much.

Dren peeled hair away from the minister's injured neck. 'Do not let the staring bother you, miss. The poor man is recovering from an accident, and he has retreated within himself.' He peered into Pearce's ear. 'Your stepfather has retained me to take care of him. So I will.'

'And does it speak?' asked Lily, wiggling her fingers at Pearce and whistling as he finally blinked. 'What are those burns on his neck?' Both Josef and Rose opened their mouths to berate her for being tart, but she silenced them with a rude noise. 'Oh leave me alone! This carriage is too small for all these secrets.' She was rewarded with a twitch at the edge of Josef's mouth. 'Tell me this one at least.'

'An unfortunate accident,' said Dren. He took some salve from his satchel and spread it over Pearce's neck. 'A kitchen fire, I am led to believe.'

'And why is he here?' Lily persisted. 'There are other coaches to take vacant-headed dolts out for countryside air. Why are we here? Why is all this stuff here?'

'We couldn't leave him,' protested Josef.

'Leave him? Leave him for what exactly?' She kicked a pile of boxes threatening her legs, sending them toppling the other way. 'Speak your mind, Josef. We're not going back, are we?' He mouthed a few responses, but put his lies behind none of them. 'Are we?'

'No.' He shrank back against the seat.

'You are perceptive, miss.' Dren was scrutinising her, his eyes shining with mischief. 'If somewhat touchy. I think you will enjoy life outside the city.'

'Too kind, sere. What the hell is going on?'

'An uprising.' Josef looked deflated, waistcoat crumpled up around his neck. 'They're furious this time, you know. Whole villages emptied against us. And we've no troops left to speak of, at least none who want to fight. Bloody gods. Half of them were up against family last time – it was too much, and I warned the chambers it was too much.

We kept rumours from the wayinns, but this time it was us being kept in the dark. Sods already knew! A ragtag army marching against us, and they already knew. Even before my man in the villages found out.' He retreated into a pile of coats and shirts, reaching out to pull in his letter box. 'Branera will open her gates this time. The mob will hang every last minister for the things we signed into law, all to appease the damn Watch.'

'Papa, please.' Rose was drained of colour.

But the confession continued, bitter and regretful. 'They deserve it, I don't. The triple draft? A disgrace! I fought it, the gods know I did. You know I did.' He shuddered, coats slipping down around him. 'We will collect Lark from his tax patrol and set up elsewhere. Dren is from Saarban. He's overseen business for me there before, and he can lead us to safety. No one will follow us over the Long Path.'

'Oh dry up,' Lily said. 'We'll be back in a few weeks and you know it.'

Four uprisings had withered against Branera's walls since she was a child. The city was unbreakable. Mobs piled up against its gates and money seeped through to send them away. Shadowy figures slipped out of hidden doors, golden promises clutched in their hands. Or different promises were sent over on threat-laden crows. Bribes, lies and gossip turned dissidents on each other, and this sent most of them home and the rest out in chains over the Long Path. Their city had never lacked for money.

'Branera will buy her freedom again. But I don't care if you can't see that.' Lily lifted her voice over his. 'A trip out to see Lark will be nice. How exactly are you hoping to find him?'

'A stroke of luck there.' Josef laughed nervously. 'Dren has offered to help us search the Splitside villages for your brother. His patrol was sent down there, you know. Dunford and the like.' This man hid every scandal in Branera behind a jovial expression, but that mask had cracks in it, and Lily could see them all. There was more to this.

Dren bowed his head in a clatter of beads. 'We will make with all speed to the Split and the Long Path, distance ourselves from the peasants. Once we have located young Lark, we can assess your options. But I really cannot recommend Saarban enough.'

'And since we've slipped away before the violence, we've got pots of coin to pay for all this.' Josef gave a weak grin. 'My spies have their uses, eh?'

'Only in helping us abandon our friends.' The whisky in Lily's stomach had fermented with her mood, souring her words as they bubbled out of her mouth. 'I'd never taken you for a coward, Josef.'

He leant sharply forwards from his coats, eyes accusative, voice taking on the flint-like quality it did when he felt wronged. 'Use your head, stupid girl. I have saved those ministers with a conscience.' He jabbed a finger at Pearce, then himself. 'We're both right here. And I know what you really mean, but your mudder friends' – the word was bitten off derisively – 'will be safe enough. Mercy help us, their fingers will tie the knots that will throttle the excess from that city, you'll see.'

He didn't know that. He didn't care either. Minister Josef Kale was a champion of the poor in policy only, a point of honour rather than sympathy. His snobbish streak ran as thick as anyone else on the boards, and he'd always forbidden his stepdaughters from wandering the mud. Even if only one of them obeyed.

The coach lapsed into silence. Rhythmic sounds of rain pattered on the roof, joining the creak and jangle of wood and harness in a traveller's lullaby. Dren rustled in his satchel, rubbing ointment on Pearce and muttering small comforts in his ear. Lily felt her eyes close, too tired to argue any further. Josef's soft snores told her he felt much the same.

'How long till we reach the Long Path?' Rose asked in an undertone. Dren's answer was inaudible, and they continued talking of the route south in an exchange of whispers.

The northern cities shunned those beyond the Split in all but trade, keeping their own accents and customs. Only merchants trod the Long Path. Their caravans traded in stories, salts and metals, and their songs spread faster than Saarban's shining coins. Corpse eaters, mystics, savages – every tale worth telling started somewhere south, and those born there were viewed with distrust by any decent householder. The Northlands started at the north shore.

Lily felt the weave of a blanket draped across her chest. Her head was lifted and laid on something soft. Some maid had scattered rose-scent on it – perhaps a last touch of the comforts she was leaving behind. She turned over to face the cushions.

Few northern children hadn't built their own Long Path in play, spanning fictional seas with borrowed planks and furniture. A younger Lily and Rose had made theirs across a low gap by the Merchant Gate. A tattooed southerner, gap-toothed and drunk after unloading his salt stock, had paused to cry his admiration at it, swaying and tipping his hat. This mistake cost him the afternoon, and he was cajoled into the game by the small orphans.

His skin was different to theirs, toasted brown by the sun of his homeland. He had a bony face and a warm smile of fake teeth that shone like scattered diamonds. Lily and Rose dragged him to sit on the south side of their bridge and watch, dangling his ink-scrawled legs high over the mud and bales of straw below. Josef sat with him. Their stepfather was stripped of his shirt in a rare day of sun, with his long hair tied back in a tail that ran all the way down to his belt. He kept Lark close, but the toddler's leg was doing the awkward dance it did when he was touched, so he was soon released into the care of his sisters. Cheerful chuckles wove into laughter as Josef sold waggon after waggon of seasoned wood for the merchant to take back home, his hands moving from pocket to pocket for paper and charcoal.

Warm memories of Branera soon faded.

How long would it take an uprising to break through the Merchant Gate? How long before they were wading through the Low Ends with torches and swords, leaving filthy prints on the boardwalks and dragging bloody stains up the stairs? In Lily's fitful dreams, it was now the gap-toothed southerner who grabbed her by the crossroads. From the shadows, Josef called frantically for her to run, but the mud sucked at her foot and held her in place.

Exodus

Lark hugged his shins, chin jolting as their waggon trundled over some rough flagstones, parting the endless crowd that trudged the Long Path. He was miserable and bored. And wet. The Split Sea thundered past somewhere below, creating the salty mist that coiled up around the ancient bridge and found every hole in his clothes. 'Sere?' he whispered, tugging on Terrano's trousers.

A low chuckle of laughter came from behind him. The other children were playing cards under the waggon awning, bickering in low voices as they huddled around a cosy lamp. Lark tried to listen, but he was distracted by a pat on his leg. 'I see it, ma'am.' He shuddered and wriggled further away from Terrano's cook. 'Another tower is it?'

She wheezed urgently at him.

He'd never heard her speak. She mostly relied on breathy gushes of air and lurid hand waving, and the other boys called her Crone, so Lark did too, but only in his head. Crone was extremely old, and he wondered if maybe her voice was just something else thing she'd lost, along with her hair and teeth and manners. He tried tugging on Terrano's cloak to get him to translate, but the scholar was lost in a distant world of his own, mumbling a song and tapping a stick over the rolling backs of his oxen.

Lark pushed away Crone's hand, and shuddered as she replaced it again, grinning wickedly. She was still pointing at the tower. Or perhaps... 'Do you mean those statues on the wall?' He tried smiling and nodding. 'I see them. They're very pretty.'

Correct. She beamed at him, her face swept up in a sea of wrinkles. Amelle – one of the other boys – said Terrano and Crone were lovers. But Amelle was a liar and a bugger, and Lark thought her too old for anything like that. Terrano was quite a lot fatter than her, but he was also a lot younger than her, and Lark couldn't picture them hugging or kissing. Though, Terrano's face creased up with a big grin when Crone fed him. And Crone would grin back, so maybe they did love each other?

That wrinkly grin was now turned on Lark. At least she'd taken her hand back. 'How far to the other side, sere?' He tugged on Terrano's cloak again. 'Is it a long way?'

Terrano winked and carried on whistling his song, leaving Crone to gesticulate an answer. She pointed up at the veiled sun, then traced a path across the sky.

'A day?' She did it four times. 'Four days?' Lark gasped. They might have to camp down among the crowd. 'But we've been going all night! Surely it's been miles and miles already.'

She gestured to the walls, and pushed her hands together, miming being in a crush of people. Her arm weaved in a wiggling motion.

The Long Path spread out again into another square, another tower. Like the others, it was dotted with tents and hawkers calling out their final stock. Their stalls were a sieve for the shuffling crowd, clever hands and voices separating coin from purse. Reductions, offers, too late it's gone; everyone seemed determined to sell all they had and equally determined to leave. Those with southern skin and gaunt faces headed south. Those with a pallor and dark mops of hair pushed back, weaving north against the crowd.

'Make way. Make way now,' Terrano murmured. He spoke so quietly that no one could possibly have heard him. Yet they did move, and sharply too, as if propelled by firm hands on their back.

'Sere?' Lark's hand was hanging off Terrano's clothes. Behind the scratchy material of his cloak, the scholar wore trousers and long white stockings, like Josef did.

'Lark Kale-Tollworth.' Terrano smiled down at him. 'What's troubling you, my boy?'

'Where are we going?' he asked, blushing at the sudden attention. His words tumbled out in a rush, earning a tut from Terrano as he stammered. 'W-where are all these people going?'

'Well, well. Two questions. We are heading to the Palace of Sells, which is in Saarban. There, I am to present my findings on life and death to my... to my colleagues.' He patted the oiled wraps that protected his special book, the one with Lark's name in it. It rested on an empty seat beside him, with Lark and Crone ranking lower in the seating arrangements and down on the bench beneath.

'And these people?'

'Civil war is brewing in the Northlands, and those that dwell on the Path rely on peaceful trade.' He gestured at the white walls around them. 'You cannot grow crops here. These merchants and pilgrims have survived such social storms before, but only by taking shelter on the most welcoming shore. That would usually be where they most fit in.'

'Are you really from the Southlands, sere? You're not very brown.'

'I am from Saarban.'

'But your—'

'Appearances are there for other people to look at, not for you to worry about.' He played fingers along his hat, adjusting its trim. 'But if you must know, I was an orphan to the city of water and light – much as you were to Branera.'

'So you're running from the uprising, too? Are we going to your family?'

Terrano beat the condensation from his hat, and Lark waited for him to explain. But he didn't. The scholar's eyes were boring into a group dragging their feet in front of them. Weary adults were pushing a couple of handcarts over the uneven slabs, and their children were taking turns to ride on the piles of clothing, or trudge along holding skirts or hands. A man leading two little girls seemed to shudder under Terrano's gaze. He ushered his charges to the side without looking back.

'Saarban is a magnificent city.' Terrano flicked his stick over the back of the oxen. 'If you wish, you will begin a proper education at the palace there. They value smart young boys.'

'Is it a busy city?'

'It is. But the palace is peaceful, quiet.'

'I think I'd like that,' said Lark, mulling it over. 'And I could write to my sisters? And to Josef?'

'Of course, of course. They may even come and visit, who knows?'

They pushed on, and the crowd seemed to thin around them. Lark tried to ask more questions, but he was hushed and sent back to sit with the others. They knew him well enough by now to give him a bit of space, so he didn't retreat to a corner and instead stayed to learn their card game. After a few hands he understood it very well, earning some notoriety and a handful of broken coins by the time another tower had passed.

Stowaway

Rain threatened Husker's grip on the coach, plotting with the rocks and trail bends to send him flying, slamming his bulk left and right. But he had ice picks for fingers – weathered for ten years at the Mountain Head. He leered and leant back into the storm, taunting it, sneering at the raging sky. The rain doubled its efforts, thrashing heat from his skin as he howled his challenge into the night.

Josef's driver had turned back to stare at him again. Husker slipped an elbow through the rail and tapped his eye meaningfully, pointing down the track. She shuddered and gathered a grip on the reins, then sunk back into her cocoon of waxed jackets. Since leaving Branera they'd passed few travellers, fewer still who paid attention to her frantic, but furtive, gestures towards the back of her coach. Or her less furtive ones. A rider for the Roaming Watch had thundered past without slowing, moving at pace towards Branera and ignoring her cry for help.

But you know, despite all that, he wasn't entirely lacking for company.

Husker twisted back to check on the caped men dogging their tail. Persistent little bastards. They'd tried to ride the coach down, fancy blades drawn and metal glinting as they cut through thundering sheets of rain. That was until a great, naked body became distinct from the luggage, and their leader had hauled hard on the reins to avoid Husker's bleeding grin and beckoning finger.

Embracing the storm, Husker threw back his head and laughed. He wasn't sure why, but he let it come. And it kept on coming. Unstoppable laughter mixed with roars of pain as his face creaked and groaned, giving bloody birth to his widest grin. Godearth's angel flew to his aid, moaning and singing as it healed his cuts. It left him dizzy, hanging from the rail by one elbow, and the next bend in the trail was almost his last.

No more laughing, then. Chin running with blood and spit, Husker noticed someone watching him, and he pointed down the trail. The driver spun back and furiously whipped the reins – as if speed could somehow separate her from him.

Forest

Josef dumped a pile of logs and branches by the campfire. His arms were bleeding from where the wood had scraped him, but he seemed quite proud of this feat. 'Should last us a while, eh?' he said. 'Don't know why it took you so long.'

Lily couldn't watch these moments.

'What is all this?' Dren flicked through the pile, tossing most of it away. 'No, no, no.'

He chose when they rested, which was rarely. He chose the roads, which were rough. They moved fast and without any scrap of comfort, dodging the city roads that were the backbone of the Northlands – all the pleasant wayinns, too. Company. Warmth. Whisky. This haste and sobriety did nothing for Lily's nerves. Her tormented dreams were plagued by pale pursuers, which woke her in gasping sweats, or once with a scream as a nightmarish shape blotted out the carriage window. Josef and Dren had stumbled from their bedrolls to grab torches and run at the nearest trees, thrusting light into empty shadows. Dren had given her a sleeping draught after that, putting it down to what he called feminine nerves.

Lily curled her lip. She only drank it because he mixed it with juni.

'Those sticks not good enough?' said Josef, looking puzzled. He watched as Dren sorted through his offering, throwing the larger bits into the bushes. 'Well. Not to worry. Be back in a jiffy with some more.' He rolled down his sleeves, wincing as they touched his cuts.

'No!' said Dren, raising his hands. 'Please, no.'

'What, then?' Josef tugged at his moustache in distress. It was this helpless look that Lily hated.

'Come, old friend,' said Dren, more gently. He was holding Josef's arm as if he needed supporting. 'Rest here and spend some time with your daughters. Let me share the labour. I fear you have lost your colour!' He scrunched up his forehead in mock scrutiny, guiding Josef to a seat and tutting. This facade wouldn't have kept Minister Kale down for more than a second in Branera, but he'd left shades of that energetic man behind with each road marker they passed. A politician's mind ran backwards out of habit. He overcomplicated everything, repeated failures dulling his razor-sharp wit.

'I am feeling a bit out of sorts,' Josef said, mopping his brow. 'A fever maybe. Is this sweat?' It looked more like rainwater. Lily averted her gaze as Josef looked her way. 'But look here, these logs will surely last longer than what you were gathering,' he said, flushing. 'What's so bad about that?'

'That pile will burn out in less than an hour.' Dren was shaking out his coat. Its baggy sleeves whipped around his arms as he tucked himself back in. 'Rest, my friend. I will take care of things.'

'If you say so.' Josef eyed the pile doubtfully. 'I'll throw one on every now and again, eh?'

'As fast as you need.' Dren lowered a lantern and sighed, relenting to the repeated lesson. 'The trees closest to us are softbark, their wood burns smokeless and quick.' He picked up another branch and tossed it into the bushes. 'One trait is good, the other is not. Use only the twigs if you want to keep your eyebrows.' He finished refilling the lantern and wiped his oily fingers on the grass, gesturing for Pearce to join him. 'Hold this up... gently now. Watch it does not tip too far! Perfect. Now, follow me.' Dren slid between the trees and vanished. Pearce followed, obediently holding up the lantern so it cast a dim circle of light over the undergrowth.

'Just us, then, girls,' said Josef, warming his hands. 'Some family time, eh?' He tentatively poked a branch into the fire, watching it fizzle and snap with amazing speed. 'Huh.'

Dren had chosen a secluded tent of leaves for their camp, a tree canopy deep off the forest trail. It was a treat for the girls to sleep out in the fresh air, as their delicate natures had thus far condemned them to be locked up in the coach with the rest of the valuables. There wasn't a lot of space, and Lily's restless dreams and sweat-fuelled shouts had woken Rose with a flailed hand more than once – no wonder she'd insisted they all sleep outside tonight. Lily stood abruptly and roamed the edges of their camp, arming herself with a stick. The leaf curtain danced beneath it, shimmering and bobbing under the deluge. It was a clever thing, this tree. The broad leaves were arranged so they ran gullies over its gnarled roots, lapping up the drips which taller canopies left for it. Dren had called it a funnel bush, then something else later on.

There was a sudden crunch of undergrowth, and a pale shape crashed through the bushes. Lily caught herself before she cried out, gasping with relief as a badger skidded away and disappeared off into the forest. More bad dreams tonight, then. Except now she could disturb Dren's sleep too, so that was something. She gave Rose a quick, apologetic hug as she returned to her seat.

'What was that for?' Rose said, surprised. 'Stop it. You'll make yourself damp. Oh, I don't think I've been dry since leaving home.' She went back to flapping her skirts, which were soaked from the dash she'd made for pots and pans. It had been raining since they left Branera, which was nothing special. Anywhere near the Mountain Feet it could rain for months. But usually they were indoors and watching streaming windows with cups of chocolate, not sitting on logs with muddy skirts and damp knickers. Lily took off a boot to let out some water, wriggling her numb toes at the fire.

'Papa?' Rose said, giving up on trying to get air through her soaked clothes. Her hands fell in her lap in exasperation, her head tilting backwards like a stroppy child. 'Did you hear what I said?'

He was still burning sticks, baffled at the speed with which each one disappeared. 'Hmm?'

'Do you think we could pick up some new clothes? No one is in skirts outside the city.' Rose hid her interest well, but Lily noticed her quick eyes and the slight blush. 'Plenty of girls were wearing trousers at the last wayinn, can you believe it?'

'Really? You should have pointed it out!' Josef laughed. He leant back as the fire fizzed and popped. 'How utterly ridiculous. Now, now, don't you worry, my dear. Saarban is very civilised. We shall find someone there to pick you out all the local fashions, great skirts and girdles and all that.' He didn't notice her crestfallen face, and shuffled up until he was right next to the flames, almost burning himself. 'Now, come on. Get a little closer to the fire if you want – it really sorts you out. I'm bone dry.'

'You are not.' Lily threw another branch on the fire.

'Careful, girl! That's got to last.' Blinking, Josef leant away from the hissing and sparks. This wood didn't so much burn as fizz. 'Well, if they're going to be gone a while, we might as well have a family toast.' He fished out a hip flask from his waistcoat and uncapped it with an expert flick. The metal clasp glinted invitingly as he waggled it in the firelight. 'Ladies?'

'Why not?' Lily reached out her hand, leaving it out patiently as he took a long swig.

'No, thank you.' Rose continued to air her skirts.

They passed the flask back and forth a few times. The spiced juni spread its relaxing glow down Lily's throat, and she tilted her head back to watch the leaves sway and drip, enjoying a moment of peace. The insistent rain pattered and pushed at their tree, until even the tight weave of leaves missed a drop, and it hit her square on the nose. A silence like this meant Josef was trying to broach an awkward subject. He'd never married, so sometimes they had to meet him halfway on matters of delicacy.

'Now, girls. A word, please.'

If he'd worn lenses, Lily had always felt Josef would be the sort to tilt them down his nose in these moments and peer over the rims. She sat up and listened politely.

'There is something, in fact, something I neglected to mention earlier. A few things in fact.' He coughed. 'I happen to know that your, erm, your father has been released.' Rose was sitting forwards with open curiosity, mouth agape. Lily had the decency to avert her head and sniff. 'Well, you know he's been writing, you saw the letters.' Josef wriggled under Rose's attention, moving his watch from one pocket to another. 'He instructed me to tell you he was coming to the city. He asked you to wait.'

The silence was heavy, broken only by the fizz and snap of the fire. Around them, the undergrowth seemed to rustle, listening to their words. 'Coming to Branera, was he?' Lily scrunched up her face. 'Good thing we left, then. Fuck him. I can't believe they let that madman free.'

'Now, now. Don't fuss!'

'I'm not fussing, Josef, I'm swearing.'

He winced. 'Well I'd rather you didn't. No need for alarm, we've left him far behind by now. One more reason we're moving so fast, you know.' His hands were clasped tight, wriggling over each other as if unknotting his problems. 'You wouldn't want to see him, would you? I promised myself I'd never let you. He's a bad man. You don't want to at all?'

'We don't want to see him,' said Rose, hurriedly. 'We're grateful for all you've done.'

'I'm glad, I'm really glad of that. I swore I'd never let you. Gods know I've done the best I can, even for young Lark.' His face cracked and another secret broke free. 'That's the other thing. Lark is in some trouble. His patrol's gone missing. Dren was passed a ransom note from some Splitside gang who've kidnapped him, so I gathered everything I could to buy his freedom. Just in case.'

'Don't you trust him!' Lily blurted out, furious. 'It's a scam. Can't you see it, you old fool? That bastard Dren's got you to collect up all your valuables for him to run off with.'

'What do you know about it?' Josef said, hands quivering in his pockets. 'We've been friends for years. Long before I took you in.' Lily wrinkled her nose, but held her tongue. 'I can't bear to think of Lark in trouble. The Taxer wrote to me just last week, saying the patrol was working out well for him. Lark was making friends, and when was the last time he had a friend?' Josef coughed, a long rattling sound that was slightly unsettling. 'It's this damned unrest that's upset everything. Morals and law cast aside. Kidnappers? I can't abide it. No, we must make haste to confront these criminals, and put our trust in Dren. We can all sit it out together in Saarban.'

Lily went over to sit beside him on the log. 'Budge over, old man. It's warmer here.' She pried the flask from his hands and took a swig, then wrapped his fingers back round it. 'And stop being so melodramatic. Lark will be fine. It could all be some bloody prank, you know. One of the wayinn keepers will have seen his troop.'

'My girl, this flask is empty,' Josef protested weakly. 'How much have you drunk?'

She put her arms around him and gave him a hug, resting her head on his bony shoulder. The shakes she'd noticed from across the fire felt stronger than they looked, deep breaths rattling in his clenched throat.

He was a good man – just too used to walls and comfort. As was she. Rose gave them a small smile, then went back to drying her clothes.

~

Food calmed Josef down, letting him fall into routine griping over Lily's cooking. Rose insisted it wasn't her turn, and as far as he was concerned it was never his. So, with a shrug at their poor choices, Lily burnt as little of it as she could.

'By the gods, girl, have the decency to eat your mistakes.' Josef held out a stick she'd dropped in the ash. 'This is yours.'

'My mistake?' She nibbled at hers. 'You know I'm terrible at this, yet you insist on me trying.'

'Rose, teach your sister something for a change.'

'I'm not a maid.' Rose took the skewer from him and stripped off the blackened exterior, exposing less-burnt meat underneath. 'I could teach you better than her if you were only willing to try. I've given up on Lils, she's awful.'

'Truly awful.' Lily grinned. 'Oh, but here's Dren. Perhaps he—'

'Another time, miss.' Dirt and branches flew as he scattered the fire with his boot. A piercing scream rang out from beyond the canopy, and Dren froze. He looked slowly over his shoulder, rainwater trickling down his jacket collar.

'What the hell was that?' Lily's heart had carried her to her feet.

'Someone dying.' Dren moved past her, holding up a fizzing branch like a torch. He started to gather his things. 'I'm fairly certain of that.' Another scream tore through the night. Startled birds flocked over-head, and Lily stumbled backwards, one hand slapping uselessly over the straps on her thigh. That bloody knife. It was still buried under piles of coach junk – she'd not had the stomach to clean it since Branera. Dren closed up his satchel and slung it on. 'I am afraid this will be safer in the dark. Please trust me on this.' With a wide sweep of his arm he threw his guttering torch out into the storm. Lily rubbed firelight from her eyes as two shadows staggered about. 'Up you get, my friend. Time for that courage of yours.'

A hand found Lily's. 'Papa, its okay,' she whispered. 'I'm here.' But the reassuring squeeze she gave him was returned as a repeated spasm. 'I'm here, it's okay.'

'Do you remember the way to the coach, miss?' Dren's voice came close to her ear. The touch on her arm was gentle, but questioning.

She shivered and turned to face him. 'Yes.'

'Take Josef. Your sister will follow with the packs.'

'Go on, Lils. I've got them.' A tall shape hopped up and down as Rose settled the straps across her shoulders, but she froze when the next scream came from nearby bushes. Full of madness and victory. A hunter, not a victim.

With a cry to run, Josef slipped free and broke towards the coach. Lily swore and took off after him, tugging at her skirt as it caught and tore on branches and brambles. Climbing the roofs of Branera in high fashion was a practised skill, as was bullying tailors into lowering that fashion, cutting straps or loosening cloth around the thigh. But in this forest such careful preparations counted for nothing. A thousand briars and nettles snatched at her as she ran, whipping blood from her face and tearing off ribbons and lace. Leaves and twigs slapped her backwards as she tried to close the gap, thorns raked her hands as she slipped and fell. Spitting dirt, Lily raised her head in time to see Josef break free into a clearing. He cried out as if in pain – lit up by moonlight and blasted by a torrent of hail. This ghostlike figure struggled on, half-drowned, before it vanished from view.

She snarled and picked herself up, throwing herself into the storm and casting around in a swamp of autumn leaves. The hail was furious, beating her back and flaying her skin with rock-hard drops. 'Get up, old man!' Lily found a forearm and dragged him up, brushing mulch from his face. 'This is no time for shortcuts.' Rose disagreed, and a flurry of leaves filled the air as she overtook them. With a few easy swings of her arms, she slung their bags up the coach and leapt after them. 'Wait!' Lily yelled, hearing her voice crack. 'Help me with him. He's gone all limp.'

Rose bent down and took a grip. 'Get off him, then.' With a grunt, she hauled Josef up by the armpits, laying him out carefully over the seats. Panting with exhaustion, Lily frowned up at her sister. Snatches of their childhood spun past, memories of a tall, angry Rose knocking down any city brat that picked on her and Lark, until Josef paid a formidable governess to watch her every step. 'Lily?' Rose's worried voice broke her daze. 'What's wrong?'

'Nothing. Help me up.' A powerful arm hauled her into the carriage with a jerk. 'Bloody hell.'

Rose didn't notice. 'Papa? Papa! He's not answering me, Lils. Papa, can you hear me?' Lily clambered over the mess of bags and boxes to her side. Slapping Rose's anxious hands away, she used two fingers and found the flutter of a heartbeat in Josef's neck. Her pocket mirror showed a faint mist rising from his lips.

'Give him some room. I said give him some room, you big idiot. Look, he's breathing.' Lily pinched his cheeks and shook him. 'Wake up, old man. I see you breathing.' His head fell back on the cushions, leaving Lily lost for words. She gripped her pocket mirror as his breath faded from it. It was his Year End gift to her, and a strange way to first use it. 'Help me get his legs up,' she said, for want of anything else to say. 'Dren will sort him out.'

They sat in silence, breathing in the smell of musty cushions and listening to raindrops pound on the roof. Rose was hunched slightly forwards and keeping very still, but Lily could see her thoughts thundering away underneath. That ripped and soaked dress had betrayed her. Hidden muscles were no longer softened by lace, or curved by layers of cloth. Lily tried not to stare, and held onto Josef's hand.

Time didn't so much drift as rot. Fear and worry broke down into sick exhaustion, and a tap against the window woke Lily just as her eyes were closing. The latch took a moment to pry open, but when it relented, a bedraggled Pearce burst inside and found himself a corner. He met Lily's eyes with a grimace, hiding behind a mop of wet hair.

'Ladies.' Dren knocked on the open door to get their attention. He was ducking under the lip of the roof to avoid the rain. 'I think that is everyone accounted for.' He leant back out to glance left and right. 'Apart from our driver, who has run off. Never fear, I am fully capable of taking over. It is not far to the Long Path.'

'What happened?' Lily rubbed her face. 'Those noises... it sounded like someone in pain.'

'Bandits. Discontent sweeps the north.' Dren's irritating melodrama defused some of the tension. 'These rascals were tracking our coach in hope of collecting a bounty. But I saw them off, do not worry.' Grabbing the roof rail he aimed a vicious kick at the coach's crest. Josef's coat of arms crunched and splintered under his boot, the next blow breaking it off. He tossed it into the bushes. 'From now on, your identity is a secret. The peasants have put a bounty on any ministers who have escaped from the city.'

'Wait!' Rose stopped him closing the door, shouldering it open again. He frowned up at her. 'Don't waste time gawping at me. Josef is sick.'

'Really?' Dren seemed surprised. He swung up into the carriage and examined Josef's prone form. 'My friend, what is the matter?' He peeled back an eyelid. 'Did he stop breathing?'

'No.' Lily handed him her stepfather's pocket watch. 'And I counted fifty heartbeats earlier.'

He gave her an approving look over his shoulder. 'Well done. You are both far too resourceful to be hemmed in by city walls.' He wet Josef's lips with a bottle from his satchel. 'That will help him sleep. Good advice for everyone, I think. We will get the poor man to a bed at the next trading post.' Dren flicked up the collar on his coat, and thumped on the front wall with a fist. 'Beat twice to get my attention, then twice again if you need me to stop.'

The door closed behind him, and shortly afterwards the coach rocked into motion. Lily shuffled over to sit next to Pearce. 'Are you all right?' She parted his hair with a finger. The minister's eyes flicked back and forth as if looking for the source of her voice. He gave a nod. A shudder rippled through him. 'Hey.' Lily touched his forearm gently. 'Are those burns new?' A thought occurred to her. 'Did you drop that lantern?'

He paused. Shivered. Another nod.

'Well, don't worry about it.' Lily sat next to him, and gave him her best conspiratorial grin. 'I've broken a few of them in my time. Josef seems to buy them cheap.' She rolled up a sleeve to show him her scar. 'When I was little, I dropped one while exploring the loft in his timber warehouse. The supervisor just about saved the place from going up in flames, but he dipped me in a rain barrel to get the hot oil off. I wore bandages and long sleeves all through the summer to hide it from Josef, you couldn't guess how itchy it was.'

She'd never told Josef that story. He'd lost a lot of his timber stock to fire over the years, flames spread by underhand competitors or started by careless employees. But if Josef heard her speak, he didn't show it. He remained still, buried deep under a pile of blankets.

Beaks and Wings

'Wait!' Husker roared, chasing the coach as it hit a bend. An arc of mud splattered his face before it careered off, lost down the forest trail. 'Damn it.'

No chance of remaining a stowaway now, not with Dren up front. That bastard was more than he seemed, standing bolt upright and scouring the bushes with piercing eyes. Sure, he had a grip on the reins, but anyone could see he was steering the horses with gestures from his other hand. Nah, that bastard wasn't all he seemed.

'Bastard,' Husker muttered. He crouched and poked at the tracks they'd left. The soaked earth ran with water, but it didn't give way under his fingers.

Spotting the Kale family crest in the bushes, he seized it and smashed it against a tree trunk, spreading splinters along the ditch. He could've sworn the bastard had locked eyes on him as he kicked it off. Everywhere he hid, those arrogant, questing eyes seemed to find him, mocking him, daring him to step out and make himself known. Husker broke the last stubborn piece of wood in two and vented a roar of frustration. Ravens took off in a flurry of beating wings, bloated from their grisly meal among the trees.

At least the coach crest was unrecognisable now – a few chips of paint that wouldn't give his girls away to more hunters on their trail. Not that they weren't travelling with enough trouble anyway.

'I'm coming, bastard.' He dropped to his knees and took a quick slop and roll in the mud, coating his skin and muttering scripture. Disguised and blessed, Husker set off at a lope along the tracks.

Those highwaymen had died badly. Probably deserved it. Their scars and drawn blades didn't set them out as godly men, creeping up on the unsuspecting camp as Lily ruined their evening meal. He'd checked one of the bodies afterwards, just to make sure, and yeah, the thief brands had been seared into him deep and hard. Like someone does when they catch a really vicious prick. So, Husker had left them out for a woodsman's burial. First the birds, then the rats and insects, finished off by a good, hard rot and you're nourishing the earth. Natural and undignified.

The ravens followed him, cawing and flapping in his wake. Glinting eyes watched him from the highest branches, whipping back and forth in the storm. The forest thought him the provider of the flesh it was feasting on. Burnt corpses and blackened hair. Scalps crisped to a dark red. One of the highwaymen was still twitching when the beaks were ripping into his skin, but a rock to his head had ended that misery.

'Bastard,' Husker panted, picking up the pace. He slogged along the trail, ignoring the rocks and pebbles underfoot. 'I'm coming for you.'

Loyalty

Crone always attracted flies nowadays. She missed her wig. Flapping a wrinkly hand over her bald scalp to drive the pesky buzzers off, she watched as Lark wavered, lonesome and uncertain in the busy drag. She'd liked this one. Quiet, obedient, the boy did as he was asked, and a lot more without being asked, and that put you right in Crone's books, yes indeed.

She edged forwards for a better view, gripping the corner post with her gnarled fingers. And she wouldn't do him this way, no she wouldn't. But Terrano had been very specific. Very clear.

Who would have thought the Old Court would be so furious? Oh but he'd been bad, they said. He had to bury the evidence clean and fast. They didn't say why though, and it was a silly shame to lose a busy worker like Lark without a good why as well. Terrano still feared his masters more than he trusted his schemes.

Lark spun around to see where faithful Crone had gone, looking as lost as a boy half his age. There was truth in that. Too much baby in him, not enough man filling out the bits where it should. A drover was working a passage through the crowd and jostled him, his obese, tattooed flesh spilling obscenely over dirty trousers, wobbling murderously as he beat at the flanks of his hapless pigs. Chains rattled and jangled and clinked as the animals squealed, snuffling in protest as the drover's switch rose again and again. He caught Lark on the backswing as he whipped and kicked them into order, and the boy recoiled – look at him! All shrinking and flinching. Ducking further into the crowd. Too timid, no doubt about that, oh yes.

A voice whispered close to Crone's ear. 'Old bitch, don't you move.'

Crone smiled amiably and nodded, keeping her attention on Lark. She felt the prick of something nasty and sharp in her back, and hands all a patter round her pockets. Leaving her visitor to his silly task, she watched as Lark squelched out of the thicker mud and onto the straw sidings of a wayinn. It was a creaking edifice of planks, nails and paint, which loomed in garish magnificence over its neighbours. A faded banner hung from the balcony, *Grand Axle Wayinn – Fine Liquors and Dice*.

Crone's visitor spun her around, so she lost sight of little Lark, but now she could take a good look and peer at her visitor instead. Not much to see. No hairs on his head, like hers but by choice, and dark eyes which peeked over a tattered hanky that covered his mouth and face. He waved a dagger under her nose. 'Where's your coin, old bitch? Don't think on it. Saw you fingering a rope of it earlier, you.'

Oh he was a new one, wasn't he? All secret and sneaky with his hanky mask and whispers. As if that didn't mark him out as one who couldn't hold his own in a fight. Crone tutted and shook her head, stroking the wisps of hair that grew long and curly on her chin.

'Well?' He shook her.

No use him asking; she'd no coins left to give. She'd had some, yes of course. Crone had robbed and choked all the poor boys and girls in Terrano's waggons to a second death, stolen whatever they had on them. On Terrano's say-so, of course. The hanky-man had seen her threading them on a rope, but not seen her pass it to little Lark. Oh yes, she'd throttled away the evidence, just as the Old Court had asked, just as Terrano had ordered. But she bent the rules for little Lark. Her favourite, she cut him loose.

The visitor was getting upset and twitchy, so Crone held out her bag of pots to keep him busy. Greed sparked in his eyes, and he grabbed it off her with a clatter. Crone kept her back against the upright so as not to worry the hanky-man, but she bent her head all sly and slowly around to see what little Lark was up to. He was done with the clamour of the street, climbing rickety steps up and into the Grand Axel Wayinn. It was as good a choice as any. It would be deserted for a while, giving him space to gather up his bits of manliness for clock-time. A few extra hours of life, maybe that's all poor old Crone had given him. She knew this place too well to ponder otherwise.

Clocking off was a daily ritual in Krans, last stop before Saarban and civilisation. The town spun on hard work, piddly wages and enough drink to forget the rest. Each day was the same hot, filthy affair, metered out in rusty minutes by the town clock down the road, and back in her day Crone had grown to be a big and beautiful whore here. Now back after all these years. Withered but crafty. Oh but happy! She'd changed. Krans didn't change. She'd said that to the other whores after the brothel madam had cut her wrists, bleeding out her troubles in bathwater. There was no money in selling flesh here – the town that earned so little and drank so fiercely.

'You're wasting my time, old bitch,' the hanky-man snapped, reaching the bottom of her sack. 'There's nothing here!'

He was forgetting to whisper now, and a few heads turned from over the street. They watched him wave his dagger at her, and now it was their turn to get greedy. The hanky-man was nothing to them. A hard man would've stabbed her up without all this jabber and robbed her corpse, oh yes. Crone shook her head at him, sad on his behalf.

The sack crashed to the ground. Her visitor grabbed her by the throat, growling threats, and settling for a slow draw of his blade over her cheek. He gave her a muttered warning to watch herself before slipping off, but that cut stung and made Crone cross. She'd have paid the hanky-man some night violence for that sort of behaviour, but even as he melted away, the real men strolled after him. No slinking or disguises for them, they'd choke him out good and proper to see if he'd stolen anything worth taking. Krans didn't change. No bath for him, no, he'd bleed out his troubles on the street.

Crone put Lark out of her mind and bent to collect up her scattered pots and pans. The money might help, might not. Buying drinks in Krans earned you friends, and sometimes friends kept you alive. A good worker like Lark deserved a dog's chance, yes. A slim chance.

Dice

Lark's eyes were lost in the vaulted ceiling of the Grand Axel Wayinn. It looked like it had been a temple once. It had pictures of old men doing miracles on the walls, and Lily had always said that gods needed more headroom than men. Would be a very funny sort of temple now, though. Everything was sticky. And the smell! The walls were seeped in so much liquor it was like someone had tried to pickle the building but couldn't find a large enough jar.

The whisky bottle rattled as Lark shifted on his stool, so he poured himself a glass and picked a scab on his cheek till it bled, wondering when Crone or Terrano would show up to collect him.

Sneaking spirits from the Taxer's pack was a habit he'd picked up since Branera. He'd liked the tax patrol at first. People had mistrusted him and given him a wide berth – friendships started with a sullen silence, then worked their way up from there at a pace he thought reasonable. But then each village brought more worried and tearful faces, the Taxer droning out more instructions from his merciless ledger. Mothers would come forward to draw from a bag of pebbles, and a plain stone sent them back to huddle with their family, together and thankful, forgetting they were now a great deal poorer. A dotted stone brought tears and threats, clenched fists and sharp words. Or worse, horrified silence. The mailed gauntlet of the draft sergeant would already be falling on the shoulder of their eldest son, or taking the elbow of their youngest daughter.

The smallest were sent off to crawl the tunnels of some distant mine. The tallest were recruited into the ranks of the Roaming Watch, anger heating their tongues as they vowed to ashen-faced fathers they'd return for harvest. It was after one of these bad days that Lark would sneak a few slugs from the Taxer's bottle, crouched like an animal over his pack. That must have been what Josef called the 'good stuff', as the whisky here was tasteless and weak. He took another swig, not bothering with a glass.

The sour-faced keeper was drifting over again, slow and regular as the tide. 'That's ten you owe me, you.' He picked up the bottle and squinted at it. 'It's ten for the whole bottle. I said that, didn't I?'

Lark cringed. The keeper's fat tongue slurred and spat words like they were porridge. And he was looming again. He always came close and loomed until he got his way, with that dirty, white shirt hanging loose like a night shift, lips drooping and sagging, his mouth hanging open. He'd rolled up his sleeves and a green snake of ink crawled down from his elbow to his long grasping fingers. 'Sere, you...' Lark found his voice, but it sounded weak, even to him. 'You did. And I paid you.'

The snake tattoo coiled as the keeper raised a finger to scratch his neck stubble. 'Nah, you didn't.'

Lark dug up more coins and a scrap of courage. He stacked three of them by the bottle. 'Maybe I didn't pay enough, sere? So ten before, now an extra three—'

The snake uncoiled as his finger thumped down on the rickety table. Lark's stacked coins slid into a puddle of slops. He stammered an apology and quickly scattered out seven more from his pocket. The keeper scraped them up with a satisfied grunt, and he was still scratching his neck as he retreated behind the bar.

Lark counted his remaining coins to calm himself. His fingers ran over their rough edges and fiddly designs, Northern sterls mostly. Squares cut from cheap metal and punctured to fit on a pocket rope. One of them was a clever forgery. Another was heavy with what might even be gold – a rare find. He'd always liked the feel of money, and the Taxer had always trusted him with the count. Before they'd all been poisoned.

Outside, a clock started to chime. The keeper started attending to the battered, dust-coated globes that were hanging over each table. They cast only dim pools of red light, but he left Lark's unlit as he passed. 'One more for that lamp, Norther.'

Lark massaged his forehead, staring at the slops and praying to whichever god used to live here that Terrano would come to collect him soon. No such luck, he got some bad memories instead. Lying in tepid ditchwater, his patrol piled around him. A mouth full of mud and grit. The Taxer's corpse leering at the sky, bloated and warped by blackened veins. Lark closed his eyes and took a long swig from the bottle, then settled in to watch the whisky puddles glisten under his freshly lit lantern. He paid the keeper using his forged coin.

Footsteps broke into Lark's glum thoughts. He wanted to believe, but Terrano always walked lightly for a man of his size, while Crone shuffled or bounced. This person hit the creaking floorboards as if to announce their coming to the world, and a chair was scraped away with just as much noise. Still, Lark held onto hope. He held onto it until a bandaged, shovel-sized hand dropped onto the table. 'That's a big bottle right there,' said its owner. Lark peeled his head from his hands to look up at the largest, dirtiest man he'd ever seen. He broke off from fondling Lark's whisky bottle, and showed some teeth in what might have been a smile. 'Road greetings, boy.' His meaty fingers drummed on the table as Lark mumbled a polite response. 'My hearing ain't good, you know.'

'Road greetings, sere,' said Lark, a bit louder.

'Road greetings. Now, need some help with that bottle? Never drink alone, boy. Especially not in Krans.'

'Of course.' Glasses rattled as Lark unstacked one and put the bottle between them. 'Please... please, be welcome.'

'I will be welcome.' The southerner wore what looked like discarded sacking material, stitched crudely together by thick twine. He'd a dozen pockets on his jacket, all filled with metal tools, and maybe even more of them hidden by a beard so overgrown it lay over his belly like a matted rug. He shucked off a layer of these soiled leathers and kicked them under the table. Showing more teeth, he nodded at the bottle. 'Empty glass. That's bad luck, that is.'

'Yes, sere.' Lark poured for them both. He was starting to feel a little faint and he couldn't stop his hand from shaking. 'That enough, sere?'

'Stop watering the table, boy.' His guest gave a throaty chuckle and caught one of Lark's wrists, wincing at the resulting scream. The keeper cursed loudly and bent to brush up broken glassware. 'Bloody gods!' Lark felt himself being held up for inspection. 'Look at that leg rattle. You're too timid for this place, you know that?' The southerner let go, dumping Lark back into his seat. 'Nothing meant by it, just facts.'

Lark's vision cleared, and his manners took over as he struggled to calm himself. 'Yes, sere,' he said, blinking. 'Another drink?' He knocked over the glass and had to pour again.

'Northers. You're a wasteful bunch.' The man's chuckles swelled into barks of laughter, and he slapped the table with his bandaged hand. He snatched it back, sucking air through his teeth. 'Shit on this cut.'

Lark had been warned about Krans before they arrived. As the two youngest children, Amelle and Lark had to wash and stack plates each evening, and since Amelle was a celebrated storyteller and liar he would attract crowds of other children to listen while they scrubbed. The mills of Krans, he said, were towering, smoke-filled death traps which claimed the hands of workers one slash at a time, turning out more blood than wood. Miming a huge saw, Amelle would scream and wave in mock agony, splattering suds over the faces of his squealing audience. And, he said, underneath the mills ran a warren of mines – a dark nest of tunnels and hellish grinding machines which crushed rocks and lives in equal measure. These two beasts of industry fought over Krans, and losing a hand to either profession was your first and only sign to retire. Because retiring with no hands isn't much of a retirement.

'Don't stare, boy, it's only a cut.'

'Sorry, sere. It's just you're dripping—'

'Now, you're making a big deal out of nothing.' The man chided him with his bloody fingers. 'Drink it off, that's the way. Meet eyes for luck.'

Lark held eye contact for as long as he dared, then quickly drank. This gave him plenty of time to watch in morbid fascination as the man approached his glass like a romance. His smacking lips inched closer and closer. His eyelids fluttered. The glass tipped, he swallowed, and with a flurry of hair and choked curses it almost came back up. Lark shrank back against the wall to avoid a flailing arm, and even he was ashamed at the cowardly squeal which escaped his lips. And he pissed himself, though only a little.

The southerner cleared his throat. He beckoned to Lark. 'Get back here, boy. You twitch too much. Nothing meant by it, just facts.' He picked up the bottle to inspect it in the lantern light, respectful as any wine merchant. 'And gods be fucked if you know what you're drinking.' He hacked up again, letting the mess splat from his hand to the floor. After some finger wiping on his trousers, the bottle was turned towards Lark. 'You've heard of top shelf? This here is what we call cellar shelf. So bad it's good. The stuff that makes you wake up with a hammer in your head, and the ugliest whore in town wrapped around your face – the second ugliest rifling through your boots for spare change. You feel that burn in your innards, boy?' He poked Lark with the bottle tip. 'That's a good time, right there. Nod your head, don't quiver. Your tongue's burnt out by this filth, no doubt.'

'I don't care for it much, sere,' said Lark, a little confused. He pulled sodden trousers away from his leg. 'I'm used to stronger, I think.'

'Aha! Some swagger in you after all. No need to lie though, no shame to grimace over this bottled arse-juice.' The keeper shot him a sour glance from the bar. The man waved a bloody hand back. 'Don't glare at me, you know I don't mean nothing by it. Just facts.' He bent close to Lark, giving him a wink and a dose of sour breath. 'I'll help you with the rest of this bottle, don't worry on that.'

'Thank you, sere.'

'My name's Buller, call me that.' Lark was getting better at spotting his smile amid the facial hair now. It was like his mouth wanted to snarl, but his eyes gave the game away. 'I'm the mill overseer and oldest hand around here. Even if I'm not actually from around here, as the bastards will no doubt tell you. I'm still the boss, though. No boasting meant by it, just facts.' He served himself another drink, then tipped the bottle towards Lark. 'You got a name, boy?'

'Lark Kale-Tollworth, sere.'

'Adopted, huh?' The whisky started to pour, sloshing up the sides of Lark's glass. 'Two families are better than one. What's your story, Kale-Tollworth? You must be pale even for north of the Split. And this don't look too healthy either.' He took one of Lark's hands and twisted it over; the dark veins seemed to pump and swell in response. 'You're not bringing sickness to my home, are you?'

Lark couldn't respond. His brain fevers held him, roaring in outrage at the grip on his palm. No scream this time, but his leg rattled the table until a glass rolled off.

'You okay, boy?' Buller let him go and picked up Lark's glass. He poured it again. 'Don't like being touched?'

'Yes, sere. Sorry.' Lark sunk his whisky with a gasp. 'I'm a little mad, sere. My birth father was a lunatic. I've got his bad blood. Brain fevers.'

'Hah, I knew it. Those marks, that's sickness if I ever saw it.'

'No, sere. It's not that,' said Lark. His head always felt clearer after a bad shake. Woozy and drunk with courage, if not from the weak spirits. 'My master says they're harmless, left over from a poison he cured in me. The ash of mortalus leaf in my veins.'

'Never heard of it. Well, it's fucking ugly, Lark, nothing meant by it.' Buller kicked back on his chair, cleaning his mouth with a few wet slaps of his lips. 'Taste of Krans, that is. That's culture in a bottle. So, where's home in the Northlands? I've been no further than the Long Path.'

'Branera, sere.'

'Bad place to call home.' Buller tossed back another glass, coughing and spluttering into his beard. 'No one seems to like that shithole – all those rich bastards and mud. Only thing worse is Cerc Reno, I hear.'

'I don't like cities much,' Lark said, in a quiet voice. 'I was born up in the foothill villages.'

'The mountains? That's pretty north, boy.'

'Yes, sere. Hillsford is the last settlement before the Mountain Feet. I was orphaned to Branera as a baby.' Lark felt himself flush. 'I hate it there, so my stepfather sent me out to gather taxes.'

'Not bad pay, following a Taxer around. Shitty business though. Spend all your time tithing honest people for the Roaming Watch.' A spread of teeth, but this time there was no warmth in his eyes. 'We've got them down here too.'

'I wasn't paid, I don't think.'

Buller swore in protest, thumping the table. 'You've had a rough time of it, Lark. Exploited, that's what you are. You ran away from this tax patrol, didn't you? Am I right?'

'Something like that.' Lark hid the coin he was playing with. The keeper had almost seen it. 'I'm on my way to Saarban, and my master says I can take on an apprenticeship at the palace there. He's a great man, a scholar called Terrano.'

Buller frowned. 'Fat bloke is he? Bald lady following him around?'

'Yes,' said Lark, surprised. 'Have you seen him?'

'Not for years, but he's known here.' Buller narrowed his eyes and spoke a little softer. 'And what does he make you do for him?'

'Cooking, mostly.'

There was a pause, and Buller grunted. 'As you say. If you need another place to work, come to me. We don't like him much – makes your skin crawl just being near the bastard. I'll find you something better to do anytime you want.' He nodded to Lark's full glass. 'You drinking or not?'

'Oh! I'm sorry.' Lark drained it and wiped his mouth on his collar. 'Would you like another?'

Buller shook his head. 'Bloody gods, boy, I don't believe this. You put that slop away better than someone your size should. You don't taste it?'

'Don't seem to.'

Buller turned and waved at an unkempt man leaning on the bar, his head bowed in low conversation with the keeper. 'Bent! Come meet this Norther.' The keeper sniffed and unleashed the contents of his mouth into a jug. The other man, Bent, shook his head and resumed his conversation. He wasn't the only newcomer. Tired, sullen men had appeared at the tables of the wayinn, dressed in grimy cuts of leather and passing bottles, muttering through the grievances of the day.

Buller smoothed his beard, and settled back into his seat. 'Mate of mine, is Bent.' He jerked his chin at the man by the bar. 'Always fixing a dice game before he starts on his whisky, but he'll be over. Don't fret, just want to show him how you put that bottle away.'

They sipped the next glass, at Buller's request. 'You know it's as much a title as a name,' he was saying. 'It came from my old man. Bastard was twice the size of me. Most respected boss in Krans, and none like him until I took his place.'

Buller rambled on, his slow and lazy movements now heavy and clumsy. It might have been the ruddy light from the lanterns, but what cheeks were visible behind the man's beard seemed to be flushing a blotchy red. Lark slid Buller over another drink, dodging back when he leant forwards to thump the table and laugh across the slops. Rose had always said liquor was poison, keeping him busy elsewhere when Lily and Josef got drunk, roaring with laughter in the study. Terrano said poison wouldn't bother him anymore.

Lark nodded along with Buller's story, pouring them both another glass. He drank his, still tasting nothing. His smile grew broader. If he could stay clear-headed, maybe he could slink away and sleep somewhere quiet. Then he could find Terrano in the morning, and tell him all about this for his book.

~

'Again, you little brat!' The ugly miner thrust a bottle at Lark, his hands clenched around the neck as if it were him in his grip. Lark flinched, expecting to be hit. He wasn't, but another drink was poured, and whisky was splashed deliberately over Lark's knees. The ugly miner stank of sweat and garlic, pressed in by the crush of the crowd and too close for anyone's comfort. The sour stench of his skin seemed to vent from holes in his tattered clothes, while mottled folds of flesh and hair showed through a rip under his arm. 'Quit staring, you.' He pushed another glass over. 'And two this time.'

'Yeah,' slurred his friend, no prettier, no cleaner. No better at this game, either. 'Too right, you.' He was incredibly drunk, and his stake had long since dwindled as Lark played circles around him. Lark had wondered if he should lose on purpose to be polite, but it wasn't his money, so was that right? The slurrer's glass eye was set crudely in a mess of scars and tattoos, and it seemed to sag and stare at Lark until the man mauled at his face to set it pointing straight. 'You watch him,' he said, pawing at it. 'You watch him.' No one else seemed to know who he was talking to, and Lark was too terrified to ask.

So Lark drank. The putrid whisky burnt on his tongue for a moment, before slipping down with no more taste than brackish water. That burning was worrying. He hadn't tasted burning before.

'Again!' The ugly miner was hysterical now, provoking roars of laughter from the crowd as he pounded the table. 'Three for him. Three for Northers, we've always said that.'

'Enough.' Bent opened his eyes. He was lounging opposite Lark, bored and sober. He played too well to need bottle forfeits. 'Buller warned you, didn't he? The kid's got an iron stomach. So you let others take a turn, you.' Bent was a grizzled mine boss, with tunnel stoop and faded eyes which only sparkled when the dice were in reach. Everything else seemed to bore him. He'd speak a word or two on Lark's behalf when his underlings slowed the game up, half-hearted barks he forgot a moment later. Not that they respected him much.

'Fuck your turn.' The ugly miner rattled the dice and poked around his last coins in disgust. 'This brat cheats. Every time he rolls bad he forfeits. Every time! Look at Buller, then look at him.'

Buller was slumped in a chair, his face lost in his beard. At first his body had fought a rear-guard against the whisky, and he'd lurch forwards to pat Lark on the shoulder, slurring advice in his ear before slumping back with a dangerous creak of the chair. He'd been snoring for some time.

'This Norther's had as many as him, more even.' The ugly miner seemed calmer now, but his hands were trembling, reined in by the presence of the jeering crowd. 'Hey, listen, kid.' He rolled the dice around his clammy palm. 'Let's say no more forfeits for me or you. How's that, huh? Just play it straight.' More insults were heaped on the miner's head. Someone clapped him round the ears. The sweating mass of the wayinn swung between raucous abuse at the Northlands and roaring support for Lark, but he wanted neither.

The crowd noise died down. Lark blinked sweat from his eyes and cleared his throat. 'Doesn't sound fair to me, sere.'

The wayinn erupted into roars and arguments. Could he let them win? It wasn't his money. It wasn't right. He couldn't. It was so obvious where the cards lay, the chance of this happening or not. And Lark had given up trying to neither lose nor win, as it was giving him a headache.

'Hurry up, you.' Bent was pushing his next stake back and forth. He had a sterl under his finger, recently minted with straight sides. 'Buy in or leave.'

The ugly miner and the slurrer held a quick, mumbled conference, then searched their pockets for enough coins to make a joint bid. Scraps of bronze dropped to the table in a meagre rain of coins. 'Sure, boss,' the ugly miner said, with his new tight-lipped calm. 'We're in it together.' A knife fell with a clatter next to the pile. It wasn't clear if this was part of their stake or to make a point.

Bent shrugged, playing the sterl around his agile fingers. 'Sure.'

It was Buller who'd started this stupid game. A drunken arm had locked tight over Lark's shoulders as he tried to excuse himself, insisting his Norther guest stay and learn to roll dice. Several forfeits later, Bent was unable to wake Buller, and the drool was dangling from his mouth like a soggy pendulum. By then the crowd was pressed in so tight that Lark couldn't have left his seat if he tried. He swallowed, trying to avoid the drooping glass eye opposite him.

'Right,' said Bent, brightening up as he shook the dice. He called the correct bet and they clattered to the table, hitting a big score anyway. He leant back, bored.

The slurrer's fingers chased a die through the slops. He'd used all his good cards, leaving him stuck with poor judgement and raw luck. 'One over yours, boss.' It was a stupid bet and a low roll. The ugly miner swore and grabbed him by the arm, but he was shoved roughly back. 'Get off, you.' The slurrer threw in a card that he couldn't possibly have, clumsily picked from his sleeve. 'I got this.' He took the smallest die to re-roll. It skidded, splattering and sliding into a puddle before showing an even lower number than before. The glass eye sagged. He fumbled it back into place and reached for the bottle. 'Forfeit, then.'

'Don't you fucking dare!' The ugly miner made another grab at him, but was pulled away and held back by the crowd. 'Let go, bastards,' he snarled. 'He's going to lose me everything.'

'Can't pay, can we?' the slurrer jeered. He held the glass up to the light and squinted at it. 'I got this.'

He missed his mouth. Half of it went over his lips, more down his shirt, but it was enough. The slurrer's cheeks bulged as he tried and failed to contain the burst of vomit, and his barstool clattered over as he doubled up and emptied his guts over someone's feet. There was a fresh round of insults and cheers.

'A lesson for you there,' said Bent, with a flickering smile for Lark. 'We all pay one way or another. Now he's got to clean someone's boots too.' He chuckled over their winnings. 'So! Just me and Buller left in. That's you.' He winked at Lark as his hands raked away coins, dividing the pot in two. 'I'll see you sick on your shoes yet, you.'

Lark was almost dizzy with relief. He even managed to meet Bent with a weak smile. This was Buller's friend – Buller wouldn't mind losing to a friend, would he? If Lark could get into the knack of losing. Bent pushed half the stake towards Lark, stopping when the ugly miner grabbed his knife from the pile and rammed it through his hand with a sickening thump. Bent gave a few panicked grunts, then pain overtook shock and he stilled the wayinn with a scream.

A warm, sweaty silence. The miner sniffed, and yanked the knife from Bent's hand before pushing it roughly into Lark's stomach. In and out. And in. Lark managed a few wet noises, and looked down in time to be splattered as the knife was pulled out again. His pain faded to confusion, his groans softened to a whimper. 'Norther bastard,' the ugly miner muttered. He slumped back in his chair. The knife clattered from his hands. 'Like fuck are you taking a single coin back across the Split.'

Bent was furious, shrieking threats as he tried to climb over the table, smearing bloody handprints on the cards and scattering dice. His lackeys wrestled him back into his seat, but everyone was spitting curses and painted red by the time they forced him to raise his hand above his heart. Lark watched this tussle with disinterest.

The table approached with stately grace. He slid forwards and sideways off his chair, knocking his chin and sinking beneath a sea of boots. Raised voices grew dull and distant, and a mouthful of vomit or something dribbled from his mouth. Wiping it away, he wondered again where Terrano was, and blinked as cards fluttered down from the table to land on his face. The ugly miner was pushed off his chair. He landed on Lark too. His lips were puckered in surprise, gaping like a gutted fish just inches from Lark's face. Someone had cut his throat, and between them they were making a real mess of blood on the floor.

With a feeble effort, Lark pushed the horrible vision away. He hated it when people got too close.

II

OLD CHAINS

Myth

Keeping to its most solemn tradition, the trading post woke with an obnoxious clatter of activity. Staff leapt from their beds to slam doors, rattle carts and call lusty greetings across the cobbled square, and Lily was now convinced they did it entirely for her benefit.

Yet by the time the cockerel had finished its own bloody racket, this enthusiasm would fade into a lethargy that settled heavier than any Splitside mist. Trade had withered under the prospect of civil war, so there were no meals to cook, no fuel to chop. Staff huddled on doorsteps and passed a bottle, or dozed in their beds until dinner. In booths where deals were once inflated and punctured by darting fingers, idle cooks lounged over their mops, whispering of patriotism stirring in the north. A peasant council ruling in Branera.

Lily flipped onto her stomach with a low growl, pulling the pillow down over her ears. A milkmaid was yelling beneath their window again. The other maids whooped and laughed at her efforts to tow a few hundred weights of noisy beef over the yard, whipping sticks at their own reluctant beasts.

'Murgghhhhh.'

Lily closed her eyes and pulled the pillow down tighter.

'Murgh.'

This was a worse sort of noise. Josef had slipped from his nightly coma into his daytime fever – the sound of his pained breathing was louder than anything else, outside or in. Louder even than the nasal half-snores erupting and spluttering from Rose.

'Gods,' muttered Lily. 'Fuck you all.' She steeled herself for the cold and threw off the sheets. 'Fuck. Fuck. Fuck.'

Rose was undisturbed by this exhortation against cold bedrooms. She was still tucked up in a large yet neat ball on the other side of the mattress, while the dark hair plastered across her face danced in the mighty torrent of air rushing from her nose. Lily resisted a growing urge to smother her sister in her sleep, and bent over some almost-clean clothes, chill air nipping at exposed skin. She growled and tugged her nightgown tighter. Of course they'd taken the cheapest room, high enough for a gale and without enough wall to keep out the clammy weather.

'Lils?' murmured Rose, her voice thick with sleep.

'Go back to sleep, nosey.' Lily rolled her over the other way and pulled on some boots, slipping her knife into its straps. Brushing the crusted blood off its handle had taken all evening and left a blister on her palm, but it was reassuring to feel its weight again.

'Where are you going?' Rose spread out, filling the bed with a cat-like stretch. She yawned. 'All this space...'

Lily turned at the door. 'I'm just checking on the coach. Don't get hair on my pillow.'

~

The barn was a short walk from the kitchen, but Lily always managed to find a long way around. Once wrapped up, she had nothing against the fog, and the lonely copse outside their rooms had long since won her over with its soft signs of life. Sleepy rodent-rustlings came from twisted roots. Birdsong drifted through the mist. Dew-laden stems kissed Lily's forearms as she waded out into the grass sea beyond the hamlet's ruined wall. The morning greeted her with a shiver.

'Is that you, miss?'

And finally this idiot, regular as any Splitside weather. Lily rolled her eyes and waded on towards Dren's voice, almost bumping into the barn door. The coach had been dragged here after a ditch ended his midnight ride to get them through the forest, and it hadn't budged an inch since. Lily's hands greeted a few of their horses as she wove through bales of straw, but she stopped dead when the coach came into view. 'Well, I see you've been busy,' she said scathingly. 'Didn't we have four wheels before?' Grabbing the rail, she swung herself up and inside.

'Did you sleep well, miss?' Dren was lounging on one of the grubby seats, tossing husks of spay out the window.

'No.' Lily wiped straw dust from her tired eyes. 'And I thought you paid the keeper's boy to have this cleaned out.' The coach was a mess of any possessions they'd failed to sort or sell. The keeper had pawed and rummaged through their old life with no real interest, dismissing most of it as city frippery. A few grudging coins were spared for any solid or practical items, but he gave nothing for sentiment or heritage. The coach would be firewood if they couldn't fix its splintered wheel.

Lily arranged herself on the cushions. There was an art to shuffling skirts and leaving a conversational gap for others to fill.

'Did you know, miss,' Dren filled, 'that this coach was a gift from a Rubean lord? A high honour. The craftsmanship is one of a kind.' He finished lacing up his boots and stood, hunched by the roof, to pull on his coat. His arms flicked left and right to find the sleeves. 'Your stepfather once raced it all the way to Cerc Reno, which is not far from here. He and Pearce bested a dozen other riders, and they did not feel a jolt the whole way.'

'Josef always tells that story,' said Lily idly. 'Is Rubean somewhere in the south?'

'Ruh-ubean, there is more air to the middle of it. Ah, you have a clumsy tongue.' Dren sat down and squeezed his fist to work spay through the cut on his palm. The air reeked of it. 'And everywhere is south compared to here.'

'Good. I do like to be on top of things. How long have you known Josef, anyway?'

He wiped his palm and evaded the question. 'You seem tired, miss. Would you care to hear a story? Rest your mind a little? I find my purse somewhat light.' Dren started to beat his hand in the rhythmic call of a storyteller. 'Young ladies of breeding pay good coin to quiver at my tales of daring and wit.'

'Excuse me if I don't,' she said, snorting. His stories rang with too much truth, and they all featured him as the hero. It was unbearable. 'Tell me useful things instead. Have you heard any more about Lark and this gang of kidnappers? Or have you abandoned that ridiculous fabrication yet?'

'Enquiries have been difficult.' Dren stiffened. 'I am not welcome here anymore.'

'These people have more sense than I thought.'

'Oh, I was well loved here, once. In better times. Debt spirals quickly under the shadow of Cerc Reno, and so here the triple draft has been enacted to the letter. They blame outsiders as much as the Grey City for their poverty. Southerners are being hounded from the villages, or left face down in streams, and would you believe that someone has been spreading rumours about me? No, do not answer.' He smoothed his hair, braids clattering. 'This is a region of idiots, taken in by the slightest ruse. Plain food and straight talking – I hate it. Branera is much more flexible.'

'So you don't know where my brother is.' Despite herself, Lily had almost started to trust him. 'You're pathetic. Why did I even—'

'Let me finish! Why must you always interrupt me?' Dren took his time, making a big deal of picking up his story again. He raised a finger. 'I have been working very hard. I slogged through the grass for days, begging for news of Lark's patrol. I demanded to be taken to the author of his ransom note and put up with no end of hardship for asking hard questions. Priests would grip my coat and hold me up, pointing fingers at my skin and wonderful nose. Here he is, they said. Here is the southern devil, here is the reason you have no money. That is laughable of course, as I am very poor, but they are looking for someone to blame. After I escaped, they would instead turn their ire on the distant walls of Cerc Reno – I tell you, these villagers are moments away from open rebellion. They are stitching uniforms in a wayinn basements, singing terrible songs...' He shook his head, sighing. 'I have come to a conclusion, miss. Your brother's tax patrol bore the crest of the Grey City, and I fear they were the first casualty in a coming conflict.'

'Impossible.' Lily flushed. 'The Taxer we apprenticed Lark to was the richest, most arrogant man Josef could find. He had a dozen guards with him at all times – one of those fools that likes to hear metal clanking every time he takes a piss.'

'And yet it was not enough,' Dren said, dismissing the powerful man with a wave. 'He should have hired a cook, they also keep officials from dying with their trousers down. Your brother's patrol was poisoned, miss. Those who carried out this act of patriotism – once suitably lubricated with ale – described the boy to me quite clearly.' He leant in closer, earnestly seeking eye contact. 'But take heart, miss. Lark seems to have survived this encounter. He was last seen heading for Saarban. Though, the description of his captor was a little worrying, I must admit.'

'Don't spare my delicate nature.'

'You know that ransom note was simply pushed under the door of my lodgings? Not that the coward would have handed it to me in person. I really should have recognised his handwriting—'

'Pay attention.' Lily's fist hit the cushion. The coach gave an ominous creak. 'Tell me who it was.'

Dren sniffed in distaste. 'My brother, Terrano.' He forestalled her indignant questions with a raised finger. 'I accept no responsibility for his actions. I hate the overweight windbag. Last we crossed paths he tried to murder me.'

'I see.' Lily eyed him frostily. 'Well then, you can help us track him down. Would you like your cut of this unspecified ransom now? Or will you wait until we've gone and you join your brother in toasting Josef's trusting nature?'

'You have such a low opinion of me,' said Dren glumly. 'I expect Terrano learnt of Josef's wealth through me, but that is hardly my fault. Fear not! Your stepfather has already paid me an extortionate fee to see you reunited with the young boy. I will see it through without further expenditure.' He shuffled closer. 'So how about a story? I have many. Two sarls or a kiss, whichever you think is cheaper.'

'Ask Josef. He can supply both and listen to the fucking thing too.' Lily crossed her arms. 'Or are you still avoiding him? He's no better this morning.' Dren's wince was a sympathetic one. He patted her arm and retreated over the seats to fiddle with his carving knife. 'Hard for you to make him better if you never visit. Are you listening to me?' Lily watched him work, her frustration mounting. 'You don't care for poor Pearce much, either.'

Fidgeting did nothing to end his odd silence. Letting her curiosity get the better of her, Lily edged closer and tried see what was in his hands. 'What are you even doing over there?' The coach creaked as their combined weight put strain on the broken wheel. She rested her elbows on his shoulders. 'Oooh. Don't sound good, does it? Shouldn't you be fixing this coach instead of fiddling with your toys?'

'Please, miss,' he said, shrugging her off. 'You will snap the axle.'

'You can't fix it, can you?' She pouted. 'Don't feel bad. I'll ask around.'

'Miss, do not mistake–'

'We had a boy in the city that did our woodwork, you know.'

'There is woodwork, and there is wood art,' Dren muttered. It was hard to provoke him, but she was getting better at it. His accent grew crisp, and his eyes seemed to darken, shedding colour as his temper slipped. 'We scholars guard our time fiercely. We have the faculty to be masters in anything we choose. Anything! I will not waste my time on simple labour. Art, however...' His changeable expression grew smug, and he turned to press a block of wood into her fingers. 'I know art.' The carving was smooth and warm from his hands. 'This is for you, miss.'

'Please,' she scoffed, turning her back so she could take a proper look. 'I expect you bought a dozen such trinkets from Branera. One for every pair of pretty legs you find on the way south.' But when she turned the carving over, she found her own face frowning up at her. 'Dren!' She made to throw it at him, but he protested, unable to defend himself while working his knife into a fresh batch of spay. 'I don't look like this!' He grinned and prised out a lurid-green pod, sap spurting from the puncture and pooling in his hand. The minty aroma of it caught Lily up the nose and she sneezed. The touch of her hand was luxuriously rough as she giggled with embarrassment and wiped snot from her face.

It wasn't the first time she'd caught a whiff of spay. The Low Ends were awash with people looking to escape the muddy drudgery of their lives – rutting in the knee-deep filth of an alley, their palms drenched in sap, pink skin exposed to the stinging rain. But that was too simple. It wasn't lust it stoked, but sensation. A lowering of inhibitions and heightening of everything else. Spay was an amplifier, a lens through which life was a thousand times larger, and for some reason she was ready to lift her skirt to Dren at the slightest sniff of it. That annoyed her enough to clear her head.

'Do you mind?' Lily managed, and turned archly away. Dren's laughter brushed up against her heart, so she gritted her teeth and leant firmly out of the coach window.

'Come back! I have put it away, miss. I promise.'

'Get lost.' She took a deep breath and held it. Tears ran down her cheeks, dripping on the piled straw.

'Miss, it is hard to talk when I cannot see your face.'

Her heartbeat slowed to something more sensible. A dozen horny aches were numbed by the chill air of the barn, and the horse opposite stared at her quizzically, chewing slowly on its feed. 'A bad habit you have there,' Lily scolded, returning to her seat. 'Are you sure that's spay? Doesn't smell like it. Seems you've been tricked, if you ask me.'

'You are very right, miss, very right. A bad habit. But for me it is merely medicinal. Come back over here, I assure you I have put it away.'

'You healers are all the same,' she said curtly, keeping her distance and guarding it with a glare. 'Given half a chance you all set about your own stock.'

'Never, miss!'

'All the while complaining of long hours as you sit by the fire of some lord and mop his brow.' She risked a glance at him, but the effects had left her. Dren was sitting attentively. His hands were neatly folded in his lap, his smile apologetic. For once she had his full attention.

'It helps me concentrate,' he said, simply.

'Oh, I'm sure. Gives your tales a bit more zest, I expect,' Lily said, unsettled by his curious calm. 'Those women quivering over your stories, were they all drugged up to the eyeballs?'

'I am afraid storytelling is the least important thing I do, miss. Nor is it the reason I turn to stimulants for relief. I beg your pardon if I gave you that impression.' Dren inclined his head gracefully. A blue feather had appeared in his braids since yesterday, and he touched it to secure its position. 'I have a curious set of talents, most of them forced on me by the Old Court in Saarban. Terrano and I were just two of many children raised in their service. The courtiers named us brothers and hollow-souls, lauded for our ability to find and hoard dangerous spirits. But no one pays me for this service; I earn my keep with more mundane professions. Most of them bore me, but storytelling is… a way to craft the mind. It breaks down the walls which hold us back.' The coach seemed to grow darker. 'Let me tell you a tale of spirits, miss.'

'What a load of nonsense.' Lily tried to ignore the hypnotic tapping of his fingertips. 'I shall have to tell Josef about this, you know. We don't hold with stories of trolls and fairies up here in the north, I'll tell you that for free.'

'And yet despite that you seem to crave them,' Dren said, with an understanding smile. 'I should know, as I have to tell them.' He beckoned, and the carving was plucked from her hands. It hovered in the air, bobbing this way and that, following gossamer shadows which trailed from his fingertips. 'Luckily, I am also a maker of such stories. Thus I always have a ready supply.' His eyes turned black, damp and glistening. With a tap from his finger, the carving started a slow arc towards Lily, and it nestled down into her palm. She couldn't breathe, but the carving could. It sighed and wriggled, moaning softly as Dren's fingers found her hair, his lips the nape of her neck.

Lily blushed and brushed him off. 'A pretty trick.' She wanted to toss the carving back, but instead found herself clutching it, and worried he might take it away. His hand hovered a few inches from her cheek. She already missed it. 'But you've ruined your gift,' she said, gathering up her hair and shaking it back into place. 'It's too easy, isn't it? Must be simple to magic up trinkets like this if you can make wood dance through the air. How many of these displays have you done in the past, I wonder? Quick twirl of the fingers and an even quicker fuck?'

Dren's hand retreated. He dipped his head in recognition of the rebuff, and he set about carving again without another word, or even a glance her way. Precise movements of his knife flicked this way and that, and he filled the coach with his work, filled it with slivers of wood and snatches of discordant humming, but he turned the new carving away when Lily tried to look. Arrogant prick. You'd think he'd never been turned down before.

She felt like slamming the barn door on the way out, but didn't. Dren had a habit of ruining her walks, and she had better ways of blowing off steam. Lily's boots scrabbled and scraped to keep her upright as she took a shortcut to the Long Path. An old map in Josef's study had it running as far as the Merchant Gate, buried under centuries of muck and soil. She'd always thought that was a city myth, but somewhere between there and here it became real, and as the Northlands fell away towards the shore, the Long Path erupted from the grass in a moss-covered parade of broken statues and white pillars. Arches held the ancient path up in the sky. Walls gave it a body, and it twisted away over the Split Sea like a pale serpent.

Lily's first rock clattered off an eagle statue, falling short of her best throw from yesterday. She was still clutching Dren's carving, and was tempted to throw that next. Maybe his strange powers would catch it. Maybe it would soar away to the Southlands, beating all of her pathetic records and she'd walk away feeling better for ridding herself of it. Shivering, she lowered her hand and tucked the carving deep into her pocket. Despite the distance, Dren's black eyes still seemed to watch her. His touch still haunted her hair.

For all the obscenities she shouted after it, her next rock didn't even reach the eagle. Letting the rest fall from her hand, Lily stood for a while, watching mist and wind fight over the white stones.

New Plans

Terrano's scratchings filled the hovel, a sound which always made Crone happy, oh yes. She'd built him a crackling fire with bundles of dried twigs and logs, until the warm, tinder smell mixed with the waft and spice of her cooking and, oh, Crone had stirred up some of his favourites tonight! Crisped and carefully burnt potatoes in a hearty stew, great wobbly chunks of meat swimming in juice and spice. A perfect evening for him and for her, and for his books.

She gripped her ladle with fierce pride, then turned to clip Lark around the ear for neglecting the dishes, then remembered he was gone. Abandoned by faithful Crone just last week, which made her sad.

'What was his name, Mrs C?' Terrano was muttering to himself as he dipped his quill over and over in an inkwell.

Crone pulled her aching feet from her slippers and wriggled her toes by the fire. She even allowed herself a contented sigh. Except she'd never had the air for a proper sigh since she'd been hanged, but she parted her lips and wheezed along just the same. Appearances matter, oh yes.

'Long whiskers. Always cursing, cussing. Thibault? Yes. Thibault.'

She watched him scrape out these long, elegant letters in his new book, and gave herself a frown. Look at him, that deep and generous neck all rolled up into sausages as he pressed his chin in with concentration. Terrano did not like these men, whoever they were, no indeed.

Crone padded over to sneak in an arm and move his supper closer, edging the inkwell aside to make room. He absently tipped a plate of potatoes into his stew, and handed the dish back to her, restoring the inkwell to its previous spot.

'And Jardus... J...'

His new book matched his mood – dark and secret. It was bound in black leather, with none of the old embellishments he loved. Nothing spared for appearances' sake, and Crone had not seen that lovely carved cover for days, the book with Lark's name in it all lost and forgotten in their bags. Gods bless and rest him, her little Lark. And who were these new names? Crone had never met them. She always met them first. They died, then she dug them up and carried them over in a sack or roll of carpet for Terrano to examine, then he did his secret magic and wrote their names in the book. Who were these new names?

With a satisfied grunt, Terrano finished a letter, and set about devouring his bowl with customary speed and neatness. Crone slopped in seconds while he was wiping his mouth, so when he turned back there was delight shining in his tiny, happy eyes. 'Ah, Margot,' he said, dabbing at his lips with a napkin, 'you've surpassed yourself again.' Crone shuffled back, nodding and smiling, clutching her ladle in two hands like a prize. He puffed on the drying ink, and placed a sheet of blotting paper in the book, turning a page. This one he simply stared at. 'I've had another letter,' he said at last. 'Would you like to hear it, my dear?'

Crone shuffled forwards, eager and willing. Oh, he was so kind and nice to a poor old lady who didn't have the breath to thank him. He was good to her, just as she was good to him.

'It's a bad business,' he said. 'The Old Court are furious. Insensible. As you know, they rejected my offer, forced me to abandon my greatest work. Now they threaten me with sanctions! Try to hasten my return.' Air wheezed through his nose. 'I can feel the pull of the Scarlet Keep already.' Terrano's head tilted as he delicately dragged an elaborate curve around a W at the top of the page. 'They know full well I cannot resist.' He paused, wrinkling his podgy nose. 'They say I am to be punished. But I think, in fact, they are the ones who are to be punished.'

He stood abruptly, his belly nudging the table and rattling dishes as he gathered up his things. With that, dinner was almost over, and soon he would be wanting his stool. Crone hurried to set it out next to his black crate. She was careful not to upset it, but it rattled and moaned as she approached, planks bending and stretching as it tried to creep, leap towards her. Crone hit it with the ladle, and wheezed a stern warning.

Sweating slightly from the roaring fire, Terrano lowered himself onto the stool and laid a hand on his crate until it settled down. He liked to write by it after dinner, as well as bringing it to his bedside at night, or sometimes he'd ask her to drag it over to the fire if he was cold. Crone pressed the bowl back into his hands.

After a few mouthfuls he handed it back with a contented grunt. 'It was a wonderful dinner, Margot. Well done.' A dribble escaped his lips, so Crone dabbed them clean, and set herself by the fire to spoon up a few remaining blobs from the pan for herself. She chewed and mashed the stringy meat with her remaining teeth, watching Terrano stare blankly at the fire, and waiting for his next words.

'It is decided.' The book was out again. Terrano's quill was dipping in the inkwell. 'We must make bold with my next project – I have grown beyond their patronage, Mrs C. Old chains, not yet discarded.'

Terrano was drowsy, but he would carry on scratching and muttering for hours yet, writing until his chin touched his chest and Crone dragged a warm and cosy blanket over his shoulders.

'We begin tonight,' he murmured, his chin drooping but his eyes gleaming. 'If I fall asleep, wake me three hours after clock-time. Krans must be deserted when we move, busy with their bottles and drink.' His eyes narrowed as he dipped his quill over and over. 'I aim to make good the promises written in this book – but I see no reason not to gather some help first.'

~

Sweat and grime clogged Lark's nose. Moaning creatures clawed through his veins, scratching their way past his heart and leaping back into his blood, until they were swept up in a scream that shattered their foul taste across his tongue. The creatures crumbled away, and this left him alone in a pressing darkness of bodies and limbs. Now this was a familiar nightmare. Tears broke the crust on Lark's eyes as he strained an arm upwards, worming past clammy skin and splaying his hand in a desperate appeal. It was gripped by wrinkly fingers.

'Pull him out, Mrs C,' said Terrano's voice. The darkness began to shift. 'The poor boy. I wish you had found him sooner.' Crone's face appeared, grinning toothily down at Lark. Clear, bright stars peppered a sky behind her.

'Get me out,' Lark pleaded, choking on his sobs. Crone was shifting bodies with a happy, gurgling determination, her thin arms showing incredible strength. 'Please, get me out.'

She hauled him out of the pile. It was a careless heap of bodies, with limp arms and legs spilling over the sides of a cart. A dull boom shook the dangling limbs and a blast of heat washed over Lark. He turned, dumbstruck, to stare up at the great, smoking mills of Krans. Their broad backs and flaming chimneys were lifting clouds of sparks up into the night, drowning out the stars with belches of smoke.

'Have you found him?' Terrano's voice floated up from somewhere.

Lark scrambled to the edge of the cart. He fell to the ground and crawled over to Terrano, sobbing and skinning his knees in his haste to lay hands over his master's buckled shoes. 'Oh, thank you.' His fingers left smudges on Terrano's white socks. 'Thank you. I—'

'There, there, my boy. Welcome back. It took us quite some time to find you, I assure you. And you died again!' Terrano shook his head. 'But you are back with us now.'

'There was a fight! They made me gamble—'

'Calm yourself. You are the first to wake, so take the chance to rest.' A thought seemed to strike him. 'That is remarkable in itself, the speed of your second awakening. Something I wish I could note. But no, this is not about you, my boy. It is not about you.' Terrano had a new book. It was small and bound in midnight leather, and he clasped it firmly in one hand as he stepped up onto his black crate. The warped planks were inches from Lark's head, and they hissed at him, but nothing would make him move from his master's side. 'How do you feel?' Terrano said, crouching to catch Lark's chin. 'Thirsty?'

'No, sere.' He clutched Terrano's hand, and pressed his cheek to it. Warmth. Life. His leg bounced and twitched, but he didn't care.

'Remarkable,' said Terrano, disentangling himself. He gestured vaguely to a heap of rags. 'Put these on. The Watch are pilfering skinflints, I am afraid. Nothing escapes their grasp, not even the shirt from your back.'

It was then Lark realised that he was naked. The clothes Terrano offered were poor even for Krans – a woollen shift with a neck cut large enough for two little boys – but Lark pulled it on despite feeling neither exposed nor chilly. He should, as nights fell cold out here, but he didn't. Running his fingers proudly over the soft material, he even found a crooked 'L' stitched on the breast, and saw Crone hovering nearby. 'Thank you.' He darted over and hugged her. 'It's lovely.' She wheezed happily and gave him a few pats on the back.

'Stand by me, my boy,' instructed Terrano. 'These others will be up and about soon. I want you to be ready to help them.' There were more carts, a dozen at least, and each was piled high with corpses. The piles were moving. 'Your silly brawl started quite the riot. Predictably, the Roaming Watch have been busy with their nooses.'

Terrano had always seemed in two parts, either lost in the little things or boring into Lark until he answered a question. The edges of these two men had now blurred, and his eyes burnt with a steady, blazing curiosity. 'You never quite believed me, did you, my boy? Even though you met others I had raised from the dead? Even as you poured whisky down your throat to no effect? Yes, Lark, I know all about that. They tell stories about the dark-veined Norther boy. Timid as a lamb, but with a stomach of iron.' He tutted. 'Alcohol is a poison – your body will not take it. The body of the dead will learn.'

'Yes, sere.'

'Yes, sere, indeed. But do not think that I reproach you. A sharp mind demands evidence.' He smiled fondly at Lark. 'What killed you this time?'

Lark ran his hands over his stomach, and found a long, puckered scar. Crone scuttled up to run her hands over it, wheezing concern. 'I think it was this, sere. A knife.'

'Wonderful! We can test that later. Again, your body will have learnt.'

'I think I believe you now,' said Lark, unsettled. He pulled down his shift. 'I don't want to be tested.'

'No, no!' Terrano laughed. 'Don't give up so easily! Have some more evidence.' He had one hand tucked into his waistcoat pocket, the other sweeping his book around as if giving a sermon to the stirring dead. 'Have some more proof.' Gasps and cries were coming from the shifting piles of bodies. It was with a stab of pity that Lark remembered the headache and whirling visions from his first encounter with Terrano, and the pain of first life after death. 'They will want water. Take that bucket and ladle.'

'Sere, why are you bringing back so many—'

'We have a job to do, my boy. I move against those who move against me.'

Confused moans turned to screams of alarm. Those on top of the piles crawled away, weak limbs failing them if they found the edge of the cart too soon, some falling to a second death as their necks crunched on the hardened clay. Crone pressed a bucket of water into Lark's hand and urged him to follow her. She leapt nimbly up onto the nearest cart to help the wretched people off, while shadowy figures were doing the same at the other carts.

'What are we doing, sere? Who moves against you?'

'Lark,' Terrano said, raising his voice above the shrieks and moans. 'Another chapter of our lives has begun, the greatest yet. Help these poor people, then let me tell you about the perverts and heathens that run the Palace of Sells in Saarban.'

Everything Burns

'He seems better today.' Lily wrung her cloth over the pot. Water pattered on the surface, imitating the endless drizzle outside. A stray drop wet Josef's hand, and he mumbled, twisting on the pillow and his froth-splattered sheets.

Rose didn't look up, still working on their ledger.

'Don't you think?' Lily laid her cloth on the water so it floated for a moment, bridging the width of the bucket. She sank it with a finger.

'Hmm?'

'He's looking better.'

'Maybe.' There was a quiet clink as Rose moved some coins to one side, measuring out lengths of string against the map scale. Each inch cost them a sarl from the stack, a wayfarer's tariff that bound honest travellers to take them along if they could. Cerc Reno enforced such laws with typical brutality. Branera offered a more flexible arrangement. Lily had no idea how southerners did things – probably ate the coins and flew you home on magic eagles. The sawing of Rose's knife filled the airy stillness of the room, making Josef croak and mumble in his sleep. Lily hushed him and draped the cloth over his forehead, before joining her sister at the table. The last route had taken some remarkable liberties with the definition of a road.

'You sure that's right?' She reached out to touch a marker and had her finger absent-mindedly bent away. 'Ow! Damn it. You have such manly hands.' Lily massaged her finger, and wandered around for a better look. 'Doesn't seem like we can get very far.'

'Far enough.' Rose touched Lily's arm in a distracted apology.

'Didn't Josef boast about having stacks of money?' Lily slumped down into a seat. 'Where's it all gone?'

Rose shrugged and hunched over the map. Her string followed paths Lark might already have taken, while strands of her hair tickled the world they were leaving behind. Her elbows covered the Mountain Feet. Branera beneath her wrists. Once the string reached the shore, it wound its way across the Long Path – a tortuous mess of curves crossing a sea with only one tide. In the Southlands it skirted strange townships. Thoke, Wisewater, Krans. And it stopped short of Saarban, whichever way it went.

'We might have to beg,' said Rose. She stretched the string taut in frustration. 'Are you good at begging?'

Lily flicked a marker. 'No. And this whole thing feels like a mistake.' Krans was just a crack and a hiss in her mouth. Everything about the south sounded strange. 'Why would Lark cross the Long Path?'

'Maybe he wants to see the world. Dren says Saarban's not so bad – it's cleaner than Branera. They wash it out once a year.'

'When did he tell you that?'

'Yesterday.'

'When yesterday?'

Josef gave an urgent shout, like he was on the cusp of making sense. But he never did. His wasted body twisted and bucked, and Lily turned her head, unable to look until he stopped. She went over to straighten his bedclothes .

'Oh.' The thickness in her throat was back. 'He's not moving again. I hate it when he lies so still.'

Rose sighed and sawed more inches off the string, moving coins aside to buy Josef another day in bed. 'We can wait a little longer. All we can do is head to Saarban when he's well enough and' – her eyes flicked over the pitiful stacks of coins – 'plead for Lark's release? Some ransom this would make. Unless Terrano has a spectacularly low regard for money.'

'Unlikely, knowing his brother.' Lily turned over Josef's arms so his sores didn't stick to the sheets. He'd never contracted the grip before. Even when his stepchildren had.

There were good memories there, between the fevers and fits. The three Tollworth orphans had been set on a waggon to Branera, bound by trembling hands and huddled under a waxed awning, with a man's hunched back and the incessant, beating rain their only view. They grew weaker, hotter, feverish, until their breath came in ragged gasps, and Rose's forehead burnt to touch. Lily remembered the squeals of baby Lark being taken from her. She remembered water pressed from a cloth over her brow, the sores on her arms being numbed with swirls of ointment. She remembered Josef, all grey beard and worried eyes. He sang to them softly, unable to carry a tune, but slowing down here and there to let Lily keep up as she mumbled along and shivered under the sheets. He read to them every night, and if the stories twisted and warped in her fevered dreams, he would reach for the book to read them again and again until they stuck right.

A knock on the door woke them both with a jump. Rose made to scoop the coins back into their purse, but Lily caught her wrist before they could give a mutinous clink. She frowned, pressing a finger to her lips, and crept over to the door.

Light taps, timid. The perverse knock of someone who doesn't want to be heard. With a hissed warning from Rose staying her hand only a moment, Lily pulled on the handle. 'Yes? What is it?' She filled the doorway. 'Oh, hello, Raub.' She crouched down in a spread of skirts, meeting the errand boy face to face.

Raub wasn't as young as he looked, just small enough to be kept carrying messages when his brothers had been given bellow handles or an axe. They had an understanding, Raub and Lily. She'd have thought her bawdy stories of whisky and vice from the Low Ends would interest a growing boy the most, earning her the sweet pastries he snuck from the kitchen. But it was her tales of finery from the boardwalks that kept his jaw dropped, and he was innocently fascinated with money in a way that reminded her of Lark. He whispered in her ear. She was wanted downstairs. Dren wanted her downstairs.

Stirring from a pile of furs by the door, Pearce looked up at her eagerly. Dren was paying for the poor man's keep but otherwise ignoring him, leaving him to roam the corridors, or trudge lonely paths out in the yard. Lily often found him waiting outside their room in the morning, huddled up under furs like a soldier on night shift. She tapped her forehead.

'Guardsman Pearce. Shall we go see what he wants?' Pearce grinned at her, so she helped him up. Taking both their hands, Lily led man and boy down the stairs, descending like a governess with her charges in tow. From the landing above, she heard the rusty slide of a bolt as Rose locked the door. 'We shall have to drag my sister out of that room someday,' said Lily loudly. 'She will make herself as sick as Josef. Don't you agree?'

No reply from either of them, but they both squeezed her hand in agreement. Raub was chewing a thumbnail, Pearce plodding along, and neither of them spared a glance for the spread of wealth at their sides. Every inch of the trading post was hung with relics and fancies, rendered dull and tawdry by repeated inspection. Lily's eyes roamed the shelves, but found nothing new, everything old.

They took a shortcut through sparkling kitchens, kept clean by idle staff used to cooking for hundreds. A few heads turned their way, and Lily's charges dropped her hands as some vague sense of pride penetrated their muffled worlds. A dozing cook opened one eye to snort at them as they passed, but she was at least polite enough to close it again, which allowed Lily to spit on her mopped floor without causing a fuss.

'Here we are,' she said brightly, pausing before the feast hall. Lily pressed a broken sarl into Raub's hand – a rare one he might enjoy. 'Thank you, Raub. Go about your chores now. Pearce and I will speak to Dren.' The boy scurried off, the coin held in two hands. Lily was watching him go, and wondering how Lark was getting on, when the feast hall door was opened. She cursed vigorously as she was dragged in by the scruff of her dress, boots scrabbling over the rug. 'Let go, bastard! Let...'

The grip around her neck tightened, but that last night in Branera held her tighter than this prick ever could. Freezing mud. Driving rain. Arm hairs tickling her nose, and gods be fucked, no, not again. Lily snarled and slapped a hand on her leg, pulling up her dress and flicking off the clip that bound her knife to its hidden sheath.

'Miss Kale, please!' said a man's voice, and Lily's wrist was quickly seized. With an unnecessary amount of sliding over her thigh, he stole her knife and sidled into view. The pervert was clean-shaven, pink skin washed raw with fragrant soap and hair trimmed razor-close to his scalp. His nose had been bent out of joint more than once, and it was set on a face so battered and beaten it was hard to place his age. In fact, there wasn't an inch of him that hadn't been scrubbed, broken, or trimmed, and he gave her a tremulous grin that wobbled on twitching muscles.

'Give me that back, please,' said Lily politely. 'So I can stab you in your dirty fucking eyes.'

'No more of that now.' The man's voice lilted in the airs and graces of Cerc Reno. He drifted off to a table, raising a hand in his wake. 'Follow me, if you will.'

It was very much her will, according to the man holding her. Lily winced as he coaxed her forwards with the barest of painful grips. More guards clattered about the feast hall, each one uniformed in polished metal and ridiculous facial hair. Two had been assigned to escort Pearce, but he could've been herded by a child with a stick and a frown if they'd known him better, and she spotted the trading post keeper giving her a particularly vindictive glare. He was dragging a bundle of logs to the nearest fire pit, and seemed to hold the unreasonable opinion that the wasted expense of heating this massive room was entirely her fault.

Lily was pushed down onto a cold bench. It was pulled out with a screech so a young guard could sit at her side, while the man with her knife perched on a cushion opposite. 'May I take this moment, Miss Kale' – he ran a hand over the short stubble of his hair, wet from grease or rain or both – 'to formally invite you into the care of Cerc Reno.' He produced papers trimmed with silver leaf from his jacket and laid them on the table. Cerc Reno had never taken a crest, but it had claimed colours. Grey and silver – that was how you knew those who served his city. No one else wanted them.

'I have been instructed to oversee the arrest of your father,' the man said, neatening his papers. 'An ugly matter, but of course that is his fault. You may address me as Militant or my lord, as you please. If you are unfamiliar with our fair city, please let me assure you that I outrank you considerably.' He placed a broken hand on his chest, fingers splayed in a dozen strange directions. It was in worse condition than his face. 'My given name is Oren, and I extend the warmest of road greetings to you.'

Lily fought the urge to threaten his eyeballs again, and elevated her speech to match his. 'The feeling is not mutual, Militant.' He was a fucking liar too. Militants were something between a soldier and a minister – she'd outrank him in any seating order. She glared at him, doing her best impression of the red-faced women that stalked Branera's highest walkways. Such matriarchs could turn crossed spears with a word, and often did so to effect dramatic entrances, haranguing those within with their sharper opinions. 'When I tell my—' Her attempt to rise was spoiled by the guard next to her, who pulled her roughly back down. Lily stabbed out a finger instead. 'When I tell my stepfather about this, you will see how out of your depth you really are. He is a minister of Branera. Any more hands on me, and he will request them as forfeit, I'll tell you that much. Good grief, trouble between our cities does not come without cost.'

'Oh, how funny!' Oren shuffled his papers, face twitching as he tittered. 'How very funny. Aha. Thank you, child.' Raub had crept in and filled some goblets with wine. With a blank glance at Lily, he took a coin from the militant, a great deal heavier and rarer than the one Lily had given him. That was her problem, always a skinflint. 'Will you call your soldiers, perhaps? We have brought enough for a fight, if that is what is needed.' Oren watched Pearce gape as he was made to sit up, his hair bunched in a guard's fist. 'Though if this pathetic thing is your only escort, perhaps we shouldn't have bothered.' Mail rustled as the guards around them shifted in some obvious posturing. Typical Reno twats, with their stupid twirly moustaches.

'So come now, no more threats,' gushed Oren. 'You are guests! Visitors in our land. And we know all about our guests. We know your stepfather is terribly ill. We know that he is wanted in Branera for a theft of...' He wet his lips. 'Staggering proportions. We know that you take morning walks to throw stones at the Long Path. What's all that about, my lady?'

'I expect you have been speaking to Dren.' Lily clenched her teeth rather than rattle off her opinion on that odious subject. She considered swatting aside the wine Oren placed in front of her, but glugged it down instead, then swatted it aside. As the goblet clattered on the floor, she found herself regretting giving up a potential weapon.

'Dren! Yes. Who is this Dren?' Oren waved the fingers on his ruined hand. Lily could hear the bones clicking. 'His name is mentioned everywhere, but we know nothing of him. We guessed you would come down here at his request. He's a guide of some sort, am I correct?' He cleared his throat. 'Let us get to business. We are hoping to secure a settlement to ease the matter, rather than force our way into your stepfather's room.' Oren flapped his useless hand at an aide. The other one was occupied with bringing a wine goblet up to his crooked nose. 'You may present those to her now.' Air whistled as it fought through his broken nostrils. 'Oh, how nice.'

A man with ink-stained fingers indicated a few spots on the silvered sheets. 'My lady, if you would make your mark here.'

'To what end?'

'To accept whatever comfort your rank affords and formalise your surrender to our laws. We will then proceed upstairs to your room, where you may sign on your stepfather's behalf. Note the intent' – he brushed a paragraph – 'is for you to deliver the stolen property to us promptly, allowing us to grant you leniency and considerable comforts.'

'Stolen property?' She scoffed at him, unable to contain her scorn at how easily they'd been duped. 'This is some lie fed to you by the mob occupying my city – farmers and thugs who want to hang Josef for fictional crimes.'

'Nevertheless.' The quill was placed next to the paper.

Lily pushed it away. 'Get fucked.'

The scribe was unmoved by her change in dialect. 'The power of the northern city has waned, child. Threat of diplomatic or military retribution from that quarter has diminished. I hear peasants run the place now.' He rolled the quill slowly between his inky fingers. 'You may have an hour locked in the militant's waggon to decide, if you prefer.' The northern city. Reno patriots never gave Branera a proper name, ever jealous of the wealth that ran past their doorstep to more pliable markets. 'Mark here, if you will. Your confession can come later.'

Her mouth still wet from wine, Lily gobbed up a prolific amount of red spit over the paper. She smeared it in with a hand, and handed it back to him, smiling as prettily as she could.

'If you wish we can prepare alternative papers,' continued the scribe, in his bored, unremarkable tone. 'Papers which the militant will sign. You're trading a warm bed for a cold cage, there will be chains either way.'

Lily snapped her fingers at him for the quill. 'Good point. I don't much care for the cold. Urgh, what a mess.' She spent some time scratching out the loops of her name around the wine. Luckily, anyone of breeding was expected to spill out a raft of titles when signing such things, and she'd inherited all of Josef's when he took her in. Counting under her breath, she spun around and slapped her guard across the cheek. Then back the other way – dainty enough for the pretence of her being something close to a lady to hold. 'How dare you!' A final slap across the other cheek, mostly for fun. 'I am not some... farm girl! Remove your hand at once.'

'I didn't touch her!' the guard squawked. And, of course, he hadn't. Lily fought back a smile as his voice broke, youthful as his downy beard. 'Militant? You don't believe this nonsense?'

Oren's face was clamped into some strange, tight lines. 'Samuel.' Lily remembered his hand sliding on her thigh, and knew she'd pitched this right. 'Behave. She is signing, after all.' Lily huffed and wriggled away from her disgraced guard, winning some precious space as she continued to scratch out Josef's lineages. She could feel the tension building across the table, and Oren's goblet was slammed down. 'In fact, you can leave us, Samuel. Go watch the door, if you can manage that. I'll be talking with your father about this.'

The young man's mouth opened and closed, working up to a rebuttal. But when Oren's breath began to growl in his throat, he coughed and hastily stood up. 'Very good, Militant.'

'Yes.' Oren chased him off with a flick of his broken hand. 'Get away.' Lily casually adjusted her knees as if adopting a more demure writing expression, trapping the goblet between her feet. 'And who have we here?' muttered Oren, turning on Pearce. 'Are you really a chamber guard? Or perhaps a whore?' He curled a hand through Pearce's lustrous hair. It had been growing back since their departure from the city, and was a shining, scarecrow mess of different lengths. The scribe was watching Lily shrewdly, and he paced around to her side of the table. 'You look terrible, I wouldn't pay much for you,' Oren crooned. 'Are you unwell? Unclean?' He kept his grip on Pearce's hair with his good hand, while feeding himself wine with the broken one. Claret spilled down his tunic. 'Do you even speak?'

The scribe leant over Lily's shoulder, watching her fiddle with the last of her titles. He frowned as he saw her delay.

'Your face is familiar though, you wretched fucking thing.' The militant's sigh was a breaking of wet air and wine over his lips. 'Ah. I do know you. Another minister from Branera, you visited my embassy just last year. One of those fools who want to stand up to the Watch.'

Lily dropped the quill on the floor, and bent to pick it up.

'Never fear, we shall have some papers made up for you, too.' Oren's limp hand caressed Pearce's cheek.

Lily's hand closed around the goblet, and she came up with all the mad screams that saw a girl clear of trouble in the Low Ends. The scribe's nose crunched under her first swing. Coloured glass fell to the floor as her bludgeon released its gaudy trimmings, and she swung again, sending him down. Oren growled and slammed Pearce onto the table, facing her defiantly as she scrambled over to give him the goblet treatment. One moment she was kneeling on his precious paperwork, dented weapon raised overhead, the next she was flat on her face.

Twisting over, she launched a flurry of kicks at the grim, bloody-faced scribe who had a handful of her skirt hem. 'Rose!' Lily screamed in the direction of an open window, kicking, stamping and finally succeeding in crushing the scribe's fingers.

But the moment was lost. She was dragged off the bench and dumped on the floor, with Samuel returning from his banishment to twist her wrist and mutter lewd threats in her ear. Oren snarled for attention. A leather glove was clamped over Lily's mouth, and she was forced to watch the Militant rant over the top of her nose. 'What was that, my lady? Perhaps those muffled noises are you apologising?' Oren's voice was tight with ruffled pride. He ran a hand over his oily hair. 'Oh surely you must be apologising. They must teach women some sort of manners in your stinking pit of a city.'

He probably didn't know there was a storeroom behind him. It led out into a copse of trees – prize information from Lily's morning walks. She'd seen a chance to relieve the cripple of some teeth and drag Pearce away in the confusion. A small chance, perhaps, but she'd felt like trying.

The glove over her mouth had been removed, as the militant had apparently asked her a question. Lily just screamed at the window. 'Rose! Get out—'

'Enough! Enough.' Oren made a gesture. Samuel covered her mouth again. 'Chains for you, Miss Kale. And a gag, too, if I've anything to do with it. Put that away. I'll do the paperwork later.'

The scribe seemed willing to overlook this breach of protocol. He cradled his crushed fingers, eyes tilting past unkempt hair to glare daggers at Lily.

'Something on your mind, my lady?' Oren muttered, watching as she struggled for space. Samuel's hand was crawling down her back. 'Rest assured, it can wait. And what about you?' Oren pressed his elbow against Pearce's neck, gritting his teeth and wrenching back an arm. 'Your mistress is in distress! Perhaps you want to rescue her? Let's hear you shout – maybe you want a gag, too.'

Oren gasped with pleasure as he earned a click from Pearce's arm, and the man let loose a wild cry. Twin moans rattled up from somewhere in Pearce's gut, the yawn of unnatural creatures birthing themselves from his body. Pearce convulsed, his jaw widening as the noise forced its way out and obliterated everything.

~

Lily's eyes opened with painful slowness. The feast hall was hot. It shimmered in front of her like a sun-drenched day on Branera's highest rooftop, and nothing moved easily. Air whistled through her teeth, and she laboured to fill her lungs enough for a scream.

Pearce was hunched over the table. His face was a pit of haggard skin where light went to die, and he was turning it slowly around, turning it to face Lily. His jaw was horribly distended, and now it was stretching wider, and wider, and then Lily realised he wasn't pointing it at her, but at Samuel.

Time was treacle-slow, but Lily's instincts laboriously flooded her with a horrible feeling that she needed to duck. Air dragged at her elbow. It swum up and into Samuel's face, and though his cheek rippled under the blow, his grip fell away with agonizing slowness. Lily had to crawl her way down his body to the floor, and she covered her head just before everything above her exploded into fire.

Life came back with a whoomph of flame. Samuel screamed. Lily screamed too, clutching her sizzling hair as his body crashed to the floor. His armour was red-hot, and his face... Lily screamed again and scrambled away on hands and knees.

~

Rose clutched the windowsill in their room, her nails edging into the wood as each shout rang out from the feast hall. Was that Lily screaming? Raub barrelled out, weeping and crying. He hammered on the shutters and cottage doors around the cobblestone yard, until a cook came out and boxed him round the ears. This left Rose hanging indecisively out of the window, wondering and second-guessing, until the next shriek came from behind her. It almost tipped her out over the sill.

'Papa, what's wrong?' She hurried over to him. 'Stop that!' Josef struggled against her. He was sweating and snarling, his bony body no longer limp but filled with violent intent. His teeth sunk into her arm, and Rose yelped, slapping him awkwardly to drive him back. 'Papa!'

She swallowed past the lump in her throat and darted in again, pushing him back before he could hurt himself. Josef rolled and ranted under the sheets, spitting in a nonsense language, and cursing her in a real one. One of these guttural words hung in the air. It crunched like the breaking of frost underfoot, and Rose stared, dumbfounded, as ice blossomed on the rafters and stalked down over the timber. Josef shrieked a welcome to some phantom spirit, tensing in a backbreaking fit that left him boneless in Rose's arms.

~

With a slow, grinding strength, Pearce freed himself from the pile of guards. One arm, then the next. Men flew left and right, crashing into walls and cartwheeling over tables.

'Kill him!' Oren's order was a panicked screech that none of them had the courage to obey. The remaining guards kept their grip on Pearce only out of fear – regret and terror written plain on their sweaty faces. An older captain with a red beard and worried eyes retreated towards the door, one hand on the hilt of his weapon.

Pearce broke loose. He leapt over to Oren and gripped the Militant's battered features in two hands. Molten spit ran down his gums. His mouth opened wide, dripping liquid fire like it was candle wax, and Oren wailed pitifully. His broken hand flailed over the table and ruffled wine-stained papers, and they started to burn. Everything was burning at this point.

Lily carried on crawling.

~

Flakes of ice stiffened Josef's downy beard, sharp shards that pressed into Rose's cheek as she held him close. An ache in her gut told her something that was hard to understand. 'I'm here, Papa.' Her tears fell on his shoulder.

Lily's pocket mirror was on the bedstand. He was deathly still, but it could prove her wrong. It could find his breath. She reached out, but her fingers had barely brushed it before it cracked and splintered, crumbling away into icy fragments. Everything was brittle and cold. Everything felt like it was about to explode, and Josef's throat had started to tremble. The room started to shake.

Another of his guttural words crunched in the air. A rafter cracked and fell. It was hard to think, harder to breath, and Rose abandoned him with a sob. She ran to the door, overturning chairs, plates and cups rolling and exploding in blooms of ice and dust, everything breaking under her flailing hands, and her stepfather's corpse twisted on the bed to bellow after her.

The door shattered under Rose's shoulder. Trinkets and baubles fell from shelves, crushed and bent underfoot as she breathlessly slammed her hands against the walls. She made it to the kitchen stairs, and fell down into the flames.

~

Pearce flew past the fire hearth, just moments after Lily had squeezed her way in. She shrank back and kicked at the logs which were stacked in her way. Only her in here. Nothing else. But the air had charcoal fingers, and it crept in from the blazing hall to give her face a warning stroke. I'm coming for you, it said.

'Fuck off,' she screamed back.

The keeper's blackened corpse hit the hearth slab, molten eyeballs running from their crushed sockets. Lily turned away with a shriek, and buried her face in her sleeve. She squeezed her eyes shut. She ignored all the noises and shouts, but a faint ringing noise drowned them out anyway. Was someone was dragging her out?

'Stop fighting, miss.' Dren's voice, close in her ear. 'It is only me.'

'You–'

'Quiet now,' said Dren. He kept her elbows pinned, his body shielding her from the flames. 'Pearce needs some time to relax, so we must run. Do you understand me?' A guard wailed from somewhere in the smoke. 'Either way, staying in this room would be a mistake.' Lily's mouth moved, but no air emerged. 'I shall take that as a yes.'

The heat returned, and Lily felt hands under her armpits. Dren dragged her away. Then, cool stone on her cheek.

'Miss, get up if you can.'

She couldn't.

'Get up, miss.'

His voice was pleading, but she couldn't.

'It would be so much better to run.'

Through watery eyes, Lily saw Dren wetting a blanket in the kitchen sluice. He wrapped it around his face and arms. 'Wish me luck, then. I will try to reason with him.'

As Dren slipped into the inferno, Lily's head fell back onto warming flagstones. The next voice she heard belonged to Rose, and the hands pulling her up were gentle and strong.

Long Path

It was a poor time for the rain to stop. Staff milled about in their bedclothes, pulling water to hurl at the flames or spill clumsily over their feet. Dogs barked and snapped at sparks. Worried grandparents swayed children on their hips. A broad lad with unbuttoned dungarees and a sleepy face spread out an arm to stop Rose pushing past, grunting with surprise when she knocked him down.

She was running now. Her boots scraped on gravel as she rounded a corner, Lily clutched tightly in her arms. More sooty faces, buckets slopping in shivering hands. The keeper's boy was standing on a crate and calling out desperate instructions that no one noticed. They obeyed the fire, not him. It roared for their attention. It ate their buckets of water and their homes, spreading with unnatural speed and exploding into life in strange places. The kitchens were already abandoned, left to fall in a groaning heap. A cry went up when the stables caught alight, but even a single spark was too much for all that dry straw and wood, too much for the Kale family coach and their screaming horses. It collapsed as Rose ran past. A gust of hot air tickled her back.

The side gate was wide open, so she waded straight out into the tall grass that surrounded the trading post. It wasn't long before pillars began to crowd around her, and white flagstones replaced the soil under her feet. The locals had done their best, but the ramp that strove up through this collapsed section was dwarfed by the bones of what came before it. The Long Path was enormous; its fallen arches and statues were so massive that the repairs had to dodge this way and that to avoid them.

'Dren?' Rose slid down against a hawk statue. It was watching the trading post burn with stately, uncaring eyes. 'Are you... are you here?' Firelight shifted shadows over the bird's feathers, touching them with movement. Its wings were flexed, drawn back and ready to beat. 'Please.' Rose's voice was thick. She took a deep breath, coughing up blackened phlegm. 'Stay,' she whispered. It was only a statue. 'Stay.'

Dren had led her here before on some pretext or another. The man had a pretty way of speaking, and they'd laughed and talked until dusk. He'd given Rose a wonderful carving that looked exactly like her, and as they wandered back he'd patted the hawk fondly. This was a safe place, he'd said with a grin. She'd waited for him here the next day. And the day after. It seemed empty without him.

'Pearce,' said a hoarse voice. 'Where is he?'

'Shush, Lils. Quiet now.' Weak hands clutched at Rose's arm. 'Lie back! I won't tell you again. He'll be fine. Don't worry about Pearce.' Lily's fingers fell from Rose's sleeve, and her eyes drifted shut. Funny she should be so concerned about him. But that was her sister – soft at the centre if not on the skin. And perhaps Pearce had even heard this rather sweet concern. He rounded a fallen column and trudged closer, his charred clothes ripped and hanging loose. 'You poor thing, what happened to you?' Rose gave her face a determined wipe and tried to stand, gasping as her leg cramped under her. 'Wait. Let me take a look at you.'

Pearce tilted his head upwards, bathing his face in the night sky. His eyes seemed too dark to be real, eating moonlight and casting shadows down his cheeks. And he was dragging something.

Rose limped a few steps closer. 'What... what have you got there?' She crouched and moved aside a coat collar with her finger. A crust of blood coated Dren's handsome features, matting his braids into untidy clumps. His chin fell limply from Rose's hands.

A few steps took her back to the hawk. She fell to her knees, trying and failing to swallow the wail that kept forcing its way up her throat. When that didn't work she rammed her forehead between its stone talons and screamed herself sore. It was hard to say how long it took her to sit up, but at some point Pearce joined her. He'd wrapped his arms around her waist and was weeping, trembling like a child.

'Don't mind me,' she said, her voice a little hoarse. 'Tell me...' Rose sniffed, wiping her nose on her arm. She felt exhausted. 'Well, I wish you could tell me what happened to Dren.'

A shudder shook Pearce's body. He remained silent.

'Stay still a moment.' Rose swallowed and took hold of a splinter in his back. He barely twitched as it slid out, though it was inches long. And in good company. 'Better?' He nodded, but flinched away when she reached for the next one. 'Wait! Don't go.' She caught and ripped his shirt in an outstretched hand. 'Don't... don't go!'

Pearce pushed her roughly back down. With a desperate look at the trading post, he slung Dren's body over his shoulder and fled up the ramp. Rose gasped, almost sick with relief, as she saw Dren stir. Not dead after all. 'Careful with him!' She almost screamed it. 'I mean, wait. Wait for us.' Rose crawled over to Lily. 'Up you get, Lils. Time to wake up.' A few mumbles, but no response. With a sigh, Rose gathered her up and gave chase, pressing her sister's head close to keep it steady. It wasn't the first time she'd carried her like a baby. At least this time she didn't reek of whisky and vomit.

Dren was proving a less willing burden. He was struggling over Pearce's shoulder, trying to free himself even if it meant sending them both down. With a final shout and twist, he grabbed a pillar, and they slid down the ramp in a tangle of limbs.

'Are you hurt?' Rose called out, picking her way up after them.

Dren grimaced as he propped himself up. 'No. Yes. A little.' He pulled apart crusted braids. 'My head is sore.'

'And bleeding,' scolded Rose, finding herself caught between hold-ing Lily and helping him. She could see the moonlight shine of blood on his hand. 'You shouldn't be charging about like that.'

'It was not like I had a choice.' Dren's every move was followed by a wince. He hauled Pearce up, but the strange man just stared up the ramp, shifting from foot to foot.

'What's wrong with him?' said Rose, hugging Lily close.

'Many things. I suggest we push on quickly, rather than talk.' Dren tore a strip from Pearce's tattered shirt. 'There is a place of refuge up ahead where we will all be safer.' He ripped off another strip and tied them into a bandage. 'Do you need Pearce to carry your sister? He is quite strong.'

'No. I can do it,' said Rose, shifting her grip. 'I think she's hit her head, maybe breathed in too much smoke.'

'And barely eaten for days, while drinking enough for a month. Your stepfather's illness has been hard on her.' Dren paused, chewing his lip nervously. 'And where is my friend Josef?'

Plumes of cinnamon smoke had chased them from the trading post, spreading red haze over a fat, royal moon – one that was large enough for a festival back in Branera. Rose could still hear the faint cries of bucket crews on the wind, but there can't have been much left to fight for. 'Back there,' she said, soft words that almost died on her lips. 'I heard Lily scream from the feast hall, then... our room froze. Papa went wild. He was thrashing and spitting. He bit me.' Tears filled her eyes. Those dents on her arm were a small hurt in all this, but one that troubled her the most. 'He stopped breathing, but his body was yelling, moaning. It was screaming at me, or with something else. There was something else in that room, I'm sure of it.' Rose choked on a sob. 'I ran.'

'Miss, I would have run too.'

'Did you do this?' Rose rounded on him, giddy with words. She blinked back tears. 'Did you? Lily said you did magic for her, rambling on about spirits and such nonsense. I called her a child! A drunk. I told her to stop listening to your stories.'

'This was not my doing. Or how things were supposed to go.' The ruined walls of the Long Path let in gusts of whistling air. They snatched the warmth from Rose's climb and stole fragments of Dren's words. 'Pearce's soul is infested by twin spirits, miss. One seized his body and set fire to the feast hall, the other broke free to claim poor Josef. Your stepfather's soul was in tatters. An easy target, I think.' He paused, and his voice was a little rougher when it returned. 'It did not take me long to lash them back to Pearce's body, but those moments have cost us a lot.'

Rose would've hit him. She would've ranted and spat curses, just like she did before a rod taught her better. But she had Lily in her arms and hugged her close instead. If her sister had been awake, she'd have complained of being crushed in that fierce embrace. 'You did do this,' she accused him, softly. 'You brought Pearce with us.'

'Perhaps. But nothing is that simple.' Dren gripped her shoulders, forcing her took look at him. 'I discovered this man's condition only as we were making plans to flee the city. Would you have left him in Branera for that to burn instead? Or would you take him far away, as fast as possible, to a place where he might be cured? Josef only knew half of this, yet he accepted my plea without hesitation.'

'But...' Dren stepped aside, inviting her to see the burns that covered Pearce's skin. He knew she had a heart, it seemed. 'What if they get out again? I heard this path was cursed.'

Dren gave a wry grin. 'Far from it.' He started to guide Pearce away. 'Come, let us press on. I can answer your questions better once we are safe. They will have food and warm beds.'

This simple promise left Rose trembling. Each step from Josef's room had drained something vital from her, and there was little of it left now. She tried to climb anyway. Her feet seemed to slip on nothing, and statues spun and tumbled. The dizziness drove her sideways, and Rose stumbled heavily into the walls of the Long Path.

And then she felt peace. The white stones whispered comforts to her. They spoke of sadness and loss, showing her all the others who'd passed over them, and how many of them had been afraid, how many of them had lost loved ones or were chased and harried from their homes. Thousands of sad souls, all crossing the Long Path and making their way to something better. Past their grief, not yet, but one step at a time. One step at a time. One step at a time.

She blinked, still pressed up against the wall. 'Dren, the Path is—'

'Keep climbing,' Dren called back, high enough that the wind was whipping his coat sideways. He'd left bright bootprints where he'd walked on the pathstones, and nothing on the dull rocks used to repair the gaps. 'The Path is more talkative further in.' Rose took a better grip on Lily, and tried taking a step. And another. The pathstones shimmered beneath her as she climbed. 'See that view?' Dren said, pointing to a large break in the walls. They were high over the northern shore of the Split. Its endless grassland was drained grey in the moonlight, and waving under the sweeping arm of the wind. 'This all used to be water once.'

'The sea came up this far?'

'It did. Though this was centuries ago, long before you were born.'

'Are you that much older than me?' Rose asked with a confused smile.

'Hard to say.' He coughed awkwardly. 'What do you think of the Path? It is usually busier. The uprising has provided us a rare moment of peace.'

Whispers in Rose's head encouraged her to come further in, further along. 'It's breathtaking. Is it really speaking to me?'

'I have not studied the appropriate texts, but I believe it is more of a resonance effect rather than true intelligence. Nevertheless, it is a remarkable trick, is it not?'

Voices called for Rose's attention, to look up, look here, look at me. Small statues were set high in the recesses of the walls, drawing her left and right to meet them. Dog statues yapped happily to her, caught in the chase of a panting wolf. Giggles came from stone children as they ran through a flock of birds. Each turn revealed more voices, and the statues called out to her, showing off, laughing and greeting her like old friends.

'When was all this built?' asked Rose, stunned. Her neck tingled as the voices eddied around her.

'I hold a few theories, everyone of intellect does.' Dren was preening slightly. A stone crow mimicked him in a fussy, squawking voice. 'Priests claim it was fashioned by a god, and built by the old three or in the name of some upstart. But this bridge commands a reverence beyond prescribed religion.' His rustling accent mixed with the whispers of the Path, until Rose seemed to hear him all around her. 'Only the weather wears at these stones – no man dares chip or shape them. Regardless of their calling.'

'But—'

'History always offers an exception, miss. The stolen statues – which you have no doubt just noticed – are the work of a man who could not hear the Path whisper to him.' Dren dodged a gap in the stones, his coat sweeping behind him as he leapt over a dizzying drop down to the sea. 'Jealousy comes easily to great men, and it is acted on all the faster. The merchants who flocked through the great man's gates told him tales of this crossing. An unbroken line of figures dancing from shore to shore, each one reaching for the next, and studying them was said to reveal a deep secret. When I was young, you would find pilgrims sitting in contemplation right along the Path.' Dren pointed at some abandoned hovels, neat huddles of tents and shacks that never touched the walls.

'Splitside culture built up around these pious travellers. Peaceful relations between the Northlands and the rest of the world began right here on the Path, yet most pilgrims reached the opposite shore without hearing more than a murmur. Many more heard only silence.' Dren's hand touched an empty plinth, brushing off wilted flowers and faded offerings. 'The man who defiled the Long Path was the only one who heard screams.'

More stone figures came into view, reverently circled by humble dwellings. A trio of stone rabbits were busy evading a farmer with a beard and flat hat, jeering and dancing as they rushed to catch up with a masked bear, who was running on his hind legs and holding a muzzle chain between two paws. He growled and chuckled as he loped along, bouncing up and down to the clink of the chain. There was so much movement in the still figures it made Rose dizzy.

'Who would do such a thing?' she said, feeling a bit sick. There was something deeply wrong about disturbing the peace of this place.

'You will know him. I expect you have even sung about him, or been clipped round the ear for pretending to be him. The Path's despoiler was Garradus Levry, King of Coin. The last man to sit on the Golden Throne.' Dren sniffed. 'I was raised in the shell of his palace. Trust me, miss, I can uniquely understand why no one has had the stomach to seat a king in it since.'

Silence, for a few footsteps. He picked up his story again. 'Before his suicide, the King of Coin's reach was unrivalled. His whims were made law by the edge of a thousand gilded swords. Each mercenary in his company took a figure from this bridge to decorate Saarban's throne room, and he hoped with time he would hear the statues speak instead of roar. But many wonder whether it was their continued screams that drove him to his final night of madness – the Feast of Ears – where he mutilated his courtiers and hung himself inside a circle of screaming statues. So passed the last of our royalty. King of Coin, but not of us.'

He stopped, turning to Rose. 'Do you not repeat that in the Northlands? "King of Coin, but not of us."'

'"Not of us",' Rose recited quickly. 'Children sing it during the summer.' Dren winked at her, whistling the law song as they passed under a crooked tower. Its ramparts sung with Dren on the wind, catching and echoing fragments of his melancholy tune. Rose felt the weariness of the tower seep into her. 'It's so mournful.' Time had woven the tower a coat of vines, which gave birth to a scattering of blue flowers when she touched it. Shy blooms peeked out from their patchwork of leaves, turning to follow Dren's glowing footsteps.

When he broke off his whistling, the tower continued it for him. 'It is sad for a reason, miss.' The wind thrummed forlornly through its ruined walls, carrying his sombre tune. He held out his hand under a flower, and it fell onto his palm. 'Like the other fortifications, it was built to guard this crossing. But unlike the others, it failed that duty. The King of Coin broke its walls and camped here to oversee the Path's desecration.' Unable to bear the windblown song any longer, Rose hummed her own melody, letting her fingertips play gently over soft petals. Her governess used to sing this after she'd put away her rod, murmuring words over Rose's hair as she cried on her lap. A dozen flowers immediately poked out their heads, following her as she stepped back. Dren laughed, touching one. 'You chose that perfectly, miss.'

'I didn't choose anything.' Rose looked up at the flowers.

'You did, and you could not have done it better. What is that song? I have not heard it.'

'A cure for sadness. Or that's what my governess called it.' Rose felt herself flush. 'It's a nursery rhyme. I've forgotten the words, but they promised something better to come.'

'And that is what this path is all about. You reminded the tower of that.' Dren waved a hand. A small patch of flowers turned sunset orange, fading through dull purples back to their original hue. 'Though, sadly, we must press on.'

Rose waved a tentative hand when his back was turned. The entire tower bloomed a rich red. 'Where are we going?' she said, hurrying to catch up. 'I'll admit it. Lils is starting to feel a little heavy. And she's snoring.'

'The second tower, miss. It is somewhere I can help Pearce, and somewhere we can rest.' There was a pause which he didn't try to fill with words, and Rose followed him as he set off down the Path at a much faster pace. After a few more turns, the bridge opened up into a wide square and second tower. This one was tall and defiant, with salt spray whipping across its exposed approach and a rumbling mass of dark water at its back. A group of fur-wrapped figures stood up from a campfire, crossbows in hand.

'Follow me, miss,' Dren said, standing out in the open. He raised his hand to greet them, and called to her over the rising wind. 'We are among friends here.'

Remains

Howling gusts of wind and spray surged around the tower. Far below, thundering waves beat at the colossal arches of the Long Path, the churning waters flinging up salt to kiss Lily's down-turned face. Her weary eyes followed the crossing south. It was as senselessly restless as the sea it bridged. The other shore would be a day closer if it simply ran straight.

'There you are.' Footsteps behind her, but Rose kept back from the edge. She raised her voice over the unstoppable water. 'I wondered if you wanted to talk.'

Lily shook her head, watching the Split surge and thrash. Rose said the Path spoke to her, offering calm words when Josef's passing bit too deep. Lily heard nothing from the stupid, silent rocks, and the weight of his absence was an even greater stone in her gut. But she had the Split. If she was angry, it was angrier. If she felt trapped, it rushed past and carried her thoughts elsewhere. The docks of Saarban. The Wayward Isles.

Rose touched her shoulder, tactfully repeating the offer.

'No.' Lily brushed her off.

'Pearce is getting ready for the ritual. The tower dwellers say it's awful to watch.' Rose paused. 'Do you want to?'

'Keep him away from me.'

'Fine,' said Rose. Lily could almost hear her lips purse, hear that frown settle in. 'But come inside and have your medicine. I didn't mix it for you to toss in the fire when I'm gone.'

'Get lost,' Lily muttered. She was pulled up with a yelp. 'Ow! Fucking man-bitch! Let go!' Rose eased up, but still insisted on marching her indoors dangled from one ear.

'Over there, please.'

'What the hell's gotten into you?' Lily let herself be led to the bed. 'Fine! Fine. Let me go. I'll drink your filthy slop.' But her throat had started to itch, tightening up as she raised her voice too loud. She tapped frantically on Rose's hand, and her sister scooped her up onto the bed, propping up pillows and holding her shoulders while the coughing fit shook her. Tears came, preying on her weakness.

'Get off me,' she gasped.

'Keep sitting up. Here's water.'

Lily took a sip, too drained to argue. She rubbed her nose on the silk sleeve of her nightgown, and let herself sink back into an deep nest of pillows. Their hosts had been generous with their hospitality. Lily took full advantage of it; she'd been sleeping in the same crumpled dresses for almost a month. Rose, on the other hand, had started dressing like a blacksmith. She had Dren's satchel out on the fireside table, and was resting a hand on it as she peered at his notes.

'Stop that. I'm fine.'

'Stop what?'

'Stealing glances at me over that book.' Lily's voice tightened. Her throat threatened to spasm again, so she took a sip of water. 'You'd make a terrible healer. You can't hide the concern on your face.'

'Ah, so you say. Wait until you try this, I've cracked it this time.' Rose waggled a flask and liquid slopped over the rim.

'Gods, don't make me drink it.' Lily wriggled against the pillows, trying to sit up. 'I was sick for hours last time. Fetch Dren, make him check it.'

'You know, he laughed when I told him about that, but he said—'

'Good evening, miss.' Dren was lounging in the doorway, grinning. 'You are looking a great deal better this evening.'

'Dren!' exclaimed Rose. 'You must knock at a lady's door. You can't burst in like this.'

'Oh, leave him alone. As if I ever passed as a lady.' Lily flushed, neatening the edges of her nightgown. 'And, Dren, no. I'm not better, thank you very much. My throat is torn to pieces from retching up the last concoction this ignoramus foisted on me. I blame you for that.'

'Impossible. My teaching is without fault. Your sister is simply clumsy.'

'That's unfair.' Rose raised the steaming flask for him to sniff. He recoiled and took it off her gingerly, dashing it in the fireplace.

'Gods, what was that?' Dren held up his hands as both Lily and Rose started talking at once. 'Quiet! Rose, stop glaring. Better clumsy than proud or unwilling. I can teach dexterity, I cannot teach a work ethic. But enough.' He shooed Rose away from the table. 'No more poisoning your sister today. Miss Lily, we will mix you a vapour instead of a tonic. If this does not fix those raw pipes then nothing will. And yes, I shall prepare it myself.'

He perched at the table and rolled back his sleeves like a penny conjurer, frowning at the ingredients Rose had prepared. He scattered them into different piles. 'We should get you one of these, miss.' The blade of his knife glinted as he held it up, his eyes busy with instructions. 'Carry only a single tool, but one good enough for every purpose. Now, from what does our patient suffer?'

'Smoke inhalation,' Rose said. 'Alcoholism.'

Lily glowered at them.

'Malnutrition,' added Dren. 'However, most importantly this was no ordinary fire she was trapped in. Shed skin from a malevolent spirit fluttered in the ash, and gnawed at the edges of her soul. Hard to treat.

For these reasons, the things I teach you will place you above other healers, and you should charge extortionate fees to reflect this. You should also remember to use more frostroot – spirits hate the cold.'

'What are you doing?' asked Rose, hovering at his shoulder. 'Can I help?'

'Of course.' Dren scraped everything into a bowl and poured in a cup of water. He handed it to her. 'Boil this.'

Rose snatched it off him. 'I already know how to boil water! Teach me something useful.'

'You must prove everything once.' Dren wiped his hands, and started cleaning out his nails with the knife point. 'Set it over the fire.'

Rose put the bowl carefully on the grate and perched on a stool to watch it. She was soon distracted. 'Lils, your room is twice as nice as mine.' She gazed about wistfully, fingers tangled in the ends of her hair. 'I don't have any pictures. That one of the shoreline is just lovely.'

'These chambers belong to Militant-Captain Rafe, custodian of this tower.' Dren was sorting through his satchel, throwing things into the fire. 'He is sleeping in the barracks for the time being. A true gentleman.'

'What are you doing now?' said Rose. She had a notebook out and was poised over a blank page. 'Is that important?'

'Very. I am tidying out my satchel.'

Rose waved her charcoal pencil. 'Is there any point me having this?'

'No. And I told you not to bother with it.' He took the notebook from her and tossed it on the fire along with some dried herbs that made the room smell of rusted metal. Rose protested, but he handed her another. 'This one has notes in it already. Do not waste your time transcribing smudged lessons, listen instead.' He tutted, showing her a limp bundle of stalks. 'You see this? So much has spoiled since I last laid everything out.'

It was hard to make yourself heard with a hoarse voice, but Lily got a word in while Rose was flicking through the book. 'Dren, which shore do these people belong to?'

'Neither,' he said. 'In the strictest sense they are criminals from the Northlands, outcasts. Each has been given an S brand, standing for southerner, and banished out over the Long Path.' His knife tapped on the table in irritation. 'It is a stupid custom. The people living on the south shore are proud – they resent taking in the undesirables of your nation. Any branded outcasts that make it to them are mutilated and sent back. So, most settle in towers on the Path. They earn an existence as peacekeepers or smugglers.'

'Great. I feel safer already.' Lily shuffled further down into the sheets. 'A den of criminals.'

'I suggest you speak to them if you want the truth of it, miss. The S brand is a convenient tool for city ministers faced with a troublesome voice. These first towers are a shelter for political exiles – anyone of low character is sent on, or simply dropped into the Split.' Dren came and sat on Lily's bed, leaning in close to feel her forehead. 'I would not recommend knocking on any doors further down the Path. Are you paying attention to your task, student of mine?' He spoke to Rose without turning, busy examining Lily's tongue. He'd had a bath recently and his hands tasted of soap. 'Would you say that water has boiled?'

Rose closed his notebook with a guilty snap. She peered into the bowl. 'Oh. No. I expect it won't.'

'And why is that?'

'Well, it's thickened up,' said Rose. 'Like porridge. I'd be covered in it before it boiled.'

'An astute observation.' Dren treated Lily to a conspiratorial roll of his eyes. 'There are rags on the table. Wrap up the bowl and bring it here.'

Rose dutifully brought it over, almost dropping it when it popped in her face. 'Oh wow.' She smacked her lips. 'My lips have gone numb. But that taste, it's delicious! Lils, it's like... it's like wild honey.'

The steaming bowl was placed on a cushion and Dren motioned for Lily to dangle her head over it. She heard them continue to talk as the sweet fumes caressed her cheeks and forehead.

'You do the basics well enough. I cannot see why you failed to correctly prepare the draught I prescribed yesterday.'

Lily heard Rose giggle, but with her head over the bowl she couldn't see what was going on. The lumpy liquid bubbled and burst, each pop releasing a soothing waft of air that numbed her raw lungs. It did smell like honey.

'Any more tips for boiling water, great teacher? Or can I assume I have passed that test?'

'No, you did well enough. But you must tilt your chin upwards when carrying hot mixtures. The gases they exude are for your patient, not for you. Some are even poisonous.'

'What?' Lily pulled up her head sharply.

'In this case they are not.' Dren put a hand on her head and pushed her back over the bowl. The bed sunk as he stood. 'If our patient is feeling well enough, Pearce has finished the preparations I set out for him.' Lily raised her head and saw Dren watching as she blinked away steam. 'Seeing him cured could bring you peace.'

The door clicked shut behind him. Rose went to check it was closed, then filled a bucket of water from the pump and dragged it over to the bed. 'Coming down, Lils? I've got a bucket here for you to wash. And another one for... you know.'

'No.' Lily breathed deeply, sucking the vapour into her throat. 'Don't you get tired of his rambling? He's like our old tutor.'

'Oh, he makes sense eventually. You just have to listen for long enough. Piece it all together.' Rose pulled small rod out from the apron she'd started wearing, which was becoming as eccentrically provisioned as Dren's satchel. She stirred the porridge on Lily's lap and released a gush of sweet air. 'I found out today that I've been learning a series of antidotes. The draught I made for you yesterday was to cure belly ache – nothing to do with your cough. Stop fussing, I didn't know! Keep your hands to yourself or you'll spill the bowl.'

'No, take it away. You two are just abusing me as you please. I'm not some wretched animal for you to experiment on.' Rose held Lily's shoulders as another coughing fit shook her. Truth be told, she'd make a pretty good healer. The concern on her face told you she cared.

'I'll come back when it's done,' said Rose, gently. 'Tell you how it went.'

When she was gone, Lily took Josef's hip flask out from beneath her pillow and had a few sips to calm herself. She'd taken to carrying it around the trading post before it burnt down, not knowing the sharp and spicy taste of its awful spirits was all she'd have left of him.

Hollow Soul

An armoured man was waiting on a bench outside Lily's door. Mail slid noisily under plate as he stood, so Rose shushed him and pulled the door shut. He smiled and spoke anyway, in a harsh croak that was at odds with his warm smile. 'A fine evening, my lady.' Grey hair tumbled down over his pauldrons and piled furs, yet he bore his armour with a calmer version of the stubborn vitality that had always driven Josef on, even when his years piled up and tried to drag him down. 'Forgive me, but I became tired of waiting for Dren to make introductions.'

'And who might you be?' demanded Rose. She gestured for him to move away from the door, out of Lily's earshot. 'What possible business do you have, creeping around outside my sister's room?'

He heaved more air through the mess of scar tissue that dented his throat. A ragged, white S was visible between the folds of skin. 'You would be Rose, then.' His lungs must have been huge, making the most of each breath in a measured flow of unhurried words. 'Branerian women have always possessed a fine quality that puts you in your place. Something we missed in Cerc Reno.' A droopy moustache quivered under his twinkling, grey eyes, and he watched her blush without any hint of embarrassment. 'Militant-Captain Rafe, at your pleasure. I hope you have been made comfortable in my tower.'

'I'm so sorry. This is your room.' Rose matched his bow with a graceful curtsy. She paid attention to such movements, because the gossips certainly did. They were nothing really – bored, half-starved girls who whispered and waited for the country oaf to trip so they could point and titter. But once she'd seen them watching, she'd never put a finger out of place. Except in the mirror.

'You move with elegance, my lady,' he said, surprised.

'And should I not?'

He bowed. 'Forgive me. It is comforting to see such niceties after all these years. And please, until your sister is well, this room is hers alone.' He drew in another huge breath and rasped more words over her mumbled thanks. 'I wondered if you and your sister were coming to observe the ritual?'

Rose brightened up, and took his offered elbow. 'Only me, I think, but I'd thank you for showing me the way. Dren has run off.'

'He does that.' Rafe ran out of breath and heaved in another as they started to walk, but the moment passed and whatever opinion he was about to voice was lost. And after a few more moments, so was Rose. The tower was a bustling warren of activity, riddled with unexpected turns and doors. It seemed impossible to keep track of which floor was which, but everyone else knew precisely where they were, and she was always in their way. A harried-looking woman pushed past with a tray of bread, giving Rose an exasperated glance.

'Would you permit me to pry a little, my lady?' Rafe's years had not yet blunted his height. He matched her with a relaxed stride that moved them smoothly down the corridor. 'Dren has been uncharacteristically quiet on you and your sister.'

'Pry away, Captain. I fear there is not much to tell.' Rose kept the smile smeared on her face, but cringed inwardly. Such vapid phrases sprang to her lips without asking permission. Branera had a lot to answer for.

'How does your sister fare? She seemed in a bad way when you arrived.'

'She's fine.' But being short with him wasn't exactly better. 'I mean, she's improving, thank you for asking. The loss of our stepfather is harder on her than any injury.'

'I heard what happened.' Rafe let his grizzled features and inclined head show the feelings that his rasping voice could not convey. 'My condolences.'

A man with a pile of books herded some chattering children past. The youngest girl had an S brand on her cheek, though the toddler seemed oblivious to her disfigurement and more interested in gawking up at Rose. She was dragged away by her friend's hand. 'It's not been easy,' said Rose, ducking under a low doorway. 'Papa was the only real family we had, apart from our missing brother. Dren's helping us find him.'

Rafe frowned. 'Dren didn't mention this.'

'He's probably embarrassed. He says his own brother's the kidnapper, and we need to bring him an awful lot of money... but Lily and I don't, well, we don't have anything like that.' Rose brushed a finger over the white stones, feeling whispers rush down her arm. 'I can keep an eye on Lils while we sort it out, but I worry about Lark. He's a bit... he's quite naive. We have an odd family.'

'It can't be so odd. You seem quite charming.'

'Our birth father killed our mother.'

Rafe didn't even blink. 'And you were orphaned to the city?' He guided her through a door, making someone wait on the other side. 'To this man Josef? Well. I am not the sort to leave you in need when your guardian has fallen.' He took a quick gasp of air to clarify. 'I will make arrangements to assist you.'

'You're too kind,' said Rose. 'But Dren is helping us.'

'Dren?' Rafe's hoarse voice rushed like metal over a whetstone. 'He is not deliberately malicious, but that is as kindly as you can put it.'

'Well, I trust him.'

They walked in silence, Rafe clanking along at Rose's side. 'Branera!' he wheezed at last, rubbing his scarred throat. 'A magnificent place. In that you were well provided for. I miss the walls and laws of a city, if not their rulers.'

'Really? Now I've left, I don't think I care for it.' Rose ran a hand over the wall again. 'I'd be quite happy here among all these voices.'

'It's a rare gift to hear them.' His moustache twitched. 'I doubt anyone else in this tower can make out more than a hum – I myself find them quite mute.' After another short stairway, and three more doors, they reached the ground floor. The upper rooms had tended towards grandeur, spacious and carpeted for easy living. But lower down they became bleak and functional. Doors were opened and slammed by uniformed men with huge rings of keys, and Rafe no longer made people wait for them to pass. In one room, sweaty youths sat in the midst of straw-ruptured dummies, blades laid casually across their laps as they chatted and gesticulated thrusts with their hands.

Rafe coughed loudly, waking the gatehouse boy with a nudge from his foot. They waited as he scampered into action, pulling back bolts and bars, cranking a wheel that took his whole body to move. Rafe dropped a coin in the boy's bowl when he was done. 'You're growing stronger, I think. No?' He ruffled the boy's lopsided hair and chuckled when it was frantically pushed it back into place.

'Your home is impressive, Captain. Though a little intimidating.' Rose nodded to greet a pair of crossbowmen stationed outside the gate. They saluted. 'You seem ready for a war, though I doubt the uprising will spill over onto your bridge. Have your really built all this with political exiles?'

'Those involved in city politics are already fighters, in their own way. We simply turn that resolve towards martial pursuits. Give them purpose. Our peacekeepers prevent the crossing descending into chaos.'

'But what I can't figure out is how you know whom to trust. They can't all be innocent.' Rose touched Rafe's arm, though he'd shown no sign of offence. 'I'm sure you are very thorough, but some people are excellent liars.'

'We find the truth eventually.' The old captain seemed satisfied of this. 'Those who deserve their S brand are shown the way south, or shown the waterside drop from our ramparts.'

Lily's balcony rose in Rose's imagination. Her stomach knotted. 'You drop them from the tower?'

'It takes a man seven seconds to reach the water.' This time, Rafe's face was as unreadable as his broken voice. 'Such a trial is sacred here, and some exiles confess willingly. They trust themselves to be spared by the Split and carried off to a new life.' He turned her away from an archway leading to the back of the tower, firmly guiding her shoulders. 'Not that way, my lady. The stone-side drop is reserved for those we find beyond redemption – I believe the gulls have not yet finished with the last body.'

A parade of ruined fountains lined the approach to Rafe's tower, and a small campfire had been built in the shelter of the only one that showed signs of life. Its bowl was a delicate circle of stone wings, while an upturned head and beak provided a determined flourish of water. This moon-touched liquid danced heroically up and into the air, before splashing down through a gaping hole in the bowl and escaping across the square. Dren and Pearce were sat at the edge of this glistening sheet, dangling their fingers in the stream and watching the ripples spread and settle. They had thick-spun blankets around their shoulders and were huddled together like old friends.

'Make yourself comfortable,' croaked Rafe, pointing Rose to a bench. As she approached, Pearce bucked away from her awkward smile and scrambled for the far side of the campfire. He hunkered down at its fringes, eyes following the windblown flames.

'I am glad you came.' Something was cluttering up Dren's busy accent. He coughed and moved to make more space on the bench, but Rafe shook his head and retreated to lean against the fountain. Clouds shrouded the moon, reducing the captain to another statue. Blue smoke curled up around his whiskers as he lit a pipe.

'Was Pearce talking to you?' Rose asked, taking up a blanket. He'd been whispering to Dren before she spooked him, but too quiet for her to catch what he said.

'Just a few words, miss. A risk, even then – the spirits inside him grow stronger when he uses his voice. It was his cry of pain that started the fire at the trading post.'

'Tell me about them,' she urged. 'Please.' His notebook weighed heavy in her apron pocket. She'd found it stuffed with torn pages and illegible writing. 'Your notes are so strange, like cottage-wife tales. What's true and what isn't?'

'That is my original journal, filled with honest mistakes and guess-work. I have come a long way since then.' Dren frowned as he warmed his hands against the fire. 'It is rare to find twin spirits. Rarer that one knows how to weave ice. Adults of their kind use these powers to spread a wasteland in which they can gorge on their host, and Pearce would wander that blasted landscape until they spat out the hard bones of his soul, leaving his ghost to roam and howl among the chasms. They would then be strong enough to bring back victim after victim.'

It was strange to see Dren without a smile. His face seemed empty when not propped up by his lips. Rose touched his hand. 'Can you cure him?'

The smile returned, but it was grim. 'I was trained to tear these creatures from the soul and consume them. I would not call that a cure, even if I have learnt enough to sometimes save the host.' Dren leant over the fire and blew out a cloud of black mist from his cheeks. A burning log climbed out of the flames, buoyed up by rippling shadows.

'My creators named me hollow-soul,' he said, watching the log turn. A gust of wind rattled the charms and beads that braided his hair. This close, Rose could see each one was cut with a mark of the old gods. 'Thousands of spirits lie bound within me. Some I have tamed. Watch closely, for you will see them only as darkness – darker than a lack of light.' Another log was enveloped in black clouds. The two pieces of wood spun and tumbled through the air, passing a lick of flame between them.

'Exercise caution, my lady,' said Rafe, pointing his pipe at the spinning firewood. 'Not all his tricks are this pretty.'

Dren let the logs fall back in a shower of sparks. 'Do not listen to him. He has gone crazy stuck in this tower. '

'Shush now, sere.' Rose placed a finger on Dren's lips. She turned to Rafe. 'You've seen this ritual before, then, Captain?'

'The Path protects the spirit eater as he feeds. I often find him at my door.'

'Nonsense,' said Dren, flicking a petulant burst of spirits at the fire. It flared briefly black. 'The Long Path protects the victim, not me. Have you not been paying any attention at all?'

Darkness robbed Rafe's face of expression, leaving only the harsh inflections of his voice. 'The first time I saw this ritual, I dragged Dren to the Split to throw him in – clear that we didn't need his kind any more than the rapists or killers that knock on my door. But he bargained with me, and promised to prove he was working against something worse than himself.' Dren bore this description quietly, playing darkness between his fingers. 'His next victim was a nobleman, further sickened than the first. He escaped from the spirit eater's care and burnt down a village. Over the next week, my tower was filled with wide-eyed children and families fleeing this destruction. Dren failed, and I shouldered the burden. I was not yet convinced.' Rafe drew heavily on his pipe. Blue smoke rolled from his mouth in an endless stream. 'The third time

Dren returned, he had a child in his arms. An infant. It was warped and twisted, but this one he managed to save, keeping it calm with a story as he teased the demons from its soul. The boy survived and opened my door for you just now.' He inclined his head. 'We have a truce. As part of the bargain, Dren has armed me with relics that protect my tower if his work goes awry. How fares this one, spirit eater?'

'He can be saved,' said Dren. Then, more quietly. 'But it will be quite the show.'

'So, my lady, you will soon see for yourself.'

'I thank you for your continued support,' said Dren. He spread his hands and bowed. 'And for not acting on your fascinating impulse for throwing people off your tower. I am actually a rather poor swimmer.'

Rose ignored him. 'Why have I not heard of these spirits before, Captain? Only travellers talk of such things.'

Dren waved his hand dismissively. 'The Northlands are a hostile environment for spirits, that much is obvious. I was only in Branera to warn your stepfather of the peasant uprising, but I found myself drawn to Pearce's mansion instead. I did not know what to make of it. He had already burnt it down. Killed his servants. Driven his wife away in a moment of lucidity. His soul was crumbling faster than anything I had seen before.' Rose watched Pearce shiver across the campfire. His eyes flicked left and right like they were trying to escape. 'Do you have my notebook?' Dren had his hand out. 'I wish to show you something.' He snatched it from her, flicking through and muttering to himself.

'Hollow-soul,' Rafe said, taking another rattling breath. 'The weak current lasts only an hour. Stop talking and begin.' A scabbard lay across his lap. It was a simple sheath – Branera handed out better equipment to wall guards – but the sword's crossguard was set with a large white stone which shone with stolen moonlight.

Dren looked up from the book and snorted. 'When was the last time you needed that, my friend?'

'I think only of my people,' Rafe rasped, resting one hand on the hilt. 'You gave it to me for this purpose.' A crowd of outcasts had gathered at his back, and they muttered in agreement. They huddled together in their furs and coats, drawn out into the cold only on the promise of a spectacle. A few held torches. Others crossed their hearts, glancing between Pearce and Dren.

'Give me a moment,' Dren insisted. 'I will not break off a story halfway. I never have, I never will.' The captain inclined his head and relaxed his grip on the sword. Dren took Rose's hand, as if worried his audience would be taken away, and blew delicately over a page on his book. Two cavernous faces seemed to wriggle and melt down the paper, their lashing tongues needled out in black lines and smeared with cursive glyphs.

'This is one of stranger inks I have come across, miss. It retains some hallucinogenic properties that are awoken by moisture. Before my time, it was used to write dire warnings to spread among the common folk.' Dren wiped the page with his sleeve and stilled its motion. 'This one warns of vicious spirits, and promises their removal. The King of Coin had opened his formidable coffers to combat this growing threat, and in this case, my brother and I were the result of his expenditure. My tutors were his servants, dubbed the Old Court by other Saarbanites, and we were educated on many terrible things under their care. Most of our time was spent on studying the strange creatures that live in the fringes of our world, and I spent years translating books at their behest, compiling great lists of benevolent and violent spirits.'

He wrinkled his nose in disgust. 'They thought it was a great joke. When we were done, they burnt our work and laughed – declaring each creature on our lists dead and why. There was only one reason, repeated a thousand times. The last of the Agran had been driven to the edges of our world and devoured by their predatory cousins.' He tapped the drawing in his journal. 'The Tar-Agran. With none of their kin left to feed on, these spirits have no choice but to emerge, moaning and grumbling as they gnaw on our meagre souls.'

Rose had been watching Pearce while Dren spoke. He kept bending into the campfire, close enough to burn himself, before pulling back sharply in a cloud of icy breath. A blanket was dumped on her lap as Dren stood, his gaunt face drenched by firelight.

'And now we must begin.' He took out his knife and tested the edge. 'Before the good captain indulges his habit of throwing people into the Split.'

Rose caught his hand. 'What are you doing?'

'Just watch.' Dren paused, sensing her real question. 'The knife is for me, not for him.' He rounded the fire and helped Pearce unbutton his shirt. It was sticking to him, but when they peeled it off and threw it into the fire, Rose had to stifle a gasp that would have been at best rude, at worst a little pathetic. The minister's skin was an artwork of cuts. Elaborate wounds divided his chest into three sigils for the old gods: an ornate spiral for Mist, a square for Earth, Death left blank. Pearce opened his mouth and spat an ivory token into Dren's outstretched hand.

'Well done,' said Dren, feeling its weight. He traced the lines on Pearce's chest with an artist's fingers. 'You have a steady hand.' At his urging, Pearce took slow, deep breaths. The fire matched him in and out. Taller each time. Hotter each time. The outcasts started muttering, lowering their torches in deference to the swelling campfire, but Rose stood and bore its assault with a frown. They treated this like an entertainment, and she hated them for that. Rafe joined her, furs sliding from his shoulders to reveal rust-flecked armour.

Dren cut his palm with a wince. 'Speak, my friend.' He clasped his hands behind Pearce's neck. 'We are ready for them, you and I.' Pearce nodded and stilled his breathing. He shivered in their bloody embrace, hands gripping Dren's braids and playing with the god-marked tokens. The fire shrank back to embers.

'Please,' said Pearce, meeting Rose's face with watery eyes. His voice was deeper than she'd expected. He hung his head and wept, bitter sobs breaking up his apology into pitiful gasps. 'Forgive... me. Forgive—' These words stretched and deepened beyond recognition, until they broke his jaw with a gristly crack. Flinging back his head, he loosed a terrible moan that goaded the campfire to climb up and spread across the night, but Dren snarled and punched him in the gut. The noise broke off, leaving Pearce to wheeze and clutch at Dren's jacket, broken mouth running with spit.

'Not good enough. We need both of them, my friend.' Pearce fell to the floor, Dren's boot on his back. Raising his fist, he squeezed a trickle of blood over Pearce's tangled hair. 'Both of them.'

A hand gripped Rose's arm. She looked down to see Rafe had stopped her taking another step forward. His drawn sword was a slice of moon-light, which hummed with voices of the Path. Its pommel stone shone even brighter as he angled it away from the fire, and flared when Pearce cried out. Dren was pulling back on his hair, opening up his mouth for blood squeezed fresh from his fist. Pearce's fingers gouged into the Path. His cries split in two. These twin voices climbed over each other in a screeching scale, and at their peak, a sheet of frost rushed out from his hands, encircling the swelling fire with a hiss.

Satisfied, Dren hauled Pearce up, and clamped his mouth shut with a bleeding hand. The campfire vanished with a muffled roar. The ice sheet boiled into steam. Pearce screamed in outrage, and they spun out onto the square, twirling and thrashing as he sought to free himself. This was an impossible task. The spirit-eater was a shadow that flowed over Pearce's back, spinning and leaping to avoid being crushed against pillars or walls. The stalls left by departed Path merchants gave neither of them much pause; Dren's feet flowed over cloth like water, while timber froze and shattered under Pearce's flailing hands. Their struggle woke the Long Path itself, which seemed to swell and glow until Dren and Pearce were standing far away on gargantuan blocks of stone. Sound ceased, and all Rose could hear was Dren. If the twin voices coming from Pearce were the roar of burning forests and the splinter of frozen lakes, Dren's voice was the shifting of mountains, the groans of the deep earth. Older. Tired. Dreadful. Even as it faded, nothing dared to fill the void, and Rose watched a young boy throw up in utter silence.

Sound returned not in a rush, but in small moments. A spitting plank on the fire. The slide of metal as Rafe sheathed his sword. 'Come, my lady,' he said, offering an arm. 'What danger there was has passed.' Dren didn't look up as they approached, but carefully pulled more matted hair from the Pearce's face. He looked almost peaceful, lying neatly on the glowing stones, even if his bloody and swollen jaw was hanging loose and draining black ichor.

'Is he...' Rose touched his forehead. That apology would linger with her forever forever. 'Is he okay?'

'Perhaps,' said Dren, in a hoarse voice. He laid a hand on Pearce's chest, and it seemed to respond, rising and falling as puffs of mist escaped his lips. He nodded to two outcasts. They lifted Pearce onto a sheepskin pallet with great care and respect.

'Where are they taking him?' asked Rose, rising with the pallet bearers. Dren tried to explain, but gave up and massaged his throat.

'He will travel the Split, my lady.' Rafe stopped the pallet and took a moment to arrange Pearce's arms. 'I have a boat ready to mount the weak current, they await only my command to launch.' He bowed, and followed the pallet bearers inside, swinging furs over his shoulder with quivering hands.

Rose sat down next to Dren, feeling for his palm. It was badly lacerated, so she took some ointment from his satchel and gently spread it in. 'Travel the Split,' croaked Dren, watching her work. 'Is a saying on the Path. A new start.' With a few coughs, and a disgusting noise, Dren managed to clear his throat. Rose looked the other away as he spat into a vial. 'Excuse me.'

'Why is it moving? Okay, don't tell me.' Rose shuddered. 'I'm afraid I don't have a handkerchief to offer you.'

Dren smiled and put the vial away. 'All gone. And do not worry about Pearce. Rafe is an expert at smuggling goods to the eastern ports. There is a temple there which tends to any broken bodies I cannot – for a fee.'

'What sort of fee?'

'It costs money to feed and wash a man for the rest of his life. Pearce's recovery is something to hope for, not to trust in.' Dren's fingers corrected her as she wound a bandage round his hand. 'Since the Split flows only one way, Rafe's people will have to return on foot, keeping their S brands a secret. Those who do this for me are paid for their bravery.'

'Do you need help?' Rose watched as Rafe ruffled the gatehouse boy's hair and dropped a coin in his bowl. 'With money, I mean. I never found everything Josef said he'd brought with us, but I had his purse with me before the fire. We could help with Pearce.' Lily wouldn't like that, but she didn't have to know.

'Ah.' Dren coughed. 'Perhaps I can clear that up. Your stepfather and I were old friends, so I understood him fairly well. In some ways he would trust me with things he had yet to share with you.'

'There's no other money, is there?' Rose's chest grew tight. 'He—'

'You are impossibly rich, even if you may not like where it came from.' Dren's hand went into his satchel and pulled out a diamond bracelet. Precious stones glinted as he turned it over. Those which hadn't been crudely prised out. 'In fact, you two have already paid quite a large sum towards Pearce's welfare.' Dren smiled weakly. 'I am glad I now have your approval.'

Rose held out a hand for the bracelet, breathless at the thought of touching it. But wanting to. 'I know what this is.' She'd seen it only behind bars and guards. 'Or what it was, before you ruined it.'

'Ruined? I have the most delicate of–'

'It's from Branera's treasury.' A small fortune hung on her hand, one of the many prizes from her city's bloodthirsty history. 'It was on only display last summer, and sent back to the vaults for another century. How did you get this?'

He cleared his throat. 'Remember I was in Branera to warn your stepfather of the uprising? I arrived after dark, so went to rest first. Except I woke to find Lark's ransom letter shoved under my door, just moments before Pearce's condition drew me to his burning mansion. These things are connected, miss. My fat brother delivered his letter, then sowed chaos to cover his retreat.' Dren rummaged in his satchel and pulled out some crumpled, mud-stained paper. He tossed it to her. 'It is not signed. It made no mention of a demand, other than for Josef to bring all his wealth to Dunford to pay for the boy's release. Your stepfather was beside himself, of course, reading it to me over and over as I tended to Pearce's wounds on his scullery table. He wanted to act immediately. But though he was a wealthy man, it was not in ready coin – his riches were in factories and stockpiles, promise notes and investments. With a rebellion marching on the city, there was little hope to gather it all.'

Rose felt sick. She handed back the bracelet. 'Josef was the city treasurer. He had all the keys.'

'Did you not think it strange that highwaymen would follow such a battered coach as Josef's? Or that we attracted the attention of Cerc Reno at the trading post?' Dren's teeth shone like the stolen gems in his blood-encrusted palm. 'Every northern man of fortune was looking for us, either for the price on Josef's head or the wealth he had stolen. When the mob took the city and found its prizes plundered, I expect they were not pleased.'

'I never knew being rich was so complicated' Rose felt a little dazed. She couldn't stop staring at the satchel. 'Why? Why would he do that? Josef was an honourable man.'

'For Lark. He loved you all a great deal. In fact, he explicitly wanted Lily to not know about this, fearing how she would take it.'

'Well, I'm not telling her,' said Rose, unable to take her eyes off the satchel. 'How much of Branera's vaults do you have in there?'

Dren's hand reached into his satchel and came up with a fistful of jewellery. 'Enough, I think.'

Stranger

The next morning, Lily found a pale man on the adjacent balcony. He was enormous, rippling with slabs of fat and muscle, leaning over his wall to watch the spray thundering below. Despite the cold of the storm, the man was mostly naked, wearing only ragged trousers and a bloody-lipped smile that would send children running.

'Hello,' said Lily, taking up her usual spot. 'Do I recognise you from somewhere?' She reassured herself of the deadly drop between their balconies. Further even than this giant could leap.

'Perhaps,' he said, giving a chuckle. His eyes were lit with an honesty that touched his terrifying appearance with some humanity. He flicked water from the black stubble of his hair as he watched her. 'Have a think.'

Lily pulled Rafe's coat tight round her shoulders, shivering despite the fur lining. Cold raindrops stung her hands. 'You're one of the men that jumped me in Branera.' It was a guess, but a good one. 'Doubt there's many people as big and naked as you.'

He laughed, nodding in agreement. 'True. But I was only looking out for you, nothing else.'

'So you say.' She shuddered. 'Guess now I know why your room's barred from the outside.'

'Is that so? People have no trust.'

Faint memories called for Lily's attention, but she couldn't place them. She shook her head. 'I feel like we've met more than once.'

The man turned to watch the sea. 'Perhaps we have.'

'Is that why you're following me?' She moved to the gap between their balconies, trying to hear him over the thundering water. 'Because you know me from somewhere?'

'Not sure we're ready for that yet. Or at least I'm not.' His hands patted the wall. 'I've been protecting you, though. Killed that man that grabbed you in Branera.'

'You don't sound pleased about that.'

'Believe it or not, I don't often kill people.' The rain hammered down over his back. 'I'm used to the mountains. The cold there keeps my impulses in check.' He pointed a thick finger out at the sea. 'That's a good view though, isn't it? I miss the views.'

'Notice how the pillars aren't worn away by the water?' Lily leant over to point them out. 'The dam up by the Mountain Feet is repaired every few years, and those rivers have nothing on the Split. This whole thing should've collapsed centuries ago.'

'Magic.' He wrinkled his nose. 'They worship this bridge as a god, but I feel far from the touch of the Earth here.'

'I don't like it either,' said Lily, shivering. 'I miss my home. There's no magic there.'

'You've got your sister with you, haven't you? Let me tell you, you miss people more than places when life takes you away.' He ripped a loose stone from the parapet and weighed it up, looking to toss it over the side.

'Don't do that,' Lily said, teeth chattering.

'I thought you didn't like this place?' But he replaced it and picked up an apple from a water-swamped tray by his feet. He bit it in two, then spoke with his mouth full. 'You know what, you seem as trapped as me, but I doubt there's bars on your door. So, why are you stuck on that balcony?'

'My stepfather died,' said Lily, softly. Easier to say it today. 'I find the water clears my thoughts.'

'Sorry to hear it,' he said in a gruff voice. The apple lingered in his hand, half-eaten.

'And my brother's been kidnapped. And my sister's a stranger. She's always in huddles with this idiot that's guiding us, hiding things from me when I get near.' She clenched her fists. 'I'm going to sneak a look in that fucking bag of hers when I get a chance.'

'Why don't you leave them to it? Do your own thing?' The giant made things sound so simple. It was probably hard to stop him doing what he wanted. 'They'd catch you up.'

Lily didn't have a good answer to that. She'd tried. The packed bag at her door from last night still taunted her. 'Josef always set me straight. He'd probably say it was a bad idea.' Her stomach rumbled, sternly reminding her that she'd sent her lunch away in a temper. 'Sere, might I impose on you for one of those?'

Sometime while she'd been speaking, the man had crushed his apple to a pulp. He wiped the mess away and lobbed a fresh one through the air to her, which she caught in two hands. It was bigger than it had looked now she held it. 'Thanks.' She bit out a chunk, and sour juice filled her mouth. 'Gods. What is this place? They have better fruit on a bridge than we do in Branera.'

'Everything good and bad passes over the Long Path at one point or another. Or so the captain who led me to this room says.' The man's frown deepened. 'I suppose he is deciding which of those I am.'

'Aren't you cold at all?' Lily's hands were shaking, taken from her pockets only so she could eat.

'I have been in a very cold place for most of my life. This rain is warm to me.' He demolished another apple in two bites, pulling the stalk from his lips and flicking it over the edge. 'You know, little things like that make people hate me. Can you believe that? Just because I unsettle them.'

'Is that why Rafe locked you in that room?'

'Who knows?' He laughed. 'People are forever locking me up for things I haven't done. But I am happy to await the moustached captain's judgement before being released. They have promised me fresh boots when I leave. That's a rare offer with toes as big as mine.' Weighing up another apple in his hand, he grunted and threw it out over the edge. It fell for several heartbeats before being engulfed by the flying water. 'Doesn't seem so far, does it? I was told it takes seven seconds for a man to hit the water.'

'You don't seem like someone who could be easily tipped over a balcony,' Lily said, amused.

'I humoured the captain. He seemed decent enough, and I have walked a long way.' The man grinned. Water diluted the crimson stream from his bleeding lips. 'What the good captain thinks is a prison is actually a brief moment of luxury – with the promise of boots at the end, no less. Here, catch.' He tossed over another apple, which Lily fumbled and dropped.

'Hey, I'm still eating this one.'

'It's to throw. So, what about you, young lady? Are you going to stay on that balcony forever?'

Lily shrugged and lobbed the apple. It did feel good. She was always good at throwing things. 'I'll be kicked out of this room today,' she said ruefully. 'We're leaving to go find my brother. Not that I'm looking forward to travelling with those two.' Images of Rose's guilty face still bothered her, lacing up Dren's satchel with excuses on her lips. She always was a shit liar.

The man was standing very still, rainwater pouring off him as he watched her. 'Well, so long, then,' said Lily, feeling awkward. 'I should go pack. Hope no one throws you in the sea.'

'So long,' said the man. He looked almost sad. 'Maybe we will meet again.'

'Maybe.' A thought struck her. 'Wait here.' Once inside, Lily snuck another peek out through her shutters. The man was squatting down to finish off his apples, rainwater pounding from his head and back. She found what she wanted and ducked back out. 'Here, catch.' She threw him the carving Dren had given her. 'Something to remember me by.'

'Ah!' he said, examining it carefully. It was a tiny thing in his hands. 'A gift! Perhaps given to you by some gentleman?'

'Given to me by a self-absorbed prick.' She grinned, feeling better already. 'Look me up in Saarban, now you've got the likeness to find me by. I could use a friend your size.'

The pale man clutched the carving and gave a solemn, deep bow. 'It would be my honour, Lily.'

Corruption

What the girls called the south was actually a laughably small and almost abandoned spit of land, dangling off a whole sprawling continent. Saarban, for all its glory, was a backwater. Branera, a myth. The scrublands stretching away from these odd cities and northern seas were vicious and widely hated, especially by those who lived there.

But not by Dren.

The dusty crags and sun-beaten clay were filled with false promises and nasty tricks, where burrowing insects grew to the size of his hand, and being bitten by one could lose you that hand. Local seasonings were so delicious they became deadly habits. Sunburn would flare to a painful red under the searing, restless sky, before the clouds rolled in and turned the road to a swamp – but Dren knew more than one road in any direction. He knew the wildlife, the Splitside seasons. He knew everything, and he loved to hold an advantage.

'Do not fret, miss,' he called back over his shoulder, taking one hand from the reins to wave expansively. Their mounts continued to labour over a vast field of steaming mud. 'Take in the sights and sounds of the south! Your sister has prepared a passable cream for the itching.'

'Find someone else to experiment on,' Lily muttered, almost inaudible.

'Endure, then. Grow strong and tough.' He made a fist and grinned. 'You will look back on these discomforts and laugh.'

'I will not,' she snarled, shaking out her wet hair.

'Failing that, you could try moving less.' He plucked a dead mudfly from his arm and rubbed it between his fingers. Few insects could break his skin twice. 'This is a breeding swarm, they will tire of us soon.'

Lily took a swipe at another bloated insect, hissing as she slapped her sunburn.

'Courage, miss. Courage.' He pulled back to ride alongside her. 'It is not far to Saarban, with so much to see beyond. Did I tell you about the ruby faults? Glistening crevasses of precious stone that open up to feed on the sun. The rituals which nurture them are most barbaric. I would hesitate to speak of them in polite company. At least while sober.'

'As if you ever hesitate to speak.' When she narrowed her eyes and turned away, Dren grinned, nurturing a swell of lust for her prickly nature. She was magnificent. Half-baroness, half-beggar. A bit of everything he had ever wanted, and Dren had to admit he loved her. Though when you lived as long as he did, love came and went with little regard for how that might seem to the rest of the world.

Dren sighed heavily. Such romantic spells spun by even faster of late, but then he was under a lot of stress. 'Let us not forget the glamorous life awaiting you in Saarban,' he said, riding around to her other side. 'My brother will be holed up in the palace kitchens, no doubt. I will free Lark and send the fat idiot packing, then you will be at your leisure to enjoy my home. We Saarbanites are masters of every craft! You will lie between sheets lighter than air, warmer than sunbeams. You will watch artisans spin silk to send all along the great canal. And the food...' His mouth watered, already tasting the crunch of roasted insects. 'You will never want to leave. A thousand ships touch Saarban's docks over the summer swell, bringing the best cuts of meat to the most talented of cooks.'

'Stop that,' she pleaded. 'You're making me sick.'

'Stop what?'

'Riding next to me and waving your arms about. I feel sick. Give me some space.'

'Those beasts do shake you about a bit,' said Dren, thoughtfully.

Lily and Rose were doubled up on the most uncomfortable mount he could find, purchased on the cheap from the last wayinn. Such half-breeds did not exist in the Northlands, and he had enjoyed their reaction to it. It was a huge and misshapen thing, a carthorse with a wolf mane and muscular legs that ended in a bony mess of paw and hoof. It was, of course, as dumb and ungainly as the other runts that the Old Court drove out of the lower gates.

'That one looks somewhat awkward,' he said. 'A touch too much lupine blood, I expect. Perhaps you would be more comfortable behind me?' He shifted forwards on his horse and patted the saddle behind him. 'This old girl is quite gentle.'

'Hah. No.'

Dren kept his smile in place but could not help feeling a little crestfallen. She was so stubborn. Or shy? He could not quite decide which, and was starting to regret not letting the trader sell him a second horse. Might as well make good speed if he was unable to get her arms around his waist.

The horsewolf continued to plod along, making pleasant grumbles as Rose scrunched its neck. 'Careful there, miss,' he said, riding forwards to be next to her. 'These half-breeds are nothing but trouble. Interesting to look at, I agree. Strong? No doubt about it. But stupid and slow. Ask anyone who owns one.' He bent over and thwacked the horsewolf between the ears. It rolled forwards in another long, wobbling step, drool shaking free from its muzzle. 'The Old Court load their best straight onto galleons at Saarban's dock. Only the runts are sold locally.'

'Oh, don't be cruel,' said Rose, slapping away his hand as he raised it again. She ran her fingers down its mane, giving it a scratch behind the ears. It howled softly, baring sharp teeth and starting to trot. 'She seems very clever to me.'

Rose had let her hair down in both the figurative and literal sense, a raven tumble that fell unbound from its wraps to cascade over her shoulders and tickle the swell of her chest. She flashed him the most wonderful of smiles and Dren felt his heart trot a bit as well. Dull men might be put off by those strong arms, or the way she stood a little taller than them, but not Dren, no. Rose was magnificent. And Dren knew he loved her, too. 'You ride with grace, miss.' He gave her his most charming smile.

'Oh, aren't you sweet? I feel quite oafish really.' He laughed dutifully as she patted the white-knuckle hands clamped around her waist. 'Lils! Look over there, I think I see smoke.' Her eyes found his, alight with excitement. 'Are we close to a city? Or perhaps a trading post?'

'Yes, something like that,' said Dren, resisting the urge to smirk. 'We are approaching the rustic settlement of Krans. A real seat of industry, with the most colourful population. Rough civilisation at its finest!'

'Really?' said Lily, tired enough for her studied bad temper to crack. 'I'm exhausted.' She dropped her forehead against Rose, then pulled it up with a grimace. 'Gods.'

'What?'

'You reek, sister. Are you washing at this next rustic shithole? Or are we skipping bathtime again?'

'Language, Lils.' Rose tutted at her. 'And I don't see the point if we're only going to get sweaty again.'

'Language? Really?' Lily snorted. 'One foot out of the city and you've been swearing like one of Ruckman's whores.'

Dren cut in quickly. 'Never fear. We shall find you both a bath on arrival. And new clothes, too. You are my wards, until I reunite you with your brother and find a suitable guardian.'

Lily gave him a sour look. 'That implication of ownership still concerns me.'

'Your duties will be light and your welfare my only concern,' he said smoothly, wondering desperately where he could buy a washtub.

'Don't be grumpy, Lils.' Rose was scrunching the loose skin around the horsewolf's neck, making it shudder with little whickers and howls of delight. 'Did we make good time today, Dren? It felt like we did.'

'We made excellent time, miss. You have handled the beast admirably.' He had always prided himself on being a brilliant liar, though it was hardest when he found the subject matter amusing. 'However, I fear my brother has too much of a head start. Given it is a lost cause to overtake him before the gates of my home city, we could all benefit from a rest in Krans. We will root him out soon enough, do not worry.'

'Why is he doing this?' said Rose, pressing him for the hundredth time on the subject. 'You never talk about Terrano.'

Dren chewed his lip, wondering how much truth was sensible. 'He has always been an opportunist, and he is always short on money. This sort of thing is to be expected. Do not fret! He will not mistreat your brother. No doubt Lark is being kept busy filling inkwells and carrying bags, or listening to his endless self-promotion.'

'Sounds familiar,' muttered Lily. Rose turned to scold her and lit up another tedious argument, so Dren left them to pursue it. He rode ahead with a wave and mumbled excuse.

The ground was hardening up, at least. Grotesque snouts emerged from crumbling holes, and soon the scrubs were littered with rodents basking in the sun. Their drying spines rattled a warning as he approached, reminding him that their venom was at peak potency during these hot months. Worse, the reek of their guts would linger for weeks under hoof. He narrowed his eyes and drove them back with a howl of spirits, pushing forwards into a canter and trusting his mare to smell anything before it was trampled.

Not that he lacked senses of his own. But today his unnaturally sharp hearing caught only the beat of hooves and the whistle of wet air. This close to Krans, every patch of the shade carved out by the boulders and clumps of bulbous scrubs should have been claimed by traders and drovers. These travellers shared stories and water flasks in the evening calm, before rolling down into Krans for clock-time, or pushing west to Saarban during the cool of the night.

Dren pulled to a stop, sensing someone nearby. 'Hello?' he called out, bright and cheerful. 'Who is there?'

'Only me, stranger. Road greetings.' A dust-coated figure unfolded himself from the nook of a boulder. His back was shaped by a life of tunnel labour. Since naming was never too imaginative in Krans, Dren could guess his before it came up. 'The name's Bent.' He padded forwards a few steps, aided by a broom under his armpit. 'I run the East Range Mine, me.'

'Road greetings, mine boss,' said Dren with a nod. He remained mounted.

'Those girls with you?' Bent gestured back down the path. They were barely visible, lost in another dip on the trail.

'Indeed. You have good eyes.'

'You'd do best not to leave them alone, you,' he said, scratching a bandage wrapped around his hand. His ink was subtle for a scrub worker, perhaps started late in life. Not that this was unusual. Krans was infamous for fortunes and failures; many travelled great distances to carve out one or the other.

'Where are your workers, mine boss? I have never seen the hill so deserted.' Dren thumbed a coin, then vanished it. No spirits, just a cheap trick done well. 'I am willing to pay for news.'

'Ah, sod that. Not much to say, me.' But his eyes had lit up at the sight of the coin. 'You'd do better to ride on to Saarban. You'll need a guide for it too – lucky I'm heading that way myself.' Bent leant precariously on his crutch, shielding his eyes to squint at the sunset. 'Weather should be good tomorrow.'

'A kind offer.' Dren stifled a laugh. 'But one I must refuse.'

'Sure about that? Bandits are about, feasters too,' he said, scanning the bushes as if enemies would leap forth at any minute. 'I can talk you past both, no harm would come to you. The ladies back there would thank you.' He grinned lustily. 'One each, eh? The scrubs are no place to travel without an escort.'

'Maybe so,' said Dren. 'First, tell me news. Perhaps Buller is still running the mills?'

He grunted, clearly annoyed. 'No one's running anything. The town's been deserted.' He was right about that. The town clock was striking, but no workers trudged from the mines. No labourers climbed the hill, seeking the last dregs of sunlight before secluding themselves in the stale shadows of a wayinn. Bent waggled a finger in his ear and inspected the result. 'If you're dead set on going down, spare us some food and I'll tell you what I know.'

'Hmm.' Dren rummaged through the supplies Rafe had burdened them with. He handed over a morsel, trying to look grudging. 'Is this enough?' He rested on his pommel to watch the miner chew. The man's mouth worked for what seemed like an eternity.

'S'good,' said Bent. Mashed apple and nuts fell from his teeth. 'So, news, then. Well, most people have left.'

'I can see that myself.' Dren felt his spirits stir, their temper fraying with his. He gritted his teeth against the sudden ache in his gut. 'Tell me why.'

'Some Norther boy started it, if you can believe that. Poor lad was learning to roll dice, and people took a dislike to it. Gods, you should see that kid drink, though. Ain't seen nothing like it, me.'

Dren was familiar with gambling in Krans. He was also utterly terrible at it, most people were. A weighty constitution for their acidic whisky was more important than any sort of luck, and Dren bled coins even when he cheated outrageously.

'The boy won too much. I protected him as best I could, of course – a young guest like that in our town.' Bent pulled himself up on his broom, puffing out his chest. 'But a few of the wrong sort of people died. So, when the killing didn't stop, the Roaming Watch rode in hard to finish it. Half the town found a noose in the end. Makes you wonder what the point was, we were killing each other pretty good anyway.' Dren watched as Bent's hand moved past his throat, stroking hair forwards to conceal a ring of bruises. 'Couple of days later, the Watch either ran out of rope or necks. Those bastards rode for Saarban, offering escort to anyone who wanted it.'

Lies and truth. Dren could sense both here. 'This Norther boy,' he said, acting on a hunch. He had Lark's description distilled down to a few things now. 'Was he a short child? Dark hair, nervous?'

'Yup,' said Bent. 'His veins all black from some sickness. You'd notice him, you. Is he a thief or something? A runaway?' That was a piece of luck. Dren had never mentioned it to the girls, but everyone who had seen Lark mentioned this mottled affliction on his skin. He watched Bent picked nuts from his teeth. 'I liked the little guy, me. Took a knife to the stomach, no fault of his own. They tossed him in the caverns with the others.'

Dren cleared his throat. 'I have an interest in the boy, and would like to identify the body. Have they been buried yet? I am not afraid to use a spade.'

Bent laughed, but he sounded nervous now. 'No burials this time of year. There were too many for the slabs too, so we had them on carts until we could sort them out. Then one morning, the under-taker goes to take their likeness for our records and they're all gone. Weird, eh? People say the Watch took them, but my money's on the feasters.'

'The bodies went missing?' Dren pulled his horse round to examine the man better. 'Quite the set of mysterious events going on here, mine boss.'

Bent laughed hoarsely. 'Hah, you know feasters.'

'They do not eat the dead.'

'As you say.' He shuffled a step closer. 'Come on, you. Take me on that horse and I'll guide you to Saarban. Across the desert, free of charge.'

'It is hardly a desert. No, no. You have aroused my curiosity now, sere. Show me your neck.' Dren laced will through his words, jerking the man's hand up with a gust of spirits. His parted hair revealed the bruises left by a quick-noose. 'A nasty mark.' He released his hold over Bent's hand. 'Was it a last-minute reprieve that saved your life, or a poorly tied knot?'

Bent buttoned up his collar, stumbling away over his crutch. 'Get away from me. Bloody witch, that's what you are.'

'Why do you always call me that here? Are you all children?' Dren growled and invoked an oath to Goddeath.

Bent's face drained. 'What the hell was that?'

'I was promising the god of death I would hang you by your testicles if you utter another lie.' He repeated the oath, syllables hissing in the air. 'Take me to the fat man. Glasses and piggy eyes? Obsession with books? Him. My brother. He is behind this, take me to him.' Spirits begged to join with Dren's tongue. Bent raised his arm with a cry, ducking down as one broke loose and shattered a boulder. 'Take me now,' snarled Dren, wiping spirit mist from his lips.

'I would! I would. But they're long gone. Please! Take my word for it.'

'Your word? Your words are weak. You strive for duplicity but lack even that substance.' Dren spluttered spirits down his jacket. With a snort, his horse became inflamed, stamping and raking the ground. 'When did my brother leave?'

'A week ago, maybe?' stammered Bent, spread flat against the boulder. He ducked awkwardly as Dren's mare reared up, her eyes bulging and dripping with shadows. 'Wait! Your brother, he's called Terrano, right? He's got the boy. He took the bodies from the cavern. Took us away.'

'Us?'

'Us! All of us. We died. I was hanged, me. Came back to life when he asked, choked the Roaming Watch in their sleep when he asked.' Bent skittered sideways on his crutch, one hand hugging the boulder. 'That Watch patrol are his now – he brought them all back. If he brings you back, you do what he says. They've gone to the city with him. Gone to the palace.' Hooves swung out inches from his face, smashing against the boulder then back to the ground with a thud. 'Mercy! That's all I know! If he reached Saarban then the Norther boy's with him there. That's all I know, I swear.' He was on his knees now. 'I can show you the way—'

'I know the way, idiot.'

Dren's mouth dripped with bitter tastes. Long-forgotten alarms clamoured in his head, urging him to take a step back. With an effort, he turned his will inwards. Rioting spirits were lashed back into order, and his fingers ran through soft horsehair, as much to calm himself as to gather up loose spirits. But when he opened his soul to take them back in, he almost gagged. Something was very wrong with this man.

Keeping his soul exposed, but tightening it, Dren swung from the saddle and hauled Bent up. He pressed his nose against the man's bruised neck and sniffed deeply. 'Gods.' Cursing in Seatongue felt feeble after the language of Goddeath, but he decided to stick with it. 'What did he do to you?'

'Who... who?'

Dren glanced over his shoulder. The girls were still some distance off; their argument was heated, but inaudible to anyone but him. 'We are going to talk before those two arrive, dead man,' he whispered, and with a growl he shoved him against the boulder. 'You have never learnt to lie well, so answer quickly and truthfully. Or I will hang you for a second time, in the manner promised.' His free hand seized Bent's groin.

'I will,' shrieked Bent. 'I will!'

'Why are you still here, if you must always do as Terrano asks? Why did you not follow him?'

'I tried, but they left me behind. My leg was slowing them down—'

'Do you hear voices in your head? Moaning sounds?'

'No. No?'

'Do you piss fire? Wilt flowers? Crumble rocks?'

'No!'

Dren released him in disgust. 'You make me sick,' he said. 'Do you not feel that thing festering in your soul?'

'What? What thing?' Bent clutched at a rabbit foot dangling over his shirt.

'A butchered spirit.' Dren sniffed deeply, tasting its abhorrent stench. 'Something old, made new by my brother's hubris.'

'Please.' Bent slumped onto his knees, his voice weakening. 'I need to catch them up.'

'You have my pity, dead man,' said Dren, stepping back and wiping his hands on his jacket. 'Take my horse. You will be with them soon.'

'Really?' Bent almost slobbered with relief. 'Thank you.'

'It is not a gift,' Dren said sharply. 'In return you will do two things.' He raised a finger, moving back as Bent eagerly stepped forwards. 'First, and most important, do not trust the fat man. Do not tell him we spoke. You can do that, even if you cannot disobey him directly. Second, if anyone complains of a moaning that seems always behind them, no matter how they turn, tell them to keep their mouth shut and wait for my arrival. Gag them if you must. Kill them if you cannot.' Not that Dren was going anywhere near that forsaken city now. But this would buy him some time before the disease spread. 'Can you remember those things?'

'I'll remember!'

'Do not tell the fat man we spoke. Do not talk if you hear voices.' He helped Bent into the saddle, screwing up his face as a muddy boot knocked into his cheek. But at least the wretch looked like he could ride. Bent reached out a shaking hand for his broom, a dumb smile creeping over his face. Dren threw the it aside. 'Ride the whole way and you won't need it.'

Bent paled and clutched at the reins. 'But the feasters—'

'They will not touch you.' Dren snorted. 'They are picky eaters and know more about the soul than most. Yours is filthy, dead man.'

~

Dren was resting in the same rocky nook when the girls caught him up. The horsewolf laboured up the last rise of the hill with a flurry of pants and snorts.

'Oh dear, Dren. Have you been robbed?' Rose was watching the distant figure gallop away. Her argument with Lily had simmered into boredom, so she seemed happy for a distraction.

'Nothing of the sort, miss.' Dren picked himself up and took their mount's halter. 'An act of charity, no more. The man was an acquaintance of mine, and desperate to see his sick wife. We used to play together as children.'

'You seem to know everyone,' said Rose, clearly impressed.

'And everything. What happened to your sister?'

'She's trying to sleep.'

'Shhhhh,' said Lily, resting on Rose's back.

'You can relax soon, miss. Look, there is Krans.' He patted Lily on the leg and earned a half-hearted kick. 'Do you like the view?'

Rose cast a doubtful eye down the muddy slope and over a row of timber hovels. They were dwarfed by towering mills and threatened by the mouth of a nearby mine. Furnace smoke hung low as if the town it had been given a shroud, and the devastated remains of a hardwood forest stretched out for miles in all directions. 'Honestly, I think she will be disappointed.'

'As long as they have a bath,' said Lily, eyes still closed. 'I don't mind.'

'And they will!' Dren was feeling much better. For Pearce his pity had come easily, as his was a healthy soul in suffering. The thing that had crawled into Bent was changing his very nature. Spreading out thin and terrible roots. 'I am looking forward to a rest myself.' Dren tugged on the horsewolf's halter. 'Though I admit that Krans suffers in comparison to the glamour of a city.'

'Those buildings have been burnt down,' pointed out Rose. 'Is that normal?'

'Merely some local unrest. Nothing we need concern ourselves with.'

The horsewolf had planted its hooves. It grumbled as Dren tried to drag it forwards, but a caress from Rose set it moving again. She laughed as Dren gave her a slow clap. 'I don't know why she hates you so much.' Rose leant back against the slope as they descended into Krans. 'Perhaps it's because you're so rude to her.'

'Ladies should always stick together,' he replied, sagely. 'But I have tackled more intractable beasts than this. Once I—'

'Is it safe down there?' said Lily, who had raised her head to take in the approaching scene.

'With me, miss, yes. Most places are.'

Hurt

L ily slid her body into the tub with a barely smothered squeal of delight. Such blessings she'd left behind without even realising it. Even the water in Rafe's tower was ice cold, dumped into the basin by a stony-faced maid. Tendons knotted from the endless, chafing days eased away in moments, and she let her head submerge, closing her eyes and losing herself in the muted echoes of her bathwater. Pine forests. Fresh rain. The shopkeeper next door had been burning this soap rather than leave it behind, but she still gouged Lily on the price of these meagre comforts

Reluctantly, she resurfaced, and resumed her watch on the dividing curtain. 'Dren,' she called out. 'If I see so much as a fold in that cloth twitch, I'm cutting your fingers off.' She continued to rinse out her too-long, greasy hair in the water.

Dren's voice rustled from somewhere beyond the curtain. 'I am starting to regret getting you that knife, miss.'

'He's just sitting here,' said Rose. 'No one wants to look at you.'

'What? Plenty of people want to look at me.'

Laughter drifted past the curtain. Lily immediately sat up, belatedly covering her breasts with an arm and spilling water on the floorboards. 'What's going on?' she snapped. 'Rose! You're supposed to be keeping an eye on him.'

'Oh shush. We were only sharing a joke.'

'Nothing to worry about, miss. Have you taken your tonic?'

Keeping herself covered, Lily stretched over for the flask he'd set out on a stool. Her fingertips brushed against it, knocking it over so it would roll towards her. She caught it and sank back into the foam. 'Rose?' she called out. 'Have you tried it?'

'It's lovely, Lils. Tastes like apple press.'

'Do you like the cinnamon, miss? Most people prefer it with a few pinches. I think two doses a day, perhaps three.'

'I have to drink this filth three times a day?' said Lily, sniffing the uncorked flask.

'He was speaking to me, Lils. Are you almost done in there?'

'No.' Water sloshed over the side as Lily sank further in, holding the flask up out of the waves. 'What's it for?'

'An disease threatens Saarban, miss, and I fear it will spread. This will protect you from it.'

There wasn't much to swallow, but it was incredibly sweet. Like a thin, sugary paste. 'Urgh, that's foul.' Lily gagged, scraping her tongue on the back of her hand. She climbed out in a rush of water. More laughter came from behind the curtain, so she gave up looking for the water jug and grabbed a sheet to dry herself, pulling on underwear while still damp. 'I'm leaving the water for you, Rose.'

'It's too small. I won't fit.'

'Then wash yourself a hoof at a time. It's disgusting to skip so many chances to bathe.' Lily wriggled into her dress, mouthing a blessing to whichever god watched over this pit of a town that she'd been wearing it before the fire. Frankly, it was a work of art, and the best set of alterations she'd coaxed from Josef's tailor. The bleary-eyed craftsman was thoroughly scandalised by the time he was done, producing only huge, sweeping ball gowns for the rest of the year.

'Did you see the clothes I laid out for you?' Rose said, mouth probably full of food. Lily could practically hear her slobbering. 'Try them on.'

'Another time,' she said, casting an eye over the pale shirts and tan trousers Rose had bought. She seemed flush with money lately. 'I'm already dressed.' Lily ducked past the curtain, wringing her hair as she went. It was an almost domestic scene. Dren with his eyes closed and feet up by a fire he'd yet to light, an open book across his chest. Rose sitting by a bowl of fruits, licking her fingers and spreading stains down her top.

'Rose!' Lily stole the bowl and hunted for a fork. 'Please, go wash.'

Rose gave her a withering look. 'Where have all these airs and graces come from? You troughed like a pig back home and I never complained.'

'I never smelt like a pig, though.'

'I think it's more wolf, the darling thing did shed a bit. Now don't get in a grump, I'll wash later.' Lily glowered at her until she sighed and stood, taking a piece of fruit with her and slipping through the curtain. 'Try the green ones, Lils. They're the best.'

'You seem very concerned with her appearance,' noted Dren, opening one eye as Lily took her sister's place at the table.

'It's your fault. You're a bad influence on her.' She waved her fork at him, and speared a slice. 'That bath will wash it all off, you'll see.' The fruit was rich and soft in her mouth, with no seeds or rind. 'Wow. These are good!'

'She did tell you.'

'Do you know that woman who owns the rag store? Scabs all over her hand? I mentioned your name and she charged me double.'

'She must have mistaken me for someone else,' Dren said, putting his book to one side. 'Is all this fussing because you are missing home? Or perhaps missing Josef?' He leant over to touch her arm. 'You can confide in me, miss. I have grieved for many friends over the years.'

'Please, I'm trying to eat.'

'Your sister tells me you used to run all over the rooftops back home without stopping to sleep, let alone wash. She said you would come back covered in mud and smiles. That is a Lily I would like to meet, not this baroness of manners.' Dren had moved his seat closer.

'I don't know what you're talking about,' said Lily. She pushed the bowl away and stood. 'But I do feel like a little air, come to think of it.'

'That is not what I meant.'

'I'll be back soon.' There was a splash from behind the curtain. 'Tell that wallowing pig she can eat whatever's left.'

'Krans is not like Branera,' said Dren, picking up his book with a resigned air. 'Take care out there.'

'I thought it was a rustic and charming place?' she said with a grin, laying a hand on his shoulder as she passed. Damp hair slipped over the patch of bare skin on her back as she closed her fasteners. She paused to give him a quick look. 'You want to come?'

He waved her out, already lost in his book. Outside the cottage, a faint smog had descended with nightfall, and it lingered beyond the porch, while the chilly air played soothingly over Lily's sunburnt cheeks. The temperature had plummeted with the sun, but the mud she stepped into had nothing on the icy slush of Branera.

Voices came from the cottage window. 'Lils, what have you put in here? It smells wonderful.'

'She has gone out for some air, miss. And probably something to drink.'

'Oh.' There was a sluice of liquid as Rose stood up from the tub. Lily caught a glimpse of wet hair and worried eyes over the curtain. 'I hope we weren't planning to leave soon, then.'

Lily wandered off down the deserted street, seeking to be distracted by something novel, but finding only memories. The streak of rotten hovels and taverns was too similar to the Low Ends – though only if they'd collapsed and lost their charm. No one came out to greet her. Everything was boarded up. Suspicious eyes harried her past broken windows, and eventually she just circled back the way she'd come. The woman with the scabbed hand seemed surprised to see her return after their heated argument, but Lily pointed out she didn't mean to spit on her counter and apologised for her language. Business can mend all breaches, and she was soon wandering out with a few of the cheapest bottles Krans had to offer. Suitably armed, it wasn't long before she found someone to share them with.

'So, you're new here, too?' Lily refused another swig of the local whisky. The wine in her chipped ceramic was bitter and thick, but still better than sipping hot razorblades. 'What happened to this place?'

'A fight,' said the child called Shana. Lily had found her wading in the twilight, splashing down the shallow waters that ran from the mill wheels. 'There was this argument and a mill boss got gutted' – she emphasised the word with a wild stab, hair flying around a grinning face – 'then the miners were angry and went after the mill bosses, and then they went back after the miners, and then the Roaming Watch came in and hanged everyone. Like this.' She let her tongue loll out, swinging from a pretend noose.

This grove was an almost pleasant refuge, a clump of trees set apart from the rest of the town. Every other scrap of bush or sapling looked to have been chopped up and fed into the sawmills, which left Krans looking much like the rest of the scrubs. Brown and dull. A sporadic trail of grass and reeds had drawn Lily here before she'd even heard the faint sounds of splashing and giggling.

'I like this stream.' Lily's fingers ran through the stiff grass. 'Everything else is so dreary here.'

'It's boring, isn't it?' said the other girl. She was called Brenne and had a long, chestnut ponytail, which dangled in the shallows as she crouched and poked a stick at the submerged stones. 'Gotta watch yourself, though. There's dead watchmen about. Feasters too.' She giggled.

'Sounds gruesome,' said Lily, with a smile. 'Are your parents leaving like everyone else?'

'Nah, we've got no parents,' said Shana. 'We're not afraid of dead people, either.'

'Nope,' said Brenne, stubbornly.

'Northers should be, though,' said Shana. 'They hate the cold – they'll smell it on you. Why'd you come down here, anyway?'

Lily shrugged. They seemed a little young to be drinking, but she'd started earlier than them so wasn't one to judge. She watched Shana drain the last of the whisky then re-cork the bottle, crouching to set it afloat. Brenne crept up and pushed her over, earning a slap that sent them both laughing and splashing again.

'Peace,' spluttered Shana, holding up her hands from where she'd been knocked down in the shallows. 'Peace, peace.'

'Peace? You sissy bitch.'

'No, no, I just want to hear what the Norther has to say.' Shana edged away to a safe distance before finding her feet, snatching up the dropped stick to arm herself. 'Stop it. Why'd you come here, Lily?'

Perhaps it was the wine, but the water looked a lot of fun. And only sober or boring people were too old to paddle with the kids. Lily unlaced her boots and dropped her knife into one for safekeeping. 'We're looking for my brother,' she explained. 'He's in trouble.'

Brenne was still eyeing Shana's stick. 'Aren't you afraid of the dead watchmen catching you? No use to your brother if you get killed.'

'Dren never mentioned anything about any creepy dead people,' said Lily, laughing as she walked down to the water's edge. 'I'll have to watch myself!' The soil squelched pleasantly around her toes, and she was struck again by homesickness. She wondered how drunk Ruckman and Withers would be by now. Or if the mob had commandeered Ruckman's brothel, turfing out his letches and irregulars to fill it with sullen farmers and smiths.

'You know Dren?' said Shana with a little squeal of delight. She splashed a few steps forwards, whipping the water with her stick.

'I've yet to meet someone who doesn't,' said Lily, resigned to his tedious infamy. 'What's so great about him anyway?'

'Have you asked him?' said Shana. 'He's honest enough if you pin him down.' She let out a dirty giggle.

'He is a wicked man,' said Brenne, snatching the stick and waggling it reprovingly. 'Tainted.'

'He's not that bad,' said Shana. She drifted onto her back, showing feet and ankles spun with a thousand tattoos. Down here, children were welcomed to adulthood with a mark on the back of their calf, and they grew the design in inches each season. Blue inking wove around Shana's tanned skin in waves a grandmother would be proud of, blending with the soft, lapping water.

'You have beautiful tattoos,' said Lily, wistfully. 'I should love to get something like that.' Holding up her skirt, she dipped her foot in the water, then pulled it out with a yelp. The stream had teeth, and it bit into her skin with a thousand tiny fangs. The two girls laughed and jeered as Lily hopped away. 'Shitting gods!' She let her foot sink into the mud until the prickling sensation faded. 'What's wrong with you? Or more to the point, what's wrong with your bloody river?'

'Something to do with the mills,' said Shana, cupping water in her hands and taking a dramatic sip.

'They burn glowing rocks from the mines to get the water hot, and run it all off here.' Brenne poked around in the grass with her stick and pulled out a dead frog. She threw it over to Lily. 'Plants don't mind it, but people do.'

'And frogs,' said Lily, staring at the blistered remains of the amphibian.

'Yeah, they don't like it either.'

'But you don't mind it,' said Lily.

'We don't mind it.'

Lily wearily sat herself down. Dren had a point – it was tiring being so far from home. 'Going to explain why?'

'Do you have feasters in the Northlands?' asked Shana, her voice gentle. Any sense of playfulness trickled away down the stream, and the children stood quietly, dripping in the water. 'Most people don't talk to us. It's a nice change.'

'Oh. We've a few songs about you. Do you really eat people?' Lily leant over her boots. Her knife rattled in one of the toes, so she reached in as if to untangle the laces and wondered if they could hear her racing heart.

'Sometimes. We eat everything, really. Twigs and rocks, kings and goats.' Shana grinned. 'It makes us strong. You lot have a narrow view of what's edible in life.'

'Going to eat me?' Lily's hand trembled as she realised she'd reached inside the wrong boot. How did she mess that up? It wasn't far back to their cottage, maybe she could run. Shit on it, she should be running already.

'No,' said Brenne, shrivelling up her face in disgust. 'You smell bad.'

She couldn't help a snort of indignation. 'I just took a bath, thank you very much.'

'Your soul, Lily, not your skin.' Shana waded out of the water, but kept a respectful distance. 'There's something spoiled about you.' Something in Shana's tone struck Lily cold. The feaster cocked her head. 'All part of the deal when travelling with Dren, I suppose. Has he given you anything to drink?'

~

Lily barged into their cottage, grabbing a bottle of Dren's tonic from the table. 'Dren,' she called out in a loud, singsong voice. He'd lit the fire and it was roaring hot. 'I have something to ask you.'

She had to steady herself on the table. Those children could certainly drink as well as eat. Feast. Weird people. Lily pocketed the tonic and picked up a water jug in two hands, wandering into her and Rose's room.

'Knock, knock... oh.' Lily felt a stab of pain at seeing her sister and Dren wrapped up in nothing but sheets and warm, sweat-infused air. 'See you've been having fun.' Taking a messy swig of water, Lily flopped down on the end of the bed, spilling some over the sheets.

'Ah. Forgive the intrusion,' said Dren, sweat glistening from his forehead. He wiped it with the back of his hand. 'Your sister said to not expect you back until tomorrow.'

Perhaps it wasn't possible to ever catch him looking awkward. Rose, however, was burning up, and clutching the blanket to her chin. Lily lay back and stared at the spinning ceiling – better than watching any more of Dren's tanned buttocks while he swung out of bed to gather his clothes. 'Don't get up on my account. Might pop out again.' Lily closed one eye as the room veered and spun. 'I just learnt a few things about you. And this.' She held up the bottle of tonic with a straight arm.

'Lily, I—'

'Shut the fuck up, Rose.' Lily tossed the tonic bottle away, letting it clatter in a corner somewhere. 'Dren, why are you poisoning us?'

'I would never do such a thing,' said Dren indignantly, hopping about as he laced on his boots.

He had his trousers on now, so she rolled her head round to give him an accusatory look. 'You're fucking feeding us one of those Tar-Agran things. The things that were in Pearce. Bits of them, all ground up in these little bottles.'

'Oh, I assure you it is not as bad as it sounds.' He rescued the jug of water from Lily' stomach. 'The tonic is made from the diluted essence of—'

'Hah,' Lily said. 'Hah, hah, hah. You said it was to protect us from a disease.'

'Tar-Agran are a disease of the soul.' Dren peered into a polished shaving glass he'd propped up against a cabinet, pouring and splashing water across his forehead and neck. 'This area will soon be crawling with them. Or something like them. Who have you been speaking to?'

'Lils, he was just telling me about all this—'

'Shut the fuck up, Rose!' screamed Lily. She snatched up the water jug and kicked her way out. The cottage door slammed behind her with a clatter, but she was followed by memories of Rose's hurt face and the sweaty, close smell of the room, and a tumble of bitter feelings that had appeared from nowhere. Lily slid down against the cottage porch and drank as much water as she could fit in her bloated stomach, spilling most of it as she shook with sobs she didn't quite understand.

'Hey, sister.' Shana was watching from across the street, a small shadow on the opposite porch. 'Got a place to stay if you want. A bit further up the road from all that.' She inclined her head to the window, where Rose was pulling on clothes and yelling at Dren. There was a crash as something broke.

'Sounds lovely,' said Lily, her voice throaty and thick. She dropped the empty jug on the porch and followed the feaster, ignoring a cry from Rose that chased her down the street.

Duty

Dren hummed an old song to himself. The refrain was always tricky, a dissonant spill of notes that paused when it might least be expected. But the last person to hum it had died a hundred years ago, and lived a thousand miles away, so who would correct him? He improvised a few bars, and started making up words.

There was a knock on the window. He stood and unlatched the shutter, then went back to fixing his chair. Rose had snapped it during her frenzied assault on the room – barely remembering to pull on clothes before chasing after her tearful sister. Dren sighed, remembering the arches of her wonderful, soft skin. Her shy, but insistent, hands.

'Hello, Shana,' he said. The chair bracket melted and ran under his fingers, spirits rolling over its surface. His mind was preoccupied and he had to do it twice.

'Dren,' crowed Shana. The feaster pushed her beaming face into the room, flush with excitement. She giggled. 'Haven't you been naughty?'

'Hardly. Now, what have you done with my wards?' Dren set the chair upright, frowning as it wobbled around the botched joint. 'They are not yours to take.'

'Not yours to keep either.' Shana wagged a stern finger. 'Lily's staying with us for now. Rose too, but only because she's so tuckered out from all the yelling and crying.' She clambered in and sat on the windowsill, swinging her bare heels to thump on the woodwork. 'But I know how it is, you're trying to behave. You've just forgotten how, you silly man.' Thump, thump. 'We like Lily, though. Going to teach her things.' The panels were splintering under the girl's feet, battered by the meaty energy all feasters hoarded. Dren irately grabbed at a heel to stop her wrecking Rose's room, but that proved to be a mistake. 'Teach you something, too?' she purred, running her toes up his arm.

Her cruel laughter mocked him as he backed away with raised hands. Like most of her pack, Shana had taken the feast early in life. She delighted in embarrassing him with her advances, knowing her body was too young to appeal even to his jaded tastes. But there was more to it than that. Feasters were a cult of old magic, lacking the subtlety to feed on the spirit world. His body gave off a tantalising, spectral smell that fascinated them.

'Don't be shy. Come closer,' said Shana, licking her lips. 'I've let myself age loads since we last met.'

Dren shuddered and tried to collect his thoughts. 'Is Rose coming back?'

'In the morning. They were arguing for soooo long!' Shana wriggled with delight and almost fell off the sill. 'Lily was snoring like a warthog in her chair when I left. And Rose was like this in the other room.' Shana made a snuffling, snorting sound, letting spit dribble over her lips.

'Charming. Did you visit only for this nonsense?'

'No, idiot. You've work to do.' Dren watched age settled over Shana's face like a veil. It seemed this conversation was going poorly. 'Doth Agren,' she snapped. 'Did you hear me?'

'What?' His mind was racing, crashing into dead ends as he sought an escape.

'You've work to do.' Shana hissed at him. 'Your fool of a brother has raised a horde of corpses using that disgusting thing you dug up in the Northlands. Saarban will be slaughtered to swell his army and feed his bloated ego. Have you not smelt the reek on the wind? This is our home!' Shana's fingertips bit into the windowsill, the wood splintering under her grip. 'It is unacceptable. Fulfil your purpose, Doth Agren.'

'You ask too much. These are no normal spirits he is creating.' Dren paused, then spoke the truth for once. 'I do not understand them. There is nothing I can do.' Or wanted to do. But Dren was grasping at the edges of an honourable twist to that idea, wondering if this was something noble stirring within him. 'I have the girls to think of.' He drew himself up. 'I must get them to safety. I am afraid it is too late for Saarban, too late for poor little Lark.'

The loss of the boy niggled him, that was fair to say. Many of these things were his fault if he thought about it hard enough. But there it was again, that honourable idea. The greater good. He had it now. He had it by the horns.

'I failed the boy,' he cried, banging a fist on the table. 'I have looked over these three for so long, but I failed him in the last. I cannot let the girls suffer, too.' He leant forwards urgently. 'You should leave with us. This entire shore will be a wasteland in days. A Tar-Agran nest! Nature twisted to protect the ruins of the city and that creature my brother consorts with.' He stood to continue packing, picking up a pile of Rose's clothes. 'Yes, you would do well to leave yourselves.'

And stashed in Rose's pack he had the wealth of a nation. Saarban was not the only refuge where he could turn those jewels into a luxurious life. The Scarlet Keep would be pulled down, and he would be rid of his tormentors. Rid of that incessant pulling to return. He could go anywhere.

'I must do the honourable thing,' he said, his voice firm.

Shana's laugh was long and insulting.

'I must!'

Her laughter stopped, which was worse. Woodwork creaked under her hands. 'Doth Agren, do you think this is a request?' The feaster's smile was sweet and sickly.

'And here it is at last, you threaten me.' Dren sat on the bed, not quite trusting the chair. He never was any good at woodwork. 'Why not speak plainly from the beginning?' It was almost a relief. Almost. Despite his instincts screaming at him to run, the bonds of the court were calling him back to give up his haul of spirits. Terrano had surely arrived by now, though they would not be making him return to his cage with a patrol of dead watchmen to protect him. 'You realise this is a trap?' he muttered, feeling a headache coming on. 'My brother knows I watch over the Tollworth orphans. The boy has always been a hook to reel me in, a lure to drag me across the continent.'

'What could he possibly want with you?'

'Nothing you would understand.' In Dren's bloated soul, he felt the spirits he had stolen from Terrano screech and scream, announcing his guilt plainly to anyone with the skill to hear it. Shana did not.

'So mysterious!' She leered at him. 'Well, well. We will come help you, then. We don't know what to do about that naughty brother of yours, but we will tear apart his dead slaves for you. If the boy is bait, then you may yet be able to save him. Wouldn't that be nice?'

Dren winced. 'Accepting your help is like setting a wildfire to warm your hands. How many of these slaves does Terrano command?'

'Hundreds,' Shana whispered. She twirled a finger through her ribboned hair and purred at him. 'Many, many more by the time we arrive.'

'How very like him.' Dren rubbed his eyes, finding himself wearier than he thought. 'Such an overachiever.'

Shana smiled, savouring his discomfort. Feasters savoured everything. 'You are a sad little thing, Doth Agren. Stupid too. Digging that creature up was the stupidest thing you've ever done. Letting Terrano steal it was a close second. He always was an insufferable egotist.'

'That is my brother, I will have you know,' Dren mumbled.

'Spare me. As if you don't hate the fucker.' Shana was leaning so far forwards she almost fell off the sill. Her eyes shone with unnatural vigour, any trace of the child lost in her age-twisted face. 'I swear it, Doth Agren. If you don't fix this you will find your friends wearing thin. Terrano protected you from us – you don't have the knack of it.'

Despite what others thought, Dren was capable of self-restraint. And of all the strange cults in the world, he took the most care around feasters. They worked in life and blood, purging themselves of anything spiritual, and therefore leaving a spirit worker with few holds over them. Terrano had never shared his tricks for scattering the little brats, scavenging up such secrets from crusty old books, and smuggling them away in his stupid fat head. Dren bowed, letting spirit mist escape from his nose. 'I will do my duty.'

'Don't fret,' said Shana, purring again. She sniffed, tasting his aroma. 'You know we love you too much to turn on you. If you behave.'

'You must keep the girls here,' he insisted, keeping his head down.

'Of course. They'll be safe.'

'And you will return them?'

'Feasters make no agreements.'

'But you do make oaths. Swear it.' He raised his head sharply, repeating his demand in death's tongue. Goddeath was not always an unworshipped deity. She had temples and priests once, and her followers would burn feasters in ceremonial pits to unlock the power trapped in their flesh. 'Make an oath.'

Shana had gone pale. 'Don't do that.'

'Swear it,' he said, words hissing in the air. Those that spoke in death were used to blisters on their gums.

'So sworn,' she said in a small voice. She hopped down and came over to hold his hand, lip wobbling. 'Do you have a plan?'

He patted her awkwardly. 'Yes. I'm going to kill my brother.'

'Good,' she whispered, giving him a quick hug. 'Will he let you?'

'Oh, come on. He is not invincible. And he keeps trying to kill me. I think I am allowed to try too.'

'Don't die.' She shivered against him. 'We need one of you around.' Dren stroked her hair as he turned a few ideas over in his head. 'What is it?' she said, nudging his palm as it stopped.

'The depressing weight of an inevitable conclusion. I know someone who may be of use.' Shana's hand had started to creep over his leg, so he pushed her off. 'Wear your years, feaster,' he said. 'This is no time to play the brat.'

Shana sighed and sat up, smoothing down her hair. 'Let me call for Brenne, then. She'd want to be involved in anything this ominous.'

Sinkstone

Husker muttered a prayer, ignoring the shawl pin fixing his hand to the counter. There was some discomfort, but not much. Pain was a distant thing to him these days, long since flayed from his skin by freezing mountain winds. To the mounting horror of the shopkeeper holding the pin, the tendons in his palm had already started to creep across the puncture, pinging and snapping as they fought around the metal. 'Come on, let it go,' he coaxed, trying to peel back her scabbed fingers.

'Demon. Demon-man!' she panted. 'Go. Leave me!'

'I'd be gone already, if you'd only help,' he insisted. Growing irritated with her furiously shaking head, he ground her knuckles until she yelped and let go. The pin made a wet sucking sound as he teased it out. 'Ah, stop that screaming. It's not your hand that got stabbed, is it? Not your face?'

His fingertips probed the cut she'd opened across his cheek, pushing the edges together. The angel in his head wept as it caressed the lips of flesh. The counter groaned as it took his weight.

'Demon!'

Husker blinked as a scatter of runes hit his face. Each was the size of a child's nail, and she'd readied another handful to throw at him. 'Mm'not,' he mumbled, pushing her back with a vague, foggy gesture. 'Shhh.'

After a few lost moments, Husker's vision returned. The shopkeeper was lying against her shelves, with all their useless junk littered around her. Bright, birdlike eyes watched him with the intensity of a cornered animal. He crouched at her side and picked up a plate, turning it over. 'You eat off that?' It was painted with some foul symbol. He snorted and smashed it against the floor. 'This mess is your fault, you know.'

'Don't care, me. I'm leaving.'

'I can see why. This town's a pit I wouldn't shit in. So, where's he staying? Tell me and I'll be gone, too.' Husker returned the pin to her. 'Here. Don't stab me again.'

Her eyes closed, and she clutched the pin to her chest like a bloody child. 'Dunno who you mean.'

'You do. Everyone knows this bastard. Where's Dren?' She shook her head vigorously, her jowly face pale and stubborn. 'Careful now, woman. Disrespect to me is disrespect to Godearth.' He felt for the cord lying over his chest, holding up the rock Priest Young had given him. His angel moaned in his head, still busy knitting wounds. 'Disrespect to a god brings misfortune. At my hand or his.'

The shopkeeper stirred at this. 'Don't you lecture me, holy-man. Demon-man.' She pulled at her shawls to reveal the stench of unwashed linen and a trio of baubles. 'I'm not a savage, me. I keep the old ways.'

'Earth, Mist... even Death.' Husker covered the last of them up with a pat. 'So you do. All three. You know, I thought that way once.' He tapped his Earth pendant. It was a larger, rougher version of her own. 'Now Godearth has me to himself.'

'Didn't see your pendant, holy-man. I never disrespect the gods, me.'

Husker shuddered at her lies, sweat flying from his forehead. He was fixated by the way she mauled at her pendants, agitated movements which pumped like a heartbeat beneath her shawls. 'Where is he?' he demanded hoarsely. He had to grip her wrist to stop it moving. Which one did this woman favour? Mist and its lies? Death and her tricks?

Only the Earth was true. He fumbled in his head for enough scripture to calm himself, then he remembered Priest Young's hand on his arm, his patient smile. 'Please.' Husker tried to smile, tried to meet her eyes. Blood speckled his lips and the shopkeeper flinched. 'I'm looking for my children. The bastard has them.'

Drips pattered from his chin as she considered his words, joining the ceiling leaks in their damp little rhythm. The shack bloomed with mould and rot, patched up here and there with sagging cloth. It looked like it had fallen down more than once. Eventually, a sly grin crossed the woman's face. 'Picked on the wrong one, has he?' She cackled and thumbed at the wall behind her. 'Dren's next door, demon-man. Tell him I'll collect his rent in the next life. Tight one, him.' She licked her lips. 'You gonna kill me, too?'

Husker let his smile fade, a reward for her truth. 'Never said I would.'

The shopkeeper stared at him for a few moments. She grunted in agreement and struggled out of her shawls, leaving them behind like a shed skin.

~

Nights were a relief in Krans, so Husker leant over the shop porch to take in some cooler air. This town wasn't much to look at – still stuck on some moment where everyone had got up and left. Doors hung open, unmoved by the wind. Windows snarled at each other across the street, their glass frames smashed down to jagged teeth. The town clock was labouring to creak out another minute, but no one else was around to notice.

Husker grunted and mounted the porch next door, ducking inside without knocking. 'Earth save me,' he muttered. 'What fresh hell is this?' The bastard was here, feet up on a table. He'd lit a fire and faded scents lingered over a dented washtub, with water stains showing its recent use. 'Bath day, is it?' Husker ran a hand through the thinning strands of his hair. 'Could do with a scrub myself.'

'Indeed,' said Dren. 'And it seems you are already undressed for the occasion.' The bastard held a book limply in one hand, pages splayed open in a garish display of literacy. 'Rafe must not have detained you for long.' He turned a page. 'I asked him to keep you for at least a month.'

'Ah, that was no great feat.' The door creaked shut. Husker gently turned the handle until it clicked. 'No great feat to make someone like me more than you. He's worried about your intentions, little bastard. He would've come himself. But you know how it is, the captain is bound to his tower.'

'So here you are.' Dren's eyes drifted up to some angry middle-distance. They returned to his book, flashing with irritation.

'Here I am. Would've been here faster if you weren't hiding in a furnace.'

'Is it so warm?' Dren marked his page, and snapped the book shut. 'Warmer than the Mountain Head, I expect.'

'Everything is, bastard.' There was a silence filled only by stares. Eventually Husker noticed another pair of eyes on him. A child was warming herself by the fire, almost engulfed by a faded armchair. Her weaving hands were full of pigtails, and she watched him approach with solemn, grey eyes. 'Good evening,' he said, crouching in front of her chair. She reminded him of Lily in some ways. Same smile, same mischief, even if her skin was scrawled with more tattoos than he could count. 'I like these.' He touched his sweat-drenched forearm to show her where he meant.

A smile tugged at the corner of her lips. 'Lily likes them, too.' She pulled back her sleeve to show him more butterflies and vines.

'Careful, Shana,' called Dren. He was putting his book away on a shelf. 'This beast is dangerous.'

'Shana,' repeated Husker. He tried to smile without breaking his face. 'You're a friend of Lily? How about Rose?'

Shana nodded. 'Both.'

'Hmm. Well we should be friends too, then.'

She whispered to him, mouthing her words. 'I'd like that.'

He fought an urge to grin wider, not wanting to frighten her. 'Want to see something pretty?' He slung his bag round to find the stone Rafe had given him. It was the size of a plum, and it shone as it rolled over his calloused, disjointed palm. 'Here. What do you think?'

She deftly took it from him and shielded it with cupped hands. It almost dazzled him, pulsing with bright light. 'Prettier like this.'

'How'd you do that?' he asked, reaching for it. He was interrupted by a sharp pain slicing its way down his back, and a wrench at the base of his spine. Twisting around, he growled and swung at Dren, but the bastard had already scampered back.

'That must have hurt.' Dren held up a fist that was coiled in smoke. It moaned pitifully. 'By the time I have clawed enough out of you to form a leash, you will regret this disgusting union.'

'Dren!' Shana gasped. 'Don't be so rude.'

'I'll be taking that back, bastard.' Husker staggered to his feet, pulling himself up on the mantelpiece. His back ran with blood, a red slick that stained his palm. 'Then maybe we'll see you bleed a little.' He flicked his bloody hand over the fire rug. No point holding back now. He hadn't seen his angel before, but he recognised its voice. That smoke was pleading with him, weeping like a lost child, and his throat rumbled angrily in response. Slabs of hot muscle pushed up through layers of snow fat. His foot slammed down in a crunch of floorboards, and Husker threw himself at Dren with a roar.

Bloody gods. It was like he'd charged into the primordial ice that cracked boulders at the Mountain Head. The bastard pushed his smoke-covered hand forward, and the invisible wall forced Husker back another wobbling step. 'So surprised?' He raised an eyebrow, conjuring up a blow that slapped Husker across the cheek. 'It was always mine. Come closer, thief, and let me complete the leash. I would wager you stole that stone, too.'

Husker strained to hold his ground, unwilling to concede another inch to this gloating prick. 'Both gifts... bastard.' But his feet were sliding on the mess running down his back. Dren beckoned to him, and raised a knife that glinted with blue light.

'Stop it!' Shana demanded. Her bare heels thumped on wood as she slid from her chair. Dren gasped and flung out an arm, but she blurred under it, and with a pretty scowl, pressed something hard against Husker's convulsing thighs. A flash of light filled the cottage.

~

Husker lay on his back for a while, ignoring the growing puddle of blood. He was trying to treasure that split second when he'd seen Dren flying through the air, thrown back by the explosion. He grinned. The bastard's face had looked like a slapped fish.

Shana poked him in the face. 'Up you get, lazybones.'

He rolled onto his knees. There was a groan from a pile of furniture at the other end of the cottage, and the stolen angel floated back to Husker in a draft of whispers. He managed to find his feet before it started fixing him. 'Thank you, my young friend.' Husker leant against an overhead beam to catch his breath. The cottage creaked in protest. 'I was told to keep that thing close, but didn't know why.' Down by his waist, Shana's tiny fingers closed his hand around Rafe's pommel stone. It was a soft, living presence – like the beating body of a field mouse. Yet it was cold and hard, too, and it seemed to draw his palm closer into an embrace.

'Oh, there's a few of them around,' said Shana, as she climbed back up into her chair. 'Dulls call them sinkstones, though we think that's a stupid name.' She coughed up a few syllables. 'See? Just because you can't speak properly doesn't mean you get to call it something else.' Her face seemed to grow older, picking up age in a breath. 'It will protect you from his tricks, but do not kill Doth Agren yet. He has a favour to ask.' Dren was steadying himself on a chair. It wobbled furiously as he coughed and hacked up smoke. 'Doth Agren,' she repeated. 'Ask.'

'You will regret this,' he muttered. Shana hissed at him, something predatory twisting her face. Dren waved her off. 'That was a prediction, not a threat. Before this is over, you will beg for me to leash this abomination.'

'Feasters don't believe in leashes,' Shana said, picking at her nose. Husker frowned as he tried to remember how old she'd seemed a moment before.

'We will see.' Dren sank heavily into his chair. 'It sounds like your friend has arrived, at least.' Behind him, the door creaked open to admit another child. She was dressed in a simple homespun dress which her mother hadn't bothered to keep clean from dirt or stains. A small, but vicious, fight ensued as both girls settled into the armchair, pushing and shoving each other to make space.

Dren ignored their squabbling and scowled at Husker. 'Do not get any ideas. I could crack that stone if I chose, it is only the cost of doing so which keeps you safe. Threaten me and the choice is made simple.'

'You hear me make any threats?' Husker was still leaning on the beam, trying to blink his vision clear. Damn room was spinning something fierce. 'People always think the worst of me.'

'As you should expect. But let me introduce you to two more freaks.' Dren opened his hand towards the children. 'Shana, you have met.' She beamed at Husker, mouthing a greeting. 'This other one is called Brenne. Have you met feasters before? They are not the innocents they seem.'

Brenne had claimed the centre of the seat, and a frown wrinkled up her forehead when Shana climbed around to perch on the back. The newcomer was the chubbier of the two, solemn and thoughtful enough until Shana got too close. A foot slipped onto her head, and she turned on her friend with bared teeth.

'I guessed that much.' Husker stretched the fresh skin on his back and dropped into a squat. He'd never made his peace with chairs since coming down from the Mountain Head, and no one had offered him a seat anyway. 'I doubt many children snack on forge slag.'

Brenne gave a guilty grin and picked a splinter from her upper lip. She proudly showed Dren the lump of metal she'd been nibbling on.

'And when are you introducing yourself, bastard? You're no less of a freak than them or me.' Husker accused Dren with a thick finger. 'Child-snatcher. Arsonist. I've seen what you leave in your wake. I'll listen, but then you'll answer to me.' He didn't try to hide his grin this time, though none of them even flinched. The feasters were watching politely. Dren just wrinkled up his nose in disgust. Husker snorted and wiped blood from his chin. 'People say I'm odd. But fuck, they've not met you three.'

'I like him,' Shana whispered to Brenne. She poked Dren in the leg. 'Where have you been hiding him, Doth Agren?'

Dren relaxed into his chair. He started pretending to clean his nails with a knife. 'Oh, it is no great story. Tollworth here has spent a decade imprisoned in the northern mountains, obsessing over the dullest of the old religions.' He waved his knife tip at Husker, giving the feasters a frank look. 'He is unnaturally strong, heals wounds in moments, and follows me around like a dog, all for reasons he does not know or understand. It is most flattering, him having crossed the Split on my account, but I suspect many wish he would walk back up the mountain and stay there. This man' – Dren ruined the word with a smile – 'left three children behind when he murdered his wife, and they all hate him. You have met Lily and Rose. His youngest has been snatched away by my fat brother.'

Husker listened to him lie without complaint. He said he'd listen, didn't he? He could hurt him later.

'I have helped out where I could,' Dren continued. 'My brother and I were doing some digging around the Mountain Feet when Tollworth was caught and chained.' He drew a sharp breath, as if the experience had been hard for him. 'Was that really ten years ago? Well, he was smaller back then, so the Watch tied him up quite easily. Unwilling to see sweet Rose, Lily and Lark left in the care of some village hag, I made arrangements to transfer them to the city. For their stepfather, I suggested a man named Josef – an old friend of mine, and sadly bereft of his own children.'

Husker snorted in contempt.

'If you must speak, then let us hear it.' Dren pulled a twig from his braids. He inserted it again lower down. 'Do not grunt like some animal.'

'What are my words against yours?' Husker said, slow enough that he had time to think. 'Mist is your way. Deceit and treachery.' He thought of the busy-sounding, pompous man who'd returned his letters. 'I walked through the ashes of that trading post. I spoke to those who survived. You call their stepfather a friend? Liar. People saw you set the flames around his sickbed.'

Dren's smile was as wet as his heart. 'You know so little. Perhaps you should have held your silence.'

'What's the point of this, Doth Agren?' Shana tugged on Dren's sleeve. 'Ask him to help us.'

'I'll give no help to this bastard,' Husker rumbled, climbing to his feet. 'Not until he tells me what's happened to my boy.' The sinkstone flared with cold as it drained away a burst of irritation. Husker looked down at his hand suspiciously. Now that was an odd sensation – like an angry sneeze that never came.

'Lark's a young man now, you know that?' Dren leant forwards, hands braced on his knees. 'You come down here, trampling and killing, bellowing for your offspring, but you know nothing of them and they want nothing from you.' A satisfied look settled over his face. 'Perhaps you want to show your affection in a more fitting way? Well, I take no pleasure in telling you this, but Lark is dead – murdered by my brother.'

Husker's heart missed a beat. It came back stronger, hotter. He blinked sweat from his eyes and started to mutter one of Priest Young's sermons, but the sinkstone beat him to it. It gorged on his anger, pulsing with cold, draining away an urge to crush this bastard's head against the nearest wall. He gripped it so hard his fist trembled.

'The fat oaf is hiding in Saarban,' he heard Dren saying, 'breeding spirits with which to infect the city. For this, the feasters and I mean to kill him. Would you do it for us? Take revenge for your son, even if it furthered my own plans?'

His words had provoked a different sort of pain. Husker's memories from before the mountain were foggy and unreachable. The baby he'd named Lark even more so. There was no face, no voice, to that tiny bundle of rags.

'Less sure of yourself now?' Dren sneered at him. 'Which matters more? Love for your dead son, or hate for me?'

'You are nothing,' Husker said calmly, over the roar of his blood. He fought an urge to bring the roof down around Dren's shit-eating smirk, and won. 'Show me my girls, then show me the man who killed my son.'

'Idiot.' Dren snorted derisively. He snatched up his book and stalked off. 'Sleep on the floor. Maybe you will meet them in the morning.' A door slammed behind him.

'Bastard,' Husker muttered, mopping his forehead.

Shana nodded, giggling in agreement. 'He's a liar, too.'

'What's your story, then?' Husker had a grip on himself now, but he still sought a distraction. He'd seen Shana's childlike features twisting into feral expressions as Dren spoke, and the chair had all but splintered under Brenne's grip. Feasters were cute, destructive little things. 'What's your secret?'

'Secret?' Brenne asked, struggling with an itchy strap on her dress. 'What's he talking about?' Shana was standing behind her, leaning both hands on Brenne's head. She whispered something in Brenne's ear and they both burst into laughter.

'How many years have you seen?' Husker pressed. 'You look young, but sometimes older.'

'Husker!' Shana gasped, one hand over her mouth. 'You can't ask a girl that.'

'There's no secrets,' Brenne insisted, with a frown. 'Just gotta watch what you eat, then you don't get old.'

'So, if I ate balls of forge slag, I'd stay like this forever?' He patted his scarred, scab-marked cheek. 'Or would I turn young and pretty first?'

'Let's find out!' Shana snatched the lump of slag off Brenne and tossed it to him. 'Eat that.'

He looked at it, turning it over. 'Not sure I know how.'

Brenne's dainty fingers plucked it from his palm. It shrunk to the size of a grape on the way to her mouth, and she popped it in, winking at him. 'Maybe there are some secrets after all.'

III

LEASHED

Light

There was a new girl in the opposite cage. 'Lark?' she whispered, clinging to the blue-white bars. A birthmark covered her nose. It was almost hidden by dust, apart from where a trail of snot had cleared a path to her lips. Lark thought she was perhaps a year older than him, if he remembered it right. Maybe as shy as he'd been? She'd taught him a funny game as their waggon had bounced over the rough tracks to Krans, the dice leaping and clattering around with a mind of their own. His hand had brushed hers more than once, and Terrano had remarked how well they'd got on.

At the sound of clanking metal, Lark turned over to face the wall. He pressed his hands tight over his ears, but he could still hear when she started wail. The blanket over his head was thick and dark, but he still could picture that huddle of bent backs. The courtiers giggled as they worked, their wooden masks knocking together as they forced a spirit into her soul. Then another, just to see.

Lark shivered in a ball of knees and elbows, feeling his brood of spirits move within him. Most souls could only endure one. But not Lark. Not special little Lark, or whatever was left of him in this dead, aching body. He tried to sleep through the drips that came after her screams.

~

Lark squealed and scrambled out of his blankets, hitting the floor with a thump.

'Wake!'

'Wake up!'

His ash-black veins had come alive, jerking him out of sleep as his brood of spirits fought for space. They churned past his belly, filling it with a bubbling, burning liquid.

'Get out!'

'Wake up!'

'No,' he groaned, crawling to the sewer grate. 'No. No.' They snapped his spine straight, cracking his head against the wall, and Lark gasped as a spray of inky blood splattered across the bricks, all the badness and filth fountaining out of him. His brood were swimming towards the cut, but Lark gritted his teeth and butted the wall again. Again. Again, until the cut was a gash and he was spluttering through a torrent that bubbled over his cheek and lips. 'Buller?' He tugged his old vest out from under the cot and tried to wipe the ichor off his face. It was soaked before the cut closed up. 'Buller?' he tried again. 'I made a mess.'

'Calm yourself, boy. I'm coming.' Keys rattled against the bars, and Lark looked up into the worried face of his only friend. The mill over-seer had been butchered over a dice table after they met, so he had a big scar running across his neck. He said he didn't mind it, and didn't remember it, but Lark thought it made him look like a sewn up doll whose head had fallen off.

Lark closed his eyes while Buller cursed and fiddled with the sparking bars. He let his head rest against the mucky bricks. He missed the dark. Darkness was a friend if you looked like him. Dazzling, soft-spined moss infested each of the cages, and it waved in the air as if moved by underwater currents. Lark hated it. He scraped it off his wall each day, but it grew back overnight.

The light dimmed as Buller bent over him. 'No! Don't!' Lark covered his head, his hands still crackling with unspent spirits.

'Don't you fuss,' Buller said, patting him with his gloves. 'I've got my leathers on.' With a sob, Lark threw his arms around his friend's chest and let himself be lifted. There was another time, another life, where he hated such closeness, but not now. He craved it. 'Careful, lad! You're kicking again.' Buller scrunched up his nose and leant back from the stench that followed Lark around. 'Earth save us, you can't wash this reek off, I swear you can't.'

Lark kept his hands wrapped around Buller's apron and tried to avoid touching his weirdly exposed chin. The leather turned molten under his fingers, smoking and melting until he shifted his grip. 'You look strange without your beard,' he whispered.

'You kept burning the bastard thing off.' Buller's chest rumbled against Lark's cheek. 'There was nothing left of it anyway.'

Thin figures stumbled to their bars as he spoke. They wiped sleep from their eyes and reached out hands in a gesture for food, hope, darkness, anything. Tainted water kept them sleeping through each other's dreams, but Buller's voice had everyone on their feet.

'Hello.' Lark raised his fingertips over Buller's back, giving a wave to the new prisoner. They'd cleaned out the straw in the girl's cage and taken her away. A man huddled by her cot, and he was clutching a blanket over his head. Most people in that cage didn't survive long enough to get used to the mosslight.

'Ease up now, boy.' Buller untangled himself from Lark's desperate hands, and set him under the sluice. He tossed the smoking remains of his apron onto a growing pile of such scraps in the corner. 'Not that I don't enjoy these moments, but you stink. Nothing meant by it, just facts.' He turned his key to unbolt the wash handle and waited for Lark to shuffle into place. Lark nodded that he was ready. 'Just facts.'

Buller pulled hard on the lever and a torrent of liquid drowned out Lark's hateful existence. Cold water, nothing else. Even the spirits that crawled through him sighed and went silent.

Terrano had smiled when Buller's corpse was thrown into the unlucky cage. Lark hadn't been able to ask why, as the courtiers were visiting, and it was hard to speak when they were working on you, but Terrano had definitely smiled – he'd given Lark a warm look that was out of place in this bright, blood-stained room. Buller had come back to life with a roar of insults. They kept coming, too, until sometime overnight when he lost his voice. The next morning, they opened his cage and gave him a mop. Buller's snarl of a smile returned after that, and he slopped out the cages, rattled buckets and kept their squalid world in order. But most of all, he cared for Lark.

'It's running out now, boy.'

The flow of water trickled to a stop. Warmth stung Lark again, and his brood resumed their slow, painful crawl through his blood. He pushed at the fouled water around his feet, trying to wash black smears down the grate. Buller grunted. 'Leave that. I'll be in with a mop later.'

'They're coming today?' Lark stood still, letting himself drip dry.

'Afraid so.' He handed over a clean vest and shorts, scuffing his boots over the lines Lark had scratched in the floor. There were two short marks since the last long one. 'You still keeping count, then?'

'Get out!'

'Escape!'

'Calm yourself, boy.' Buller was moving around the cage and setting everything in order. 'You're mumbling again.' He lay Lark's blanket neatly over the cot and rinsed down the grate with the last trickles of sluice water. Fresh straw. Scratchy clothes. The smell and feel of these things, as much as Buller's concerned face when he did these chores, kept Lark sane. The other prisoners held their silence, straining out their hands in an appeal for attention.

'I don't want another,' Lark pleaded. His brood were grumbling at the prospect of a newcomer. It was hard to tell when they spoke to him, or if he spoke for them.

'No more.'

'No.'

'No more,' screamed Lark.

'Hush now, someone's coming.' Buller turned his back on the door, uncorking and tapping at a small box. 'Don't stare at my hands, look at something else.'

Rhythmic clanks, as always, came first. The tool cart mounted the spine of the Scarlet Keep one step at a time, clunking away from far below. A cage minder strained to pull it up over the last lip on the stairs, the big one that kept Lark's blood from running out past the door, and she had to lean back quickly to avoid some sharp points that jabbed up against the covering cloth. Rolling it into place, she took out a key and started to unbuckle the manacles on the central table.

'What's that?' said the man in the unlucky cage. His hands flailed for the wall as he tried to stand. 'Who's there?'

The minder didn't answer. Her eyes had a bit of a glazed look, which meant maybe she liked drinking cage water too much. Swaying slightly, she tugged the cloth from the cart and started to clip it up across the middle of the room. It didn't reach all the way down, so Lark could still see if he crouched. Bare feet scampered in. The courtiers minced about, pushing each other impatiently, rasping and giggling as they made bulges in the curtain.

'Hold still now,' croaked one.

The man screamed when they dragged him onto the table. And then he really screamed. The gutter filled up, and the courtiers splashed about in the big red puddle they'd made. Someone dragged the black crate in, and there were a few seconds of drips and silence while the courtiers waited. A spray of gore shook the curtain.

'Couldn't even take one,' mumbled Lark.

'I've got something, if you want.' Buller turned Lark's face away with a hand on his chin. 'A healer's cure. Stop looking at that now.'

'There's no curing me.' Lark's smile trembled as he took the fungus from his friend's glove. The canopy of pink splodges would warn any forager off, but Lark didn't mind it very much, even though it tasted a bit sharp. They'd tried a lot of things. Poppy juice, sleepleaf, gallons and gallons of cage water... that just made him wet himself, and it wasn't nice to die with damp shorts on. Yet this fungus worked. They fed it to the creatures chained up in the palace pits – beasts that never saw daylight, but were grown and bred, cut up and patched up, and bred again until the court had what they wanted. Buller would only touch it with his leathers on.

'Chew quicker, boy,' he said in an urgent whisper. 'They're coming.' The echoes of his voice were already foggy and deep. Even Lark's brood sounded like they were very far away, trapped in a bottle under a lake, and that meant they couldn't scream at him like they normally did. Lately they'd become obsessed with just one thing.

'Escape,' mumbled Lark. He steadied himself on the side of his cot, keeping up appearances as the courtiers approached. Each was a brownish blur, naked apart from the wooden masks which covered their mouths and ground up their voices.

'We thought knives again, little Lark,' said the first of the three, in a tinny growl that rattled through the grill over her mouth. She leant over, her pendulous breasts swinging before him in a ponderous, swaying motion. Ants crawled out from behind her mask, scuttling in busy lines over her collarbone and tearing holes in her skin. The work of the fungus, or something real and worse. Not knowing helped.

'Our special little boy,' an older male said. His bony hips and stomach were ridged by starvation. His hands were covered in a downy white fluff. When he chuckled, the cage swam with a scatter of fireflies, which burst into sparks against the white-hot walls. 'You really do defy all expectations. And our standards are so incredibly high.' He ruffled Lark's hair.

'Yes! Yes. Since you lasted so long last time, we thought it prudent to explore your limits. With knives. Why, if we changed to something else, we wouldn't learn anything at all.' The third courtier was only a boy. He spoke in a piping, happy voice that had been educated with little trills and flourishes. He'd lifted his mask to reveal his face, but Lark didn't want to look. The boy held a serrated dagger in both hands. They all did now. 'We've sharpened everything this time. Don't be a poor sport, see if you can keep it together.'

Lark looked. The boy's cheeks and brow were flecked with frost, which was how you knew Terrano was watching. He spread ice around the palace to make dead people do what he said, and Lark's skin ached as it tried to settle over him too. But his brood were too numerous, too vicious. They grumbled and snapped, melting the ice before it sunk in.

The boy replaced his mask. 'Deep breaths, now,' he growled. 'That's the ticket.' Buller dragged the crate of spirits over, shivering as the frost spread onto him. He wasn't Lark's friend anymore, not for a while. 'Leave that there, minder.'

'No, over here,' demanded the female, one hand on her hip. 'By me. Quickly now.' Buller jerked closer, pulling the crate towards Lark's cot. The wood was swollen with spirits. Its planks dripped with black sap, and it bulged and rattled, hissing at Buller's fingers.

The courtiers began to cut. Lark slipped into the fungus fumes and felt nothing, sinking from his narrow cot to the floor. The ceiling of his cage had lots of little cracks in it, and some of them almost looked like pictures. But he had to squint. If he squinted really hard, he could see a horse. One of the knife blows rolled him over, and then he couldn't look at the ceiling anymore. A spirit crawled from the crate. It inched through the bloodbath, winding around the ankles of the sweating courtiers.

It nudged them, cooing at Lark.

It bobbed its head at his limp fingers, sniffing.

It crawled up his arm, tiny feet gripping his skin.

It nibbled him behind the ear and nestled in, speaking in whispers.

'Escape,' it said.

His brood screamed in protest, squirming and fighting for space. The newcomer watched patiently, cooing, bobbing and waiting for a gap to be rent in Lark's bloated soul.

~

He woke, as always, in brightness.

'Buller?' Lark's voice trembled and broke. 'Buller!' His brood were exhausted, drifting slowly about. His straw hadn't been replaced yet, so maybe he'd woken up early? It looked like Buller would have to mop the walls again.

'Get out.'

'Escape.'

Did his lips move? He thought they did. Someone had left him a fresh change of clothes on the cot, so he put them on.

'Escape.'

Buller was still nowhere to be seen. The other prisoners writhed and snored in their drugged sleep, and for some reason Crone had been thrown in the unlucky cage. Lark was used to thinking of her as younger than she was, despite the fact she was bald and toothless and smelt funny, but being in a cage had robbed her of that. She let out a sob as he moved to his bars.

'Where have you been?' he asked, feeling a bit hurt.

Footsteps were coming from the stairwell, and very bad whistling. The cage minder that entered wasn't dead yet, and he was dressed in bright green robes, swinging a sedative-tipped prong like he was out for a nice walk. Buller refused to use his, calling it a coward's tool.

The minder crouched by Crone's cage. 'Fall from grace, huh, old ma?' He wiped the tip of his prong, cleaning off the venom, and jabbed Crone in the arm. She continued to sob without looking up. 'You don't remember me, old ma. But I remember you.' He jabbed her again. 'Stings a bit, huh? Bit of payback.' Her arm was covered in cuts before he gave up. 'Mad old bitch, you shush now. He wants you to have this. Said you could still have it despite the scene you made.' He took a blond wig from his bag. But rather than toss it past the bars, he dangled it from his prong and tried to drape it on her head. 'So pretty,' he crooned. 'Pretty old ma. Not pretty enough, I guess, not for him. She's with him now.'

Crone snatched his wrist and twisted. There was an audible crack of bone, but the man choked rather than screamed; her other hand had shot out and seized his throat in long, gnarled fingers. Lark remembered that grip from when he'd been wasteful when chopping carrots. Her reddened eyes watched the minder struggle for a moment, then she took his prong and stabbed him cleanly through the cheek.

'She wants you to open the gate,' said Lark, helpfully.

'G'rk.' The minder's eyes trembled with shock. They roved left and right as they searched for an escape, but he had more chance of bending back the blue-white bars than peeling away any one of Crone's fingers. An odd, crispy smell started to fill the room. The bars hated dead people, and they were snapping at Crone's arm with the same ferocity that they attacked Lark. Not that she seemed to care. Crone pulled the minder closer, until he was sizzling too, and ripped the prong from his ruined cheek. She wheezed and rattled it angrily between the bars.

'She still wants you to open the gate,' Lark pointed out. The man's flailing hands found the lock, but it did him little good. Crone leapt forwards with the swinging gate, without letting go, and trapped him against the wall. She glared at him as he roasted, spitefully keeping close enough for the bars to crackle.

'Can I come out?' Lark asked, softly.

Crone let the cage minder fall to the floor and shuffled over, stroking her wig like a pet. She put it on and stood up on her tiptoes to flick back the bolt. Lark felt like crying when the gate swung open. But she was crying too, so that seemed okay.

'Thank you,' he said, hugging her. His nose was buried in her wig, and that made him want to cry even more. It smelt clean, and not at all like blood or shit, or anything else in his cage. 'I like your hair, It's very pretty. Why did Terrano lock you up?'

Crone pushed free with a sob. She stumbled back to her cage and pulled off her wig, slamming her back against the wall and sinking down with a wretched wail.

'Well, I don't know why I was locked up either,' Lark said tetchily. 'No need to be like that.' His fists bunched as a hundred shadowy hands clenched around his own. With a shriek he hit the central table, breaking off the gleaming trough that drained away little girls' lives, stomping on it again and again until it was as twisted beyond use. Sleepy faces turned to him from the other cages. Crone stayed slumped over her cot, watching his tantrum with hollow, uncaring eyes. 'I'm going to escape,' Lark said, panting among the mess. 'Do you want to come?'

'Get out.'

'Escape.'

'Escape?' Lark whispered.

Crone crawled under her cot and ignored him. Well, he could come back for her later. And he certainly couldn't stay, because voices were coming from the stairwell. Was that Buller?

'Kill.'

'Kill him.'

'No,' Lark whispered. He slipped out of the room. 'Buller's my friend.'

'Kill Terrano.'

'Oh,' said Lark. 'That.' He dodged through a nearby door when the voices got too close. They didn't sound very happy when they saw the mess he'd made, so Lark started to run, and for some reason he was now very, very good at running. His brood screamed joyfully as he rounded a corner and sped down a long, straight corridor, and people started to run away from him. Strange to think he'd come this way only a few weeks ago, with one of his hands clinging to Terrano's cloak, following the twists and turns of a dusty corridor, until he was nudged into a room that turned out to be a cage.

'Kill him.'

'Find him.'

Lark ducked down behind a chest of drawers. He stifled a yawn as some men ran past. Perhaps he could kill Terrano tomorrow? It would be very nice to sleep in the dark tonight, and maybe somewhere less busy. He tried the stairs, because he didn't remember wall moss growing on every floor. There were a lot of people in the Scarlet Keep. Every room was filled with cages, or turned into one. He passed a study with some men chained up to a bookcase. He snuck through a kitchen filled with bunk beds and leather straps. One of the bigger libraries had huge birdcages suspended from the ceiling, but they didn't have birds in them, and they creaked and swung as prisoners stirred in their drugged sleep.

Thankfully, there was no moss on this floor, just torchlight. Flames sputtered around Lark as he ran, and he let his spirits fill the shadows he left behind. His feet skimmed over the ground. His haunted eyes turned darkness into soft greys and edges. Lark's world twisted as he scrambled up onto a wall and scuttled through an archway upside down, the stone melting and dripping as his toes sunk in to give him grip.

There. A room of complete darkness.

'Kill her.'

'Her?' Lark dropped to the floor. He tucked himself into the shadows, nestling between some sacks of flour. 'What do you mean, her?' But that was the way it went. His brood was only quiet when he wanted something.

Going Alone

L ily could see Saarban from the top of this stupid sawmill. Achingly close. It seemed to wink at her, its famous beacons flickering in the encroaching dusk, and that hump of lights at the back could only be Highwall.

A sail creaked past. Lily rubbed her eyes and rolled over to watch the cogs and shafts spin instead, sawblades unlatched and waiting their turn to dance. Rose was sunk in a chair on the other side of the room, and the mad bitch hadn't started snoring yet, so Lily continued to wait. Shana had left a few hours ago, trusting her feasters to enforce a truce. They were dozing in a big heap in the middle of the room. Each one was a girl too young to have felt the ache of her blood, but also eerie and old. When they weren't yelling and tripping over each other in odd little games, they prowled around like wildcats. Most things they touched they broke. Most things they broke they ate. Earlier, an excited shout had the whole pack scrambling down the sawmill, and Lily had watched them pass a lizard carcass around. Bloody hands and cheeky smiles, that was them.

One of the feasters mumbled in her sleep, kicking another's face and rolling her off the pile of furs. Neither of them woke, and Rose let out a great, honking snore.

Dressing was the noisiest part, so the trick was to do that elsewhere. Lily gathered up her boots and clothes, and crept over to the open face of the sawmill. Her nightgown snagged on a few loose nails as she navigated the rope ladder down, but she was mostly dressed and kneeling to fasten her boots before she heard a massive thump and the sound of cursing behind her. She gritted her teeth and drew herself up. 'What the hell are you doing?'

Rose picked herself up from where she'd fallen at the bottom of the rope ladder. 'Stupid thing.' She brushed angrily at the stains on her trousers, and strode over to wash her hands in the mill's boiler exhaust.

Lily darted over and slapped her hand away. 'Don't, you fool!'

'Bloody gods, Lily!' Rose turned on her, eyes flashing. 'What's wrong with you?'

'Fine, stick your whole snout in. See what happens.' Lily dipped her fingers in the tainted water, ignoring the sting, and flicked some up at Rose's face. Rose yelped, rubbing furiously at her cheeks. 'See? So, what the hell do you know about anything? Go back to bed and wait for your lover to bring his cock around.' She left Rose wiping her face and started kicking her way through the bushes. A few torches had already gathered by the hill. Cursing her sister for the delay, Lily pushed on faster.

Behind her came inevitable, clumsy footfalls. 'And where are you sneaking off to?' Rose marched up and grabbed a handful of her cloak. 'Stop being such a child and—'

'Child?' Lily shrieked, flailing about until Rose let her go. She backed off, panting. 'I'm being the big sister. Lark's stuck in that city, so that's where I'm going.'

'Alone?' snarled Rose, taking a step forwards. A few nails were still hanging loose in that oversized head of hers. 'I don't bloody think so. You wouldn't last a second without Dren.'

'Who's the child now?' Lily sneered at her. 'Go back and hide behind your lover.' She started walking off in the direction of the hill. 'I'll tell Lark you're dead.'

'You've got no money!' Rose was at her side again, furious.

'I can steal what I need.'

'You've no idea where he is!'

'I've got a name.' Lily sniffed, tossing her hair. 'I know he's fat and called Terrano. I know him and that poisoner back there grew up in the Palace of Sells. I also know I can handle a city better than you and him, or any of this feaster shit.'

'And how are you going to get there?' This was the trouble with arguing with Rose – the lanky bitch had twice the stride and lungs to go with it. Lily glowered at her and carried on marching towards the lights, while struggling to keep her breathing even.

The cart came into view. A pair of bearded travellers in dusty capes and broad hats were already settling into their seats, and Lily tried to climb over the last of the bushes without looking too suspicious. The driver stopped counting his coins and strode over to confront them, snatching up a quarterstaff.

'I see.' Rose pursed her lips. 'Well, there's room enough for two.'

Lily said nothing, brushing leaves off her skirt and chewing over exactly how hard she wanted to argue. She'd been in Rose's pack. No idea where she'd got those jewels – but they'd be useful. 'Hold this, then.' She shrugged off her own bag and swung it up into her sister's arms. Lily approached the cart driver, adjusting to a pleasant smile as he neared. 'Road greetings, sere! We seek passage to Saarban.' She curtsied to the cart's occupants. 'Will you accept the wayfarer's toll?'

'Don't take her,' snapped an old woman, rushing around the cart to clutch at him with scabbed hands. The store owner from earlier. She was probably still annoyed about Lily spitting on her counter. 'She's trouble, she is. All of them are. I've had nothing but grief today, me. Trust Granny.'

The quarterstaff wobbled as the cart driver pointed it at Lily, poking her like it was a blunt spear. He'd clearly never swung it at anything more dangerous than a tree stump, puffing up his chest and muttering orders as he fancied himself a soldier in some long-forgotten war.

'Right,' he barked. 'How do you know we're going to Saarban, you? Don't seem very trustworthy, sneaking up here all unannounced.'

'Your granny likes to talk, my dear.' Lily put a delicate hand on his staff. 'She was muttering about your cart as she robbed me for soap. In any case, Shana and the feasters said to tell you they'd be pleased if you could take us.' Lily flashed him a liar's smile and stuck a thumb back at Rose. 'My porter will handle the payment.' His staff had wilted at the mention of feasters, so Lily patted him on the shoulder and stepped past. She settled in beside his granny and gave her a solicitous smile, trying to ignore the smell. The two men opposite touched their hats.

'Road greetings, gentlemen,' she said, leaning towards them. Or more accurately, leaning away from Granny Scabs. 'What takes you to Saarban?' They were pale rather than tanned, with no inking or marks. 'Are you also from the Northlands?'

They conferred with a confused glance, then replied in a string of guttural words that sounded apologetic. Granny was fiddling with a bent shawl pin and shot Lily a scathing look. 'Not Northers, them. From the coast. The Wayward Isles.'

'Oh! Like my friend Withers,' Lily said. They looked even more uncertain. 'A famous diplomat? Retired to Branera?' She gave up trying to remember his full name and just tipped her own imaginary hat at them.

The cart shook as Rose rammed the driver up against its wheels. 'The wayfarer's tariff,' she said, a few inches from his face, 'is not two sarls a mile.' He winced and mumbled an apology as she lifted him higher. Shirts crumpled around his chin. 'And I'm carrying that stick of yours until we get there.' It dropped willingly from his hands. The cart creaked as Rose put her foot on it, and she stared at the two Waywards gentlemen until they shuffled over and made room for her oversized arse. Rose thumped the side of the cart, calling impatiently over her shoulder. 'Let's go.'

'My sister Rose,' said Lily, nudging Granny Scabs. 'She's the real troublemaker.'

Rose's face twitched at her name. She had dark rings under her eyes, and her hair was in a rare tangle over her shoulders. 'He tried to take advantage of us.'

Granny smirked at this, settling back as the cart lurched into motion. 'My grandson. Troublemaker too, he is.' She mimed hitting him with the staff. 'Hit him next time, around the ears.' She cackled. 'I'm too old to do it now, I am.'

It was slow going up the hill. Everyone was uncomfortably close, their eyes picking out spots in the distance. Lily fidgeted for a while, but felt the unbearable knot in her stomach ease as they crested a rise and Krans fell away. Sure, the scrubs were as bleak as ever, yet on a clear night her eyes were drawn to the stars anyway. Faint washes of green daubed a black canvas, some night god painting his glitzy art above Saarban. A suitably gaudy welcome to the City of Water and Light.

The cart jolted as its wheels kicked up over a dirt ridge. 'I think I prefer travelling at night,' said Lily, to no one in particular. Saarban twinkled at her in the distance. 'Less sunburn at least.' Rose sat in silence, her eyes narrowing at every bone-jarring jolt. Lily sighed and leant over to gently pry their bags from her sister's white-knuckle grip. 'What did Shana leave for our dinner?'

Two dead mice. Some smooth pebbles. A sweetloaf wrapped up in leaves. Lily broke the bread in two and handed some to Rose, then tipped the rest away onto the road. They sat and chewed in silence, until one of the Waywards men took out a little flute and played a ditty, his comrade singing along in their bizarre, guttural tongue.

Deep Water

Damp air snatched past Husker's face. The deepening chill and still weight of the air whispered to him; they were deep in the arms of Godearth now. Each flooded tunnel took them further from Krans, and deeper than he thought a mine could go. Yet there was peace here for someone like him. A better peace than he'd left behind on the Mountain Head, where Goddeath ate her fill in the snow and Godmist spewed ice over the peaks. He wriggled his toes, letting the current lap against them.

'You hear that?' said Dren, crouched on the barge roof.

'I hear you.' Husker shifted his bulk and caused the vessel to rock out of turn. 'I'm always hearing you. Hold your tongue a while.' The pouch around his neck pulsed with cold, and his irritation was drained away. He felt for Priest Young's pendant, but held onto the sinkstone instead.

'Husker, look here!' Shana trilled at him as she swam past, leaping up and out of the rushing water. She fell back with a splash. 'Look!'

'No one likes a show-off,' said Husker, picking nuts from his teeth. He flicked a shell at her.

Their barge was drifting out over a pit of obsidian water. A crack of light touched its surface, nurturing long vines that hung down from far above to dip their tips in the underground lake. Chittering mammals skittered and swung around this breach, dim shapes which occasionally fell with a distant plop. More feasters had joined them since they set off, and on hearing such sounds they would squeal and dive off in search. The girl-things were as sleek as otters, carving through the spray thrown up by the chop of the bouncing vessel, and spreading out to cavort and play as it slowed in the caverns. If the feasters fell behind, it hardly mattered – they'd dive underwater and catch up with a few strokes of their delicate arms, the water erupting with bubbles as they soared up and out like leaping fish. Apart from these odd moments, they looked like a gaggle of farm girls out for a swim, with plaits, bunches and floral dresses floating around them like lily pads.

Dren sniffed the air. 'I could swear this cavern has changed.' His pole nudged them around a finger of crooked stone. A current snatched at the barge and pulled them into a tunnel so low he had to squat on the roof.

'Looks like you're hunting rocks,' Husker said, pushing one away with his foot. 'Are we even close to Saarban, little bastard?'

'Oh, hours yet. Tell me though, why do you think your girls ran away rather than stay to meet you?' Dren's laughter broke like dry leaves underfoot. A quick rustle then gone. 'Quite the effect you have, driving them further into danger.'

Husker spat a nut over the side. 'Funny that. My guess would be they ran from you, not me.'

'And you were so hoping to speak with them!'

'You know, I'm not so sure I was. It's been a long time.' Husker stretched, feeling the pull and ripple of muscles under his back. The sinkstone nestled up cold against his collarbone. 'I'm taking it one step at a time.'

Dren smirked. 'One step at a time?'

'That's what I said.'

'No, no. That is what the sinkstone said. Can you feel it changing you yet? When so much of you is hate and anger, to have those things sucked away must leave you quite empty.'

'Let me see.' He held up his fingers to count. 'It keeps me cold. Keeps me focused. Annoys you. Yeah, we're getting along just fine.' Husker scattered a handful of shells over the deck. They bounced overboard, bobbing then vanishing from the swaying lamplight. 'Is your brother as annoying as you?'

'He is.'

'Is that why you want me to kill him?'

Dren started humming a discordant tune, his hands playing over the pole in idle patterns. Shana floated past on her back. She was slinging lazy, ink-scrawled arms overhead, somehow keeping pace with the racing barge, before she sunk with a surprised yelp. Brenne rose first, giggling and splashing as she swam away from Shana's angry retribution.

'I'll sink you, bitch!'

'Catch me first?'

'Catch you? I'll drown you—'

'Enough! Enough,' said Dren. He made to poke Shana with his pole, but she bared her teeth and snapped at it. 'No! I need this.'

They drifted out into another cavern. The water here wasn't dark at all, but glowed with blue undertones, swaying with such subterranean life that it left the lightless expanse above them seeming dead and heavy. Enormous fronds of weed quivered beneath the barge, pulsing as they were pushed apart, brighter and brighter, until the barge begun to glow and Dren's face was drowned in marine light and shadow. Without a word, the feasters climbed back on board. They sat in damp huddles and braided their hair in silence.

'Got crinkly skin?' Husker asked Shana, offering her a handful of nuts. She shook her head. 'Water too cold?' The feasters shushed him, each one putting a finger on her lips. Dren too, the smug bastard. Husker opened his mouth, but something in the water chose that moment to brush up against his heels and scratch him. Then again, harder. He reluctantly swung his feet out of the water, making room for Shana to duck under his arm and sit on his lap. The feaster ignored his offered handful of nuts and solemnly tore off some sacking to chew on. 'Getting a bit rough' Husker eyed the frothing water and edged back against the cabin. No honest villager from the Mountain Feet would take a deep bath, let alone go for a swim. 'Is this normal?' Shana pressed her finger to his lips and carried on chewing pieces of sacking.

Dren was leaning left and right with the sway of the barge, his eyes fixed dead ahead. Seemed pretty pointless. True darkness lay beyond their lanterns, the depths-of-forest stuff that swallowed up a man's lantern and made him feel like a child. Then there was the flying water, broken up the thumping prow and hurled back as ragged sheets through the air. Husker mopped his face, watching sceptically as Dren spun his pole for an overhead grip. It shot out. Shadows swelled around the bastard's shoulders as he strained, swinging their vessel around a tight bend, and the barge groaned, its lanterns guttering to nothing as his efforts sucked the light out of their fiery hearts. With a loud crack, darkness enveloped the barge. When the lanterns flared back, their flickering light showed rock walls tight on each side, and Dren tossed his snapped pole overboard. He spread his arms, clouds billowing from his sleeves to buttress the hull, and a growing rumble of falling water drowned out the creak of tortured wood.

'Brace yourself, Tollworth,' Dren roared, spluttering through the spray. The barge leapt into the air and landed with a deafening crash. Husker took a moment before opening his eyes.

'Earth take you, bastard. What was all that about?'

'A shortcut.' Dren was lounging on the cabin roof. They were floating along in a steady current. 'We have reached the underducts of Saarban. Can you not swim? You seem very tense.'

The mine tunnels had dropped them into a wider, tiled corridor of clear water, and its mosaic walls were infested with a moss that outshone their lanterns. With a purr from Shana, the feasters started moving about the deck again, swinging over rails and leaping into the water, laughing and pushing each other in. One was handing out clumps of wall moss, glowing stains already smearing her dainty mouth.

'What's an underduct?' Husker said, peering at the water suspiciously. The tiles were riddled with weeds.

'A passage for water. Saarban is the city of water and light, so what more fitting way to bring us in?' Dren was cutting his palm to grind in more of the green root he was addicted to, and he spoke through gritted teeth. 'The feasters say... ah, that the girls left shortly after dusk. This barge will beat their cart to the city, with twice the comfort and four times the speed. My brother and his spirits will be dealt with long before they wander in. Do as I say, and your offspring will not be at risk.'

'You think so little of them. They're not stumbling into danger – they're riding into it.' Husker's skin cracked as he grinned. 'My children were born brave.'

'Those that survive, I suppose. There is no bravery where Lark has gone.' Dren twirled his knife elegantly. 'Tell me, do you feel that, Tollworth?' Husker grunted, snatching at the rail as his legs shifted beneath him. It was Dren's turn to smile, more horrible than his bloody lips could ever be. 'Do you feel the pull of my city?'

The last of the exhausted feasters climbed back on board. They draped themselves about in puddles, unable to contend with the racing water and steep upwards gradient. Husker stepped over one and took a firmer grip on the rail. 'Shit. That's not normal.'

'Tollworth, we are climbing into Highwall, the most exclusive and unnatural district of Saarban.' The knife spun again, its blade as bright as his too-white teeth. 'Many things will soon cease to be normal. It is my home, after all.'

Rock Lesson

S hana gripped the pebble, feeling out its smooth, dead surface. They'd played the rock game in harder places, but this was still tricky.

... darting lizards hugged the wall, small eyes flickering from inside nests of glowing moss. Unlikely creatures wiped mould from their bulging eyes and uncurled from murky corners to stalk the barge, stirred from years of slumber by the eddies of their passage. Weeds, bloated with stagnant life, expelled clouds of bloodsucking worms as the hull violated ancient dunes of silt and grit...

Shana blocked out all the pulses and tastes of the underduct, and concentrated on the game. 'Silly bitch,' she muttered. 'Get a grip.' An expectant hush fell over her sister-feasters as she raised the pebble, fighting to keep it steady.

'Take it back.' Dren was crouched by her side, rocking on sinewy calves against the tilt of the barge. His skin reeked of spay. 'You gave it to him, you can take it back.' The pebble chose that moment to wobble and take Shana's hand sideways.

'Damnit! Dren, get lost.' She pushed him away. 'Gods you're... ewww! Look how sweaty he is.' Shana waved her hand at her sisters, and they all laughed and groaned. Wiping it on Dren's jacket, she clung to that childish reaction and resisted the urge to claw some respect from his face. 'Go away, sweaty-man.'

Seizing a moment when the pebble relented to her whims, Shana spun and threw. She gasped as it tore free from her hand, and the girls clapped and shrieked when it landed neatly on the furthest chalk square, sliding down the slanted deck to rest against a bundle of moss. Grinning hugely, she skipped across the chalk to claim her prize. This clump was different, they could all feel it. A tiny flower hid in there. They could pull as much from the walls as they wanted, and from these tender hearts it would regrow. Neater than human hearts, in that respect.

'Shana, you—'

'She said get lost, Doth Agren,' snapped Brenne, shoving him so hard he hit the cabin. She'd never had much restraint. 'Go and find your own game.'

The moss squealed as Shana's teeth tore into it. Nothing Dren or the other dulls could hear, but a symphony of teeth to a feaster. She giggled, wiping fluorescent dribble from her chin, and the others sighed and smiled. They all wanted to land on that square, but they left it for her, because she was Shana.

'Your turn, sister,' she said to Brenne. The pebble veered and sunk as she tossed it over, but her mastery was well practised. Like all rocks, this bundle of sediment was too lifeless to sense. Easy to crush. Hard to hold. Since stones and dead things were important, Shanna made the most vicious feasters win this game before they left her side. Not all of them survived the process, but Brenne was smart enough to not try and leave yet. 'Take it slow, you big silly.'

Brenne fumbled the rock, snatching at it amid taunts and jeers. She chased it down the deck, and cracked it before she took control. That was the rock lesson. Keep your dull senses, too. Learn to handle the stupid rock, and learn restraint in a delicate world.

'Go on, Brenne,' one of the younger feasters urged, hands full of her pairing's hair. The other girl butted her impatiently until she resumed grooming.

But Shana could see from Brenne's slumped shoulders that the rock had crumbled in her hand. Gorging on life was a rich, wet joy, but it left a feaster without balance, and this one still had a lot to learn. They all tittered when the bits fell from her fingers, and she spun around, her hungry gaze silencing everything before resting on Dren in a way that he wouldn't understand. Shana dragged him around the cabin. 'I've had my turn, Doth Agren. Let's talk.'

Dren scowled at her, blinking drug haze from his eyes and confused at these simplest of cues. She'd never actually eat him, but he was hers regardless. 'Where are we going?' he hissed, glancing back down the barge. There were few obstacles in the water now, so he'd grudgingly left Husker with a steering pole.

'Mmmm' – Shana looked around for inspiration – 'the prow.' She squeezed his hand and felt the texture of spirits within him, a tantalising meal always out of reach. Her mouth grew moist, her stomach warm. Her feaster core wanted to rip into him, lick him, cover his guts in kisses, and yet the dull parts of her were sickened and confused at the idea. She cultivated such reactions, kept that girlish part of herself innocent. Feasting was all about balance.

'Enough! Where are we going?' Dren pulled his hand away, and she had to let go or crush his fingers.

'Here.' Shana climbed up to perch on the handrails. 'You can sit down there.' He frowned, and the spirit aroma swelled. Shana's belly rumbled in response. 'So, sweaty-man, what's this thing you want me to do?' The wind of their passage pushed fingers through her hair, russet tendrils that reached out towards him. She let her age slip a bit. 'Speak your mind. I will listen.'

'I have been quite clear,' he said frostily.

'You're never clear. It's part of your charm.' She twirled a lock of her hair and nibbled it, drinking in the anger of his eyes, sniffing the mist seeping from his mouth. Her little appetiser.

'Take back the sinkstone before I am forced to break it.' Her feaster core had nothing pleasant to say about being given orders, so Shana went with the little girl and stuck out her tongue. Dren's jaw clenched. 'Act your years, Shana. He must be controlled! Think of the damage he could do.'

She wound more hair in her hands. 'He won't. He's nice.'

'He kills without thinking, unstoppable by anyone but me.' Dren snarled at her, spilling spirits down his chin. 'And only without that sinkstone.'

'He struggles with his nature, you're just too stupid to see it. Perhaps you want to control us, too? We're not so different.' Shana's hair fell from her hands, her child-self receding from such a boring conversation. 'You hate no chains but your own, Doth Agren. This hypocrisy is sickening.'

'Take it back. With it gone, I can handle him and my brother without risk.' Dren lowered his head, mist trickling from his mouth and nose. 'In return, I will assist you in claiming Highwall. I know that is why you have come in such force, despite me bringing him to do any killing that is required.'

His tone of his was starting to grate. 'What bargain would I make with you?' she said, gripping the rail. 'You are steeped in deceit. You told me the boy was bait, for whatever sick reason you won't disclose. But that means he is alive, or at least alive enough for that lonely man back there not to care. Yet you made him believe there was no hope, took the cruellest path.' She bared her sharpening teeth at him. 'Slavery is all you know, and so you will never be free of it. I know what they did to you in that keep, Doth Agren. I know how much of you they cut out to make the spaces in your soul. I can see...' She licked her lips. 'I can taste the chains on you. Even now you wonder if you are acting of free will, or if the cages are reeling you in.'

Shadows bled from Dren's smile, darkening its shine. 'You know nothing of chains, feaster. If I slip them, things will be less simple.'

What remained of Shana's innocence slipped into age. Years piled on her shoulders, and the world burst into life, throbbing with prey and wet beating hearts.

... skin tore as Brenne ground a girl's cheek over barge planks and chalk. Damp air rushed between sharpening fangs as her pairing hissed a challenge. Underneath the hull, frothing water pushed against fin and muscle. Long, scaled tales beat through clouds of silt...

'Threats, Doth Agren?' said Shana. 'Should I end you now, then? Which danger is greater, your brother or you?' She crashed her hand through the rail, breaking it into jagged splinters. First by mistake, and again to see him flinch. 'You are pathetic,' she hissed. 'Knife-made freaks, walking my territory only by my allowance.' Footsteps approached her over the deck, and she felt her child raise its head. With a deftness that made her Shana, and not some unspeakable horror, she pivoted on that thought and let the little girl take control.

'Husker!' She giggled and ran over to him, dodging past Dren and climbing up the giant, her nimble feet finding purchase in his rolls of flab. Her child loved this one. His hands caught her as she climbed, quick and gentle despite his size, and he swung her up onto his shoulder. She patted his balding scalp like a drum. 'Hello! Ewwww, you're sweaty too!'

'Easy, little one.' Husker's deep voice was as unhurried as ever, but there was urgency in the way he stood. 'And take a better grip. I just dropped the pole.'

'There are no obstacles here,' said Dren scathingly. 'Do you think I would leave you to steer otherwise?'

Now she was up on Husker's shoulders, Shana could see out further over the prow. 'Maybe we're lost, then?' She hugged his head. 'Okay, I'm ready.' The barge smashed into a pillar, kicking up violently, and they all staggered backwards. The underduct had started to froth and swirl. It was snaking its way around a series of green pillars, each one trailing weeds to point a way left or right.

The wilful barge chose neither; it spun and crashed into the next one with a defiant crunch of wood. Dren's eyes bulged as the collision sent him back over the broken handrails, snatching at splinters and air. He spluttered through murky foam as the barge righted itself, clinging to some tow ropes like a drunken spider. 'Tollworth, you—'

'Turn around!' Shana cried, tapping Husker's head as urgently and delicately as possible. There was something worrying happening in the water. 'Get back! We need to get back from the rail.'

'Ow! Watch who you're slapping,' Husker grumbled, swaying as they bounced off another pillar.

'Please!' Shana patted him again, trying to move him away from the massive hearts and lungs that were climbing up the listing barge. Scaly talons clamped around Husker's ankle, slamming him down and sending him sliding, crashing through the rails. Shana threw her arms around his neck and rode him down into the water, twisting to bare her teeth at the monstrous lizards that were swarming up over the hull. Husker was too dull to notice. Too panicked. He hit the water with a thunderous splash and was immediately crushed between the barge and a pillar. His flailing limbs caught a tile and pinked the water around them.

... blood swirled and spread. Scaled nostrils flared. Mandibles, venom, gills, everything sharp and deadly was pointing at that fat, bleeding flesh...

Shana snarled back as she sunk to the weed-riddled bottom, bubbles racing from her mouth. She smothered her child and ate the world in – every breath, every pulse. On the barge, Dren's damp throat was full of spit and panic, gargling for air as he shrieked her name. In the water, scales shrieked over ancient hide as a bitter rush of flavours bloomed around her, and Husker roared as a lizard's claws peeled skin from his back. He was unable to fight, unable to swim. It was only a matter of time before that dull heap of flesh and lungs inhaled, too stupid to do anything other than choke and drown. Cowering deep inside her, Shana's girl screamed for someone to help him.

Fine. Gripping an armpit, she started swimming up. But this was a rock lesson. Husker's joints groaned in protest, tendons popping and ripping until she gave up and let him sink. With a hiss of frustration, she kicked him around a pillar and snatched at the next lizard that swam past. The water slowed her hand, fetching her a bleeding tail rather than a severed head. She let it drift to the bottom.

They were funnelled up against the shallow edge of the tunnel, and Husker broke water, filling his chest with an almighty gasp of air. Shana vaulted up to mount his neck. She gripped his ears and twisted, exerting every rock lesson she knew to keep herself from pulling them off. He bellowed in pain. Blood squirted between her fingers. But his head turned, and he slogged them up onto a ridge that ran along the walls, ducking to avoid the curved ceiling. Wary of the shallows, or wary because she was Shana, the lizards wriggled back to their weed beds. She'd tasted old reptiles like this before. If they were one thing, they were patient.

'Ouch! Husker!' Shana rubbed her head. 'Mind the ceiling.' He mumbled an apology, still snorting and spitting water. The barge had pulled away, even if it was only limping along and kept afloat by clouds of spirit mist. Shana could dive in and reach them by staying this deep in the feast, but her child wanted to stay with Husker, so she stayed. Pulses faded around her, and the barge vanished from view.

Husker batted Shana's hands away from his torn ears. 'Let go.' She released him, and watched in grim horror as he pushed them back into place so they could mend. The skin seemed to quiver for the chance. It reached for its rightful place as he fumbled to hold them true.

'Sorry,' she said, tears in her eyes.

He grunted. 'No harm done.' He was trying to feel if he'd fixed them on right. He hadn't. When you got this close there were many bits of him that seemed wonky, or bulging out in the wrong places. 'How do I look?' he said, strangely worried.

'Ugly. And stupid too.' She scowled down at him, peering around so he could see her face. 'Why can't you swim?' He muttered something about baths and mountains, then started wading forwards. 'Where are you going now?'

'To meet the man who murdered my son.' Shana squealed as they almost tipped over, and Husker swung her around to his other shoulder so he could balance better against the wall. 'Terrano will be dead before my girls arrive. They will think their brother is still missing, and I can save their grief for a better time.'

'But... but Dren's a liar.' Shana let her child speak, knowing she'd spent too long in her core lately. 'He's lying about everything.'

'I know that. Mist is his way.'

'No, I mean, he's really lying. Lily and Rose are going to get there first. He said they wouldn't, but they will.' Husker grumbled at this, and started to move faster. Water flew around his shins as he forged a path through the shallows. 'And Lark's not dead,' Shana blurted out. 'Or at least not really. Terrano uses spirits to bring people back to life, and so he'd have done that to Lark, too. Dren says he's bait. Dren thinks—' Groaning inwardly, Shana wrenched back control from her child. But it was too late. Husker's agitation was growing. His shoulders were hardening, his skin hot to touch. 'I shouldn't have said that,' she said, keeping the girl pushed down. 'The thing you should know about Doth Agren is—'

'I will kill them both. One is a liar, the other a thief.' A snort rattled through his nostrils. 'Between them they had me convinced I would never meet my son again.'

'I don't know why they're so mean to you.' Shana gave him a hug and a squeeze. It always felt odd pretending to be a child, rather than letting her actual child do it. 'Have you met Dren before?' She let him consider her words while her agile fingers worked.

'Not sure.'

'He says you have,' she said, withdrawing her hands from his neck and taking the sinkstone with it. The surge of guilt she felt at this betrayal was drawn away into the cold, pulsing stone. 'He said you met when your wife died.'

Husker grunted, unaware of her theft. It was hard for a dull to follow any feaster's movements, and she was Shana. Even her child-self had been a pickpocket. 'You know, I can barely remember that day. Everything is scattered. But I've got enough memories left over to know that bastard's story is full of holes. He was the one who woke me up, I remember that. They believed him, and blamed me for everything.'

'But why–'

'My wife was dead at my side.'

'He killed her?' Shana struggled to keep her years. Her child wanted to snivel, confess, hand back the pretty stone. A failed thief right to the end. At this rate she'd have to spend weeks letting her run things, or that side of her would weaken and shrivel.

'The more I learn of him, the more it fits.'

'Could you hurt him a bit, instead of killing him?' One last chance, if Husker would listen. 'I can help! We need one of the hollow-souls alive, though. They eat the bad spirits blown here by the Split. His brother is worse.'

'We can figure it out. Trust in the Earth, little feaster.' He smiled up at her, filling the cracks of his teeth with blood. 'Before you can plant a crop, you must first till the soil. I will kill them both.'

Shana combed sadly at his thin strands of hair, parting it back the way he kept it. She let a sliver of her girl-self through to weep silently over his head. 'You may find that hard,' she said, pocketing the sinkstone.

Blacksand

S hade enveloped the cart, waking Lily from her doze. An armed patrol was thumping past, and crowding everyone else up against the base of a cliff. 'What's going on?' she protested, rubbing her eyes. It looked like they were queuing to enter the city. And it looked like the Roaming Watch had decided queues were for other people.

Granny pushed Lily off her shoulder. She waved a scabbed hand at the watch riders. 'Always in the way, they are.' Few of the them spared the cart a second glance, despite Rose menacing them with bloodshot eyes and a tightly-gripped quarterstaff. One of the Waywards gentlemen tipped his hat, and Granny slapped his knee. 'Don't you make them welcome, you. Bad news when the Watch show up. They bring it or make it.'

Lily discretely wiped her chin and tried to recover a bit of decorum. Saarban was a mountain city, and its gatehouse sat across a cliff breach hewn open by some god's drunken axe-blow, shamefully mended the next day with stone blocks as large as houses. The formidable size of these defences made them more ornate than practical. After all, Saarban was made famous by a merchant king; he was not prone to turning people away, and his death seemed to have changed little in that regard. Everyone in the queue had retained their good mood, despite the crush. They were dressed in bright colours and exchanging loud greetings, waving hands at each other over the noisy crowd.

'So these are the people that keep Saarban looking pretty from our side of the Split?' said Lily, watching ash-smeared men and women haul wood up to the cliff braziers. 'They look exhausted.'

'Need a lot of wood to keep those beacons fed.' Granny scratched at her wrist. 'Spend most of their time on the stairs. Got nice legs, their men do.' She cackled.

'What a waste of time.' Lily nudged Rose. 'City of Water and Light, sister. You're missing it. Stop gawping at the soldiers.'

Rose glared at a loitering rider. He snorted and gave her a wink, then kicked his horse on to push through the crowd. The Roaming Watch rode without formation, but not without order. His mount fearlessly skirted a rocky slope before joining a long file up and over the gatehouse bridge. A deep-throated horn soon had them riding on and falling back into distinct groups, and locals rushed down the stairs, missing their chance to tempt the disinterested riders with water and cakes.

'Filthy lot, aren't they?' Lily said. She turned around to watch their receding, disappointed faces. 'Given they live next to a river.'

Granny snorted and shook her head. She was binding up the lower part of her face in a wrap of cloth. 'Need to get into the city, they do. Can't wash out here.'

The stink of the river proved Granny's point. Men with poles were leaning out from the bridge to poke at blocked sewage, uncovering more stench with each thrust. Rose's face screwed up as she tried to endure it, but then she wilted forwards and retched quietly over the side. One of the Waywards gentlemen patted her on the back in sympathy. His mouth and nose was covered by a damp handkerchief.

A watch rider tapped on the cart. 'Want one?' Lily grabbed the scented rag he was holding out and mumbled belated thanks. He gave her a tight-lipped smile. 'My pleasure. Hope you like oranges.' The watchman touched a small pair of tinted spectacles as he surveyed the cart. 'It's oranges or sun-boiled shit until we pass the gatehouse.'

Lily bunched up the rag around her nose, trying to not let it touch her lips. 'You must really hate oranges.'

'Ah. I was born on these stairs, the smell is something I miss.' He briefly removed a straw hat to wipe his forehead. Unlike the other riders, his armour clattered from the sides of his saddle, and he rode topless in the warmth of a scrubs sunrise. He splashed scent on another wad of cloth. 'Does your sister want one?'

Rose snatched it off him. 'What makes you think this runt's my sister?'

'I've got one myself,' he said, wiping scent from his fingers. 'Sat across from her like that too many times to count. It's a comfortable sort of hate, that's what gives the game away.'

'Hate's a strong word,' said Rose, flushing a little. She was folding up the cloth into a neat square.

'As you say.' He adjusted his hat. 'So, Northers, why are you travelling to Saarban?'

'We're looking for our brother.'

'Run away, has he? My sister did that, too.'

'Kidnapped,' Lily said, eyeing the spears and horses marching past. 'Perhaps the Roaming Watch would take an interest?'

'You know us,' he said, scratching a muscled torso that was impressive for his age. 'We're mostly here to keep things ticking over. Keep things civil for the cities and earn our tributes. But maybe. Got a name for this kidnapper?'

She shrugged. 'That's about all we've got. He's called Terrano.'

The man frowned and swore softly, fidgeting with his keys. 'Hells. Really?' Grumbling to himself, he snapped his fingers at the two nearest watchmen. They pulled their horses smartly about and blocked the way forwards. 'Get off, then, please.'

Granny sniggered as Lily got a prod with a spear. The two Waywards gentlemen glanced at each other in confusion, so the old woman translated something complicated in their guttural language. They turned admonishing looks on Lily. One of them muttered a halting curse in Seatongue.

'Well, same to you too,' said Lily, sniffing. 'Some hospitality we've received down here, isn't it, Rose? Stop waving that stick around, please. These men have bigger ones and theirs have points on the end. That's it, off you get.' She coaxed her wild-eyed sister off first, tossing her nose rag to Granny. 'All yours, Granny dearest.'

The topless watchman loomed over them. His mount snuffled as he brought it about, looking for someone in the crowd. 'Examine the others,' he said, gesturing curtly to the watchman holding their carthorse. 'Let these others go if they're not infected. But not into the city.' Granny hissed, suddenly not finding things so funny. 'Your friend can take these two girls to the quartermiss for safekeeping. I'm riding slowly' – he emphasised the word – 'to get the watchboss. Very slowly, on account of my age. See to it that you're faster than me.'

'Sere.' The watchman holding the cart reigns nodded. The other tapped his forehead in the barest of salutes.

Shaking his head at Lily, the topless watchman trotted away towards the city gates. The cart was towed back the way they'd come, and the two Waywards gentlemen started gabbling frantically and shouting at Granny. One of them hit her with his hat, which she grabbed and threw away into the crowd.

'Northers.' The remaining watchman banged his spear against the dirt. He'd crossed to the far side of the road. 'Over here, out of the way.'

'Quite the force you're riding with,' said Lily, as more of his sullen comrades rode past. 'Very martial. Taking a holiday in the city? Or has Saarban not paid her taxes?'

'They've paid. That's why we're here,' he said, catching a slumped rider's attention and exchanging a forehead tap. Watchmen took pride in looking scruffy. A straggly beard was as mandatory as the burgundy robes, with only a glimpse of chainmail flashing underneath loose hair and cloth. Neatness was for warriors with something to prove.

Their watchmen stepped forward to meet an approaching carriage. It was drawn by four of the wolfish half-breeds that Lily and Rose had ridden to Krans, but whereas their beast had been ungainly and lumpy, these were sleek and quick-footed, shaking out manes and bushy, lupine tails. Their sultry black skin matched that of the elegant woman lounging across the driving seat, who was draped in as much cloth and hair as her male peers. She'd grown a fearsome mass of curls, shaved off on one side and left wild on the other, and when she spotted Lily, the woman's painted lips drew back in a smile.

'Quartermiss,' called their watchman, raising his hand. The carriage veered towards them, clattering to a halt. Lily watched in mild horror as Rose reached out a tentative hand to touch the mane of the nearest horsewolf, undaunted by its flare of gums and sharp teeth.

'What do you have here?' The quartermiss rolled over and lay on her stomach, looking down at Lily. Her bare feet curled up behind her. 'What treats have you brought me?'

'Two girls with the potential to be prisoners. Our soft-hearted treasurer would prefer them to be guests.'

'Why would he want that?' She cocked her head, her fingers playing along the shaved side. 'Are they to be his whores?'

The watchman smirked. 'No. But they mentioned our man by name.'

'Then they know something, and they are prisoners. To be interrogated.' She laughed, eyes twinkling, and rolled away out of sight.

There was a commotion further up the path. Four riders were pushing back against the crowd, with the topless man trailing behind and complaining at the pace. The man leading the group was a thin-faced southerner with long, gangly arms which dangled at his side. He guided his mount with knees and clicks of the tongue, head tilting curiously as he caught sight of Lily.

'I am only teasing, girls.' The quartermiss appeared again, this time holding an ornate key. She slipped from her seat and unlocked the carriage door, banging on the frame to loosen it up. 'Climb in quickly. You will prefer my hospitality, however humble, to that of the man approaching.'

Lily was already scrambling inside. If that was the watchboss, he reminded her of the backstreet merchants that ran the Low Ends – vicious, calculating bastards that sized you up and sold you in a single scathing look. None of them dared touch a minister's daughter, but she'd often seen them mulling over the risks. 'Rose,' she hissed, holding out her hand. 'Come on.' As prisons went, Lily thought it seemed pretty comfortable. It was dark and smelt of grease, but it had an unmade bed and a mirror instead of chains and drunks – better than Branera's night waggon. But Rose's face still twitched when she peered inside, perhaps not blessed with as many life experiences with which to measure this one.

The quartermiss moved forwards to meet the riders. 'Road greetings,' she said, raising her chin. Unfurled from her seat she stood at least as tall as Rose, and held herself with the loose authority of someone who didn't care for anyone else's. 'Why are you here, Watchboss? You know I do not care for you.'

'Them.' The watchboss remained mounted, leaning over his saddle and pointing. 'Give me them.'

'Give?' She laughed. 'So, you accept they are mine. They are in my carriage, after all.'

'That one isn't.'

The watchboss spoke haltingly, with an accent Lily couldn't quite place, and he was staring at Rose with open-mouthed hunger. The quartermiss turned, wincing with displeasure. She claimed Rose's staff with a few quick prods. 'In there, my darling.' She tossed it into the carriage, giving Rose a firm push after it. 'Go play in there.'

'Give them,' the watchboss said, pointing and snapping his fingers. 'Give, give, give.'

The topless man rode forwards, his face studiously blank. 'Honoured quartermiss, our watchboss formally requests that you hand these Northers over for questioning. We need fresh intelligence on our quarry.'

'Torture,' the watchboss said, clicking his tongue and advancing his horse. 'Need to know about hollow man. They know about hollow man.'

The quartermiss cocked her head. 'But they're mine, aren't they? I have them in my home, and I don't torture guests.' She clapped her hands twice. A pair of boys in burgundy robes appeared on the roof of her coach. 'Drive us on, little ones.' She put a foot up into the carriage. 'I shall interview our guests in my own manner. Bring a scribe to our evening meal, if it pleases you, and you will have my account.' The quartermiss swept inside and shut the door, locking it with a satisfying clunk of her key. The carriage rumbled into motion. 'Road greetings, my darlings,' she said in a whisper. It was almost pitch black, but Lily could make out the shape of her hands as she touched their cheeks. 'What do you think of my home?'

'It's dark,' said Rose hoarsely. 'Don't you have anywhere to sit?'

Chuckling, the quartermiss took a stool from the corner. She handed it to Rose and sat elegantly on the bed. 'And you, sister-second, would you like to sit here?' She patted the covers.

'I'm fine.' Lily stuck near the crack of light around the door. 'Is there no lantern we could use?'

'There will be no flames or light in my home. Are you sure you are comfortable there on the floor?' Lily nodded. 'Very well. Now, guests, may I have your names?'

'Guests, huh?' Lily scoffed at her. 'Fine. I'm Lily Kale-Tollworth, and that woman snoring against the wall is my sister Rose.'

'Perhaps' – the quartermiss helped a mumbling Rose onto the bed and took the stool for herself – 'we should swap. That's better. Rest now, darling.' Her hand lingered for a second on Rose's forehead, then she turned to Lily. 'You will stay awake, I hope? The watchboss holds no sway over me, but we abide by the same rules. This patrol must hear what you know of Terrano, one way or another. His way, or my way.'

'Torture now or torture later, right?' Lily thought back to the naked aggression of the watchboss. He seemed surrounded by people put there to keep him on a leash. 'I doubt that's a man who gives up once he's set out his peeling knives. In what way would you be able to refuse him that?'

'In the Roaming Watch way. I am Thora Onan. As a quartermiss, I decide when to hand out the worst weapons we have hidden away. I am only attached to his patrol for this task, thus he holds no sway over me, and I a lot over him.' There was a puff of scent as Thora splashed a vial over her hands. Saarban's river stench was still creeping in through the door, and it mingled with the smell of oil and lavender. 'The Watch, as you have seen us before, are just local patrols – gathered from the villages and trained in our ways. They send word south if there is trouble they cannot handle, and if the occasion deserves it, we send a quartermiss. Each of us has his or her own gift to lend, each offers weapons unlike those any city can harness. The threat of these weapons, and our prowess in using them, is how we earn the tribute you send us.'

'Tribute? Depends on how you see it, I guess. It's obvious how little choice we have but to pay.'

'That is, of course, true.' Thora laughed, slapping scent on her hands.

'So, what weapons are you bringing to Saarban?' Lily looked around the darkened carriage. 'I've always said the Watch are obsessed with new ways of cutting people open. This should be a story worth telling.'

Thora didn't laugh this time. It was too dark to see if she was smiling. 'Hold out your palm.'

Lily hesitated for a moment, and stuck out her hand. 'What for?'

'You are brave, my darling, so brave.' Thora held her wrist and drew it close, rubbing scent over her palm. She made another gesture, and something tickled Lily's skin.

'What's that?' said Lily, keeping her hand steady. 'It's like sand.' Her eyes were still adjusting, but she could see Thora pouring from a pouch.

'Yes, like sand. Blacksand. Without protective oil, it burns your skin. Burns it like fire.' With a flick she let some scatter over Lily's arm, making her gasp at the patter of stinging grains. Thora's grip on her wrist was like a vice. 'And when blacksand touches fire, it explodes – corrupting all it touches. Smell it, Lily darling. Not too close, only a whiff.'

'Urgh.' She crinkled up her nose. 'Rotten eggs.'

'It is the smell of death,' Thora said, still gripping Lily's wrist. 'It is worth knowing this smell.' She cupped Lily's hand and twisted it over the pouch, so the blacksand fell back in. 'And how do you harness death?' She flicked open the cupboard beside her bed. Inside were no clothes or belongings, but rows of weapons, greased and wrapped in cloth. The exposed metal shone with a faint, greenish aura.

'Rifles.' Lily touched one. 'Though not exactly like the pictures.'

'You had a tutor, I see,' Thora said, chuckling. The cupboard was closed with a click. 'And one that did not neglect the Northland's past.'

'I only remember the horrible bits.'

'You have it backwards, then. People prefer to forget such weaponry exists.' Thora stroked the rifle cupboard with her fingertips. 'They wanted these secrets lost.'

'Conveniently, it is you who enforce that.'

'There are laws, yes.'

'Your laws. Not that we ever produced anything as exotic as this.'

Thora was still staring at the cupboard. 'Exotic, my darling? How apt – like a strange animal brought home from far away. Yes, they wanted these secrets caged. Then brought out. Then caged again, never sure whether such things are better lost or preserved. I am the one who takes the choice from them. They must convince me before death is harnessed and handed out.'

'And how did they do it this time?'

Thora hummed, pursing her lips as she considered this. 'I am not yet convinced, pretty darling. But our spies say the hollow-soul we hunt has broken his chains. The court of your last king created him to hunt spirits, but he now hunts people and threatens our honour.' She shook her head. 'Do not laugh at me, Lily Kale-Tollworth. Perhaps you would prefer I say reputation? Fine. Yet it remains true that one of our patrols has been corrupted by this hollow-soul. He had them murdered, and in death they now follow his orders. They sent me to correct this.' She rubbed her scented hands over face and neck, bathing in the odd smell. 'Your turn, my darling. What do you know of this hollow-soul? This necromancer?'

'Not much,' said Lily, edging back against the door. Thora was leaning in, close and fragrant. Rotten eggs lingered somewhere beyond the flowers. 'He's kidnapped my brother, that's all. We've travelled from Branera to free him.'

'I will need more than that, pretty one,' said Thora. Her hands were planted either side of Lily's lap. Their cheeks brushed as she whispered in her ear. 'The watchboss needs information. He has a hunger for it.'

'Well.' Lily's heart raced. 'Terrano's brother was our guide, he's mixed up in this somehow. He delivered Lark's ransom letter to us.'

'Ah, the runt.' She sat back, appeased for the moment. 'He never had the strength of his brother. We believe he is still bound by the palace, and not a danger to the city. Do you know where he is?'

'Back in Krans? I don't know.' Lily felt a weight settle over her again. One she'd tried to leave behind in that muddy shithole. 'I guess he's coming here.'

'You are certain of that?'

'He's been dogging us for too long to stop now. He's obsessed with us in some way or another, I don't trust him to stay away. Or at all, really.'

'He is a devious creature,' agreed Thora. 'I wish I had never invited him into my bed.'

Lily clenched her teeth. 'He really makes a name for himself in that regard. So, these dead men that Terrano's resurrected, they're hiding in Saarban and killing people for him?'

'Dead men,' Thora scoffed. 'More than dead men. Dead watchmen. Even the patrols know too much of our ways to be left in the hands of another. These creatures lack a will of their own, yet others will see them as members of our order.' She took a pistol from her robes and sniffed the barrel. 'The city faces a man who communes with death, so they sent for one who harnesses it. I shall decide if they are worthy of my blacksand.'

Fine Ladies

A hand shook Rose awake.

'Mmmm, get off,' she grumbled, turning over with enough frustration to knock the wall. Not her bed, then.

'Pretty darling,' a woman's voice said, chuckling. 'Time to get up. Quickly now, before the watchboss returns from his prowling. You have made it safely to Saarban.'

Rose peeled open her eyes. She was in a prison, or perhaps a coach, with bright daylight and the noise of a bustling city coming from the door. A boy in Watch robes patiently held it open. 'Urgh.' She dragged fingers through her hair, wincing at the knots. 'Have I been drinking?'

'No, sleeping. Do you do much of that?' The woman urged her to stand, pushing her towards the door. 'Hurry now.' The world spun as Rose was herded out into an alley. Saarban's air was heavy with moisture and boiled by a lazy sun, which swam high over a slope of whitewashed buildings. Every window in the street was shuttered, presumably to keep out the racket of a market at its far end. Lily hovered its edge. She was leaning out to take it all in, her head moving in excited, birdlike leaps.

There was a thump as the woman threw a pack out of the carriage. A clatter as a quarterstaff followed it. 'What's that?' Rose asked, still feeling groggy.

'Your weapon.' The woman smiled. She reached down and touched Rose's cheek. 'Are you also brave, darling? Like your sister? I pray you have the courage to do something brave together. Your brother may need it.' She clapped her hands twice. 'Boys.' Two robed children flew out from under the coach wheels and scrambled up to take the reins. Rose wrinkled her nose as they trundled off, trying to rub the smell of rotten eggs from her cheek.

'Hey!' Lily was waving to her. 'Over here.'

Rose drank a flask of Dren's tonic while pretending to look around. She furtively wiped her lips. 'Wha... where are we, Lils?' Her gums had gone numb again. But it eased her headache enough to cope with this market.

'Saarban, you dummy. Didn't Thora tell you?' Lily's face was full of mischief, predictably coming alive at the sound of hawkers, goats and butchers.

'And who might Thora be?'

'Hmm? Oh, the woman who just threw you out of her coach.' Lily's eyes were still on the market. 'I told her about Lark. Nicest person we've met for weeks – she even let you sleep in her bed for a while.'

'This place reeks,' said Rose, rubbing her nose. 'No doubt you'll be making me bathe here, too? I'm not sure I'd come out any cleaner.'

She snorted with laughter. 'Agreed. Come on, we've been waiting.'

'Who?'

'Prepare yourself, sister dearest.' Lily placed a dainty hand on her chest. 'For we have a gentleman escort.' Grabbing Rose's arm, she grinned and reversed them into the marketplace. It was a dirty, impatient sort of place. Workshops disgorged their wares directly onto ramshackle stalls, and no one spoke, they only yelled – screaming about their fish or books or reasonably priced jars. A filthy canal struggled down from the upper city to slice the market in two. Any choke points, such as foot bridges over this dubious water, were staked out by teams of formidably overweight women, who thrust out arms of jewellery and dazzling beads as Rose pushed past.

'May I introduce our guide,' said Lily, over the din. She pulled over a sour-faced man who was buttoned up in a black jacket, one that pinched around his neck but flapped loose at the sleeves. 'His name's Hardus.' She wove her arm through his and smiled. 'He says that fine women like us should take lodgings higher up in the city. Thora suggested that we ask after Lark up there.'

Their guide's sullen eyes slunk away when Rose tried to meet them. He couldn't contain his distaste for everything around him, though his scruffy hair and creased looks hardly put him in any place to comment. 'He thinks we're fine women?' Rose smoothed down her dirty apron.

Lily huffed. 'Well some of us are. Sometimes.'

'We should climb,' said Hardus, in a dour voice that was as slovenly as his appearance. He could barely be bothered to move his lips. 'It smells down here.'

Hardus showed them a staircase by the canal, pushing market boys out of the way when Rose found herself stranded. Lily hung off his arm as he trudged upwards, alternately pressing him with questions or being dragged on when she stopped to gawk. Workers wore white shirts loose against the sun. Glass bracelets caught and threw fragments of sunlight. On one roof terrace, men in colourful robes were busy getting in everyone's way, dodging loose tarpaulin as they tested benches and kept up their animated discussion.

'Shameless,' muttered Hardus, glowering at a crew winching wine barrels up onto a roof. He ran a finger around his collar, briefly revealing the tips of some southlander tattoos. 'Frivolity in the Wet Rings. Didn't think I'd live to see it.'

'Is that where we are?' Lily turned back to admire the slope of buildings below them. Without a hangover to curb it, her enthusiasm was relentless. 'What an odd name. Is it something to do with that canal?'

'Yes. The Rings are washed each year to clean out the filth.' Hardus looked around and sniffed. 'You've arrived on flood night. These social climbers are mimicking our celebration of it, calling it a festival.'

'Why were we in that woman's carriage?' asked Rose, tapping Lily on the shoulder.

Lily allowed herself to be dragged on by Hardus, but turned around to pass on a look. 'You should try sleeping more. Thora was trying to stop us getting tortured. She's a big deal in the Roaming Watch, a sort of fixer they send in when things go bad—'

'Be quiet, please,' snapped Hardus.

Lily rolled her eyes. 'Apparently it's a bad sign when someone like her turns up, according to Hardus here. Not that I've seen anything out of the ordinary.' She prodded their guide in the ribs. 'And you, remember that we're fine ladies. We're paying you in jewels, so keep a civil tongue.'

He hissed, his head bobbing back and forth as he climbed. Not unlike the birds pecking around his feet. 'Enough! The peasants down here would kill for a few coins, let alone jewels—'

'Why don't we ride that up?' Lily gasped. 'Can we? Look, Rose!'

It seemed the chains over the canal weren't just for hanging up awning. A caged enclosure was being hauled up from further down the slope, and its haughty passengers were pressed together on benches, clutching scent cloths to their mouths and ignoring a gaggle of traders running at their side. A veiled lady at the back reached through the railings and exchanged a few coins for a small bag, scandalising those sitting around her.

'Yes!' Hardus gasped with relief. 'At last.' He ran to a platform and furiously waved a small handkerchief. A bored-looking attendant inside the enclosure tugged on a smaller chain, and they clunked, swayed and slowed to a halt. City guards stepped smartly forwards to position some steps, one of them barking orders and holding back the increasingly desperate traders.

'How marvellous,' said Lily, holding up her skirt hem as she climbed on board. She beamed at the garishly dressed ladies inside, her boots clopping loudly on the plank floor. It creaked when Rose ducked in, earning her some stares. This was like the worst bits of Branera. Women kept to one end, men the other. Except for those who'd brought a husband or wife, where the couple suffered to meet in the middle and look uncomfortable.

Hardus found some empty seats and stuck to his side of the line, wearing a warm, if greasy, smile. 'There we go,' he said, settling in. He unbuttoned his collar. 'There we go.'

'Seen any other Northers lately, dear Hardus?' Lily was leaning out through the railings, screwing up her nose and watching the canal swirl below them. 'Our brother arrived recently. In strange company, too. Which is why the you-know-what-watch was sent for.'

'We are still in the Wet Rings, Miss Tollworth. Hardly a place to discuss—'

'Kale-Tollworth, if you please, or just Kale if you don't. So, what can we talk about, then? What's that place down there?'

'The Smoke District,' he said, flushing at her interruptions. 'It's not a place we concern ourselves with.' In Rose's opinion, it seemed worthy of concern. After terrorising the market, the canal fell down to a pit of factories, which bristled with chimney tents the same way Branera's bakery stacks did. Smog gathered in this lower tier, creeping up to tickle the sandals of any unfortunate vendor forced to the market's lowest point. The canal plunged bravely down through this haze. Its tormented water was repeatedly snatched away to pummel against wheels, or be thrown back and forth from pipes and drains.

'Weren't you down there when Thora grabbed you?' Lily asked Hardus, brimming with innocence.

'You are mistaken.' His jaw clenched. He tapped the handrail and raised his voice. 'The air before flood night is so foul. Have you noticed,

Northers? We've a saying in Saarban – water reflects intent. If it brings tears to your eyes, so will those who drink it.' Either reassured by this pantomime, or tiring of it, the other passengers resumed their low conversations. Hardus trailed off into a mumble. 'Keep that in mind.'

Someone tipped the attendant a coin. He pulled twice on the chain and they lurched forwards, and even Rose's greasy hair found the life to fly around her, flicking up in the faces of the women sat behind. They soon grew tired of huffing and tapping on her shoulder, but the enclosure slowed anyway when they passed up through finer streets. Couples strolled under pastel canopies. Softly-spoken merchants waved manicured hands over selected wares. Pairs of servants idled with buckets and mops, ready for the gusts of smog which stained everything they touched – yet there was an edge to the calm here. A silk merchant called too loudly over the crowd. He drew the attention of a city guard, and a whisper in his ear had him packing up his stall, pale-faced and shaking.

'Funny place this, isn't it?' said Lily. She was oblivious to the looks they were getting. Or enjoying them. 'Prettier than Branera, though.'

'I don't like it,' said Rose stubbornly.

Lily looked amused. 'You don't?'

'I know you do already. But the more we climb, the more I hate it. It's like they shove all the misery and dirt downhill. Even the mudders in Branera had a better life than that.'

'Since when did you go down to the mud?' Lily tapped Hardus on the shoulder, who was talking with another man mired at the gender divide. 'Are we almost at your lodgings? It's very fancy up here, I must admit.'

He smiled, unbuttoning more of his collar and tilting his chin to catch the breeze of their passage. 'Oh, you've seen nothing yet. The Wet Rings aren't even part of the city.' He pointed upwards to an approaching cliff and waterfall. Some buildings were visible through the misty spray. 'Highwall is where the true Saarbanites live.'

Their enclosure slowed to a crawl as it strove to meet the height of the cliff. The chain passed through towers and church spires, until they hit some cogs and started to rise directly upwards. Rose grimaced and moved away from the increasingly sickening drop, squeezing a space between two men when none of the women would move. One of them froze up; he kept his hands on his lap and withered under the expression on a thin-faced woman opposite. Rose's other neighbour pulled a grim face. He nodded at the drop, and she rolled her eyes in agreement, but her attempts at conversation were drowned out by the approaching waterfall.

She managed to snatch a quick look down. Pink and red tiles formed a spiral mosaic that spread out from the basin, sending warm colours down the canal. Some ancient architect had earned a smug moment. That spiral was a sigil for Godmist – water temples were always hidden in plain sight. The Wet Rings were a sloped half-wheel that an army of stoneworkers had chiselled out of Highwall's cliff, leaving two curved arms as a city wall. Four waterfalls fell into the Rings and filled the spokes of the wheel, while rich idiots did their part and built glorious mansions to adorn the highest points. Their towers strained up towards Highwall, their gardens pushed away rivals with hedges and grass. The lower city was a water decoration with people living in it.

The enclosure jerked sideways, hitting another junction of chain and wood. Rose gripped the bench, shivering as colder air found damp patches on her neck. Barefoot workers were swarming over the approaching clifftop and making ready for their arrival. They swung ropes to each other, shouting and curling their toes around treacherous rocks as they unhooked enclosures and threaded chains as thick as their arms. Rose's neighbour nudged her. He raised his finger in warning, and widened his eyes just as the cage was unbuckled and dropped a foot. Rose shrieked, gasping with laughter. The man winked, matching the sway of the enclosure while he collected belongings from under the bench.

'Make ready, please,' called an attendant.

'Be welcome, Northers,' said Hardus, who seemed more at ease. His grimace relaxed further as he held out a discrete hand. 'If you please.'

'What does he want now?' said Rose suspiciously.

'Paying,' said Lily, pointing at their bag. 'Give him one of those diamond chains so he can barter it for us.'

'I thought it wasn't safe to discuss such things?'

Hardus bowed. He clasped his hands together inside overlong sleeves. 'My lady, this is Highwall. If you think your wealth matters here, that is rather charming.'

Festive Gifts

Lily hugged her knees and watched the Wet Rings flood. It reminded her of the lake ceremonies back home, where children floated out candles for the many unnamed gods. Around dusk, she'd watched the canals swell. Streets turned into rivers, and the lower city rang out with distant cheers and drums. Flat roofs became islands where people could dance around their piled belongings – but not everyone was so fortunate. Possessions for Saarban's poorest were keepsakes they could carry in a cart, or things they replaced once a year. Waggons had worked all day to empty the most humble dwellings of furniture, burning it in bonfires or hauling it out to a tent city, which was stocked with enough meat and wine to forget this pointless sacrifice. Hardus had explained all this at great length, without offering any reason other than tradition.

She glanced over her shoulder at his roof terrace. String music and a dozen languages were still clashing as his guests toasted the view and their good fortune, their hands waving in the lantern-light to underline clumsy translations. Lily had excused herself from this noise to go hide among the chimney pots, pleading a headache. The maps in Branera didn't go much further than this, yet these people had travelled from all directions, riding or sailing for a year just to reach the festival. They hadn't heard of the Northlands, and thought it funny how much life clung to the barren shores of the Split.

'Shana?' Lily held up her candle, briefly illuminating the feaster's cheeky grin. She was fiddling with her toes and acting the child, rather than whatever older thing she was.

'Thought I'd see how you were getting on.'

'You came all the way from Krans? Just for that?'

'We took a shortcut. Dren's here, too, you know.' She cocked her head as Lily snorted. 'Don't care, huh? Well, guess who else. Go on, guess!'

'Lark, I hope. This is supposed to be a wayinn for foreigners, but no one's seen him. Or heard of Terrano.'

Shana flapped a hand. 'Oh, they wouldn't have. Terrano's a palace dog – he's rarely allowed out in the city.' She patted Lily's knee with gleeful excitement. 'Someone else! You were close when you guessed Lark.'

'Move over. You're spoiling the view.'

'How about your father?' she crowed. 'Mr Tollworth. What about that?'

Lily's heart wedged itself in her throat. 'What?'

'He's followed you from the Northlands. Can you believe it? Ever since he was released from the mountain. Now I know you don't like him, but he was telling me—'

'He's not with you, is he?' Lily's hands were trembling. She hid them under her armpits. 'You haven't led him here?'

'And should I not?' Shana snapped, some of her age showing. She clapped her hand to her mouth. 'Oh! Sorry. Sorry. I'm out of balance, ignore that.' She rolled onto her knees and took Lily's hand. 'I haven't brought him here, though I wanted to. He's a nice man really. I don't even think he killed your mother, not the way he tells it... no wait.' The feaster was a dead weight on her arm. 'He's sort of sad and I... I did something bad to him. And I want to make it up. He just wants to meet you.'

Lily shook her head. 'No.'

'But you got on so well before!' Shana tugged on her arm. 'The man on Rafe's balcony? That was him.'

The huge, pale figure loomed clearly in Lily's mind. That near-naked body. The way everything seemed small and fragile next to him. Those kind, almost disappointed eyes. 'Sod him. He's missed his chance.'

'He's shy!'

'He's a freak.'

'He can be both,' said Shana hotly. 'He's been stuck up a mountain his whole life. The poor man was following you and working up the courage to say hello. But when he heard Lark was in trouble, he made a deal with Dren to come help.'

'What sort of deal?'

Shana looked nervous. 'It's complicated.' She was rolling a glowing stone around her hand, gnawing at her lip. 'I mean he would have come anyway if he thought Lark was here, but Dren told him Lark was dead to trick him, and that was really horrid, so Husker wants to kill him, too. But we need someone to eat all the spirits when Terrano's dead, so I.... I helped Dren leash him.' Tears were creeping down Shana's face, picking up speed with her babbling. 'That's why you need to see him! He's going to die and he's come all this way, and it's my fault!'

'I didn't ask him to come, did I?'

'Oh.' Shana wiped her snotty face on a sleeve. 'I know. But Dren and your father really hate each other. I'm not even sure if they'll get Lark out of there. All those two are good for is causing chaos, not saving little boys.' She sniffed sadly. 'Much like me.'

'You know where Lark is.' Lily caught Shana's wrist. 'Why didn't you tell me that instead of blathering on? I've been looking for him all day.'

The feaster grinned and sprang to her feet. One of the table guests turned, startled by a blur that flashed past his chair. Lily followed at a slower pace, waving him back to his food, and leant against a chimney stack on the far side of the roof. Hardus' mansion was one of the tallest buildings in Highwall, yet it had nothing on the Palace of Sells. Shana was crouched on the lip of the roof and pointing up at it.

'In there.'

'Well, no wonder I didn't bloody find him. Hardus said it's forbidden for anyone to go in.'

'Nope, only the Scarlet Keep. And that's just a trick.' Shana's posture aged. She hunched over the lip of the roof and narrowed her eyes. 'That keep is left dark, but its courtiers still scurry around inside. City laws prohibit them leaving, but the king's servants were permitted to outlive that fool and tend the cogs of his city.' The roof lip crumbled under her hands. 'We do not care for them.'

'And Lark?' Lily stared breathlessly at the towering walls. Red vines cascaded over the ramparts, like jewels encrusting the ancient mass of stone. 'Do they have Lark in there?'

'Yes. He is part of Terrano's scheme in some way – perhaps simply to bait Dren into a rescue. The Scarlet Keep is full dead slaves, raised into Terrano's service and waiting to be unleashed on the city.' She glanced at Lily. 'There are a lot of them.'

A boisterous crowd had massed to hurl paint and insults at the palace gates. This was, apparently, part of the festival. A guard stood up to kick a burning effigy of King Garradus to one side, then went back to his stool.

'What are you thinking?' said Shana, cocking her head.

'Mostly that I don't trust Dren to get Lark out of there.'

The feaster sat herself up on the wall. 'So, if I help, would you go?'

'I'd go anyway, thank you very much.' That was stretching the truth, but with a feaster at her side surely nothing could stop her. She spotted something glowing between Shana's knuckles. 'What's that?'

Her fingers unfurled and light bloomed from her palm. 'My help.'

'Wait... what? You're not coming with me?'

'Don't be a sissy bitch.' Shana glared at her. She slipped off the wall and stamped her foot. 'They hate us in there. That palace is full with wards that would turn me inside out.' She pulled a face. 'Urgh. Even Dren will have to trick his way in to kill Terrano.'

'But what about the dead people?' Lily ran a hand through her hair in exasperation. 'I thought you'd be protecting me.'

'I am! Look. Listen, it's very simple.' Shana's eyes looked about as if taking inspiration. 'Terrano uses a spirit to bring people back to life, but he has to trap it in their body. He lures it in, and then he gets his magic, well its not really magic just a lot of practise, and then he...' Shana's hands mimed something, her little nose all wrinkled up. 'He sticks this thing into them and binds it, then sews that up with some more bindings because when the spirit realises there's no soul in there it will want to get out, and this sinkstone will mess all that up. Go on, take it!' A horrible weight of age washed over Shana's face, wrinkling her skin and sharpening her teeth. Lily's neck prickled as instincts older than she was screamed at her to run, to throw herself from the roof and take her chances with the drop. 'Feast on it,' Shana purred.

'Shana.' Lily found it hard to breathe. 'Do you take pleasure in scaring those weaker than yourself?'

The feaster quivered and blinked a few times, each one seeming to restore her youth. Her skin tightened as she blushed. 'Oh.' She shook her head. 'No.'

'Gods, you're ugly when you do that.'

'I can't help it! There's violence coming. My body's making itself ready.' Shana placed a hand over her heart. 'Feaster oath. Dead people can't touch you if you swallow this. Get your brother and hide somewhere safe, let us handle the rest.'

Lily shook her head, not quite sure what she was refusing. 'I–'

'Don't be such a wimp!' Shana scolded. 'I'm trying to help.' She struggled with her age again, scrunching up her little face until the wrinkles faded. 'Feasting's all about balance. The child part of me is crying right now, crying because of what I did to get this stone. Do me a favour and take it? I can't concentrate with it sucking half my thoughts away.'

Lily sighed. 'Will it hurt? Swallowing this?' Shana's face was damp with tears. She wiped them away and shook her head. 'Stop crying and give it to me, then.'

'He was so nice to me,' the feaster snivelled. A violinist started playing a jig, and the thumping noise of feet dancing on a table drowned out Shana's pitiful wail. 'And he didn't even get to meet you.'

'I said give it to me!' Lily snatched the stone, gasping when Shana scuttled forwards and buried her face in her skirt. 'Oh gods. Get off me, you little freak! What–' A scream cut through the night. The musician cursed as he missed his note, bow screeching savagely over the strings, but he still held up his hands in disbelief as his audience abandoned him in a clatter of seats and cutlery. Grudgingly, with his violin and bow dangling from his hands, he wandered over to join them at the roof edge. Everyone was pointing at the street below, clutching each other and gabbling in different languages.

Shana pulled back, tapping Lily's hand. 'Eat that, with my blessing.' There was something funny about the way she said that. 'If you keep it down, follow the palace walls until you find the Night Gate. You will know it by the smell. The wards there will not hurt you.'

'What's going on?' Lily turned around, trying to place distant cries and shouts of alarm. Down in the Wet Rings, rooftop bonfires were being extinguished one by one. Burning buildings lit up in their stead.

Shana prowled the lip of the roof, sniffing. 'The Scarlet Keep has been opened.' Feasters started climbing up onto the roof, or creeping out from between chimney stacks, or landing with a thump as if the night itself had just tossed them down. Shana drew herself up and addressed her pack, raising a hand that had the weight of ritual behind it. She tore out ribbons from her hair. 'This is not a night for balance, sisters.' Dresses fell in a pile, until they were crouched in their undergowns and purring quietly. 'Where's Brenne?' Shana surveyed the pack, her eyes narrowing. 'We need her.'

'Too far gone,' one muttered. 'Bitch tasted meat.'

Another feaster hissed in agreement. Her cheek was covered in a nasty scab. 'Too wild for us. You talk to her.'

Shana snarled in frustration. She folded up her dress carefully and handed it to Lily. 'I won't want this back, but try and make me take it.' With a gasp, Shana's face twisted monstrously into age, far further than ever before. Her thin arms grew meagre, and she stumbled backwards, smashing through a chimney. She looked up at Lily from the rubble, teeth as sharp as a wildcat. 'Go, you fool,' she croaked. 'Find your brother.' Her head fell back. Then she was on her feet and stroking a girl's hair. Then raising a chin with a finger. Her eyes glinted as she turned them on Lily. 'Avoid us till sunrise.' She hissed, gesturing sharply at the other feasters. There was a scuttle of bare feet, and their pale gowns soared briefly before being lost in the night.

Lily let out her breath. 'Well, fuck.'

From this vantage point, Saarban didn't have much of a chance. Especially if every guard in Highwall had drunk as much as the one getting treated up against Hardus' gate. The city was as oblivious as he was – lost in a stupor of wine and excess, caught with its trousers down and goblet in hand. Drums and music filled the square outside the Palace of Sells. Dancers twirled between the light of coloured lanterns. A few streets away, a long table had been set up under a beautiful awning, and some of the diners were already slumped over their food. Dozens of them. As they were dragged off, one by one towards the palace, and as the remaining guests wiped their daggers and strolled to the next street banquet, laughing and dancing to blend in, Lily wondered why this all seemed so perfectly reasonable and fine. Flashes of terror lit her up like a distant storm, but something was draining it away.

She opened her palm and winced at the dazzling light. Just take it one step at a time, it seemed to say. Take it one step at a time.

Angel

'That all, bastard?' Husker gritted his teeth and pushed forwards into Dren's room. It was like someone was pouring hot sand around his ankles. 'I got this far. You must be worried.'

He waded on until the sand reached his belly, and fumbled for something to throw. A candlestick hit the latrine door with a clunk. A chair hit the wall beside it.

'Come out, little bastard,' he yelled, curses slurring over his lips like dribbled soup. The sand had reached his chin, tilting it up. 'Want to die with your arse out?' But behind the door he could sense Dren's fist curling up, tightening the leash and pouring on pain. Husker's guts crawled up his neck and boiled in his throat. He should've found that sodding sinkstone before trying this. 'Bastard,' he choked, before nausea and heat slammed him to the ground.

'Hush now, Tollworth.' The latrine door swung open. At least he wasn't taking a shit. 'I will be ready soon.' Dren finished washing his hair, rinsing it over a bucket with long twists of his hands. Without the dirty braids it was glossy and long, and all the feathers and charms were scattered around his toes, or left floating in the water. He flicked this mass of hair over one shoulder and padded past.

'A bit much?' he said, rubbing his face dry. Dren turned a critical eye over the garish robes he'd draped out over a chair. 'But then, these are poor clothes for Highwall. And you...' He crouched to inspect Husker, flipping him this way and that with a spinning hand. Godearth's angel moaned for help, trapped in a stain on Dren's palm. 'I am afraid you play the part well enough.'

Tossing the towel aside, Dren approached a full-length mirror with almost predatory lust. He shook his hair out and breathed on his palm, running it through his locks in a howling cloud of spirits and steam. Husker got a dose of it too, and he gritted his teeth as heat and finger-nails flooded down the leash. The bastard hummed tunelessly while he finished dressing – a bloody torture in itself – then spun and presented himself with a dramatic flourish. He raised an eyebrow over Husker's burnt and crusted skin. 'Ah.'

Husker coughed, air sticking in his boiled throat. 'Bastard.' He kept his watery eyes open with as much intensity as he could muster. 'You still look like shit.'

Dren sighed and crouched down. He dug a finger into one of Husker's sores and inspected the result. 'Pathetic. You are of no use to me like this.' He slapped his stained palm over Husker's heart, driving what felt like a steel spike through his ribs. Blood wheezed from Husker's lips like a sputtering fountain. And then... things felt different. Angel crawled through his flesh. It hissed, roaming his body as it closed scabs and sores. 'Try moving.'

Husker wiped drool from his lip. He raised a hand to crush Dren's throat. 'How about this—'

'*Manost,*' grated a voice in his head. *'Be cautious.'*

'—bastard. What the fuck?'

Angel's voice was like flint striking over his ears. *'The eater is a blight on these lands.'* It flowed into his arm and forced him to lower it. *'But dangerous. Our time will come.'*

'Do not take me for a fool,' Dren said, irritably. He batted Husker's conflicted hand away. 'You are still leashed, even if I have used a less punishing, and in many ways brilliant, paradigm.'

Husker gritted his teeth, fighting Angel for the gods-given right to choke this prick to death. 'I'll show you punishing.' His arm shook. 'If this sodding thing will let me.'

'That thing has more sense than you, it seems. Now, stand up and be quiet.'

Hidden hands ran over Husker's body. The leash hauled him up, bending his joints and straightening his spine. 'Pervert,' he growled. 'Stroke me all you want. When I—'

'Manost. I demand caution.'

'And fuck you, too.' Husker winced as Angel snarled at him in rubble and stones. 'Gods, you're a noisy bloody thing.'

'So it speaks to you, then?' Dren pulled Husker's chin down and looked him in the eye. 'Tell me, what do you think that is? Whisper it. With its gag removed, the spirit is free to feed on your words.'

'Angel,' Husker muttered.

The roaring in his head stopped. *'I am no angel.'* Calm and gravelly, coarse with wry humour.

'Incorrect,' snapped Dren. 'It is a spirit. A true Tar-Agran, and nothing so profane as the half-spawn that Terrano is spreading.' He circled Husker with trailing fingers, like he was searching some stitching or seam. 'This one was only a runt. I wove it through your corpse to save my life. Yet, you have bonded with it in ways I do not understand. In ways I loathe.' The fingers stopped, resting on Husker's lower back. 'My brother now wishes to do the same to a whole city. As you can see, the fat idiot tramples where I tiptoe.' The leash thumped Husker down onto one knee. His nostrils flared as Dren's elbow caught him a dizzying blow across the temple, and the bastard stepped in close, wrapping an arm tight around his neck.

'Perhaps you want death?' Dren whispered, squeezing. 'You could restrain the spirit. We could do it together.' Husker growled his answer, and the knotted cords of his neck pushed the bastard's grip apart. Dren pulled away, patting him on the shoulder. 'Something to think about. When Terrano has been dealt with, your purpose will be fulfilled.' His hand slid over Husker's collarbone and seized the rock pendant. 'At least we can dispense with this.' Dren shoved him down, or the leash did. Fucking puppetry, that's what this was. The bastard circled back into view, dangling his pendant by its broken chain. 'It is a delusion to think such strength comes from the gods. An annoying one, too.'

The leash relaxed around Husker's mouth. 'Liar,' he grunted. 'Mist is your way.'

'No, manost,' Angel grated in Husker's head. *'Truth.'*

'You always were stubborn.' Dren slapped him, and Husker's neck twisted an inch as it took the force of the blow. 'Was that what happened up on the mountain? Too stubborn to die and keep the runt trapped until I return? No one survives winter on the farms.' Dren gripped him by the shoulders and stood him up, his smile suddenly warm and inviting. 'What happened, my friend? You can tell me. Maybe there is another way out of this.'

'Godearth,' Husker muttered. 'Angel.'

'A mystery, then,' said Dren, his smile porcelain. He waved fingers around Husker's mouth, binding it shut with the leash. 'You feed the spirit with this nonsense. So, no more speaking.'

Husker fought to produce the tiniest of smirks. Too little, too late, bastard. He could feel Angel now. He'd named it. It was real and solid, and he let it ride his tongue. *'You are a fool, manost.'* Pebbles rattled as Angel laughed. *'But I accept your welcome.'*

'A second chance for us tonight, Tollworth.' Dren was testing the point on a cattle prod. 'We will finish the work I created you for.' He held the prod limply, eyes lost somewhere. 'And then we can discuss an end for you, too. Find you some peace.' A moment of silence. Dren dismissed it with a frown and strode out, clenching his fist to tug the leash along with him. Husker let his feet thump forwards a few paces, then threw himself against it with a strength he'd kept hidden. Stumble over a bed. Knock over a dresser. He staggered one final time and snatched up his pendant from where it had rolled into the dust.

'*Leave that foolish token,*' Angel hissed. '*You know the truth of things now. No god made us.*'

Angel may have ridden in his head for ten years, but it must have been blind or asleep for most of it. Husker let himself be pulled through the door, knocking down a shelf as he went. Dren watched him with raised eyebrows.

'Why fight it?' he said. 'No spirit can best me. You are as much spirit as man, what do you hope to achieve?'

~

Festival crowds filled the courtyard. Revellers parted, gasping at Husker's huge, steaming body. The cattle prod stabbed at him, a dull pricking that barely registered over his ice-flayed hide. It was the leash that moved him, the rest just theatre for the horrified crowd.

'Back! Get back,' Dren croaked, flinging out an arm when someone got too close. His voice was roughened by a bottle from his satchel, his skin darkened by some staining liquid. Long, unbound hair swung a curtain around his face, and he clutched rags to his nose. 'The creature is sedated. Take care not to touch it. Breathe not too deep!'

Husker stumbled forwards.

'*Manost, I will have the truth.*' Angel was wound around his knuckles, urging him to release the pendant. '*What use have you for this trinket? Why devote yourself to some god, now you know your powers were mine all along? Ours, all along?*' It crept away and curled up around his spine, reaching into his head. It hissed and dived in, skimming over the turbulent froth of his thoughts. Angel was a gull over a raging ocean, plucking words as they leapt from the surface.

'Not god,' Husker thought at it. *'Priest. Obeying priest.'*

'Priest?' It growled, tasting these ideas. The storm in his head was gathering strength. A strong wind gusted over the waves.

'Blind? Stupid?' he thought. *'Seen it. Were there.'*

Angel hissed at him, dodging a crashing wave. *'I was gagged. Asleep.'*

The sea vanished, replaced by cries and shouts from the crowd. A guard had caught Dren, wrenching his wrist until he fell to his knees. The bastard struggled to keep his disguise intact, but he was punched savagely in the face for his trouble. Blood splattered across the cobbles.

Angel climbed out of Husker's head, dripping from his thoughts. *'That rock reminds you of a man.'* Its claws pushed into his memories again, reading them like a seer fingering entrails. *'It was the priest you valued, not the god. Ritual, structure, reform.'*

Some old memories had been raked up. Starvation sent Husker a different way to the others, and he learnt the signs for when a prisoner would fall. They sung first – normal songs, and not so normal songs – then their tools would drop from their frozen fingers and they would roll slowly into the deep drifts. The cold crop would already be creeping over to envelope their latest victim, but the maddening howl they spread on the wind would quickly turn to indignant squeals. With the deadly roots busy, Husker's knife was free to hack at their fleshy, blood-swollen leaves. Prisoners were meant to starve. Meant to fall. Meant to feed the crop. The faces of those who did as they were told watched him as he chewed on the bitter leaves. Silent faces, cold and bloodless. Leather and bone in the snow.

'Give way! Give the man some space.'

The guards had been converted. Dren's hands were quick with his purse, and they were his for a time. Several of them held back the gaping crowd. Their leader stood below Husker, staring up into his face and clutching the coin Dren had given him. 'What do you call it?' he said, awestruck.

Dren coughed and spoke in his harshened voice, clutching a blooded rag to his nose. 'That is for the Palace to decide. It only looks like a man, that much I know.' Husker saw him throw a pinch of dust as he passed from shoulder to shoulder. 'The palace cages will hold it. Sere? Are you quite well? Gentlemen, some assistance!'

Guards hurried over and took their dizzy leader from him. 'What happened?' One of them forced his eyelids up to find fluttering pupils. 'What did it do?'

'I warned him not to get too close,' moaned Dren, wringing his hands. 'Sedative fumes still linger on its skin. I could not wash them off.'

They backed away after that. A runner brought news of riots and fire in the Wet Rings, and the guards hurried off to answer the alarm. Someone uncorked a fresh wine barrel, cheering the downfall of the dead king, and it was kicked away to roll over the cobbles. The crowd quickly dispersed, chanting songs and chasing a red stream with their goblets.

'My brother's assault has begun,' muttered Dren. The prod started up around Husker's back again, moving him towards the Palace of Sells. 'No doubt he will be directing matters from the safety of a kitchen some-where, stuffing his face while others bleed.'

'This place is death,' rattled Angel. It turned Husker's eyes upwards to take in the towering palace walls. Viscera-red vines tainted the ramparts. *'Something has been released here. Something old, something cold.'*

Husker ignored them both, lost in his storm of memories.

Mountain

The priest was wrapped in a sheet, stained red from where the iron snow had slashed through his meagre defence of cloth and skin. He huddled by a fire as if in prayer, but his eyes shone with a fervour that put the flames to shame. This was one of the worst ruins on the Mountain Head. No one else sheltered under the glowing symbols and stained-glass windows, each one smashed and showing only slices of their profane subjects.

Husker dumped firewood at his feet. 'Take it.'

The priest looked up. 'You don't need it?'

He shrugged. The man he'd taken it from didn't need it. The priest had snapped his arm earlier, and the wound putrefied from snow sickness. Husker had fed him to the cold crops, then fed himself.

'Don't need it,' he said, wiping blood from his chin. 'Don't care.'

'I can see that.'

'I want to know,' said Husker. He was getting cold, so he took the priest's blanket and wrapped it around his shoulders. The priest didn't blink, just watched with a frown.

'What do you want to know?' His teeth started to chatter.

'How.' Husker massaged his jaw. He didn't speak much these days. He thought a lot, but speaking was different. 'I want to know how.'

'How?' The priest rubbed his hands over the pathetic lick of flames. He bent so close he almost embraced them. 'You will have to be more specific than that.'

Husker growled and smashed his scrawny fist into the fire, knocking logs away. 'Tell me how!' Even forming these words opened a crack in his head. 'How to get down.' Why did he want to get down? He knew why, but he didn't want to talk about it. He didn't want to think about it. The crack of memories widened and tears stung his face, until Husker bowed his head over the remains of the fire. His hand rested in the ashes.

'You should stay here, my friend.' The priest sat back on his haunches, shivering like crazy. Snowflakes whipped through a crack in the ruins and sliced his cheek. 'You have a sentence to serve, blood on your hands.'

More blood every day; this place wasn't curing that. Some men had gone missing from the fields last week. Husker had found them last night, some dead, some almost. He'd offered them all to the crop anyway.

'Your hand...' The priest's eyes grew wide. His finger shook as he pointed, and Husker looked down at his palm. The blisters from the fire were already healing, melting back into his skin. He hadn't even noticed the moaning in his head. 'Earth save us.' The priest took Husker's hand and turned it over. 'This is a miracle.'

Husker snorted and pulled out his bootknife. He slammed it into his palm, barely missing the priest's thumb, then held the wound up and twisted the blade slowly as he drew it out. The priest grasped at the wound. Blood ran over his trembling fingers as he watched it heal. 'Does the snow sickness not infect it? A cut like this should be death.'

'A cut like this is nothing.' Husker wiped his knife and put it away.

'And what is it like?'

'Noisy.' Husker grunted. He tapped his head. 'Moaning.'

'An angel,' said the priest in wonder. His nails pressed in as he tested the skin.

Husker snarled and pulled his hand away. 'Tell me how to get down.' The dam in his head was broken, so he was ready for the pain. Tears froze on his cheeks, as the Mountain Head never did leave room for grief. 'I want to see my children.'

The priest watched him suffer, apparently without pity. 'But you are guilty. The Roaming Watch say you killed your wife.'

'Don't remember.' And he didn't. A few happy memories was all he had. They hurt too much for that story to fit. 'Wouldn't do it.'

The priest thought for a while. His lips had turned blue. 'I can show you the way down,' he said at last. 'But it will take ten years.'

Husker growled. 'Ten years? It took you ten years to climb up here?'

'No. A few days. Less if the Watch continue to hide from this storm. But would you really come down? Or would this blood-drinking thing you have become?' He started to gather up the scattered firewood, his hands shaking with cold. 'The monster can go down in a few hours, or the man can go down in ten years. Think on which your children would prefer, but you will need my help for either.'

Husker sat and thought. He hadn't let himself think for a while. Eventually, he handed the priest his blanket. 'Here.'

The priest smiled at him. 'My name is Young.' He had crooked teeth. 'What do they call you, friend? Do you have a profession? A home?'

'The Watch call me Tollworth. I've forgotten the rest.'

The priest handed him a rock pendant. 'Keep this, Tollworth. Follow me until you can follow yourself.' The moon framed itself in a window on the tainted ruins, and red light fell over his crooked grin. 'An angel resides in your twisted heart. I shall teach you of it, and you will be a man again.'

Corrupted

The Scarlet Keep was deserted. Lark had seen people singing and tying up lanterns out in the square, and all the men and women Terrano had gathered in the keep went out to join them. They were dressed in bright colours and laughing, handing out gifts as they spread out into the city. But they had knives strapped under their robes, so Lark thought this was probably just pretend.

A few of the older ones had stayed behind, and they were working hard to clean the dining hall. Lark scrambled over the rafters for a better view. The soup smelt really good! Every empty bowl had a spoon and a cup, and a weapon of some sort next to it, ready for people to come take a seat. Some children were the first to enter. They were being herded in by a rich couple, and they had the dazed look people got after waking up on a strange, bloodstained bed, with vague memories of being stabbed or drowned, and a terrible thirst for water. The youngest had woken up too early – Lark had been watching from under another bed – and the boy had screamed and screamed, cowering behind a pillow as the courtiers closed in on Terrano's crate with glowing stones. The spirits never wanted to go back in.

Lark watched as the boy sat down to eat his first dinner as a dead person. His hand kept shaking and spilling soup.

'Climb up. Kill him.'
'Kill her.'

Lark clenched his teeth. 'Shh!' He squeezed his arm, feeling his brood writhe and squirm. 'Please? Please be quiet.' They growled at him, trying to force his fingers away. 'I said be quiet!' His voice echoed around the rafters. The boy dropped his spoon and looked up in alarm, so Lark fed himself into a shadow. Perhaps his brood had a point? He hadn't been up to see Terrano for a while, and it was a nice climb to the top. Bread first, though. He slid down a tapestry of some men planting a flag on a hill, and one of the servers turned, frowning at the breath of sour air that marked Lark's passage. She turned again, puzzled by the smell still swirling around her. Crumbs pattered in the dead boy's soup as Lark scuttled along the rafters.

The rich couple were being sized up for their job. Everyone was going to have a job. Terrano had killed some watchmen, and their job was recruitment, and probably also fighting. They were all as big as Buller, but also creepy and unkind – give them a weapon and they sprang about like festival tumblers, sweating and swearing, pushing each other back and forth over the dusty floor of the drill room. The one below was the meanest. He dismissed the rich couple with a jerk of his head, and Lark could hear the tiny spirits mewling in them when they passed by. His were much louder, of course.

'Kill him.'

'Climb. Climb. Climb.'

'Shush,' hissed Lark, slapping at his mouth to push them away. 'I wish you'd just shush.' He worked his bruised jaw while they grumbled and fought for control of his tongue. He didn't enjoy these tussles, but it was better than locking them up in his head. They hated it up there. Lark had struggled to cope with their thrashing, unable to sleep as they buffeted his dreams with eerie images of a world beyond the sea, and shaped his tongue into the guttural sounds that fed them. Being sleepy made Lark cross with everyone, so now he chased them around his blackened veins, not letting them grow agitated in his head, or settle in the warm flow of his blood. Each evening he'd sit in the dark, hugging his knees and muttering to himself, and every spirit got a taste of his tongue, but no more. There were hundreds of new voices last night, which was a little worrying.

'Off we go,' he whispered. One of his hands refused to let go of the beam. He teased his fingers apart and splinters tumbled down into the room below. 'Everyone ready?' They moaned and screamed back at him, so he swung up into the veins of the Scarlet Keep.

Buller said the last king was a crazy bastard. He had a lot of spies, and each spyway was high enough for a man to run along at a stoop, wide enough for two to pass if they angled their shoulders. Lark had their draughty confines all to himself. He blurred along in a gale of spirits, letting them seep from his skin and roll as clouds at his side. Spotting a mark he'd left earlier, he leapt and let them buffet him upwards to catch the top rung of a ladder, flying up into a floor that was brighter than the others. Glowing moss sunk its roots through the stone, giving the passage a faint, sulphuric glow.

'Margot?' he said, dropping into his old room.

Crone looked up from her book. It still sounded funny to him, her real name. She liked to scrape it on the floor when they tried to talk in more than nods and wheezes. Sometimes she scraped out a letter taller than the others, or really carved a line in thick, but Lark had no idea what any of that meant.

'You've already looked through that one!' Lark dashed into the small library next door and returned with a stack of books, dropping one guiltily as his spirits crinkled the cover. He pushed the rest through the bars, keeping back so they didn't snap at his wrists. 'This big one looks good, there's pictures on every page. Did you like the last one?'

Crone wheezed and nodded.

'Good. And would you like to come out yet?' She recoiled in horror from his outstretched hand. Crone shivered, and crawled over to sit with her back against the wall moss. Lark slipped down to sit beside her, though he kept his distance from the blue-white bars. 'I would've died in there, Margot.' He was looking at the stinking grate in his cage. The tiny cot. 'I think it's only right I go up and kill him. Should I do it?' She looked up and bared her teeth. In Crone-speak this was a very strong yes. 'I will, then. I will.' Lark twiddled his thumbs. He hadn't thought to ask her this next thing. 'Is there someone else up there? Is there a woman up there?'

'Kill him.'

'Kill her.'

Lark bit down hard and growled to force some spirits from his mouth. 'My brood seem to think so.' Crone's lip curled in disgust. She grabbed her scraping rock and started to write her name with so much force the tip snapped off.

'Hey.' Buller was hovering by the door. Lark waved at him. He entered, glancing back down the corridor. 'You seen what's going on downstairs, boy?' Lark nodded. He couldn't talk because a spirit had his tongue in a knot. 'Terrano's sent them out. All of Saarban is going to pass through this keep by the end of the night, one way or another. That's what they say, anyway.' Buller spoke in a whisper, afraid Terrano would overhear and send his frost after him. 'So, I reckon tonight we can move, too. Clear out of here, what do you say?'

'Sure.' Lark looked up at him. 'Do you think I should kill him first?'

Buller looked uneasy, scratching the stubble on his chin. 'Tough to say. Could do.' He'd slipped further out of Terrano's grip than the others, but this was pushing his disloyalty hard. 'Could do.' He put down a plate of mutton and started to sort the softer bits out, chopping them up for Crone. 'And what about you, old girl? Who's going to feed you when I'm gone? You might have to come out of that cage.'

Crone growled. She'd finished scratching on the floor, and it seemed she did know at least one other word. 'Whore,' read Lark. 'He's up there with a whore?' Crone wheezed angrily, stabbing her fingers up at the ceiling. She pulled out a locket from her top, a tin heart with a folded-up sketch in it. 'Is that Terrano? He's so thin! Who's this?' Lark pointed at the woman with him. She was beautiful, in an unkempt, cheerful way, and she was resting her head on his shoulder. Long curls of hair fell over Terrano's shirt. Crone parted her lips in a moan that made no noise, and she seized her wig, tugging at its length and wheezing.

'It's you?' said Lark, in a moment of tragic insight. Crone threw the locket down and fell after it, smashing it over and over with her scraping rock. She dashed the pieces away and sulkily grabbed a handful of meat from Buller's plate. 'Oh, please don't cry. That was you, wasn't it? You and Terrano were married.'

She stopped crying and eating long enough to snort with laughter, and wobbled her hand in a sort of almost-there gesture. Crone brushed the last bits of locket under her cot and sniffed noisily, opening a new book. The odd angry tear dripped on its page.

'Well.' Lark thought this over. 'So he's left you for someone else. That's not very nice. Would you like me to kill her, too?'

Crone bared her teeth at him. Buller put a hand on Lark's shoulder and cleared his throat. 'No one said you've got to kill anyone, boy.' But his fingers were gripping him quite hard.

'Is that a yes or a no?' said Lark sadly.

'Kill her.'

'Climb up and kill him.'

Crone did one of her airless sighs, just an opening and closing of her lips. Buller moved to the door, beckoning for Lark to follow. 'After you've done... whatever it is you're up to.' His hands were clenching and unfurling. 'Meet me back here. I've found us a nice way out.'

'Will she be okay?' said Lark in a small voice. 'She seems so sad.'

'Listen, lad, that woman is tough as nails. Tougher than you and me – nothing meant by it, just facts. Womenfolk put up with a whole lot more than you or I do.' Lark met his eyes blankly, thinking of all the nights he'd woken up screaming in his cage, feeling knives and rope at his neck. He nodded. 'Beautiful girl she was too, from that drawing.' Buller tapped his lip. 'I can't put my word to it, but I'd swear there's a portrait of her hanging in my old lodgings. Whorehouse, you know how it is. The best beds in town, and those damn matrons like to make spare coin even if you're not putting it away. Anyway, there's a painting of a lass who set the whole thing up, smart as they come, and that would make our friend here a few hundred years old.' He glanced at her. 'But sacking up with someone like Terrano, who's to say what's normal there?'

Crone cocked her head, batting eyelids at Buller and letting out a sultry wheeze. He either didn't notice or ignored her, but Lark thought his cheeks had gone a bit red.

'You run along now.' Buller patted Lark's shoulder, sucking air through his teeth when a spirit bit him. 'Ah, shit on these things. First thing we do in the Wet Rings is find a tanner. I need gloves.'

'It's not as bad as it was!' protested Lark.

'No, it's not. Keep exercising them, boy. It's doing you good.' His eyes glazed over a bit, and his voice got all throaty. 'Go for a run upstairs if you want, there's still time.'

Lark slipped out of the room and ran up the central stairs. Only the Old Court dared climb this high, and since he'd killed a few of them they'd left him in peace. He hated them. He hated their knives and ropes and tinny voices. He hated their nakedness and strange masks. The people downstairs were like Buller or Crone, nice or bad as they were before they'd died. Terrano made them do what he said, but they were still people. The courtiers weren't people. Every night they would come up here and talk over who had died in which cage, and what they had learnt, and then they would wash their bloody hands and sit down to a big dinner. Sometimes Terrano would join them. After more discussion, and coffee, and nuts, they would disappear into the huge wings of bedrooms and glass-roofed gardens, but one evening they'd come up to find Lark waiting, and then they'd started sleeping somewhere else.

Lark stepped over a rotting corpse and padded towards Terrano's door. Silken portraits looked down on him from both sides. Each courtier had picked a pose, but this was the only way to tell them apart. Their faces were obscured by wooden masks, and their nudity was hidden by robes. The last two held up their arms and framed a pair of massive, crackling doors, which were made of the same blue-white metal as Lark's old cage. 'Knock, knock,' he whispered, staring up at Terrano's door. He had to steady himself on a bookcase. The humming grew louder, and sparks swept across the metal in gusts of crackling wind. 'I've come to kill you again.'

He left quickly, in case it actually opened.

Secrets

Pain bent Rose's head into her hands. Dren's tonic didn't taste like that, shouldn't hurt like this. She flicked irritably through his notebook, blinking away red spots. Some of the pictures were clearer in the dark. Why? What was the point in that? You still needed light to read the rest of it.

Rose relit her candle. She'd swear on any altar that the pages swapped places every time she put the book down. Forwards two pages. Back one. There, the top of the recipe. A moaning noise meant... too much spirit essence. And maybe she needed that green pulp? Dren didn't describe it well, instead rambling on about a maid who bent over to do the dusting. It was more of a diary than apothecary manual, and a filthy one at that. Rose rinsed her mouth and picked up the pestle for another go.

The door crashed open, flooding the room with light. 'Lils?' Rose stood up so quickly her stool fell over. 'What do you think you're doing? Didn't I ask for a moment to myself?' Her hand slipped off Lily's wet clothes, and she yelled at the latrine door as it slammed shut. 'Didn't I?' A servant was standing in the doorway, lantern in hand. Rose held her arm up against the glare and noticed yellow mucus dripping from her fingers. 'What...' She touched her nose and found more there. 'Oh gods.'

Almost tripping over her stool, she pushed the servant back and shut the door, slamming the bolt across. Her fingers smeared everything she touched. 'Lils?' she called out. 'Are you nearly done in there? I could really do with some privacy.' All that came was the sound of Lily being noisily sick. Rose stopped trying to wipe the pestle down and pushed the latrine open, turning excuses over in her head. 'Hey, have you—'

Lily waved a hand at her to shut up, fingertips and sodden sleeves dripping with more of the glowing mucus. The gown Hardus had bought her was ruined, smeared down over her narrow back and sodden with yellow gunk.

'Oh.' Rose shaded her eyes. She winced as her sister retched over the privy drop. 'It's coming from you.'

'So?' Lily pulled herself up one limb at a time. She tried the water pump, but found it broken and rattled the handle viciously. 'What's so strange about that?' Rose shrunk back as Lily wandered unsteadily past. There was hardly more than a thumb of her hair left, plastered flat against her skull like thick, yellow paint.

'Lils, what have you done?'

'This? I snuck into the kitchen and hacked it shorter.' She ran a hand over her scalp. 'It was falling out anyway.'

'That wasn't what I meant! Why are you...' Rose realised she was clutching her own hair. 'What have you been up to?'

'Could ask the same of you,' Lily retorted, flicking spots over Dren's notebook. 'Sneaking off every night to play apothecary – you're so addicted to this poison you're cooking it up yourself?'

'What would you know about that?' Rose felt her colour drain.

Lily's grin was wicked. The gunk was in her mouth, too, staining her teeth and gums. 'Your first time, darling? Please. Part of the reason I didn't touch any more of that tonic was because I can recognise a taste. Not sure if spay is an optional extra or a necessary ingredient, you'll have to ask him yourself.' She picked up the pestle. 'Is this all his?'

'You little brat.' Rose snatched it back. 'You could've said something.'

'Not like we were getting along at the time, were we? Thought I'd let you figure it out.' Lily swore as a fastener ripped in her struggle to undress, then growled and tore the rest of it off. The room dimmed as she wiped herself down. 'You're a mess, Rose. Admit it.' She sneered and tossed her sopping clothes on their bed, picking up the tattered dress she'd worn since Josef had died. She hadn't wiped her teeth, which still shone like bog lights. 'The green pods on the desk, that's spay. Don't take it out on me.'

'Wait, wait.' Rose pressed her fingers to her forehead. 'You haven't told me why you're glowing like that.'

'I ate something.' Lily clicked her fingers to find the name in her memory. 'A sinkstone? Maybe you don't normally eat them, I can't figure out if this is normal or not.'

'It's not!'

Lily shrugged and ran a hand through her hair, showing only the faintest hint of embarrassment. 'Shana suggested it.'

'Don't tell me that creature's here.'

'A whole pack of them, dear sister. Terrano has sent spirit-infested corpses out to kill everyone and drag them back to the Scarlet Keep. The feasters are here to stop him.' Lily scraped gunk off her cheeks and flicked it away. 'Anyway, you should go hide somewhere. Shana told me where Lark is, so I'm going to get him. She said that feasting on the sinkstone would protect me, though neglected to inform me it would be so fucking disgusting. You should see what came out of my nose—'

'Oh, Lils.' Rose sighed, feeling weary all of a sudden. 'I can't believe you sometimes.'

'Like you're all sensible this evening.'

'Compared to you, yes, I'm always sensible.' Rose bent down beside their bed and hunted for her quarterstaff. 'I'm glad you came to get me at least.'

'Nope, I came for a change of clothes. You can't come.'

'And you're going to stop me, you little rat?' She thumped the staff on the covers. 'I'm afraid I'm not in the mood.'

Lily scoffed at her. 'You're a liability. Where's your magic pebble, huh?' She flicked damp fingers at Rose's face. 'Where's your glowing gunk? You'll get eaten by Terrano's monsters. Or have a spirit crammed up your knickers, and then you'll be a slave to both of those hollow-idiots.'

Rose wiped mucus off her forehead and moved to the table. 'I'll be fine.'

'Trust me. Shana's centuries old. She's wise, she's a feaster—'

'You don't even know what that is.'

'More than you, fuckwit. She knows what she's talking about. If she thinks we need protection, we need it. I've got it, you don't.' She paused. 'What are you doing?'

Rose raised an eyebrow and picked up her bowl of tonic. Her spine seem to wriggle as she gulped it all down, shaking off tiredness and aches. The room grew less dark. Her senses sharpened, picking up the aroma of her untouched dinner, before she was utterly crushed by a triple dose of side-effects. 'Urgh. Bloody gods.' She clutched her temple and risked a glance at Lily. Her sister was leaning back against the wall and looking a little unwell herself.

'Getting spayed up, huh?' she said, clutching her stomach. 'Nice way to spend your evening in.'

'Shut up,' said Rose, and bent over the table. 'Remember what Dren said before you stormed out? This tonic wards off spirits.' She winced as her headache briefly blinded her. 'I'd take his word over those little tramps and some magic pebble any day. I'm just looking forward to what it does to you in the privy tomorrow.'

'Huh.' Lily was massaging her belly. 'Think it's dissolving, to tell you the truth. Not sure how I know, but it feels that way. Hurts too.' She paused. 'That a headache you got there?'

'Maybe.'

They watched each other a moment, Rose rubbing her head, Lily finally bending into the stomach cramps she'd been hiding. Through blurred eyes, Rose thought she could make out a wry grin on her sister's face. 'Guess we're ready, then,' said Lily. A moth fluttered over, finding her brighter than the smouldering candle wick. She swatted it away. 'Except you've drunk enough spay to floor a horse. Might slow us up when that hits.'

'Is this it?' Rose picked up one of the green pods with her fingertips. 'I didn't even put it in. Dren isn't very clear in his instructions.'

'And you still trust that man?' Lily laughed, straightening up with a wince. She held out a dripping handshake. 'Bet on it. My glowing pebble against your headache juice. Winner gets to spend the jewels on whisky.'

Rose clasped her hand, but it felt a little strange. 'I don't like whisky,' she said weakly, passing her fingers through the vortex of light and shadow that was growing between them. Darkness clung to her like a glove, driving back her sister's light.

Lily withdrew her hand. 'Let's get going.'

~

Rose watched as more revellers abandoned their food, flocking to point and laugh at the pale-skinned giant lurching towards the palace. City guardsmen barked orders, holding back the crowd as a scuffle broke out.

'You seeing this, Lils?' she whispered, kneeling behind a low wall. Festive lanterns painted the freak's skin a lurid green. His stomach lolled about as he was prodded into another thumping step. 'Some city. Parading that thing around like a backwater circus.'

'Stop gawping. Let's get ahead of them.'

'Freaks and beasts.' Rose watched a moment longer. 'Remember? Like they had at the summer fete.' Lily had already slipped off, keeping low as she crossed over to the next alley. 'You'll hurt your back crouching like that. They're too busy to worry about us.'

'Which of these men are Terrano's slaves? Do you know? I don't.' Lily slipped behind a cart, hugging close to the wall of a bank. A teller ran down the steps towards the commotion on the square, a trail of paper fluttering from his hand. Lily waited for him to go, then beckoned to Rose. 'Follow my lead, stompy sister. I've been doing this for years.'

'I expect this is a little different. You're glowing like one of those lanterns... and it's leaking from your nose again. Come here.' Another teller ran down the steps. He almost stumbled, and Rose gave him a look. 'Keep moving, sere.' She had Lily's cheeks gripped in one hand, her apron in the other. 'There's a monster out on the square if you want to stare at something.'

'Get off.' Lily pulled away and scowled at the teller. She vanished into a side street, and Rose frowned, jogging after a yellow blur that moved from shadow to shadow.

Eccentric storefronts lined every street and corner of Highwall, filled with all manner of crafts and follies. Rose had toured the more famous districts before sunset, rolling her eyes as Hardus bragged about his ancient family and how they'd built six of the squat towers that protected the city's fabulous wealth. Josef would've loved to hear that; he'd have laughed in their faces, taken it off them in a year. He'd taught Rose that Branera's power lay in the motion of money, not the hoarding of it. Which made these Highwall shops and bazaars the beating heart of Saarban's wealth – not some treasure-stuffed towers.

'Since when have you been so quick?' said Rose, leaning against an apothecary window to catch her breath. It was full of too many things with too much fur, and gave you the strange sensation of being watched. 'Urgh. I'm not enjoying the humidity of this place.'

'There's the gate.' Lily looked tired. Her hand seemed to blur as she rubbed her forehead. 'What's your plan to get in? Shana said—'

'I'll handle it.' Rose led the way to the palace, flapping her apron to air out some of the sweat.

Lily sneezed and splattered gunk on the cobbles. 'Fine, but I need you to wipe my face again.' She wobbled over unsteadily.

'Keep it on you, please. I want you to look unwell.'

'I look more than unwell!' Lily shivered, shaking yellow spots against the wall. 'This might raise a few questions, don't you think?'

'Only the right ones. Can you' – Rose gestured encouragingly – 'leak more? Force it out?'

Lily gave her a blank stare. Gunk trickled down her forehead.

'Perfect! How did you do that?'

'Shut up.'

'Oh. Well, it worked. Take this and lean on it, like you're really ill.'

Lily snatched the quarterstaff and made a fair effort of hobbling off. 'Hurry up, then,' she snapped. 'That crowd's getting closer.'

'What's the rush?'

'I've met that giant before. Let's not complicate this with a reunion.'

By custom, the palace gates were defaced during the festival and not cleaned for a fortnight. Crowned effigies lay at its feet like fallen invaders, while the bulging scars of board and nail were smeared with enough vegetable stink to make you pray for rain. Two uniformed men were sat beside this festering portal, slumped in the posture of a long shift, and they were watching the approaching crowd with a mixture of boredom and distaste.

'Wait there,' one said, his curt voice muffled by a mask. A painted fingernail was pointing at the white gravel that spilled out from under the gate like a welcome mat. 'Don't stand on it. And no more throwing stuff, either.'

'My sister's sick,' said Rose, mimicking a drawl she'd heard in Krans. 'Needs to see the court healer, she does.'

'Your accent's shit, Norther,' said the other man, taking in Lily's pained slump with a frown. His eyebrows were painted with ash, and a golden chain hung between his ears. 'Right?'

'Too right,' the first man bleated. 'And how sick is sick? Expensive to see our healer for something an apothecary can fix.'

'She's sick enough,' said Rose. 'If you'd take the time to look.'

'Ah, sod it. Let them through.' The ash-painted man wrinkled up his face in disgust. 'This one looks like she's dying in an interesting way. You know how the Court feel about that.' He pointed at Lily, who was bent over the staff like damp washing hung out on a stick. If it was an act, it was a good one. Which in itself was cause for concern.

His partner stood up, looking disgruntled. 'You're dripping on my gravel.' He waved to someone up on the ramparts, and the gates started to groan open. 'Don't die before you get to a bed.'

Rose crossed her arms. 'If I had to guess, sere, you don't sound that interested in helping her.'

'The Court will be interested, one way or another. They may even help, that's their call. You know the way to the Scarlet Keep?' He grabbed Rose as she snorted and walked away. 'Straight over the lake. Don't go wandering, I'm too sober for hide and seek.'

'Strange way to behave,' she said quietly, glancing down at his hand. 'If you don't want to come, why are you holding my arm?'

He sniffed and let her go. 'Clear out of here, then.'

She smiled at him, mastering the urge to pat his head. Rose had been taught her manners by a governess with a kind smile and an iron jaw. It wasn't that she didn't get angry, she'd just learnt that you can't punch your way out of problems by the age of seven. Spearmen sat in various sullen poses along the gatehouse tunnel, watching her as she passed. None of them whistled at her, or tried to bully her, they just watched her enter and leave, cards and dice in hand. The iron jaw of the gatehouse. There was nothing kind or smiling about the stiff-necked men out front, but her governess would have approved of the ordering.

Warm air greeted them outside, with a gate slamming shut in farewell. This was punctuated by the rattle and thud of a portcullis. 'Oi.' A woman leant over the ramparts to thumb them a direction. 'That way. End of the street, then across the lake.' Her hands fumbled for her crossbow as she walked back to her post. 'Bloody gods, what's this next thing?'

Lily was already hobbling away along a wide thoroughfare. This road had been built to receive the richest merchants from Saarban and beyond, though perhaps not today. Everything was boarded up. Hastily painted signs blamed the water festival for this rare closure, while others loudly declared that this was the place to get the best books, or to come back soon for the finest pottery, or that half-breeds ploughed your fields in half the time. Rose hurried to catch her sister up.

'That went well.' White gravel crunched unevenly under Lily's staff. She was supporting herself on the wall and unwittingly painting the shopfronts with a glowing streak. 'Didn't know you could lie.'

Rose glanced back at the gatehouse, where they were shouting warnings down at the giant on the other side. 'Hardus carried on lecturing me for hours after you slipped out. The Scarlet Keep handles any illness the city can't, or at least catalogues it.'

Lily stopped as she rounded the last building in the street. She leant on a street sign. 'And how many die before reaching their sick bed?'

The rest of the grounds were flooded by a lake of clear water, leaving narrow, torch-lit walkways to join the dozen keeps that squatted around it. Each one was crowned with beacons and draped in golden banners, apart from the smallest, which was a strange gap in this gilded ring. Yet its importance was unmistakable. Its forbearance set it apart from its garish neighbours, with only one walkway daring to make its approach. Rose tried to visually untangle the lattice of paths. 'Is this one of those garden puzzles? If not, why did it take them so long to figure out the King was crazy?'

'Not sure.' Lily was trembling, bracing herself against the signpost. 'Terrano's trying to bring the whole city through here by sunrise. Let's go bribe him before he's too busy slaughtering people.'

'Are you actually in pain, Lils? Or is this an act?'

'Both.'

'Come on,' Rose said, nudging her forwards. 'We want this path.'

'You think?' Lily set off, wincing with each crunch of the staff. The courtyard lake would have been peaceful if it wasn't so ornate. Solitary figures were out trudging the other walkways, raking delicate patterns from one keep to the next and pausing only to relight the guttering torches that marked the way. One of them was following Lily at a distance and using a bucket and mop to rinse out the gravel she'd dripped on. He frowned at his feet when they stopped to look at him.

'He hates me.' Lily blinked, staring about as if confused.

'Just be careful near that edge,' warned Rose. 'Ignore him and watch where you're walking.'

'Is it cold out here?'

'It's pretty cold.' Rose coaxed her on. 'Not far now.' The Scarlet Keep didn't seem that small once they were close, and definitely not after they'd been directed all the way around it to the healers wing. Red vines infested the keep's mortar, gripping each massive stone and reaching out greedy fingers over a thatch skirt at its base. 'Lils, do you remember what I told you about King Garradus?' The silence of the lake was profound, and Rose had dealt with it for as long as she could. 'He stole statues from the Long Path to decorate this keep.'

'So?'

'Well, I think he stole these vines too. There's a tower there that's covered in them.' Rose still had dreams about crossing the Long Path, where empty plinths lay like wounds on the ancient brickwork. 'He seemed more of a thief than a merchant king.'

'You keep banging on about that ruined tower. At least distract me with something novel.' Lily sent a shower of gravel into the water, and Rose had to catch her as she slipped. 'Oh, get off.'

'If you think we're going to charge around demanding to see Lark, without first showing you to this healer, I'm afraid you're mistaken.' Rose grimaced and wiped yellow sweat from her hands. 'Get in there, right now. And don't faint.'

'I don't want any help,' mumbled Lily.

Rose caught her and carried her inside. 'Tough. You eat stupid things, this is what you get. See, look it's nice.'

A gloomy interior held several neat rows of beds, with tiny fire-places and basins lining the walls. The marble floor gleamed with polish. The bed linen was crisp and white – except for where it had been softened by the butchered neck of a corpse. There were dozens of them, and their shocked, blood-spattered faces had been turned to face a wooden crate that dripped with black sap.

'Hello?' called Rose, letting Lily slide to the floor. A screeching figure reared up from behind a bed. He snatched up a serrated dagger and vaulted towards them, utterly naked apart from a wooden mask that rendered his war cry tinny and indistinct. Well, even her govern-ess would have given her a free pass this time. Rose crouched to take the quarterstaff from Lily's limp grip and swung it from her hips, grunting as it smacked him clean in the ribs. There was no meat to his wasted body. He flew across the room, stumbling over a bed and pulling off sheets with a trailing hand.

'You keep back,' she warned, pointing at him. A naked woman stalked out from behind a screen. 'Both of you!'

They screeched and charged in, blundering into her staff like she wasn't even there. Except, of course, she was. Rose shouldered the woman hard enough to flatten her out, and spun to catch the man with a monstrous crack across the mask, snapping his head back-wards and sending him sliding over the polished floor. He rolled to his knees and touched a confused hand to the blood running down his chin.

'Lils?' Rose whispered, nudging Lily with her foot. Mucus was dribbling from her sister's nose and mouth, pooling on the floorboards and finding cracks to the lake below. 'Say something, you idiot.'

Worry untangled the little knot of anger which Rose had carried around since she was seven, and she lost control. The man's next screech had her screaming at him, swinging at nothing. She beat furiously around the room, thrashing at beds when they moved, or kicking at a pile of laundry when a sheet twitched. 'No! No, no, no.' Dropping the staff, she sprinted over to Lily, but the female maniac was already crouched over her neck, serrated blade in place. A steadying hand was pressed down on her sister's mucus-covered jaw, and Rose wailed, knowing in her heart that it was too late.

Lily coughed and opened her eyes.

The maniac screeched, and her ribcage broke open in an explosion of blood and light. Rose tried to stop. She skidded to a halt by grabbing a bed, tangling herself in a stack of sheets rather than slide into that carnal mess. Cursed gods! The stench was unbelievable. There was a series of wet pattering sounds as bits of maniac detached from the ceiling, and Rose had to steady herself on a wash basin or take the time to fill it. Incredibly, Lily was laughing. Her face was smeared with blood and black ichor, which was fountaining from the woman's ruptured chest and filling the room with a putrid, unnatural smell. 'Behind you!' Rose screamed, pointing at a bed.

The naked man kicked a pillow at Lily's face. He leapt at her, his body bent back in an arc, dagger held overhead in a double grip. Lily blurred to her feet and met him with a hug, giggling when he broke open against her. She let the mess slide to the floor. 'Oh, Rose. That feels...' Her sister flicked fingers down her skirt to clean off bits of gut and bone. 'So much better. Like the best sneeze you ever had.'

Rose felt her way towards the door, gasping as she brushed against a cold hand strapped to one of the beds. 'What just happened?'

'We met some dead people, I think. Shana did say they wouldn't be able to touch me.' Lily picked up the hem of her skirt and delicately stepped over the mess, disappearing behind a screen. There was the sound of water splashing. 'I'm impressed with your tonic, though, don't get me wrong. Takes a lot to make someone like you invisible. You kept whacking them about, and they kept running back in for more. I would have laughed if I wasn't busy dying.'

'Lils! You made them explode. You touched them and they exploded.'

'Actually, I pulled something out of them – their ribs just got in the way.' There was a clatter and curse as Lily knocked something over. 'I could feel the sinkstone sort of gripping on the spirits in them, then bam!'

'This isn't right,' said Rose, trying to breathe, trying to find somewhere to look that didn't make her feel faint. The black crate filled her vision. It stretched and warped, its planks rattling with a moan that was echoed by the slack-jawed bodies scattered around the room.

Rose rubbed furiously at her eyes.

'I think it's going perfectly,' said Lily, emerging from behind the screen. She wiped her sleeves with a cloth. 'I also think I'm winning our bet. Being invisible isn't as exciting as making things explode.'

'Let's not do this. I don't want to kill anyone.'

'Well, we can warn them in advance, then it's up to them, isn't it?' Lily poked around the floor with her boot. 'You seeing this?'

'You're making me sick.'

'Take a look, you big numpty. See that?' Her toe nudged a slug-like shape which was congealing on the floor. 'These are the things I pulled out of them.'

'What's that?' Rose watched in horror as it reared up and mewled plaintively. 'Is it coming towards me?'

''Yup. Watch your back.' Lily pointed at another slug on the bed sheet. It made a cooing noise and threw itself at Rose's hand, splatting against her skin and dissolving into dark mist. Rose shrieked and belatedly leapt away, shaking her hand. She almost stepped on the first slug, but it purred and hurled itself against her boots anyway. The mist from the two creatures climbed up over her apron and settled around her shoulders, hovering there like ephemeral lace.

'Are you going to help? Or just laugh?' She tried to waft the mist away, but it crept lovingly back into place, moaning softly.'I can do both,' said Lily, giggling. The mist fled from her glowing mucus-fingers, spinning and swirling in panic. 'Guess I could keep my hands around your neck.'

'Fine, get off.' Rose pushed her back. 'I don't want those hands anywhere near me. Let's find Lark and get out.'

'I like the sound of that.' Lily crouched down next to the mutilated bodies and poked one in the face. 'Who do you want to ask for directions? This guy?' Lily inspected her finger. 'Urgh. Need to wash again.'

Rose moved to the door and took in some much needed fresh air. The sooner she could get Lily out of that room the better. She was watching the flickering lake torches, and chewing over ideas, when she heard a polite cough. The cleaner with the mop and bucket had finally caught them up. He frowned up at her, so Rose shrugged and stepped away to let him see inside.

Feaster

The thatch skirt around the Scarlet Keep was warm and cluttered, a warren of cosy rooms littered with straw and debris. Lily had stolen a wedge of cheese and was taking bites out of it as they went. It tasted good, but didn't touch the odd emptiness growing in her stomach.

Rose tetchily shifted the weight of her pack. 'Are we almost there? Please say we are.'

'Just this next room,' the cleaner replied, neatening his clothes for a change. He kept darting off to scrape away odds and ends with his foot, or lagging behind to straighten chairs. 'But you must know my superior is a very busy man. There is no guarantee he will have seen your brother.'

'And what does he know about masked maniacs with serrated knives?' asked Rose bitterly. 'Or people with slugs in their chests?'

'Oh dry up,' Lily cut in. 'And thanks ever so much.'

The cleaner shrank away from the damp hand she placed on his shoulder. 'Wait!' His eyes bulged. 'He's difficult. He doesn't like women and—'

With that invigorating thought in mind, Lily stepped through into a disappointingly empty room. An ancient door into the vine-clad keep stood ajar, with a heap of snapped boards and nails lying at its base. A palace guard was perched on a stool nearby, and busying himself with a well-stocked bookshelf. He tore out a page. Touching it to a candle, he held up the flaming paper, and vines peeled away to reveal grey, crumbling stone. They crawled slowly back when it withered over his gauntlet.

'Where is everyone?' The cleaner ducked under Lily's dripping arm, frantically searching the room. 'Guardsman, I have a murder to report! Someone has been dressing in courtier masks and—'

'Shh now.' The guard looked up from a half-filled pipe, amused at the small man's fluster. His mask only covered his jaw and mouth, revealing blue eyes and a ragged mop of hair that he kept shaking from his face. 'There's been a few changes. Head inside for me, and someone will explain it to you.'

'We don't go into the keep.' The cleaner seemed confused, steadying himself on a chair. 'Are any of my colleagues through there?'

'Sure.' The guard touched a wad of pages to the fire, wafting them back and forth. He lit his pipe from the embers and lifted his mask to put it to his lips. 'First on the left.'

Lily touched her forehead as she walked past, watching his eyes wander over her saturated dress. Rose came through with less grace, bodily carrying the reluctant cleaner with her; the guard averted his gaze so quickly he choked on his pipe. 'I see that tonic of yours is still working, sister dearest.' Lily took a final bite of the cheese and tossed it away. It wasn't coming close to satisfying her. 'These dead men soil themselves every time you get too close. Did you feel the slug in him that time?'

'I don't want to talk about it.'

'It can't be that bad,' said Lily, pausing to cradle her stomach. The build-up of sinkstone gunk was making it hard to think straight. And then there was the gnawing hunger, which had been growing since she'd spoken to Shana. She yawned. 'Relax a little, sister.'

'I don't want to talk about it, and I don't want to relax.' Rose looked like she was trying to breathe lightly. She covered her mouth with a sleeve. 'This place is disgusting.'

Lily sneezed and splattered a wall hanging with glowing drops. Rose was right, you couldn't make it any dirtier. Someone had tried to clean the carpet, but they'd only succeeded in pushing out its mould into garish sweeps. 'What's it like?' she said, catching her up. 'When you're near them? I get a sort of pulling coming from their chest, like the sinkstone's trying to grab them.' She mimed a twist and pull. 'Rip them right out.'

'Stop being so weird.' Rose's face was twisted up with worry. 'I hate this. They're all terrified of me.'

Lily chased the mist swirling around Rose's neck. 'Can you still hear them moaning?'

'Now that, I definitely won't talk about,' Rose said emphatically, pushing Lily along. 'And I mean it.'

'Please! Let us go back.' The cleaner tried to turn. Rose stubbornly blocked his way with the staff, so he put his hands on it and pleaded up at her. 'Both of you are sick, please go back to the healers' wing. If you're unwell there is no reason to spread it around.'

'Don't you wonder why he hasn't got one?' said Lily, patting him on the head.

'I've been meaning to say something about that.' Rose herded them both forwards with the staff. 'You can't just go around touching people to see if they explode. You've gone all strange and I don't like it.'

'Stop worrying.' Lily's nose was itching fiercely. She braced herself against a cupboard and sneezed again, splattering gunk everywhere. 'Or worry about something else.'

The cleaner was looking longingly back down the corridor. Rose shooed him forwards. 'Go on, keep going. Weren't you telling us to hurry up earlier? We need you to introduce us.'

'It won't help,' he moaned. 'They'll say the same as me – you two need to be put into a bed and sedated.'

After a few nudges with the staff, he started trailing along again. One of his hands was clutching Lily's sodden dress, and his nerves were infectious. She found herself growing steadily more worried. Or irritated. Both came out the same for her. 'Is this it?' She slapped her palms loudly on the door and leant in to push it open. 'Let's see this man who kidnapped Lark, then.'

Beyond the door was a dining hall, its aroma of soup and baking bread now tainted by the rancid air they'd let in. There wasn't much dining going on. Racks of swords and cloaks filled the room, with tables pushed up against the wall and crates piled in every dusty crevice. Dour watchmen were tending these stores, oiling and sharpening with a care that showed where their true love lay. Metal glinted under cloth. Points and straight edges were held up for inspection. Lily took a few steps into their midst and turned slowly around, feeling their spirits squirm at the sinkstone's presence.

Their guide yelped as he was seized and dragged to the hall's high table. A grim-faced watchman continued to wipe down a helmet in slow, careful movements. His eyes flicked up. They returned to the metal, as if they found it more favourable. 'Your name?' The cloth flicked out dust from a delicately wrought pattern around the eye slits.

'Yarras Farrier, sere. I've cleaned the thatch most of my life, my father too. I know I'm not supposed to be in here, but the guardsman—'

'A sword for our cleaner.'

Two blades were considered. Yarras barely tried to grip the shorter one before dropping it with a clatter. 'Oh, sorry. I mean...' He bent over to pick it up, but a watchman was already straightening with it in his hands.

'Not a swordsman, then.' The cloth left a speck of lint and provoked a frown. 'Fetch him a dagger and show him to his bed. Bring him back when it's done.' There was no such thing as a small watchman, though the one that hauled Yarras off must have been grown twice. The cleaner was still fussing and asking questions even as he was carried away an inch off the ground.

Lily stepped forwards. 'Good evening.' It was hard to remember how the boardwalk women talked now. The prim tones, the steely eyes. She drew herself up a bit. 'Do not think you will be treating me in that manner. Do you have a name?'

He put down the cloth and grudgingly raising his eyes. 'Marne,' he said. 'My patrol has pledged itself to a new master, but we keep the ways of the Watch.' He inclined his head. 'At your pleasure, for the little I care of it. And you, child, I assume you are also named?'

'Well named, I think you'll find. I'm Lily Kale-Tollworth, daughter to the late Treasury Minister of Branera.' She whispered to Rose without turning. 'Stay handy now, sister.' This was a phrase they'd say when walking a rough district in Branera, and Rose, still unused to being the least obvious person in a room, dutifully stepped forwards. She raised her staff. The watchmen saw nothing, eyes slipping over her as they continued to oil, sharpen and sew.

'Perhaps you will talk less as a host, Lily Kale-Tollworth.' Marne returned to his polishing. 'Fetch her a sword.'

'Oh, no, thank you.' Lily waved away the blade. 'Hosts? Is that what you call yourselves?'

A flash of irritation lit up his eyes. The rag didn't stop moving. 'We each died and now care for a guest. As will you. As will everyone in Saarban. Give her the sword.'

'No. Is Terrano here?' Lily raised her chin imperiously. 'He has my brother and I formally request his return.' Rose had some of those jewels with her, but to hell with mentioning that yet. 'Call for your master.'

A watchman tried to press his sword into Lily's hand, and the staff came down with a whistle and a crack. The man grunted in shock, turning over his wrist to inspect swollen fingers. Since Rose couldn't get enough of swinging that thing, Lily sighed and flicked her fingers for effect; the butt of the staff smacked him viciously in the gut. The watchman who'd dragged off Yarras sneered at this and strode over to grab Lily's wrist, failing to hesitate when she grinned. The sinkstone struck him with the joy of a lightning bolt finding its steeple, and his strangled cry was punctuated by a loud metallic thump. Lily watched him crumple, suppressing an odd giggle as he slipped on the ichor running out from under his dented breastplate.

The sounds of polishing and sewing stopped. Lily picked up Marne's helmet and held it up to the light. Sinkstone gunk stained the gleaming metal, a sloppy handprint that dribbled yellow liquid over its finely etched crests and patterns. Her eyes flicked over to its owner. 'I will not go until I have spoken with Terrano.'

Marne rose slowly to his feet. 'Grin all you want.' He took a step back and unbuckled his cape. 'There is nothing impressive in what you do. My patrol has travelled further than your shore-hugging dreams, and we are never troubled by heathen magic. Wherever we find it.' He continued to stare when Lily held out his helmet. She rolled her eyes and tossed it to him, but he stepped aside and let it fall, kicking it away with a clatter. 'Tell me, witch. Why would I let you speak to our king?'

She laughed. 'That's a lot to take in. If you mean Terrano, I've already told you. He has our brother and I want him back. My brother, I mean. Only me here.'

Marne's face twitched. That helmet was probably the one thing he loved, and she'd ruined it. 'It is no surprise you are related to that creature,' he said. 'You would take the boy away?'

'Why wouldn't I?'

He probably didn't smile often. 'If you do not know, then you will find out. Our sentinels say he left around dusk, with plans to head for the Long Path. See that he goes further, if you get the chance.' A pack of watchmen had gathered around him, tightening straps and settling helmets. One handed Marne a sword, which he spun expertly to test its weight. Another was weaving in and out of the ranks, muttering and waving his hands over their shoulders.

'What's he mumbling about?' Lily pointed a dripping finger. The man's cloak was a deeper brown than the others, tasselled with ceramic shards that clattered and rustled as he moved.

'A warding ritual,' said Marne, loosening his shoulders. 'Something we learnt in our campaigns to the south. Worried, little witch?'

She sniffed, feeling her sinkstone throb in time with the man's chanting. 'Tell him to save his voice. Now I know where my brother's heading, I'll leave.'

'You'll leave only if our king wishes it. He's being consulted.' The strange grin again. 'As you wished, of course.' He muttered something to the two men flanking him. The air around their shoulders had started to glow, agitated by the hands of the brown-cloaked watchman.

'Too kind, but there's no need for him to get his robes on.' Lily looked over the racks of blades and spears. 'Don't let me interrupt your evening.' Raising her hand in farewell, she turned and strode towards the musty corridor, trying to ignore her aching guts. Rose's fingers found her sleeve. 'Keep moving,' Lily hissed, not acknowledging her. 'Gods, I've got another stomach ache.'

'Lils, earlier you asked if it was cold and I lied. It was really warm.'

'So what?'

'It's really, really cold now. But I don't know why, and I don't trust you to know any different.'

Lily could see it, at least. Her boots were slipping on a strange, creeping frost. 'Just keep moving,' she whispered. 'Is that Yarras?' The cleaner was on his knees, tracing awe-struck lines in the thickening ice, and he wasn't alone. A crowd of cloaked hosts blocked the musty corridor at his back. One helped him stand, buttoning up a torn collar and draping a cloak over the bloodstains. Lily spun around. 'Make them move, Marne.' The sinkstone gurgled in her stomach, agreeing with this threat. 'Or they'll all die. Again.'

'No!' Rose stepped in her way.

'Learn to be quiet, girl,' said Marne. 'The King will decide who dies.'

Something foul was gusting through the hall. It fell from the rafters and roamed the corners, eating the air and leaving snow on the tables. Sour breath tickled Lily's face. Cold fingers ran over her neck, down her back. She shook herself vigorously and stepped sharply away. 'You can fuck off!' she snapped, spinning around as she tried to evade the creeping presence.

'He speaks,' rasped Marne, chin tilting upwards. 'He says...' Metal scraped as the watchmen drew their weapons in unison, teeth bared behind ice-flecked beards. 'The King smells his brother on you, little witch. He says you are his brother's whore. You and another with you. One we cannot see.' Marne's face hardened with resolve. He turned to face Rose, and his eyes squeezed shut. When they opened again, they were small spheres of ice, an unbreakable stare that belonged to someone else. Ice crept over his brow, moulding his features into a gaunt, lean expression, and he breathed out a dusting of snow. 'Ah, girls,' he said, in a soft, cultured voice. 'You are looking for your brother, perhaps?' He chuckled silently, and coughed. A chunk of ice and flesh broke free, exposing cheekbone. 'I could ask you the same question. Where is my brother?' Marne's head tilted curiously, his frosted skin cracking around the folds of his neck. 'Is Dren coming? I can smell him on you. I would take my spirits back from him.'

'You can smell me?' Rose's hands shuffled up the staff.

'More than I can see you. Poor girl, what has he done to you?' He blinked, snowflakes drifting free. Cracks appeared in the mask as he shuddered. 'And there is—' Marne groaned as the mask shattered. His quivering hands felt for missing patches of skin and cheek, and with a stagger that didn't quite reach the table, he fell to his knees and screamed miserably into the stone floor.

'Did I do that?' Rose whispered, appalled. Marne's cries grew louder when meltwater ran down his chin, fingers hovering over empty eye sockets.

'How do I know?' said Lily. 'And you, what was that about whores?' She kicked the howling Marne in his ribs. 'I never got to whore with anything. It was this one here that did all the whoring.'

'Lils, they can't see me!'

'Of course not, you just blinded him.' Lily kicked Marne again, fingers crackling and dripping with gunk.

'Let's just go.' Rose's hand found her sleeve, drawing back with a yelp as a spark jumped the gap. 'And don't touch anyone!'

Lily curled her lip, disgusted by Rose's dullness.

... rasping throats and thumping hearts called to her from across the room, slopping with blood and panic-tainted tastes. And those hearts encased in armour were the biggest and most delicious...

'Maybe I want to touch them,' she whispered, glancing over her shoulder at the watchmen. 'Feast a little.' Their wrists were flicking left and right as they stalked forwards, spinning weapons in a vicious flourish of skill. The watchman with the brown cloak urged them on, picking up Marne to drag him to one side.

'You'll get diced!' Rose shouted, pulling her back. 'Are you mad?'

Sensible old cow. Bet she tasted awful.

'Fine,' snapped Lily, darting for a different door. She petulantly slapped a cloaked host out of the way, a tap that was enough to spin the dull bitch right around. A spray of blood and ichor cut a slow arc through the air. Her mouth creaked open in shock, her lips drew back over missing teeth, wrinkled skin stretching as a spirit tore its way up and out of her brittle ribs, and Lily almost turned, almost went back and buried herself in all that warm life and blood, and then it was too late and they were out in a musty corridor.

Rose slammed the door shut behind them. 'Lils.' She was panting, eyes wide as she leant against the handle. 'You've gone all weird again.'

Lily tore her gaze away from the sweat beading on her sister's skin. They had to get out. That was important, for whatever reason. The corridor melted into a blur and she ran upstairs to a window, banging on it, hissing in frustration when she found it locked and growling at the fiddly metal bar holding it shut. Rose kept saying something. She sounded worried. She always ways. Stupid, foul-tasting cow. Hard to think with that great, thumping heart pounding away over your shoulder.

'Lils, what are you doing?' Bones slid over gristle, and fingers gripped Lily's shoulder.

Maybe she had a reason to be worried? Lily did feel a bit weird. A bit hungry. She flipped the latch over, thinking on what it was, and what one did with it, and the odd hunger seemed to fade

'Give me a moment,' she managed. 'It's rusted up.' She pretended to fumble with it some more. 'Got it!' A tangle of red vines provided grip as she vaulted over the window ledge and landed in an awkward roll on the thatch roof. Rose followed with a cry and a thud, raising a straw-covered look of surprise from where she'd fallen. 'Look before you leap.' Lily pulled her up and dusted them both down. 'You just jumped blindly out a window, didn't you?'

'I followed you,' Rose mumbled. 'Thatch roof. Good idea.'

'Seemed safer than running through that warren again.' Lily started to pick her way towards the courtyard lake. The straw roof bent beneath her, slipping here and there as it took her weight. She counted under her breath until Rose put her foot through. 'You okay?' she called back, adjusting to the dim light coming from the keep windows. There was no moon out, but the sky was making up for it in stars. 'They're not following us.'

Rose pulled her leg free and followed in a low crouch, arms held out for balance. 'They want to kill us.'

'You. They want to kill you, for screwing around with Dren. Haven't you washed since?' Straw was stuck to the grazes on Lily's shin, so she stopped to pick bits out.

'Just shut up.' Rose was trying to move faster over the unstable roof, careering around like a pissed jester. Lily picked off a last piece of straw and looked up to see how far they had to go. Her mouth drifted open. Terrano's hosts were flooding out of the other keeps, fighting for space on the narrow paths that wove over the courtyard lake. Lanterns were knocked over in the crush, with darkness following in their wake.

'Shit.' Lily tried to stand, cursing as her boot got wedged.

'Why do you think I'm running?' Rose swore quietly as she dodged another sagging patch of roof. 'This was a terrible idea.' Lily ignored her, slipping and tumbling to reach the edge first. From behind, a loud thump and a shout suggested her sister had got her foot stuck again.

'Catch me up!' she yelled, eyeing the drop. Rose would be fine. What was this next leap to a bloody giant like her? Flipping on her stomach, she crawled backwards until her legs were dangling over the edge. She scrabbled for grip in the loose straw, and her heart lurched when she slipped an inch. There was a crash from below. 'I'll fucking kill you!' She screamed, kicking downwards. 'Let go! Let me go!'

'Stop kicking! It's me.' A dust-covered Rose pulled her down, catching her as she hit the floor. Lily wobbled up onto her feet and tried to get her bearings. A door into the thatch rooms had been forced open. There was a hole in the roof, straw everywhere.

'You fell through?' Lily turned around to find herself alone. 'Wait!'

They had one advantage: the paranoia of a dead king. He had permitted only one bridge to cross the path to his home and built the other keeps at a wary distance. Cloaked hosts were leaping between walkways to try and reach this crossing first, spilling from paths to wade over and cut them off. Dead watchmen were easily spotted. Their hulking shapes cleared paths as they ran, swatting lesser beings into the water if they didn't make way fast enough. In her panic, Lily found herself moving too quickly, moving past Rose in a blur of sickening speed.

... bones slid and slipped in joints, skin creaked and stretched as it plunged into freezing water. Muscle thudded over gravel, hot air rising from chainmail as bearded throats growled violent threats...

With her mind anywhere but her feet, Lily slipped. Hissing at a sharp pain in her ankle, she limped on, scattering gravel as she flailed past the bridge like that was all that mattered. Thumping footsteps grew nearer. Rose thundered up behind and scooped her up with a grunt of effort, and Lily gritted her teeth, trying and failing to keep her ankle from bouncing awkwardly against the bag slung over her sister's back. Shana had tricked her in some way – that much was completely fucking clear. The fleshy bits of the world were beating loudly in Lily's ears, pathetic details engorged into a horrible display of sinew and sweat. Lily gripped Rose's neck and struggled not to listen to the blood slopping around her veins. More watchmen were waiting for them at the end of the path. Torchlight glinted off rods of polished metal, and you didn't need feaster senses to catch the stink of lavender and rotten eggs.

'Rose!' Lily shrieked, pounding her shoulder. 'Put me down.' She was dumped straight on the gravel, and her sister raised a sweat-drenched face to accuse her with a glare. 'You were running right into them!' Lily gasped, pulling herself up on Rose's arm. Her ankle was obscenely sore. 'Watchmen at the end of the path.'

'They cut us... cut us off?'

'No,' Lily whispered. 'That's the real deal. It's Thora's patrol.'

'Then why stop?' Rose winced as she straightened up. 'You said she helped us before.'

The stench of eggs and lavender was stronger now. Lily could make out Thora standing in the centre of her patrol, raising something long and metallic to her lips. 'Those are blacksand weapons,' she said, clutching her gurgling stomach. Something had provoked the sinkstone. It was draining away the feaster hunger that blurred her hands and sharpened her mind. She felt weak. Dull. 'They might shoot us.'

'They'll recognise us!'

'You think so?' Drops of gunk spattered over the water as Lily shook an arm. 'I didn't look like this before.'

Dead watchmen reached the bridge behind them. They vaulted over the edge and leapt down in pairs, legs absorbing the drop in heavy crunches of gravel. The leading watchman raised his fist and stalked forwards with careful, crouched steps. At his side, cloaked waders pushed doggedly against the water, fighting an icy breeze that whipped over the surface.

'What else can we do?' said Rose, looking up and down the path. 'We should just trust this Thora.'

'I agree. But we need to earn it.' This was truly the most stupid of ideas, but the ravenous sinkstone had left a void where her common sense should be. Fear and doubt? Both missing. Feaster senses? Utterly gone. Lily rotated her ankle, and felt pain shrug its shoulders and vanish. All that was left was her stupid plan, and this stupid stone. 'Listen, I'll try exploding a few of them. If Thora sees that, she'll know we're on her side. Whoever we are.'

'Lily!' Rose said, aghast. 'What is the matter with you this evening?'

The sinkstone was whispering to her. 'I'm just taking it one step at a time,' she said, limping back towards the bridge. 'Stay handy, sister.' She only had to touch them. That was easy, she'd knocked enough teeth loose in a fight. Though, that only happened when she was drunk or angry – or both because someone had confiscated her drink. Lily whimpered as a wave of terror fought past the sinkstone.

Her first victim stood alone on the narrow path. 'Witch.' He made a fist. 'You think I can't cut off those hands before they touch me?'

'I can tell you,' she said, sniffing, 'that is the last thing on my mind.' She'd have to get his armour off somehow. Or his gloves. That helmet completely covered his face, which hardly seemed fair. 'You watchmen are really not my type.'

'No, girl. We're not.' His eyes swam over Rose as she slipped past Lily. 'I've razed cities before. There's nothing but pain waiting for you out there.' Watchmen waited at his back, swords held limply in their hands. 'The King wishes you to join us. He says we can make your death more pleasant than this.' Lily tried to concentrate, ignoring the gathering chill that was eating into her skin, or the rising wind that stirred their clothes. The watchman's helmet cracked as it was encased in a layer of ice. 'My dear girl.' Terrano's rich voice was muffled by metal. 'Could you tell me where my brother is? He is here somewhere, but I can't find him.' The tip of the watchman's sword quivered, frost shattering on the blade.

'Oh, Dren's around. He's going to kill you.' Lily wasn't having much luck with massaging her stomach and visualising what she wanted. She tried holding her breath and mentally screaming.

'I assure you he is not.' Terrano's voice drifted off, like it was carried away on a breeze. The watchman howled in agony, but it was hard to see how much of his face had melted off through those small eye slits. Rose seemed keen to push the advantage. She beat him down to the gravel with big overhead chops of her staff, stamping her boot on his sword when he tried to reclaim it. But this man was both pissed off and huge. He brushed away her staff to regain his footing, and lashed out blindly, covering ground with big swings of his fists and legs. Rose staggered as a lucky hit caught her across the chin, hitting the water with a huge, tit-slapping crash.

'Come on,' Lily muttered, resorting to begging. 'Stop trying to help. Please? Shana did this to me on purpose.'

Seems like she only had to ask. Pain and hunger staggered Lily as the sinkstone withdrew its protection. The berserk watchman tore off his helmet, his cheeks crushing into Terrano's icy features as he scrambled for his sword, but Lily screamed and blurred towards him, closing in on a thundering heart that was fat with blood and ice. He swung for her head, fast and clean, enough to take down anyone but a feaster. Lily ducked under a humming blade that crept ponderously through the air, and rose up close to his chest, gripping his neck robes in one hand and snapping teeth in his face. She paced over to the water's edge and dangled him over the lake.

'Please...' he croaked.

She hissed and slapped a hand on his face, ripping off his armour so the explosion showered her in blood and ichor. She dropped what was left of him in the water. Tainted meat, not worth a meal.

... lungs creaked. Feet crunched on gravel. Cold air sang as it parted around two swinging blades...

Lily leant forwards and back. Falling swords cut the air around her, and she crouched, her bloody hands flicking out and finding exposed shins. Two watchmen bucked and twisted, screamed and fell. Another stepped up, roaring a warcry and thudding his blade into Lily's shoulder. She snarled and gripped the gap between his robes and helmet, pulling him down with her as she collapsed under the weight of his blow. What air was left Lily's tortured lungs escaped in two blows; he crashed down on her midriff and exploded against her with a damp thud.

Pain and darkness threatened Lily's vision. Her lips moved noiselessly as she begged for help, desperately grasping at her feaster powers when they were then drained away into the throbbing pit of her stomach.

'No.... I–'

The sinkstone ignored her. She felt empty. No fear, no pain, and Lily was pinned down by those she'd killed. She watched with distant concern as slugs rose from the mess of their wounds. This close she could hear them hiss, smell their spectral reek as they wriggled up her body, over her chest, gripping her hair with a thousand tiny legs. One crawled up to her shoulder and sniffed the blood-drenched fabric.

'Death?' it whispered.

Cold water splashed Lily's face as a soaking-wet Rose swung her staff like she was hoeing weeds. Slugs flew through the air, falling with a splash in the lake. Another thump clubbed away a dripping figure who was climbing onto the path. A watchman ran forwards, stabbing wildly with a spear, but he couldn't see Rose was already too close for that. She cracked him with her elbow and shoved him back with the staff. Powering her legs, she kept on pushing, collecting another watchman, and another, sending them into the water as they tripped and fell. Rose threw her staff after them and ran back to Lily, heaving and rolling bodies off her.

She touched the wet patch on Lily's shoulder. 'Lils, is this blood?'

'Come on!' Lily grabbed her and started to stumble towards the gatehouse. The sinkstone was fading, leaving her to handle the mess of her tired, bleeding body. 'Please, Thora. Please understand. Please.'

~

'Stand ready, my darlings.'

Thora closed her eyes and smiled, thanking the Watchful Prince for this moment. Was it to be so easy? A small skirmish to take the gates, then her foe gathered on open ground – slowed by water and clumped on narrow paths. Shuffling ran down the ranks. Rifles were raised, matching an elegant gesture of her hand. Thora could see the lake forever tainted by this moment. She could hear her imperious command that the gravel be left red as a reminder for those who would cross the Roaming Watch.

Thora opened her eyes to a lake of disappointingly clear water. 'Lay our troubled friends to rest,' She luck-kissed her pistol, tasting lavender and death. 'And any who stand with them.'

Squinting to account for her sand-blind eye, she aimed. Barrels drifted this way and that. Watchmen sought a clear shot, wooden stocks slipping against their bulging shoulders, and Thora sighed, regretting the blacksand that would be wasted this day. The Watch were peerless with common weapons. Spear, bow, sword – each chose their favoured tool. None chose a rifle, as none of them could. They were forbidden from touching them until these moments.

'On my signal.' She watched a scuffle break out on the path, punctuated by screams and flashes of light. 'Pick your targets, dear ones.'

The lanterns showed glimpses of haggard, snarling faces, each one flecked with unnatural frost. Her informants had insisted these things wouldn't die the same way twice. But then, you hadn't truly died until you'd been hit with hot blacksand. Peasants said the stinging sensation was your soul dying, but Thora knew better. It was the death of flesh itself. She'd watched blacksand turn many a wound into something worse, rotting away at healthy tissue.

Two of the creatures were closer than the rest. They disentangled themselves from the pack and ran down the path towards her patrol. One was glowing as bright as the lake lanterns, and pulsing with a sickly yellow light.

'Fire, my darlings,' she said. 'And try not to hit the two pretty girls.'

Broken

'Tollworth! We have no time for this petulance. Must I move your feet every step?'

Husker had seen them. A father should recognise his girls, and Husker had, even if Lily was dripping with glowing sweat. Even if Rose was a woman tall enough to reach his shoulder. The leash lifted Husker's knee, extended his leg, thumped his foot down. Then lifted his other knee.

'Fuck you!' Dren wiped the staining oil from his face, poise shattered. 'Fuck. You.' He ripped off the elegant jacket and tossed it into the court-yard lake. 'You chose this path, remember that.'

Husker was surprised how pretty they both were. An ugly creature like him shouldn't sire pretty things like that. Lily seemed sick, leaning heavily over a staff, and one of the gate guards had caught Rose by the wrist. He'd noticed that too.

'*Manost,*' said Angel, the spirit's gravel-voice rattling in his head. A spectral talon tapped him on the shoulder. '*You are losing yourself.*'

Yeah, that sounded about right. He'd dropped Young's rock pendant somewhere. It didn't feel like it belonged with him anymore. Faith in Godearth? Faith in Priest Young? Faith in himself? Didn't matter which it was, but gods be fucked he'd lost it.

A blast of cold wind chilled him as they approached the rear of the Scarlet Keep, frosting his skin and melting over the furnace being stoked in his heart. He only noticed the man impaled on a metal sconce when he felt blood running over his knuckles. Something sharp snagged his side. Husker looked down at a snapped spear shaft; the rest was waving back and forth in the hands of a terrified palace guard.

'Kill him too,' demanded Dren.

Husker crushed the man's skull and dropped the mess at Dren's feet. Angel hissed in displeasure, swimming to the spear wound and knitting it up. It had to yank out the spearhead using Husker's hand, because Husker couldn't be bothered to do it himself. *'Manost. Calm yourself!'* Angel probed his mind, searching for something and finding it. It poked it with a talon, releasing a wave of frost. *'Something is not right here.'*

The doors to the Scarlet Keep cracked under Husker's shoulder. He lumbered inside and scooped up the broken slab of wood that barred them. The splintered end knocked men clear across the entry hall, and he heard a wail from under his foot. Nice place. Cleaner than you'd think for a forbidden keep. An army of servants were beating dust from wall hangings, stuck up their ladders and gawping at him.

'The stairs,' hissed Dren, pointing at them. 'Kill anyone that tries to stop us.'

Husker pulled a man's shortblade from his belt and shoved it under his ribs, yet for some reason the fucker wouldn't die. He scrabbled and clawed, managing to pull the weapon out and wedge it into Husker's shoulder. Scabs fell away when he lifted the man's shirt, revealing fresh, raw skin. 'Like me,' he mumbled. 'Healed.'

Angel laughed as it stemmed the blood pouring from his shoulder. *'Nothing is quite like us, manost.'*

'That spirit knows how to knit flesh. Choke him instead.' Dren paused, a grape halfway to his mouth. These workers had been taking a food break. 'And how are you speaking, exactly?' His fingers wired the leash tighter around Husker's mouth, but Husker didn't care. They climbed. More men died.

'I was made here,' Dren said pensively, leaning over a table. Manacles hung on opposite walls of the room, a desk and stool by each. There were two of everything. 'Terrano was kept there. Me here.' Dren picked up one set of chains – pathetic things that would only close over a child's wrist. Mist bloomed from his shirt cuffs, crumpling and melting the links, and he turned his hand to let the slag drop into a water butt. The steam took on a darker quality as it traversed his troubled features.

Husker touched one of the blue-white knives, which were hung by their dozens around the wall. 'Takes a lot of cutting to make something as messed up as you.'

'I am a hollow-soul,' Dren snapped. 'The clue is in the name.' His smile returned, but it did nothing to hide the pain behind it. He hated this room. 'And again, how are you talking?'

The leash grew tight round Husker's face, crushing his teeth together until his jaw popped. Husker didn't care. They climbed, more men died. He tossed the last of them down the stairs, leaving a trail for anyone who followed. Let them know what was up here – couldn't say fairer than that. Luminescent moss clung to the walls on the next floor, wriggling contentedly in the air. *'The next room, manost. It smells interesting.'* Angel rose from his thoughts and tugged at his feet, so Husker turned himself inside, pulling down a shelf with a lazy swing of his arm.

Dren followed him. 'How are you—' His voice cut off abruptly. 'Margot? Is that you?'

An old woman was caged here. Someone had treated her well, giving her books and plates of food. And by the only-slightly foul smell, that someone had also been chucking buckets of water down a grate she was squatting over. She stood and pulled up her trousers, sneering at Dren and adjusting a dirty wig with one hand.

'Terrano has turned on you, then?' Dren drew close to her cage. His words were almost lost under the vicious crackle of its blue-white bars. 'So much for love. He could never truly let her in while he held on to you.' The woman jutted out her chin, gesturing at her neck and wheezing angrily. Dren rolled his eyes and reached through the bars, wincing as they bit him. His hand closed around her throat.

'Trap,' the woman croaked. Dark mist rose from her mouth and spilled over Dren's hand. 'Trap, trap.'

He withdrew his arm. 'As if he is capable.' Dren rubbed at the scorch marks on his sleeve, and ignored the disgusted hand she waved at him. 'Even if that is the case, I have brought a weapon that he cannot contend with.'

Husker had broken everything in the room that would break. He was eyeing up the bars of the nearest cage, and wondering if they'd bend before he was driven back by their sparks.

'I will release you when it is done.' Dren drew himself up. 'I have always said you picked the wrong brother.' She spat on the floor and wheezed angrily, waving him away.

They climbed. No more men died, because there were none. Husker's hands itched. They entered a library at the top of the keep, which was filled with old scrolls and tapestries of masked people. This was a temple for books, and instead of a holy statue or tree, it had massive, blue-white doors. Husker watched as Dren stepped up to inspect these towering slabs of metal, remembering a faraway temple where Priest Young had sat on his altar and allowed himself to be robbed.

'The end of the maze,' muttered Dren, staring up at the door. 'Now, where is the bull?' Husker's fist caught him across the ribs, carrying him sideways into a pile of books. He rose with the drunken-limbed affront of a prize fighter caught with a dirty blow. 'How dare you?' Dren rasped, mopping blood from a gash on his face. Looked like he'd landed against some sharp edges. 'How could you? I have you leashed!'

Dren frantically dodged as Husker swung a chair at him. Just a glancing hit, the slippery fuck. He threw away the snapped pieces of wooden leg, trusting his fists to hold together better, and sweat flew from his arms as his knuckles thudded hard into skinny ribs. Dren wheezed blood over Husker's shoulder and tried to fall to his knees, but not yet, bastard. He clamped Dren's neck in one hand and slammed him against a wall, pinning him there like an insect.

Husker's hands were stilled.

'Eater,' rasped Angel, through his mouth. 'It is time we talk.'

Dren babbled with laughter, and his swollen face melted that rustling accent into a fat-lipped mumble. 'He lets you ride his tongue? He always was a fool. Has he named you, too?'

'Yes,' Angel grated, struggling with Husker's mouth. 'Manost has named me.'

'And?' Dren clutched at the meaty fingers gripping his throat. He had his toes up on a nearby cabinet, which left him just enough space to breathe. 'What has the idiot dubbed you?'

'Angel.'

Dren's body shook with laughter, which turned to frantic choking as his toes scrabbled for purchase. He pressed down on Husker's forearms. 'He is undeserving of his body. So, given it is yours, what will you do with it?'

An avalanche rolled in Husker's head as Angel laughed. Out loud, it was his own voice that chuckled, but that didn't seem so strange. 'That is not how we do things,' said Angel. 'I have only stepped in for a moment.'

Dren scraped a finger along Husker's arm. He sniffed it, licked it. 'The leash is frayed.'

'Your brother broke it when we entered the keep. I can smell the spirit he couples with, eater. Once fire but now ice. She is beyond old.' Husker's nostrils flared as Angel sniffed the air. 'Older than any you have trapped, despite their number.'

Dren's eyes flicked over to the imposing door. 'And are you proud to be used this way, spirit? My brother guessed I would bring you here. He knew you would be mindless enough to turn on me, given the chance.'

'We don't care.' Angel pulled Husker's mouth up into one of his ice-scarred smiles. 'What is it you call me, eater? A runt? Manost was a runt too, before you joined us. We will take what revenge we can.'

'Put me down, spirit.' Dren gasped. 'Let us bargain.' He'd gone red in the face. Husker moved his arm an inch higher, watching the bastard's legs kick and thrash.

'Manost does not care for that idea. When I withdraw my will he will break you apart.'

'Tell him I will help the boy. I know what my brother has done – he will need my help.'

'Eater, without trust there can be no bargain.'

'Why are we talking, then?' Dren's eyes were draining of colour. Puffs of mist escaped from his lips and desperation sharpened his voice. 'What assurances can I give?'

'None.' Husker and Angel widened the smile together, breaking so much skin his jaw ran red. 'We wanted you to know your brother had tricked you.' They tightened his hand, seeking the popping noise of a crushed throat. Dren started to kick. He spat words that made no sense, hissing with a tongue made of spit and hot coals. With a final heave, his knee flew up high enough to rattle Husker's jaw, and when his hands came back down they slapped broiling mists over Husker's face. Howling spirits burrowed in, dragging Angel down to some murky, corporeal pit, and Husker lashed out as his body fell. He broke something hard, sent something soft flying away. He snarled, hoping either was Dren.

Angel was whispering advice. Husker wiped blood from his chin and rubbed it over his eyes; the mists hardened into a thick, slathering thing that peeled off in chunks under his fingers. It dragged out the invading spirits like thorns with a poultice.

'*There, manost!*'

Dren was prostrate before the doors, caught in some act of bizarre worship. Except his fists were clenched. His back was arched in pain. He flung back his head and wailed, and his body seemed to empty itself of everything dark and ethereal. Clouds rose from him, chattering with voices, and they swirled, whipping around to funnel over the metal doors. Husker lumbered forwards. Heavy tomes dangled from the ceiling by long chains, and he caught one as he passed, tearing down its anchor in a crack of masonry. With a snap of his wrists, he whipped the rubble over to lash Dren across the head. The bastard's liquid-black eyes flicked his way at the last moment. Spirits peeled off to bat it aside. Sparks flew as the chain pinged into two lengths.

The door groaned open. Dren scrambled up to sprint for the widening gap, and Husker leapt, swiping for a fistful of hair, and missing by fingertips. But he was close enough to hear the bastard whimper. Close enough to smell seared skin.

'Manost, wait!'

He already had his hands on the door. Husker strained, pulling the gap wider and wedging his chin through to roar a challenge. The metal bent as he forced his fat arm through, and Angel screamed with him, flesh and soul punished for this intrusion.

~

Husker lay still, face pressed against a snowdrift. 'Angel?' he croaked, spitting out snow that tasted of smoke.

Silence.

The doors behind him were twisted and black. Memories slipped through them, and Husker's fingers scraped furrows in the snow. He lay still a while longer. Eventually, he started to crawl. These were mountain instincts; sometimes you fell and didn't want to move. You had to start crawling. You had to start crawling, because the cold crop was creeping closer, and you had to crawl to keep warm and...

Packed snow fell from Husker's face. This wasn't the Mountain Head. A glass roof was tinting starlight and bathing some rolling snowdrifts in blue light. Statues filled every recess of the room, with icicles hanging from the arms of dancing women, dogs, cats and pigs, and each was turned to face a golden throne. The withered figure that was slumped in it seemed too gaunt for life, yet he raised a shaking hand in welcome. 'Is it done?' he asked, in a soft voice.

The man bowed his head, succumbing to the weight of his rank hair, which was matted with grime and woven through the folds of a shirt made for someone many times his size. His hands quivered under the burden of raising a battered crow, but when it was in place, his eyes rose from this rotten mess. They were lit with a curiosity that demanded answers. 'Are you my brother's protector?' he asked, a little louder. A noise rippled around the room as the statues echoed his words. A scream, but no louder than a whisper.

'Couldn't say,' said Husker, rubbing snow from his face. 'Not been myself lately.'

'You broke my door.'

Husker breathed deeply and held the chill in his chest. He felt safer here, where people could be safer around him. It was a shitty world that made it this way, but this snow was home. He looked back at the crumpled metal. 'Not much use as a door, is it? Doesn't let anyone through.'

The man chuckled. 'It costs a lot for creatures like us to pass.' His head tilted in contemplation. 'Perhaps you have lost something too, my friend? No Tar-Agran can pass the door unscathed, a lesson I learnt too late. The weakest are killed. The greatest are weakened.'

He had a point. Normally Angel wouldn't shut up, so this silence didn't bode well for a runt. Husker forged through the snow, searching for a sharp edge in some bones buried by a shallow drift. Elaborate weapons and gilded armour; these poor bastards were royal guard. Sealed in after the kings death, or something crazy like that. 'Nourish the earth, my friends.' Husker crouched down and gripped the point of a halberd, tight enough to cut his hand. 'And apologies.'

'They are dead,' said the man, peering around his throne. 'I am sure they will not mind.'

Husker winced. 'Be quiet a moment, will you? I can't listen with all these statues screeching at you.' The man dutifully fell silent. Husker watched his cut drip on the snow, just bleeding away. Seemed odd after all these years. Husker stood and turned his attention to the strange king. 'So, who the hell are you?'

'Terrano. King of the Split.' The statues whispered and screamed his name.

'You're the one that stole my boy, then. Brother to that other bastard that leashed me like an animal.'

'Dren? Did you kill him?' Terrano seemed only half-interested. 'I knew he would bring you. I broke his hold over you.'

'Damn it.' Husker cleaned out an ear. 'Why do these statues make so much noise?'

'They are mistaken!' Terrano hissed and leapt up on his haunches. He threw his crown at the nearest one. It gave a heavy clunk, dislodging an icicle. 'An age has passed since King Garradus looted the Long Path to decorate this throne room, but they think I am him. Can you believe that?'

'Seems fair. You're in his seat.'

'You will find that it is my seat.' Terrano leapt over the arms of the throne. He moved in large, elegant gestures, his oversized clothes and robes flowing behind him as he bent to pick up the crown. 'Who else is king, but he who sits on the Golden Throne?'

'Not you. Anyone would tell you that, if you let anyone up here.' Husker made his own seat in a snowdrift. He was only delaying the inevitable, but he relished this feeling of control.

Terrano scurried back and sat down. 'We have plenty of subjects. Every host below bends to my will, they carry my children.'

'I've met them.'

Terrano smiled, hugging his knees. 'I feel like you want to kill me. Perhaps I should say something?'

Husker settled into his snow throne. 'You will anyway.'

'You are worried about Lark, no doubt.' Terrano pursed his lips and nodded. 'Be at peace. I treated your son like my own, yes, even when I used him to lure in Dren. We all care for him. Under my guidance, he has taken up a mantel of great importance.' Terrano's eyes dipped momentarily, sent somewhere far away. 'I caged him only so he would not follow me up here. He would not survive the door, and the dear boy was destined to die for a better cause than loyalty.'

Husker's thumb stopped tracing Earth lines in the snow. He was behind on his scripture practise and couldn't remember the next phrase. 'Not the sort of words that save your life.'

Terrano chuckled silently, shoulders wriggling under his robes. 'Is that what you think? It is you who are dying, I am simply offering you comfort before you go. I am not like my brother.' He raised his arms and snow flew around his lap, piling up into the slender form of a young woman. Gossamer strands of ice grew out from her crystal skull. Snow hardened into glassy eyes. 'As I said, the greatest spirits are only weakened by the door.' Terrano nuzzled her face, his cheeks sticking to icy skin. 'My hard-hearted brother and I dug her up in the mountains – the same day he made you his protector, in fact. I feel I chose my ally better.' The spirit melted between poses. Sitting in Terrano's arms. Standing at his side. Standing behind him. Her hands settled over his shoulders and she was taller now, looming over the throne.

'She is from another age,' Terrano mumbled. His eyes lost their focus, and his fingers wandered over the rim of his dented crown. 'An elder spirit who has come fully into our world. Why subjugate her, Dren? Why waste her on the wards?' The spirit's hands melted down his face, soothing his mad whispers with a caress. 'We are fond of each other,' he snapped. 'Fonder, stronger. I will not use and discard her.' The spirit pulled back her lips in agreement, revealing a mouth filled with icicle-sharp teeth.

'And you.' Terrano's focus returned as he smiled. 'You are like her, or something similar. So angry. So hot. The mountains near your home were once as hot as you, do you know that? My love cooled with them over the years, bones and memories at the Mountain Feet. Until we dug her up.' Terrano ran his fingers down her arm. 'I offered the Court a queen. No need to keep me as a slave and hunter if they could breed spirits of their own.' He raised his head suddenly. 'Where is Dren? You did not tell me how you killed him.'

'He got away.' Turned out Husker had remembered some scripture after all. He'd got a whole verse down while this prick was rambling.

'Oh. He stole my spirits.' Terrano struggled in the spirit queen's arms. 'A moment, my dear, I am finding it hard to breathe.' His words became strained. 'See, we are very close. She will not let you harm me.'

'Yeah.' Husker brushed scabs off his palm. 'Where's Lark? Sounds like he's still alive.'

The spirit's smile was filled with affection. Her fangs disappeared behind perfect, crystalline lips. 'Our boy!' cried Terrano. 'My little Lark. We had him released.' He stroked his clothes, feeling every mouldy stitch. 'Taken away into the city, and there he will be opened up. He will give his life so more of our children will be born. Lark is their nest.' Terrano sighed. 'And such a sweet child. I wish he had not proved so unique in his resilience.'

'I think I preferred Dren to you,' said Husker, bowing his head. 'And that's saying something.' He felt the furnace being stoked within his heart, and started to loosen his neck.

Terrano frowned, sniffing the air. 'You brought a spirit past my door?'

'More than a spirit,' Angel rasped, rolling words up Husker's throat. It raised his head. 'This flesh is my fortress, eater.'

Husker lunged at the throne. Statues screamed as the spirit queen melted forwards. She stretched up in a screech of ice, nails elongating into talons, shoulders bristling with spines. With no time to turn, Husker saw only a blur of claws before blood was running down his face. He growled, blinking furiously, and stumbled to a halt. One of his eyes had gone dark.

'Do without it, manost,' rattled Angel, flowing into his hands and filling them with heat. *'We shall ruin her anyway.'* The spirit queen struck again, but this time Husker met her forearm in a grip as hot as forge tongs. Steam billowed as she melted, snapped and vanished. Husker stalked backwards, watching the snowdrifts for movement.

With a glacial creak, the spirit reformed and spilled his guts. Husker staggered, hitting the snow with his hand and knee. Hissing victoriously, the spirit stepped up and raised her talons. But fuck, ancient spirits make the same mistakes as everyone else. Husker was big, but he wasn't slow. He savoured the way her crystal eyes widened as they rolled down to see the hand he'd pushed through her abdomen. He relished Terrano's wail as he pulled out a fistful of ice. It crunched in his grip, and the spirit recoiled in a series of eerie shrieks, throwing up clouds of snow as she retreated behind the throne.

Like any good brawler after landing a lucky hit, Husker took a moment to gather himself. He scooped up his stomach from the snow. It squelched as he pushed it back into place, and his skin tore as he straightened up. But not bad, though. Not bad, given the mess she was in. 'Need a hand?' he asked. Blood dripped from his smile and joined the pink slush around his shins.

The spirit was gathering up snow with her claws, packing it down over her chest in awkward, shaky movements, throwing him looks like a cornered animal. Husker strode over and smashed her back with a double fist, cursing as she vanished in a gale of snow. Angel rasped a warning, so he planted his heels and barrelled backwards, crashing into her as she reformed, running onto some spines for his trouble. Things were getting to that desperate, bloody stage, the one where both fighters slapped on whatever blows they could cobble together. Husker's teeth took out a chunk of ice. Her swinging elbow broke his jaw. He tried to crush her in a bear hug, but those icy talons scythed in quick, vicious arcs that butchered him into red streaks. Husker wiped his eyes as they pulled apart, and tried to follow her movements.

'*Keep going, manost,*' Angel snarled. But the spirit sounded weak. A gash across Husker's back hadn't closed. His calf buckled under a severed tendon.

Now or fucking never. With a shove from his remaining leg, he threw himself at the throne, roaring and opening his arms wide. The spirit queen screeched in panic and darted across to block him. Husker's arms slammed together, smashing her into pieces and slapping his hands around Terrano's crown.

With a final, fleshy crack, it was over.

Lark

Another deafening storm of rifle-fire. Small flashes. Belches of flame lit up a line of raised elbows and cocked heads. Lily winced at the lingering screams and carried on limping towards the gatehouse. Fingers gripped her wrist, and she turned, but Rose pulled her away from Thora's flushed, excited face.

'You can thank her later.'

More orders were cried out. Some torches were raised. A line of crouched watchmen handed up loaded rifles and carefully tended to those that were passed back. Blacksand bullets were hellish projectiles, tearing flesh where they struck and leaving rot in their wake. Lily knew this, as one had ripped a hole in her hand.

'What's wrong?' Rose reached the relative safety of the gatehouse, but still ducked as the rifles cracked out another round. 'Is your ankle hurting?' Lily nodded. The sinkstone had crumbled away, but the pain and fear it left behind were better than the terrifying numbness eating its way up her arm.

Highwall was still lit up by beautiful festival lanterns, even if the revellers had been slaughtered and scattered over the cobbles. Fires roasted the remaining darkness and flecked it with embers. Scuttling shapes ran between slumped bodies.

'How are we going to find Lark in all this?' Fingers lifted Lily's chin. A palm was laid on her cheek. 'Lils? You're burning up!'

No comforts were whispered in her head, no light shone from her dry skin. Everything was dull, dead and quiet. Lily hung on to Rose, hiding frightened tears against her apron. 'You stink,' she whispered. Each flutter of her heart pushed the rot further. Past her shoulder, past her neck. The poison was a cold hand that cupped her chin and started to squeeze.

'What's this?' Rose had found the rotting hole in her palm. Lily's lips were forced apart, and something small and hard was forced in, which she swallowed.

~

'One step at a time,' Lily murmured. 'Right?' The sky rolled past. Each star was dragging a trail of violet flames, streaking paths across the inky void. Clouds boiled up to form Thora's lips, which parted and vanished in a crack of gunfire.

'Lily?' a voice said.

'Rose? Where are you?'

The clouds forming Thora's face fell and became everything, thick as a thunderstorm and crackling with life. Whispers and moans rippled through the smog, and they pushed past in currents that tugged at Lily's feet. She stumbled, almost losing her balance.

No, wait. She was lying down.

'Lils! I need help.'

Lily stood up. Her hand had a hole in it, but the wound was warm and wet. 'It hurts,' she said, tearing up as she cradled the injury. 'You saved my life.'

'Oh and I'm very happy about that, dear sister. Can you come and repay the favour?' Rose's voice was starting to take on a strangled, high-pitched quality. 'Please? Now?'

'Where are you? There's smoke everywhere.' Lily waved at it, and shrieked as light burst from the wound in her hand. Smouldering rubble. Burnt timber. Prone bodies and abandoned tables. The light faded, and Lily gasped as a wave of pain rippled up her arm, like the wound had sucked it all back in. 'That was weird.'

'You've missed the weirdest bits.'

Lily took a few steps towards Rose's voice, fighting against a damp and sticky dress. 'I've figured out how you saved me.'

'Oh yes?'

Rose sounded desperate, clinging to the stilted conversation much like she did driftwood when they went swimming. But Lily must have become muddled somehow, as her sister's voice was now behind her. She walked in that direction instead. 'You found the rest of the sinkstone in my pocket.' Glowing gunk pattered on the floor as Lily walked. 'How much did you give me?'

'All of it.'

Lily grimaced. Earlier that evening she'd chipped some off and ground it up, pinching it into a glass of cheap whisky. It's not that she didn't trust Shana enough to swallow the whole thing – well okay, that's exactly what it was. No stomach cramps this time, at least. 'I can't see you,' she said, frowning at the swirling smoke. 'Say something else.'

'How about, hurry up?'

Lily sighed. 'This is ridiculous. Either I'm going crazy or you keep moving around.'

'Something keeps... tugging me away.'

'How did you know the sinkstone would drain away blacksand? Was that in Dren's book?' Lily listened, turning around to pinpoint her reply.

'I just guessed. Your skin was hot, but your belly was freezing.' Rose was moving again. 'It seemed like it was fighting off the poison. So I gave you more.'

Lily wiped gunk from her forehead. 'Well, it worked. What's with all this smoke?'

'It's coming from me. Can you make that light again?'

Now there was an idea. Lily raised her hand and squeezed, forcing out another burst of light. Rose wasn't far away. 'You know, that really stings,' she said, fumbling towards her as the light sunk back into her hand. 'So, what's the problem?' She could make out bare shoulders and torn clothes. Fingers clutching at handfuls of ragged hair.

'I don't know,' whispered Rose.

Lily reached out to comfort her and missed. She swore and clapped her hands, darting forwards in time to drive off the smoke creatures which were dragging Rose around. They had spindly, gas-like forms, but scattered and broke when Lily drew near.

'There was a scream.' Rose was on her knees and didn't look up. Maybe she couldn't. 'I swear it sounded like Lark. Then all this liquid came flooding out of a side street and I tried to run. But more and more of it kept chasing me, and now I feel so heavy I can't move. It's getting heavier, Lils. I can't move and it's hard to breathe.'

'Shh, keep calm.' The gunk on her hand was glowing enough for her to examine Rose's back, but gods be fucked if she knew what she was looking at. 'It's some sort of black stream? It's running up over your shoulders and dissolving, that's what's making the smoke.'

'Please,' begged Rose. 'Help me.'

'I will. I need to find out where it's coming from.'

'No!' Rose's objection was weak and distant – she'd been moved again. Lily tried to ignore her and pushed her fingertips into the black stream, feeling out its strange current. It was cold and scratchy, like liquid grit, but it would do to lead her through the smoke. Keeping crouched, she followed it upriver.

Spirit slugs mewled at her from under cloaks. Rats ran over painted faces and festive baubles. Each of these details became clear only when

Lily trod on them, but the sinkstone was helping her keep a steady pace. It whispered to her, and its comforting mantra slowed her quickening breath. 'One step at a time,' she muttered. 'One step. At a time. One step.' It was too much doing this blind. On an impulse, Lily clapped and lit up the square. 'Oh gods.'

The black stream was weaving her between a dozen corpse piles. Each Highwaller was sorted by age and gender, and left here ready to be hauled into the Scarlet Keep. Some of them had even been dragged part way towards the gatehouse, before the person doing the dragging had been summarily dismembered. Feasters scuttled between the piles, hissing and leaping back up onto a rooftop. When the light faded, Lily decided, on balance, that she preferred being blind. Though that didn't stop her screaming when she stumbled into one of the piles, and it certainly didn't stop her discarding the elegant words of the sinkstone for a rendition of muttered fucks.

The smoke started to fight her as she pushed on into a side street. Ethereal creatures snatched at her for purchase, howling in frustration as they were sucked away towards the square. There was something not entirely present about them, with a smell that eluded memory. In fact, it was this annoying trait that Lily at last recognised. Back in the palace, Rose's tonic had lured in spirit slugs and splatted them up into this stuff. She'd worn a little cloud of it like a fashion accessory. Now, you'd need a hell of a lot of slugs to make a cloud like this, and there were a lot of corpses back there for them to wriggle into. So... bloody hell. That tonic of hers had driven a horse and cart through Terrano's plans. Rose Kale-Tollworth, slayer of spirits. Winner of bets.

'You going to let her get away with that?' Lily gritted her teeth and pushed on another step. 'She doesn't even like whisky.'

The sinkstone gurgled. Glowing sweat burst from her skin like she was overripe fruit. It ran down her shins and mixed with the black stream, weaving golden cobble-trails and gobbling up smoke in flashes of light. The storm of spirits screamed and swirled, eventually parting to reveal a small boy.

'Lily?' he asked, tentatively.

'Wow.' She crouched next to him, keeping the distance he liked. 'Good thing you recognised me. Because you've changed your hair.'

'Not just my hair,' said Lark glumly, clutching at his side. Someone had dressed her little brother in rags. His black veins wriggled under translucent skin, and he shone with a sickly hue.

'I'm glowing, too. What's so bad about that?'

'Yours is nicer.' He started crying. 'Look at what they did to me.' Lark peeled his hands away. Spirit slugs crawled from a gash on his midriff and spilled down over his belly. They tried to wriggle away, but the black stream swelled, sucking them up and melting them down in belches of smoke and spray. Lightning flashed as the sinkstone drowned Lily in protective sweat.

Lark covered the cut. 'Did you see them?'

'Just about.' Lily scraped gunk from her eyes.

'So why are you glowing? Mine's from these things. I think they're making babies in me.'

'Oh, I ate a magic rock.' Lily tucked stray hair away from his eyes, waiting to see how he'd take it. Sometimes he let her. 'What's with all those veins, Lark? Have you been sick?'

'Sort of.' He was crying again.

'Don't worry. We can fix this.'

Lark winced. 'I can't keep–' His hands slipped and slugs sprayed from the wound, feeding the stream and filling the air with shrieking voices. Ankle-deep in rising black liquid, Lily bent into a smoke storm that rushed past and stripped the gunk from her skin. Trailing claws left cuts over her cheek. Her dress was scythed with a thousand tiny rips.

She carefully replaced Lark's hands. 'What's going on under there? Does it hurt?'

'Can you take a look?' he asked. 'I'll hold them back a bit.'

She nodded. 'Ready? Oh, hey.' The hug he gave her was unexpected, almost as surreal as the calm that settled over the street. 'Well, this is nice,' she said, awkwardly peering past his shoulder. The cut in Lark's side was long and ragged, like someone had tried to open it up as wide as possible.

'Buller did it,' said Lark, mumbling into her hair.

'Who's Buller?'

'My friend. He's over there somewhere.' Lark waved behind him. 'He stabbed me, then started crying and went over there. He's quiet now.'

Lily moved Lark's hands back into place. 'Press down tight, I need to think.' She stood and squeezed her hand to create more light, but it guttered, barely pushing back the smoke. 'Come on,' she said, patting her stomach. 'A bit of help?' No response from the sinkstone. 'Come on!' Lily slapped her palm against the wall in frustration, but it took a while to scream her way past that decision.

She opened her eyes to find Lark watching her. Sinkstone gunk was pumping from her hand in a nightmarish stream. 'That's disgusting,' he said, still clutching his side.

Lily inspected her palm, grimly fascinated at how light surged from it in a beam that didn't fade or dim. 'I'm sorry, Lark.' A large man was slumped up against a rain barrel. He didn't move as she passed the light over a nasty scar on his neck. 'I think he's dead. Was he really your friend?' The knife he'd used to open his wrists had been hurled against a wall, chipping its blue-white blade.

'He didn't want to do it.' Lark's face twitched as the beam illuminated him again. 'But he had one of these spirits in him. They're nasty, cold things, and Terrano makes you do things through them. Buller thought he was free but he wasn't.'

Lily crouched next to Lark, moving her hand slowly over his wound. He screamed in pain. 'Sorry!' she said, aghast. 'What did I do?'

'Again,' demanded Lark.

'What?'

'Again!' he yelled. 'Again, again!'

Like they were back in Branera. Lily always made up the best games. Rose was too stuck-up to throw mud from the rooftop or chase fish in the stream. 'Again,' he'd shout as she loosed a handful of mud at the chickens pecking around the Merchant Gate. 'Again!'

'Again!' He gripped her shoulders, his dark-veined face monstrous and joyful. Hesitantly, Lily hovered her hand over the wound. He flung back his head and gritted his teeth, and the smell of singed flesh filled the air. He pressed their cuts together. Lily gasped, eyes watering at the cruel strength in her brother's fingers.

'Lark?' she said, wincing at the pain.

'Don't worry,' he said in a small voice. Light poured from her hand to sear his corrupted flesh. 'I'm ready.'

A Beautiful City

'My lords, the creature hid its cunning well. It is hard to blame the Court for not noticing, even if that is your agenda.' Wine flasks slammed against the table and the council's grumbling moved to open rebuke. The informant remained standing, ignoring their gestures at the door. 'We believed Terrano could barely speak without our permission, let alone assault the city. Our oldest courtiers had bound him to their masks—'

'Brazen child.' Saarban's minister of justice was on his feet, though barely. One of his arms shook against the tabletop. 'Are we to openly talk of the King's ways now?' He gestured for the informant to explain himself, collapsing into his seat to wheeze and pant.

The informant bowed his head respectfully. 'We thought your attendance at our banquets indicated approval, Minister. We thought you shared our fondness for the old ways, if kept suitably discreet.'

He did that a lot, laying out their indiscretions before the rest. Lily liked to watch the glint in his eye as he dismantled them so neatly. Her hand hovered over a loaf less mouldy than the rest.

'Can I take another of these?' she whispered.

The ration keeper urged her to take it, picking it up and laying it in her basket. 'Please. Any word from Highwall? Will the lifts open soon?'

Lily smiled. 'The lifts are open now.'

The woman shook her head. 'I mean, when will it be safe?'

'Perhaps soon.'

Banging fists gave way to more coughing. Every window had been flung open to let in the unwholesome air of the Wet Rings, but the council's lungs were slowly rotting anyway. The flood had lingered too long, with waterlogged bodies still being found in the most unlikely of places.

The informant's voice remained steady as he wiped broth from his face. 'I understand your disbelief, gentlemen. I was abroad on business until yesterday, so I can only give you a partial account. My final account, too, until you resume my pay.'

Coughing. Hard stares. The informant shrugged.

'Your choice, of course,' he said. 'The hollow-soul tried to bargain with us, a dangerous sign of independent thought. He was recalled to his cage, yet he returned with a patrol of watchmen and slaughtered everyone in the Scarlet Keep. Every courtier he raised from the dead became his slave, a host for a new kind of spirit he had created.'

He paused as a merchant indicated he wanted to speak. Everyone watched as the red-faced man struggled to his feet, then struggled to clear his lungs. The informant put down a glass of water and raised his voice again. 'The festival was his opportunity to strike. House guards were isolated to their rooftops. City militia were stuck outside the walls. Your best peacekeepers were sent out to keep order among the displaced working class.'

An heir to the red-faced merchant helped his struggling father find a seat. 'Don't insinuate that we were unprepared, courtier. My family paid for boats to patrol the flooded streets, as did every man around this table. That has been enough to deter looters and troublemakers for years.'

The glint in the informant's eye was back. 'Terrano drowned men in his cellars, creating slaves that could breathe underwater. Some took sword thrusts without slowing.' The informant's open hand addressed each council member in turn. 'Which of you spent enough money to repel such an attack?'

Lily shared a look with the ration keeper. 'He's going to lose his pretty head, speaking like that.' She waved a dismissive hand. 'Anyway, so long. Stick it on my slate.'

The ration keeper gave a shy grin, tucking her pigtails back up into a hair wrap. 'You don't have a slate. Just get us our homes back.'

Lily could make out the places where jewels had once adorned her neck – empty bands and hollow circlets. Some Highwallers adjusted. Some didn't.

~

The trudge up to the Highwall lifts was as depressing as ever. The armoured clank of Lily's escort made her twitchy, the stench of the Wet Rings made her nauseous. Despite their obvious failings, the city council still commanded a few soldiers, and the leader of this ragged troop was waiting for her by the waterfall basin.

'About time,' he said, banging his chest to dislodge something. He noisily filled a handkerchief with it. 'I can't chew this air fast enough to catch my breath.' None of his men would work the lifts anymore, but Fammadi was too ambitious to admit something as commonplace as fear. He waved her escort back and opened the gate for Lily to board.

'Try it further down. The council won't last much longer.'

'What a tragedy.' Fammadi stood at the bars, swaying with the enclosure and watching the Wet Rings fall away. He was still patriotic, in an everything's-fucked sort of way. 'I wonder if they've taken a look at the mob outside their door this evening?'

They passed the enclosure he was using as a bedroom, suspended from another lift beside a church spire. He'd wrapped blankets around the bars to keep out the wind and claimed his new perch was for the health of his lungs. A weak excuse. Without him issuing a single order, his men had slowly deserted the council and the ration house, camping down in his church instead. Lily thought he had the look of someone biding his time.

Fammadi breathed deeply, taking in a lungful of the freshening air. 'Anyone come in through the gates yet?'

'Opening them wasn't the problem.'

'It's just tents,' he said sourly, spitting over the edge.

'They're a better home than the Wet Rings. With all the debris and sickness, that's too small a place with too many people.'

'The wrong type of people.'

Lily grinned, gripping the bars as they rattled through a chain junction. 'You should make a move soon if you want to keep those Highwallers alive, and stop waiting for your militia to come back. Trust me on this, the tent council they serve are as charismatic as they are ruthless. They don't fawn and scrape over me like those idiots in the ration house – and I'm pretty sure I fancy at least two of them. Give them any indication a plague is breaking out in the Wet Rings and they'll bar the gates from the outside. People will love them for it.' She let him chew over this latest news and looked out over the lower city. From this height Lily couldn't smell it. She couldn't see the gaunt faces of people who'd spent their vast fortunes on rationed chunks of mouldy bread. The mosaics in the dried-up waterways were bright under the sun – it was only up close you saw the city's cracks and smears.

Feasters prowled over the approaching platform. They were sniffing the rattling chains curiously, and one leapt up onto the enclosure roof. Fammadi secured the brakes, stiffening slightly when she purred and swiped a hand through the bars. Lily stepped briskly out. 'Come on, now. Get down.' She pulled the snarling creature off by a foot and tossed her back to the others, hissing to scatter them. Baleful eyes watched her from the lift sheds as she juggled baskets, searching her pockets for a sarl.

'They're going to turn on you if you do that.' Fammadi joined her outside the enclosure, probably just to prove a point.

'Hah. Feaster's don't get hurt that easily.' She held out a coin. 'Almost time for your revolution, surely?'

He pushed his windswept hair back into place and retreated into the enclosure. 'Too tired today.' He waved away her money. 'No need for that.' Lily watched him descend, letting cliff winds blow the smell of decay from her clothes.

Feasters scrambled at her heels when she left. She had to kick one off her boots, and the girl-thing skidded away, too crestfallen to make another attempt for her baskets. 'Shana says no meat. No meat!' Lily held back the basket, watching their eyes follow it. 'But I've got something else.' She opened a drawstring bag and flung out its contents. Delicious crunchy pebbles, fetched all the way from Krans. The feasters scuttled after them, squabbling and hissing as they pried these treats from cracks in the crumbling street. After watching for a moment, Lily shrugged and held up a metal puzzle box. A dozen small heads turned her way. 'There's meat in here.' She tossed it to them. 'Figure it out.'

Lily carefully picked her way over a ruined mansion, which was her latest shortcut to the palace. Highwall was fading. It was bound to the Scarlet Keep in some way, held together by a force stranger and weaker than stone and mortar. Her exploration of the palace cellars had found many machines and cogs, with empty vats that should be filled, and pipes with symbols for water. There were plenty of things that looked like they should be turning, but weren't. Plenty of things that should be alive, instead of dead. There wasn't much she could do about that. Even if the Wet Rings desperately needed their waterfalls back. Even if the mansions of Highwall were crumbling. Lily hurried past the street where she'd found Lark dying, still strangely intact. Too many bad memories.

The Palace of Sells was still an imposing sight. It didn't seem capable of fading, and it stood imperiously over the growing ruins at its feet. 'Road greetings, sister,' called Shana, raising a needle as Lily approached. She looked so tiny in her oversized chair, her sewing so delicate a pastime under the looming arch of blacksand-shattered gates.

'Don't call me that.' Lily threw her a ragged dress. 'Found this. You sure you don't want me to get them new clothes?'

Shana shook her head and carried on sewing. 'They need their old ones.' She pricked her finger and tears welled up in her eyes. 'Ow!' Lily waited for the crying to stop, unwilling to play mother. Shana had been the first to recover her balance since slaughtering Terrano's assassins, but she was still indulging her inner brat at every opportunity. After a while, the feaster wiped away her tears and resumed sewing.

'Still got her chained up, then,' said Lily, holding her ground as Brenne clinked out into the daylight.

'Sorry about last time. If she's jealous, that's a good sign.'

'Jealous?' Lily watched Brenne's face quiver with hatred, all wrinkles and fangs. Her chain clinked as it drew taught.

'She thinks we'll be a pairing.' Shana put down her needle, looking Lily over with weary concern. Her age flickered. 'I cannot fathom why the sinkstone did not drain away my blessing. I only meant to lend you our senses.'

'They've gone. Stop worrying.' Lily ignored the wet pulse of Shana's small, fluttering heart. 'She's not recovered, then? I see she's still wearing her dress.'

Shana giggled, twirling her hair around a finger. 'You still wearing it, Brenney? Still in your pretty dressy?' She turned back to Lily with a breathless whisper. 'I've stitched her into it. She's a naughty bitch and takes it off otherwise.' Her expression grew heavy and old. 'Did you give the council my message?'

Lily sighed. 'No. I'm not the type to kick a person when they're down.'

'I have faith in you.'

'They think I'm taming you or something, driving you out of the city.'

'This cliff was our home long before they came,' said Shana. She cut some thread with her age-sharpened teeth and played it around her fingers. 'It is ours again now.'

'Isn't that a bit underhand? Using Terrano's rebellion as an excuse to claim it? There's thousands of people down there without a home.'

Shana frowned, her needle glinting as it pierced and pulled. 'History is a long series of people taking things off each other.'

'You sound like Dren,' said Lily. She picked up her baskets, trying not to make it obvious that she was giving Brenne a wide berth.

'Get me some more thread, if you would.' Shana's needle paused. 'I found one of your puzzle boxes. Didn't I say no meat? Some might call it cruel.' Shana turned on Lily with an impish grin. 'I watched them try to open one.'

'It's a good idea, that's what it is,' Lily protested. 'They're too weak to force open the clasp, but if they—'

'I understand.' Shana dismissed her with a flick and turned back to her sewing. 'It nurtures their senses, drives back the feast. You're not as stupid as some dulls.'

Lily sniffed. 'Want me to get you one of those boxes, too? Might prick your fingers less.' Shana smiled and continued her clumsy needlework. But she was making a worrying purring sound, so Lily hurried off.

~

Living in a palace was not as glamorous as it might seem. It was Rose who'd found the drain for the courtyard lake, leaving behind a pit of bloodstained gravel and tainted bodies. It was Lily who'd thought to ask Shana for help with the rest.

Not the best idea she'd ever had. The next morning feasters were everywhere, draped over walls and dozing off swollen bellies, and the sound of them pitifully spewing black liquid was quite disgusting. Shana had started them on their diet the next day, and Rose had started to mop.

'Missed a bit,' said Lily, standing over her on a lake path. Rose looked up from the basin, shielding her eyes against the sunset. Her spot of clean gravel was set against a vast expanse of pink-and-black-splattered pebbles.

'New clothes, Lils?'

'Do you like them?' Lily wiggled a boot at her. 'A gift from the council. My old ones were stained.'

'It's the trousers I'm shocked at.'

'I'm done with dresses. Too similar to those little monsters outside.'

'Well, that's fair enough. Shana still won't let me pass, you know.' Rose shuddered. 'Not that I want to. All those little faces everywhere you look. I don't know what they see in you.'

Lily shrugged. Air roared in Rose's nostrils, swelling and draining her lungs. 'I've traded some more empty promises for dinner, if you're hungry.' Rose nodded and threw her dirty water down one of the drains. She ignored Lily's offered hand and climbed up herself.

'Just keep a hold on those baskets. I'd pull you in.'

'Doubt it. They feed me so much the lifts have started to creak.'

Rose led them through the thatch rooms. She'd marked doors with different dyes to indicate which ones were clean, or safe, or suspicious. The palace was a strange place, and even if they ignored all the dead things in cages, there were a lot of tasks that needed addressing quite urgently. They'd already flooded three cellars. Lily nudged open a door and reversed into the Scarlet Keep, angling her baskets to fit through the gap. 'Lark,' she called. 'I've brought food.'

Rose sat down in the nearest armchair, coughing at the resulting cloud of dust. She waved her arms and sneezed. 'Didn't we clean this room?'

'Who knows? They all look the same.'

Lark dropped straight out of the ceiling, wrapped up in a cloud of chattering spirits. He spun between them in a dance, and darted over to Rose for a hug. She yelped and dodged, fending him off with a basket. 'Not yet! Go see Lily first.'

His face fell. 'Sorry, I forgot. Father doesn't mind.'

Lily beckoned him over. 'Come over here, you little freak. Shirt off.' He dutifully trudged over, scolding his spirits to keep them quiet. 'Arms up!' She helped him out of his shirt. 'Good boy. Now, let's have a look.'

The wound on his side didn't bleed, but it didn't heal. The liquid that wept from it clung onto his skin, creating a dark crust that Lily had to break off before tending to him.

'I think it's getting better!' She rolled up her sleeves, grimacing as she peeled away the scab. 'Oh gods.' She gagged, turning her head away.

'Is she lying?' Lark asked Rose.

'Yes. But she's only trying to be nice.' Rose craned her neck round for a look. 'It's not getting worse.'

'That's good,' he said. 'Lily! That hurts.'

She ignored him and concentrated. The glow from the sinkstone had settled into a scar on her hand, bright enough to make Rose bitch and moan until Lily agreed to sleep in a separate room, hand tucked under a pillow. Pressed up against Lark's wound, the latent sinkstone fragments came alive, angry and bright enough to sear it clean. It stung like anything. Or more specifically, it stung like sticking your hand in a wasp nest, waggling it about, then counting to ten.

She got as far as six and had to stop because Lark was copying her, and she couldn't laugh and swear at the same time. 'Enough!' She threw his shirt at him, flexing her swollen hand. 'That's it. That's all you get for being cheeky.'

He grinned and threw himself at Rose, who enveloped him in a hug that shook him left and right. 'Oh, Larky! Aren't you the huggable one?'

'Mmmm-not. You're almost as soft as Father.'

Rose made a face. 'Hey!' She looked around. 'He's not coming down, is he?'

'No.' Lark snuggled into her arms, leg twitching. 'He prefers it up in the snow room.'

'You feel anything?' said Lily, gesturing and raising her eyebrows. Rose shook her head, and a smile warmed her cheeks. Their brother's tearful stories had helped them understand some of what had happened to him, but couldn't account for what he didn't understand himself. Rose had finger-shaped scabs from where he hugged her after a nightmare last week, a shoulder rash from where he cried. They managed as best they could.

Something urgent was happening in Lily's stomach. She mumbled an excuse and bolted through the thatch rooms, not quite making it before throwing up athletically into the lake basin, vaguely missing the nearest drain. Sinkstone vomit was bright enough to see in the gathering dusk. 'Drat,' she mumbled, eyeing the smear.

A shadow fell over her. 'Miss, your sister will never get this place clean if you don't help.'

Lily wiped her mouth and fixed Dren with a venomous look. She left her scarred hand over the edge to drain it, gunk dripping down onto the gravel. 'Push off, Dren. Leave me to my new and glamorous lifestyle.'

'I have come to help – is that any way to treat me?' He offered her a bottle that smelt of juni. 'I am both celebrating and commiserating the loss of a brother, if you would care to join me?'

'I don't drink.' Lily stood up, wiping her hand and looking down at his bruised and battered face. 'Are you shorter? Your coat doesn't fit and you look like shit.'

He smiled, teeth still oddly pristine despite his swollen cheeks and grazed face. 'The last courtier whose mask bound me to this keep had secluded herself near the throne room. Unfortunately, your father found me on the way back down.' He opened his coat to reveal a bruised ribcage and, thankfully, some trousers. 'I am diminished. With my spirits spent on the door, I could not defend myself.' He buttoned up his coat. 'But never fear, the bonds of the Old Court are broken. I am ready once again to help.'

'Take your sodding help elsewhere. Rose has forgotten you, I'd prefer to keep it that way.'

'Ah, please do not misunderstand.' He fidgeted. 'My feelings for your sister have... moved on. I am sorry.'

'I wouldn't worry.' Lily started walking back to her dinner, and Dren darted around to cut her off, his eyes flashing with irritation. Yet they didn't fade to black. No puffs of mist escaped his lips. 'Huh. You mean it, don't you?' she said, looking down at the shrivelled hand clamping her wrist. 'There's nothing left in that hollow soul of yours.'

'Why are you being like this?' he moaned. 'I have always protected you. I have always looked out for you.'

Lily broke his nose. The sky was dark enough to see the glow between her knuckles as she stood over his groaning body and thought about what to say. 'Shana said you owe us a debt. Now might be the time to tell me about it.'

'Norther brat,' he hissed, wiping blood from his lips. 'You are beyond ungrateful.' Lily crouched and stroked Dren's swollen cheek, drawn to the smell of bruised flesh. He gripped her hand and nuzzled it. 'Miss, I never meant for any of you to suffer.' He kissed her fingers. 'It is true. I wronged you, replacing your father with that monstrosity in the throne room. But I have been unwavering in making amends! I found you a rich foster home in Branera. I helped you track down Lark. I taught Rose to mix a tonic that kept you safe from my brother's spirits.'

He gargled in shock as Lily put a hand to his neck. 'How kind of you,' she said, leaning in. 'You know, Terrano kept asking for you when he was trying to kill us. He said he wanted his spirits back, the ones that made you so fancy and dramatic before. He might have kidnapped Lark, but he was really after you, wasn't he?' She leant in a little harder, feeling his cowardly heart thump and spurt. 'Have you met my little brother? He's not the same as he was.'

'Not my fault,' he croaked.

'I'm different too.'

'Miss, my—'

Lily let him stagger to his feet. She turned, unwilling to show him her face. 'I'll say it plainly, because you're too arrogant to see it.' She wiped her eyes, and in a blur she was at his back. The gentle shove she gave him sent him staggering. 'Whatever you did, we don't care. Kindly fuck off and stop trying to fix things.'

Dren stood there a moment, shoulders wilting. Then he started walking, and surprised her by not looking back.

~

Lark left Rose dozing in the chair, as he wanted to go climbing. But first he'd checked her over to make sure his hands hadn't bitten her, because last time she'd lied and he'd hated that.

There were a lot of stairs in the Scarlet Keep. Normally he relied on his spirits to do the work, but Lily had killed a lot of them so he was soon very much out of breath. It was better, though. After some practice he'd learnt how to push the nastier spirits out through the cut, and keep the nicer ones in his head.

'You are a monster, manost.' A spirit clawed at his thoughts to show him it was angry. *'You let our brothers die in that witch's light.'*

Nicer, but not nice. 'Shut up,' he whispered. 'You hurt me often enough.'

'One day you will suffer again at our hands.' It slunk away.

Crone was snoring on her cot. She didn't want to come out of her cage, but Father had helped him play a trick to make it bigger. The blue-white bars had lost their spark, so they'd taken them all out when she was sleeping, and leant her cage door against the lip leading to the stairs. She'd grumbled when she woke up, but accepted that she was still on the same side of her door, still inside her cage. They'd just made it bigger.

He watched Crone open an eye. She pulled her wig apart to look at him suspiciously, and made a few gestures with her hand. He replied with a few of his own. He'd found a book on it, a way to talk with your hands. Luckily, it had pictures and was for babies. Otherwise he'd have to teach her to read, too, and that seemed too hard.

Lark reached the library on the top floor. 'Father?' The metal doors creaked open and admitted a blast of wintry air, so Lark pulled down a tapestry to wrap around his shoulders. He'd burnt all the ones with courtiers on them.

Husker padded over and picked him up. 'Hmmm. You're not stinging so much today. I sort of miss it.'

'Lily's getting better at cleaning me. You don't mind, though, do you?'

His father laughed, setting him down and placing a battered crown on Lark's head. It was too large, and he had to tilt his neck to keep it on. 'Nothing can hurt me, little prince.' Husker poked Lark in the belly. 'Angel keeps me safe.'

'Am I really a prince?' said Lark. He wrapped the tapestry tighter around him.

'I killed a king, or a man who thought he was king.' Husker wore that mock-serious face that adults used when playing with children. Lark pretended he hadn't seen it. 'By rights that means I have his throne.'

'Do you want to come and have dinner? Lily and Rose are there.'

'I'll come down when they're gone.'

'They'd like it if you came down,' said Lark. 'They—'

'They fear me,' he said. 'As they should.'

'But it was that other man that made you kill everyone,' said Lark stubbornly. 'Terrano's brother.'

'It was me.'

'It was the thing in you, then, the spirit. I've got them too. I know what they're like.'

'Angel is different.' Husker sat down and held out his arms, letting Lark climb into his lap. 'No, son, I've done this before, I can do it again. I'll remain up here in the cold until I can come down as a man. Did you send my letter?'

'To the priest? Priest Young?' Lark fidgeted with his hands. 'I gave it to Lily, I didn't want to go out too far.'

'She's a good girl, she will send it. Just let me know when he arrives.'

'I have something for you!'

'My pendant?' Husker's massive, dented face looked hopeful.

'Maybe something better?' Lark stammered, suddenly unsure. 'I did look for it, but I found this instead. Lily said you'd want it.' He handed Husker a carving of Lily's face. 'She said you must have dropped it, and to tell you that you're a bastard for throwing away a daughter's gift.'

Husker turned it over in his hands. 'I'd forgotten about this.' Tears welled up in his eyes, so Lark put his arms around his father and squeezed, hugging him until his leg started to bounce.

Thanks for reading, manost.

The Split Sea encircles many kingdoms. As these kingdoms spin, the water slows. And it was moving for a reason.

~

In *Book 1: A Handful of Souls*, the Golden Throne has frozen over. Lily's family has been re-united, for a time.

In *Book 2: A Kings Feast*, the Deathlands have been bought. It is here that Lily must seek answers, or fall to the ravenous hunger that is consuming her body.

~

Want to be an advanced reader?
Want to create a character?
Want to decide which path these poor sods will take?

I have a mailing list. Some of these things may happen if you sign up to it.
Join at stephenrice.co.uk

A Humble Request

If you enjoyed this novel, please share your thoughts with a friend.

Or perhaps with a few thousand strangers?

Reviews are strange things.

Printed in Great Britain
by Amazon